Right Talents

jay gee heath

Also by jay gee heath
Right Skills

Dedication

Sam who just might read this one.
Didn't know what you started did you?
This is only the first book!!!

Acknowledgements

Thank you to my first readers, my proofers. I know this first book is your favorite.

Vivian Horak

Janet Benjamins

Jo Anne Sullivan

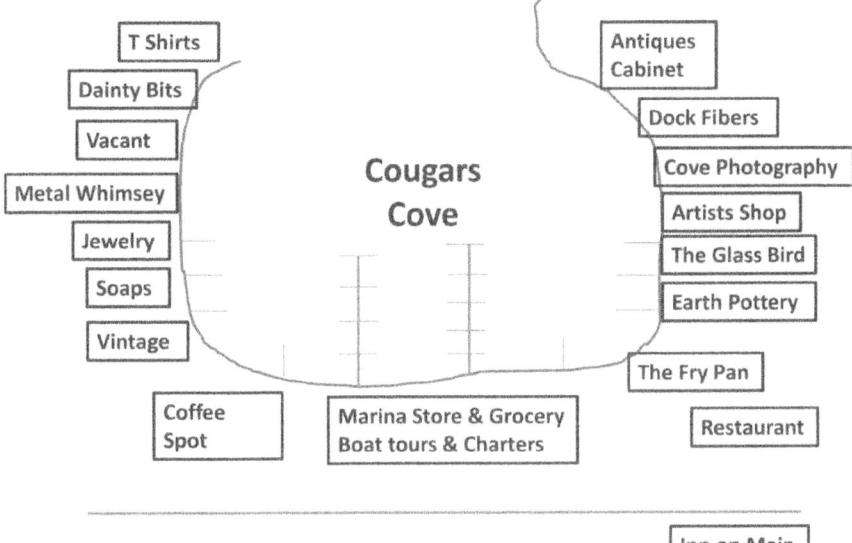

T Shirts

Dainty Bits

Vacant

Metal Whimsey

Jewelry

Soaps

Vintage

**Cougars
Cove**

Antiques
Cabinet

Dock Fibers

Cove Photography

Artists Shop

The Glass Bird

Earth Pottery

The Fry Pan

Coffee
Spot

Marina Store & Grocery
Boat tours & Charters

Restaurant

Inn on Main

Week 1: Monday

May couldn't believe it had happened so quickly. Went bad, so fast.

She had been thrilled to find herself pregnant. Could not wait to tell him. Maybe she was a little nervous because he had never actually said he wanted children, just said that they should probably let it happen. She had run to his office as soon as the doctor confirmed her suspicions. Rushed past his secretary.

"I'm pregnant," she said gleefully as she entered.

"What?" he asked looking at her puzzled?

"I am pregnant" she said again. She watched as he understood and saw anger? He was angry because she was pregnant?

"You can't be," he said. He was angry.

"Yes, Yes I am."

"No, you can't be. Not by me."

It took a moment for what he said to sink in. It didn't make any sense. Now it was her turn to say, "What?"

"I'm sterile."

Confused she said, "What," again. "What do you mean?"

"I am sterile," he repeated. "If you are pregnant, it's not mine."

"Of course the baby is yours." What was he saying? How could he be sterile? "What do you mean you're sterile? How can that be? You can't be sterile. How can I be pregnant if you're sterile?"

"Yes, that is the question, isn't it? How **can**," he emphasized the word, "you be pregnant if I am sterile?"

1

"No, no. You can't be sterile. When did that happen? How do you know? You never said." None of this was making sense. She had been nervous that he might not be immediately happy. But this? This made no sense.

"I've always been sterile. I never told you because it wasn't important to me."

"Not important to you? How could you not tell me? How could you marry me and not tell me? You knew I wanted children."

"I thought you might not marry me if you knew. You were the perfect wife for a man in my position, so I didn't tell you." As if that made it OK.

"You really believe that don't you?" she said amazed. "That you are sterile. That I didn't need to know." She was amazed at his self-righteousness

She was still trying to understand how he could have just dismissed, so callously, her wants, when he continued after a moment of silence, "Yes, of course. And now, my dear, you are pregnant. Who is the man? Tell me." He sounded dangerous.

"What do you mean? There is no man. Of course I am not sleeping with someone else. This is our baby. How can you say these things?"

"Easy. Go to your lover. Go tell him you're pregnant. See how he likes it. Go to him, honey. Go move in with him, because you will not return to my house."

"You love me. I love you, Derek. You know this baby is yours. Don't do this." Begging, because she was sure that he was serious.

"My attorney will contact you this evening with divorce papers. You will sign them. Security will escort you out. Go now." He turned his back and called down to security.

Shocked, reeling, frightened, she turned and fled. Before she was subjected to the further indignity of being escorted out of his building. How had this happened? What was he saying? He couldn't be serious. They had been married for 10 months. He wouldn't just walk away. Send her away. He would rethink as soon as he calmed down. She would call him. He would get a test and see that he was not sterile. How could he think such a thing? How could he not tell her that he was sterile? What was she going to do if he wouldn't believe her?

She walked in a daze. Too bewildered to think, she just walked. Found herself in the park and sat. Her mind was blank. What had just happened? Had he actually just thrown her out? How could he do that? He loved her. She sat there, running the conversation over and over. Trying to find some detail to grab onto. To anchor her. Surely this was not happening. She had been so thrilled. She was pregnant. With his baby. How could he accuse her of adultery? How could he believe that she had a lover? She loved him. He knew that.

Round and round the thoughts went. Over and over.

The chill of evening finally cut through the fog and confusion in her brain. She roused as if from a stupor and was surprised to find she had been sitting here for hours.

I'll call him she thought. Call him now. He's just waiting for me to call him. He is frantic because he doesn't know where I am. He always knows where I am. He'll be worried. He'll be remorseful and beg me to come back. He didn't mean those hateful things he said. Yes, I'll call him now she thought. And opened her cell and pushed his name.

His attorney answered the phone. His attorney! "He will not talk to you. You will not come back to his house."

"Just like that? Just like that? It is over? Can't you get him to listen?" she begged.

The attorney only repeated smugly, "He has decided. And you know when he makes a decision, its final. He will not talk to you. You will not go back to his house. Meet me in the lobby of the Ritz, this evening, at 5 PM. I will have paperwork for you to sign tonight."

"No," she said, "I won't." At that moment she realized that she had never said no to Derek. Or his attorney. "I am not signing any papers in the lobby. You will leave them with me and I will call you when I have read them over and am ready to talk with you again."

"You will sign the papers. Or Derek will be forced to make your adulterous behavior public."

"No, he won't." There was one card she could play and she played it. "He won't want the world to know that his wife had to go outside her marriage with him for satisfaction." She knew that. She knew Derek. He would never allow the world to think his wife might be unfaithful.

"So, you admit then to your illicit affair? As if pregnancy is not proof enough." The attorney made that a statement, not a question.

"No. I did not have an affair. The child is Derek's. He is not sterile. But if he goes public, he will become a laughing stock. I guarantee you." Well she was pretty sure. And the attorney didn't have to know that.

The attorney folded. "You have 24 hours. Meet me in the lobby, tonight. I will leave the papers with you overnight. You will return them to me, tomorrow at five, in the lobby."

One day. She had one day. What could she do in one day? She better get her brain working. Make some decisions. Make some plans. At least she was fighting back. Standing up for herself.

She suddenly realized she was freezing, the temperature had dropped. She was wearing only a light dress. A dress Derek had bought her, had selected for her to wear today. And how had that happened? How had she become such a passive child that she let her husband select what she would wear. She could almost understand that she let him buy her clothes. Husbands did that, didn't they? Select and buy their wives' clothing? Hunh? But how could she let him pick out what she would wear. Yes, it seemed to make him happy, but why had she never said, "I don't feel red today, I want to wear blue."

Those were thoughts she could deal with later. Right now she needed a place to go. She couldn't go home. As she had no lover, she couldn't go to him. Probably just as well there was no lover. If she went to a lover, Derek would probably follow her and have him beaten up. The Ritz she guessed. That's where the attorney expected her to be. Go to the hotel, get a room.

She shook herself and set off. Good thing she had her purse. She took a mental inventory as she walked. Wallet, maybe $150.00 cash, her personal checkbook, the one she kept in her maiden name for little presents for Derek, credit cards. And, of course all the "girl" things. She should be OK for a few days. No luggage though. Getting a room should be interesting.

The desk clerk looked at her funny. Maybe it was because she had no luggage. Or maybe he recognized the name or her picture from the society pages. Or maybe he thought she was meeting a lover. She laughed at the idea as she went up to her room. Single room, not a suite.

She freshened up and went back downstairs to meet the attorney.

He looked as smug as he had sounded on the phone as he handed over a large envelope. "Deliver these, signed, back here tomorrow at five. That is all the time you get. You cannot handle the public fallout either." He stalked off.

She went back to her room and shut the door. Sank down onto the couch.

Realized she had the envelope in her hand. She opened it. A check, a large check. Was he buying her off? The note said he would endorse it once he received the signed forms. She shuddered. No way was she taking that money. She would support herself and her baby.

Of course, there was the Petition for Dissolution of marriage ready for her signature. It already had a case number. Copies of the summons forms. His signatures were already there and notarized. Pretty quick work she thought. But then he did have an office full of attorneys, a top notch legal team. She noted the three to six weeks' time for an uncontested divorce. Is that all it took to end a marriage she wondered sadly. She was sure he would speed that up.

How could this man, this man she thought she loved, how could he, in a fraction of a second, reject her? Not given her a chance to explain? Did he have no faith in her? Didn't he know she would never take a lover? She knew in her heart, that it was over. She could never forgive him. For his treatment now, for his deceit about his believed sterility. She knew him well enough to know he never changed his mind. He loved only himself, his power, and his money. The divorce was to be her punishment for the apparent transgression. He was a powerful man. She supposed she should be happy that he had not selected a penance or retribution more befitting an immoral, straying spouse.

Divorce. She would sign the papers, she knew. She would not contest it. Meet the attorney in the lobby as instructed. Try to get him to see the truth, try to get him to talk to Derek. She had not cheated, but she would not go back to Derek now. She knew she would not be able to convince the attorney, though she would try one more time. She knew that the attorney did just what Derek said with no thoughts of his own and no free will. Always waiting for Derek's next instruction. A go-fer. A lackey. That was all Derek kept around. And why was she thinking the attorney was such a pitiful creature. Wasn't she exactly the same? Hadn't she done just what Derek wanted when he wanted? She laughed at herself again. That was all changing, beginning right now, tonight.

The divorce form didn't really surprise her. But she was surprised by the vile notarized agreement in which her husband renounced their child. How could he even suggest the baby was not his? Was this agreement final? Would he change his mind if he found out the truth?

That question scared her. Her mind was suddenly working, her brain was functioning again. Good. She was not going to trust his notarized letter. She needed to be sure Derek would never be able to come back and take the child. She would have to take this agreement to another attorney. Ensure that it would be binding forever. Derek must give up all rights to the child. She would not have him coming back at a later date demanding visitation or even shared custody or sole custody. She would protect her baby now. She should also have the divorce agreement reviewed professionally. Her friend Kathy was dating a child support activist, maybe she could get him to review the paperwork and make sure her child would be safe. Draw up a legal revocation. She had a day. She was sure it could be done.

She would call her friend, Kathy. She was sure Kathy would be able to help.

Good, she was thinking again. Her brain was functioning. She would deal with her immediate situation and when she was settled and secure, then she could examine her feelings. Sit down and cry. She should want to cry, but instead, she felt... relieved? Well, if it were not for the baby, she would feel relieved. How come? Later. She would deal with her feelings later.

When she told Kathy her situation, her friend offered sympathy and support. "That self-important jerk," she said. "I never liked him. Or the way he treated you. Like some sort of object."

"Why didn't you ever tell me how you felt about Derek?"

"It wasn't really any of my business. You seemed happy to have him in control. Though it did grate on my nerves whenever you just did what he said."

"I guess. I didn't realize. Only just recently I have started to feel closed in. Locked up."

"Well girl, I am glad you're out of it. How do you feel about the baby? You must feel good since you are protecting it. You can come and live with me for a while if you want. I have a spare room."

"I don't know what I am going to do. It is all too soon. But I'll let you know. Thank you. Can you ask your boyfriend to give me a call? You said he is a child advocate, he might know exactly what paperwork I need to protect my baby."

"I'll call Sydney right now and have him contact you. Take care of yourself and let me know if you need anything."

May was in a stupor all night. She didn't sleep. Didn't even undress. Just paced and thought. Lay on the bed. Got up and paced again. There wasn't much she could do. She already knew that she would not contest the divorce. His admitted betrayal by not telling her he was sterile devastated her. Didn't tell her because it didn't suit his purpose? He knew how much she wanted children. He had always just said, what will be, will be. He had lied by omission. He didn't even give her the chance to make her own decision. He had already been making her decisions for her before they were even married. And she had just complied, never questioned his instructions. Agreeing with everything he did as if she were a delicate fragile flower that needed to be protected. When, how, had she stopped being herself and become Derek's windup doll? Maybe when he told her they would get married. Told her when and where too. She thought he had been so manly. So decisive. And then he wanted to go with her to pick out her gown. When she had told him she wanted to make her own gown, he had simply smiled and said she deserved the best, maybe Vera Wang. And she thought that was sweet. He picked the upscale shop. And she was so thrilled with his attention, she let him talk her into a gown much more formal and expensive then she really wanted. But he seemed so happy to be able to buy it for her, she'd yielded and let him.

That was the way it started. She had let him take control of her life. How had she become such a docile wimp? She had been a strong person. Her father had disappeared before she was born. Her Mom had raised her alone. Now, she would be doing the same thing with her child.

May would fall back on her skills. She had taught herself to sew and worked in a fabric store when she was 14. Then she worked in a department store, first folding women's clothes, then selling them, and then helping to purchase them. Assisting with fabric, color, and style decisions. She developed a fascination for fabrics and shades. She put herself through college with an apprenticeship at the museum, in the historical clothing collection, repairing men's, and women's garments and accessories. That's where she had met Kathy, who was the conservation and restoration expert for the museum. And later, when May volunteered at the museum, they had spent many hours together while Kathy was repairing paintings. Derek didn't want her to work, but he had allowed her to volunteer when she begged. He did so because he said there was prestige with volunteer work.

OK, maybe she did have a nearly useless art history degree with a minor in dressmaking and design, but she had supported herself and clothed herself. She was making a name for herself and had received an award for designs which replicated women's clothing of the 19th century.

She was starting on a Master's Degree when she first met Derek. She had set up a 'Costumes through the Ages' exhibit at the museum and she had been flattered by his interest. He was on the museum board. Such a good looking, important man had noticed her. And not just noticed, but liked and courted her. She had been excited and infatuated by his attention and quickly fallen under his spell. She was awestruck and fell head over heels.

Was that all it had been? Infatuation? Someone, anyone noticing her? Enough of these thoughts, of the past. The future, she had to plan her future.

What would she tell her baby when it, no she, May was sure the baby would be a she. What would she tell the baby when she asked about her Dad? Time enough to worry about that.

Tomorrow. Well today, the sky was already getting light. She would take a shower, get ready for the day and her meeting with Sydney. He was bringing the completed paperwork to ensure sole custody of her baby.

Tuesday

She looked at Derek, pleading, "Derek, please don't do this. Don't abandon your child. Don't forsake me"

He said nothing, simply nodded to his attorney to take over.

"Did you sign all the papers?" the attorney asked.

"Yes, I signed all the papers."

"Hand them over," the attorney said.

"First, Derek needs to sign this form rejecting all parental rights to the baby. I've already signed. The desk clerk will notarize it."

Derek nodded to the attorney who read through it quickly and passed it to him. "This is essentially the same form we created. Just more formal."

All three of them signed both sets, one for her, one for Derek. They were both notarized.

As soon as she received her notarized copy, she handed over the uncontested divorce agreement.

"Good," Derek said. "I was sure the money would influence you."

"Yes, it convinced me you were determined to end our marriage. I'm sorry for you, for us"

"I don't ever want to see you again. I suggest you leave town. Soon. Your charge cards have been cancelled, your cell no longer has service, and your checking account is closed. You can't afford this hotel, go move in with your boyfriend," he said with a hardness in his voice. He nodded to the attorney, turned, and walked away, the attorney scurrying after.

She wondered that they had not even checked the paperwork. Guess Derek trusted her enough, knew her well enough, that he believed her when she said she had signed all the papers. How long before he found his check with the divorce papers. Would he reconsider? Probably not, he never changed his mind. Never doubted himself. But it would make no difference to her. Her life with him was over.

She went back to her room to decide what to do next. Didn't have long to worry as the hotel clerk rang. Her belongings were on the way up. She opened the door and waved in only the meager items she had brought to the marriage. Only what she owned before the marriage. Stunned, she numbly watched the man roll in the large suitcase and put down her sewing machine. And she was still standing in the doorway long after he left.

She found her old clothes in the suitcase. The ones she had designed and worn before she met Derek. None of the clothes which he had bought for her were included. None of the jewelry. Not even her make up case. Who else could use that? Would have to be someone with her coloring. Not that she would use it ever again. She wore make up because Derek insisted, she hated it. That was another way she had let him control her life. She had never considered him small or mean spirited. She had never noticed. It hurt, the meanness she now recognized. The loss of things, not so much. She supposed she should be happy he hadn't burnt the things she treasured. Her sewing machine, her clothes, her designs. She would be happy to be able to wear them again.

He even thought he could tell her to leave town. That was a little overblown. But she had already decided that she was leaving. She wanted the baby to grow up in a small town.

Oh, my God, how was she ever going to manage? Homeless, jobless, pregnant. She had no family. She was alone. And broke? She did have that small personal accounts which she had never closed when she got married. And a credit card of her own. Both in her maiden name. Ones she kept so she could buy Derek presents with her own money.

It wasn't much. But it could pay for a doctor and just maybe for the delivery of the baby. And her license was in her maiden name.

She would have to leave by bus. And she knew exactly where she would go. She had accompanied Derek on his trip to Ft. Myers, on the west coast, last month. He had sent her shopping while he conducted his business. She had the chauffeur drive along the coast. Just drive. Even then she understood that if she bought something, she wouldn't get to wear it or use it. It would never be as suitable as what Derek chose for her. So why bother. She would just look at the scenery.

They had wandered south and ended up in a place called Cougars Cove. The area was beautiful and peaceful. There was an Inn on the water so quaint that she just wanted to get out of the car and settle in. The dock was lined with shops. From the road they looked like specialty shops, an artists' colony. But the chauffeur said they should head back. To be close by when Derek called. She wondered now if Derek had paid the chauffeur to watch her and report back. She wouldn't be surprised.

She would go west, west to Cougars Cove. It would be fun to work in the town or on the dock. Soon they would be hiring seasonal help. She had that degree in art history. How useless was that. But she had a good job history except recently, since she hadn't worked since she was married. She wouldn't make a lot of money, but she could get by on a little. She had before, she would again.

She was computer literate, could do office work, and could waitress. She had been a pretty bad waitress, though, that should be a last resort. Sales clerk, she could get a job in a clothing store.

So, yes, go west. She looked at her meager possessions and contemplated her old sewing machine. Derek had not let her make her own clothes after he married her. Insisted on haute couture. She was surprised he had let her keep the machine and that he had sent it. Maybe that was another way for him to hit out at her. But she was an excellent seamstress and sewing could be another source of income. A good job for a pregnant woman and a new mother.

Actually, her decisions were not so hard. If you discount the feelings of desperation, desertion, and abandonment. Being unwanted and unloved. The decisions were simple. She had a child to consider and needed to be strong. And she was strong. She could make her own way. She had been independent before Derek. Somewhere along the way, she had let him take over. Make all the decisions. Run her life the way he wanted. Tell her what to wear, how to act, where to go, when to go, and what to do when she got there. When did he think she had time for an affair? He was always watching and knew her every move. He planned her every move. She shook her head. Enough.

Wednesday

She took the first bus west. Her final destination Cougars Cove. She was ready to stop when the bus reached Ft. Myers. She got off the bus and picked up her luggage. This was it, now how did she get to Cougars Cove? She was sitting eating a snack as she watched a laughing family get on a small shuttle type bus heading south to, Cougars Cove, was posted in the front window! How lucky could she get? A good omen? She trusted omens.

She asked and was told the shuttle regularly ran between town and Cougars Cove. She really knew nothing about the town or the people. It could be the Stepford Wives for all she knew. Nervous, she bought a ticket and joined them. Two more people got on the bus. They all seemed to know each other. All friendly and happy and trading stories of where they had been, what they and done. The father of the children looked at her and asked if she was on vacation.

She looked at the family and decided it would be safe to talk. She didn't want to lie, so qualified her answer, "I'm looking to resettle and thought I would try out Cougars Cove, it is such a pretty area. I will be looking for a job."

"Season starts in another month, there will be a lot of jobs soon in the shops on the dock. Little slow right now," he added.

"Do you have a place to stay?" the Mom asked.

"No, probably at the Inn for a while."

"The Inn on Main Street. It's friendly, nice, and reasonable. The shuttle will stop right in front. The shuttle bus runs regularly between town and the Cove so you don't need a car."

"OK, that is good to know, thanks."

They let her off in front of the quaint inn she had loved on her last visit. She should be able to get a job, even off season, if not she could always get on another bus to another area.

She didn't think she would go back to school, to finish her Masters. She had been on the fast track. But she wasn't anymore. A year would make a big difference. There were too few jobs available in her field and no one would take a chance on a person who had dropped out for a year. And would need to drop out again for the baby. Also she had left her connections behind. Something else she could thank Derek for.

No, she couldn't blame Derek. She had let him convince her she didn't need to get her degree. And he didn't think that she should go back and visit or socialize with her art department friends. Hindsight, didn't they call that 20/20? It was so clear now how he had cut her off from everyone.

She walked into an old fashioned lobby. Flowered wall paper, beam ceilings, comfortable chairs. Small but colorful flower arrangements. No one was at the front desk but she heard muttering behind an open door. She put down the sewing machine and left the suitcase and peeked around the door and called, "Hello?"

The man inside was muttering deprecations to a tutu, she saw. He appeared to be a strong, well-built, older man. Mid fifties. Why had she thought gay? Just because he was playing with a tutu? Better hold that thought.

"Excuse me," she said a little louder.

He looked up at her angrily. But she knew it was the costume he was angry at not her. She almost laughed, his distress was so comical. "I wanted a room. But maybe I should help you first?"

"Ya, you can help me. Shoot this thing," he snarled

"What's wrong with it? Did it break a leg? And how can you tell it needs to be shot?" She did smile now.

He laughed, "OK, you got me. Not a broken leg. Probably just that I am a helpless man. Take pity on me. Go ahead and laugh at me, but help me please. I beg you."

"Let me see. You're sewing? A tutu? Wait a minute, I have to laugh again. It's just so incongruous. A strong he man like you terrified by a piece of netting."

"I promised my little girl that I would fix it for her."

May thought he looked a little old to have a daughter young enough to be wearing the tutu.

As if he read her thoughts, he said, "My granddaughter. Jesse is my granddaughter. Her mother is visiting her sister and I am in charge of all things tutu." He didn't expand on where Jesse's dad was and May didn't ask.

"It's Jesse's favorite piece of clothing. All her friends wear tutus to play in. And it is just about worn out and, my daughter says, too small. It looked pretty simple to fix, but I think it is alive. I can't get a handle on it."

"Give it to me," she said. "This is obviously woman's work. You do want me to fix it?" she asked double checking.

"Of course I want you to fix it. Can you? I will give you anything."

"Give me about 10 minutes and then I will want your cheapest room."

"OK, I'll begin the registration. And make you a cup of tea?"

"Sure," she said, already engrossed in the project. The tutu was pretty well used, but it could be retied.

She was done by the time he came back with the tea. He set one cup in front of her and sat down with one of his own. "You saved my life. Jesse lives in that tutu. She had a crying fit when it came apart."

"Well, she will be happy now and feel free to call me when you need a seamstress. It would be pretty easy to make a new one. And relatively inexpensive. And I don't think this will last much longer."

"Thanks, I owe you. I have the perfect room for you, a small bedroom, and bath on the second floor, the grunt of the Inn, so it is cheaper and always the last to rent. It's still off season too." He quoted a price she could manage.

"You will like it here. Are you looking for a job? Or just passing through?"

"Job. I'll be looking for a job."

"There are lots of jobs in season, which will be starting soon. We house some of the seasonal help." She finished the registration, using her credit card and her maiden name, May Johnson. Not Elizabeth May Stratton. Derek had felt that May was too plebian for a woman of her social status, but she preferred May. The room was affordable. She could live here for a week or so, until she found an apartment. She had her savings from her own personal account which meant she would not be desperate for a couple of months. Then, by the time season ended, she might have enough saved to get her through the pregnancy and child birth. And she would have to find a doctor.

The man led her to the elevator and upstairs carrying her sewing machine. She dragged the suitcase. He unlocked the door for her. The room was charming. He said, "Come on down when you get cleaned up and I'll make you another cup of tea and a snack. Call if you need anything. I'm Ryan, Ryan Gibbs. And I already know you're May Johnson. We have breakfast, well coffee, tea, and muffins from 7 to 8 in the lobby."

She was still high from the excitement of actually getting to the Inn, her first step in her future. After she scrubbed her face and hung her few things, she went down for the tea and true to his word he had snacks, scones, of all things.

"Scones are leftover from this morning, but they are still good and it is OK to eat them in the evening. Mind if I sit with you? I could use a cup of tea with a pretty lady." He had such an open smile, she warmed to him immediately. Like the Dad she never had.

"I'd love your company. You can tell me a little about the town."

"It's an old Florida cracker town. Cracker simply means folks born in Florida. Or where they live in Florida. And that's pronounced floor ee da. This is an old town, settled in the early pioneer days. Laid back and quaint. Artists and fishermen mostly now, down on the Cove Dock. That's the Cougars Cove Docks and Marina, a short walk that way," he said pointing. "You probably didn't see it coming in through town, Cougars Cove. We like to think we are pretty self-sufficient, but we still need to go to the 'big city' for big items."

"I can't wait to walk around. What about you? You don't look like an innkeeper." She put her hand to her mouth. "I'm sorry, that was very snoopy. You don't have to answer that."

"Anyone will tell you. Just filling in for my daughter-in-law, Liz. She's in Orlando taking care of her sister who fell last week and needed some help. It's off season still and Liz has good help here. So I just fill in as needed. I live in the house out back."

May wondered, but stopped herself from asking, what he did when he was not 'filling in' and where his son was. Instead she shared, "I'm going through a nasty divorce. I like to think when one door closes, another opens. So I am starting a new chapter of my life here. I liked this town when I drove through once before. So I'm looking for a job and want to make my home here." Why had she told him that? Because he was friendly and interested? Maybe.

And suddenly she was tired. Exhausted, she excused herself went upstairs where she fell onto the bed and was instantly asleep.

He watched her leave and wondered what caused her to be starting a new chapter of her life away from family and friends. Shrugged, and went back to work.

Thursday

After perusing the local want ads, May set out job hunting. It was a long day. Three interviews, waitress at a fine restaurant, clerk in the used car office, and salesperson in women's lingerie in the department store. She wasn't sure about the waitress job. She had never been very good at it, no matter how hard she tried. She was always racing back to the kitchen for something she forgot.

She had also looked at two apartments, well efficiencies. Though both had adequate room for her and the baby, she couldn't afford either of them. By the time she got back to the Inn, she needed a cup of tea and a sit down.

Guess she was going to make it herself today. There were tea bags and hot water. She was sitting down with her cup and had just taken her first sip, when a whirlwind in a tutu danced into the lobby. She couldn't help but laugh. The little girl stopped suddenly when she saw May.

"Hi, I'm Jesse."

"And I'm May. I thought you might be Jesse, I recognize the tutu."

"Oh, did you fix it for me? Grampa said a nice lady guest fixed it. Thank you so much. Isn't it pretty? Grandpa said he may have to buy me a new one. But I want pink and green."

May laughed some more and drank some tea, while Jesse danced. May had forgotten to eat, so she had another scone. Note to self, she thought, eat breakfast tomorrow.

Friday

May dropped off applications for 2 more jobs. Looked at 1 more apartment. Again, more then she would be able to afford. The landlord suggested a roommate, but May wasn't sure that would work with a baby on the way. If she couldn't find anything she could afford, then maybe she would advertise for a roommate. But she really wanted something by herself, she would keep looking.

As soon as she got a job and a place to live, she would have to find a doctor and an attorney.

She picked up the newspaper on her way back to the Inn, to read in the lounge. With a cup of tea. The job advertisements were the same. She would have to wait for the Sunday paper before she could do anything more. But she could go online and look, the Inn had a business room for guests. She asked at the front desk and was given the code to access the web. But there were no jobs, so she decided to see what the web had on the town. There was a lot of information and pictures. She lost track of time, looking at maps, shops, historical places, hiking trails. The Dock looked fascinating and she decided to explore it tomorrow. If the shops and crafts were even half as nice as the pictures online, she would spend the day there.

Jesse came in as she was finishing and then Ryan came in and said, "Come on Jesse, let's go to town and see if we can buy a new tutu." He turned and saw May and continued, "May is coming with us to help." He looked pleadingly at May.

"Sure that sounds like fun." She forgot being weary, put her cup in the tray and followed them out.

As she expected, they could not find a tutu in the department store or the children's shop. Jesse was trying to hide her disappointment, but her giggles had stopped a long time ago.

"There is a fabric shop across the street, let's try there," May suggested.

"Won't do any good, Grampa can't sew and I'm too little," Jesse whispered sadly.

"I can sew. And you can help. A tutu doesn't take much sewing. Let's go see if they have the fabric. We need tulle." It was the only chance to make the little girl smile.

They trooped in and May spotted the tulle immediately. Thank goodness. She led the way to a rainbow of colored bolts. They would need at least 8 yards. 10 would be better. And as she expected, it was pretty cheap.

Jesse was dancing up and down again. "Can I pick out a color? Can I pick more than 1 color? Can I have pinks and greens?"

She looked excitedly at May who nodded. "Sure you pick them out Sweetie."

The sales lady came over saying, "Hi Ryan, never expected to see you in here."

"And I never expected to be in here. How are you doing Marge?"

"I'm doing fine. And how about you Jesse? What are you after today?"

"We are going to make a tutu!! We wants pinks and greens and we want tuuule."

"Oh, you and Ryan are going to make it?" She grinned at Ryan who turned red.

"No, me an' May," Jesse corrected her. "We are going to make it together. She's staying at the Inn."

Marge smiled at May and said, "Nice to meet you May, are you in town visiting?"

"Not visiting. If I can find a job and an apartment, I plan on staying a long time."

"Good luck with that now. Things will be a little tight 'til season starts."

Jesse finally decided on three shades of pink and two of green. Marge measured and cut them efficiently, 2 yards each.

"Jesse, do you want a matching headband with a tulle flower?" May asked.

"In pink and green?"

"Absolutely." At the last minute May remembered they needed elastic. "And let me get elastic for the tutu and some thread."

She found Jesse and Ryan gathered at the register. A woman had come over when she heard Jesse giggling and laughing.

"You're going to make a tutu?" she asked. "My little girl, Sabrina, really wants one. She is so envious that Jesse is making one. Is that all it takes? 10 yards and a little elastic? And Jesse says there is very little sewing."

"That's right. Do you both want to sew with us? It will be much more fun with more people. Want me to help you pick out fabrics? Or maybe your little girl would want to do that. And you could come over to the Inn tomorrow and we could work together, all of us. No reason the girls can't help, it is a simple job." May stopped, a little shocked. It had been so long since she had talked with a casual acquaintance or been able to offer to help someone. Not something Derek ever allowed. It felt good. And how would Ryan feel about her using the Inn?

"Would you really do that? You don't even know me," the woman said.

"We can fix that. Ryan or Marge could introduce us."

Ryan made the introductions. "May Johnson, meet Marla Rogers. Marla is married to the Sheriff David Rogers. So she is probably safe,"

Now Marla was giggly. "Can I bring Sabrina? Tomorrow afternoon? We can come to the Inn around 3? I am so excited. I can't wait to tell Sabrina. But I will give you one chance to back out. One chance to change your mind if you want."

"Tomorrow will be fine. I am job hunting. But I can't job hunt on Saturday."

"My husband, David, is looking for a lead, plain clothes detective. Do you have a law enforcement background?"

"No law enforcement, but I could nail the plain clothes part."

They all laughed.

"Tomorrow at 3." She looked at Ryan for an OK and he nodded with a grin. "We'll have fun. And bring a pair of scissors with your fabric and elastic. I have a sewing machine and we can use that."

When they got back to the Inn, Ryan sent Jesse off to play and made tea and sat down with her. "Thank you from the bottom of my heart for going with us today. I really appreciate how well you took charge. I'm glad that you happened our way and settled at our Inn. You'll like our town if you like quiet, small towns with friendly, nosey neighbors. Wish I could help with a job, you would be great on our front desk. But unfortunately the Inn is fully staffed right now with long time local people. What type of work are you looking for?"

"Oh, I can do almost anything. Office work, I am good with a computer and I have some accounting and advertising background. I worked my way through college in those positions. I also sew, as you already know. I design clothes and sew them. That's my love. Most everything I wear I created. Not jeans or T-shirts. No one can improve on those. Except by adding designs which I sometimes do."

She didn't know what it was about him but she found herself spilling her whole story.

When she finished, he looked angry. She hadn't meant to tell him the whole sad story. "Your husband is a jerk. How he could let you get away is beyond me. You don't really sound broken up about this. How are you feeling?"

"I'm not broken up. I have had a lot of time to sit and think. On the bus. Once I got over the immediate crisis and after my pity party over abandonment, I had time to think about it and I found that I am actually relieved."

"Why relieved?"

"Well Derek just sort of ran my life. At first he would suggest things and I would go along. They made sense. And then he took more and more control. And I let him. In fact I didn't even notice. He selected my clothes for the day and my meetings and duties. He alienated my friends. About a month ago I suddenly realized that I had become mindless eye candy for him. I was trying to make my own decisions, but it was like pushing water. Nothing moved or changed. I was drowning."

"I used to be self-sufficient. I don't know how I became a paper, cut-out doll with no ideas or interests. I did manage to have one volunteer job which he approved of and had one friend there. So after my pity party, I realized that this divorce was a good thing. An end to a bad marriage. But that is a whole 'nother psychiatric session. This is the beginning of a new life for me. A new start. A new start with a baby."

She shook her head. "I can't believe I just told you all that." She couldn't believe she had spilled not only the ugly story but also her feelings about the divorce too. "Enough, no more. Let's talk about you." Enough? She had told him all of it. There wasn't any more to tell him.

"Oh, I am pretty much what you see. A grampa filling in for my daughter-in-law who is taking care of her sister. My son asked me to come and I had a lot of vacation time piled up. So I took time off to help out. I'm actually enjoying it. Jesse is a handful. But the Inn runs itself. Liz has good help and I do very little. Just pick up a little of the slack and Liz and my son feel comfortable that someone they trust is in charge."

"Now you look exhausted. Go on upstairs and get some rest." He took the tea cups and headed to the back.

She was tired. A long hot soak would feel good. And she could try to figure out why she told her life story to a stranger, even if he was a grampa.

After a nap, she went across the street for a late meal and then back to her room. Her message light was on and when she pushed the button she heard Marge saying that word of the tutu class had spread and 2 more ladies wanted to come with their kids. Marge had double checked with Ryan and he was happy to have them all use the conference room. And he would supply refreshments.

"Hope you don't mind adding Moms and kids. It will be a great way for you to meet people. Oh, call me if you have any questions," she ended. May just laughed. This was one time it felt good to have someone make plans for her. She was excited at the prospect of meeting new people, people in town. Maybe one of the moms could recommend a doctor. Maybe a lawyer.

Saturday

Since she would have to wait until Monday to job hunt she set out to visit the Dock shops Saturday morning. She could see it from her room and could easily walk there.

A pretty spot. Cougars Cove Dock. Quaint, small, shops with locally crafted gifts. A coffee shop, The Coffee Spot and something called The Fry Pan. She might try those.

Delightful shops. All open. The weather was beautiful. Shoppers were strolling, laughing, and eating ice cream. She could while away a couple of hours here. She walked through a pottery shop, Earth Pottery. Fantastic shapes and glazes. She looked with admiration at a luminary. Made by the owner, Gordon. The curved style, made her want to touch it. The shapes of the cut outs, fascinating. They would cast an intriguing light pattern in a darkened room. Maybe when she got settled, if she got settled, she could get one for herself. It was a happy thought.

The stained glass shop, The Glass Bird, was right next door. Cheerful colored birds hung in the window with ornaments of all shapes, and vases, and glass catchers. Brightly colored flowers and fish. Happy colors and designs everywhere. She gave in to the pure enjoyment of the shop, looking and touching almost everything. Forgetting her own problems.

Next she stepped into the art shop. Missed the name. Went back out to check, The Artists' Shop. Well that was original, she thought and went back inside. Full of water colors and oils depicting the local natural areas. Trees and animals. Flowers and birds. Some of the bird paintings were superb. She thought they were good enough to be in her museum in the local artist room. Well her ex museum. And here was another item for her want list, the Louisiana heron (renamed a tri-color heron now she reminded herself) standing on a half-submerged branch. She liked the blue grey tones of the bird and its reflection in the water.

And in one corner of the shop, origami. One thousand cranes, the sign said, with their story. They were made from papers of many colors and designs, in all different sizes. The clerk explained the story, that in Japan, the tradition of folding 1,000 cranes is done when someone has a wish, be it for peace, health, or luck. And according to Japanese lore, folding 1,000 Origami Cranes is truly a labor of love. Tradition holds that the bride who finishes this task, called sembazuru, before her wedding day, will be richly rewarded with a good and happy marriage since the crane mates for life.

May laughed out loud. "That's what I did wrong," she said. "I didn't even make one crane. For my next marriage I will make two thousand. How long will that take? Should I start now I wonder?"

"It is just a story. A nice story," the clerk admitted. "And you don't need to make them all yourself. Your family and friends can make them for you and gift you. That works for good luck also." The clerk told her that she had made the cranes. The more expensive ones were from paper she had designed herself. She filled the quiet moments while working in the shop, painting the paper and folding the cranes. May bought a small green crane with more tiny cranes painted on the paper.

The next shop was devoted to photography. Cougars Cove Photography. Some photos were almost three dimensional. Did all these birds live here in this tiny area she wondered? Then noticed that each had a description, date, and location posted below. And she was sure the same identification would be on the back.

They had delightful greeting cards. She bought one for Kathy. And a posted sign mentioned that the owner/operator did human portraits also.

The next shop, Cougars Dock Fibers, showcased handmade cloth treasures. Marvelous woven throws and shawls. Hand painted silk scarves and runners. Purses in delightful fabrics. Some hand painted. Some with smaller matching bags or wallets, or phone covers. And many more phone and eye glass covers. Wreaths, a spectacular one of handmade hydrangea in that coppery blue color with green leaves. She wanted that bad. Ohh, $250.00. Maybe not today. Maybe not ever at that price. But certainly worth it. A lot of hand time with many hours of work went into that wreath.

She stopped at The Coffee Spot, what a great name. She could just hear herself saying, "Meet you at The Coffee Spot." The menu included simple breakfasts and lunch sandwiches, soup, and desserts. She suddenly realized she had not eaten and ordered coffee and a breakfast sandwich.

She sat and watched the boats come and go. And the tourists walking by. She loved this spot. She and baby were so lucky to be here. She was so glad Derek had kicked her out. Where had that thought come from? She smiled, it all felt so right. She was glad she hadn't made the cranes.

She would wait until tomorrow to visit Cougars Cove T-shirts. Of course there would be a T-shirt shop. There was also an antique shop, The Antique Cabinet. A hand made, natural, soaps shop, called appropriately enough, Soaps. They also had lotions. The next shop had handmade jewelry, a chocolate shop with ice cream. A restaurant, which looked to be open for dinner only. The Fry Pan, open for lunch. Metal Whimsy, that sounded like fun. Maybe tomorrow. And of course the Marina store and charter and tour boats. She might need the whole day tomorrow. But now she needed to be heading back for the tutu class.

She turned back toward the Inn and saw a sign in the window of the vintage clothing shop, again with the appropriate name, Vintage. The sign said, 'Job with housing' and a phone number. She could go inside and ask now. What could she lose by checking on the job now and then coming back on Monday?

She went inside but became distracted by the dresses and purses. The textures and fabrics appealed to her. And again she found herself touching and feeling. Instead of the smooth cold glass in the Glass Bird though, these were cottons, soft laces, and silky satins.

"Can I help you?" asked the girl. She looked like a teenager. Petite, long, black hair in a ponytail. No makeup.

May pulled herself away from the clothing, as she said, "This is a great shop. Where do you find so many wonderful period pieces?"

"The owner, she travels off season and has many contacts."

"Oh. I really came in about the sign in the window. Maybe you can give me a heads up on who is hiring, the type of job, is it sales? And the accommodations."

"It is sales, nights and weekends mostly. The accommodations is a small apartment right over this shop. One bedroom with small den, 1 bath. Reasonably priced. But it is reserved for whoever is hired. The two go together."

"That sounds perfect for me." She hadn't meant to say that out loud. Could she be so lucky as to fall into a job in her area of expertise, one that came with a place to live? "I will give a call Monday and set up an appointment."

"Why wait until Monday?" the girl said. "Let's talk about it now."

"I don't understand. Are you saying that you will do the interviewing?"

"I'm the owner of Vintage. I saw you feeling the fabrics and I saw your delight in the gowns. Let me ask you a few questions," she said and then slapped them out like cards on a poker table, not even waiting for answers.

"Do you have any sales experience? Do you know anything about vintage clothing? Are you able to recognize fabrics by sight or feel and do you know the care of same? Are you able to describe the history and antiquity to a buying public that barely recognizes the value of dated clothing? Can you alter clothing to fit the customer?"

"Yes, all of that," May replied when she got the chance. "I worked my way through school as a sales clerk in a clothing store. I have a degree in Art History, which includes styles and fabrics through time. I am a seamstress and select my own fabrics to fit my own designs. I'm wearing one now. It's a little old, but it is not too dated."

"I wondered. Your outfit didn't look like off the rack. I like it. Turn around, let me see the fit." May slowly turned. She knew the outfit looked good. And fit perfectly.

"OK, let's do a test." The clerk picked a dress off the rack and said, "Tell me about this dress."

"Flowers, mums, in pink and red against a dark green background. A polished cotton fabric. It has embroidery around the neck and sleeves which makes it very feminine. Circa 1960. It can be washed but will need to be ironed," May just said what she knew.

"Good, Now this dress."

"It has greens and navy on tones, um, waves of blue in a sateen. Maybe a little dressy. The buttons down the front are covered with the same fabric. As is the belt. Might want to dry clean this one. And I would say it was first sold around 1950 or '51, in an upscale shop."

"OK. Now sell me this dress," the clerk said pulling out a pretty sundress.

"No. I don't think I can do that."

"Why not? Aren't you applying for a job as sales person?" That was a little testy.

"Yes, but this dress is all wrong for you. The color will make your skin look sallow and the design is wrong for your body type. It will make you look dowdy." May pulled a similar dress out, in a deeper shade and said, "Now this color blue will make your blue eyes pop. It will make your skin radiant. And give your hair a healthy shine. Also the style is perfect for your body shape and the knit will fall loosely. I know you love this other dress, but go try them both on."

'Wow, you do know clothes. You're hired, but I still want to see a resume. Do you have one?"

"Um, no, but I can make one for you. By Monday. Are you really saying I can have the job?"

"Yes. And I will expect you to attend some Dock Artist meetings with me and help with advertising. Will that be OK? Can you do that?"

"I did some advertising with some charity groups at the museum."

"When can you start?"

"Just like that? You don't even know anything about me."

"Remember, I saw you looking at the dresses, I saw the look on your face, I saw how you felt for textures. And I can see how well that suit is designed and cut for you. I don't need anymore. Let's give you a one week probationary period and see if we mesh. I'm Sheil Burke," She held out her hand.

"May Johnson." They shook, both smiling. There was little doubt that they would be friends.

"And the apartment. Do you really have an apartment to go with the job. I am looking for a place to live. I'm at the Inn right now."

"After your first week, if we are both happy, the apartment will be yours."

May nodded. "Wait," she said. Worked up her courage. "There is one more thing you need to know, I'm pregnant and due in 7 months. But I think I could still work."

Sheil looked surprised and then looked at May's belly, back into her face. "By my quick calculations, the way I see it," Sheil said thoughtfully, "that will take you through the season. All the cleanup work from this season will be completed. And prep for next season is not labor intensive. Oh, I made a pun. A new mother can work at home. Or watch the shop with a child nearby. It should work out. When can you start?"

"I can start working tomorrow." May was relieved that Sheil took the pregnancy so well and happy she had been brave enough to mention it.

"Maybe we should go upstairs and see the apartment before you make that decision," Sheil suggested.

They went up the inside stairs, "There is also an outside staircase out back." She unlocked the door and May walked into a furnished living room in tans and blues. A couch, recliner, rocking chair. "Oh, a rocking chair," she exclaimed. Coffee table, end tables, small TV. The kitchen, a modern kitchen, was off to the right, separated by a counter with four high stools. They walked to the left, past a large, luxuriant bath across from a small den set up with a desk and 2 chairs, and into a large bedroom with a walk in closet.

"Wow, this is spectacular."

"You like it? I used to live here and I might have spoiled myself."

"Oh, I am so glad you did, because now I can be spoiled. I almost want to move in right now."

"Soon. Tomorrow, Sunday, 12:30, be here. I will walk you through the shop procedures. Can you do that?"

"I will be here." May couldn't believe it. She felt like dancing. What a great job, terrific shop. A future. And Derek had actually made it all possible. Packing only her old handmade clothes! Wasn't that a kick? She wondered what he would say if he knew. But, she wasn't going to think about the past, only the future.

She ran right into the office when she got back to the Inn. "I got a job, I got a job." She shouted joyfully. Jumping up and down like a kid! Like Jesse when she got the tutu. She grabbed Ryan and started dancing around. He followed, caught up in celebration. "I am going to work for Sheil at Vintage. I am the new sales girl. I start tomorrow. I get my own apartment after a week of probation. And I start tomorrow." She wound down. And went from a happy high to a sad, "But I'll have to leave you and Jesse."

"Oh, we'll be right here. It's just a short walk. We'll still be close. Sheil is great. You will like working for her. And I hear she has a great shop. Never been in it myself. Wouldn't be at all manly," he said with a smile, remembering the tutu. "Now go get ready for your tutu bash this afternoon."

May carried her sewing machine to the conference room. Found Ryan just finishing up with a tray of sandwiches. He had already set out veggies and dip. Sodas, water, decaf coffee, and tea bags. Little dessert cakes. She was amazed and pleased that he had gone to so much trouble. Granted it was for Jesse too, but he didn't have to do so much.

Jesse was already there with her friend, Sabrina. And Marla.

The other 2 moms and their daughters came in together.

"Oh, food. I am starving. And my kid is also. Can we eat?? Please. Please."

Marla laughed and said, "Meet Carol, she is pregnant and always, always hungry. We keep feeding her, but she never gains any weight. Go figure."

Carol mouthed "Hi," around a rolled turkey snack. The other Mom laughed too, she was the clerk from the origami corner. "Hi, we met this morning, I'm Joan Waters and this is Kit. Carol's little girl over there is Carly. Marge told us what we needed to buy and even printed out a list." Shaking her head. "I know I'm an airhead, but I think I should be able to remember something this simple. Maybe. Who did I say I am?"

They all laughed. Carol asked if May had fun exploring the Dock and May said it was terrific, but she hadn't gotten to all the shops yet. "And I got a job. Which I really need if I want to eat."

They crowded around with questions. Carol was first, "Why do you need a job? Aren't you just visiting?"

"No, I'm moving here." May took a deep breath and looked at the women. If she planned to live here, she had better share some of it up front.

"My sad, sad story is that I am in the midst of a divorce and decided to start my new life here. And that is enough about me, let's get to the tutus."

The afternoon went quickly. Gossip, some small town history, and lots of laughs. May demonstrated how to measure the fabrics and tie the knots. The Moms measured and cut their own fabric and the kids were excited to be able to knot the fabric on the waistband, making their own tutus. May made the final hem in the waistbands.

The girls had to put them on as soon as they were done. The kids danced around in their tutus. Ran out to show Ryan. Then they made the flower hair ribbons. Shorter pieces of voile tied and rounded to make a ball, sewn to the stretch headband. They made them in different colors. The first was the hardest, but the others went together quickly.

May gave the instructions for wings in case the kids wanted those later. She felt comfortable and welcome in this group of friendly women.

The Moms put everything away and cleaned up after themselves. They agreed to do another project together and would check with Ryan if they could continue to use the Inn conference room on Sunday mornings. Or, if they would all need sewing machines, maybe Marge would let them set up in the store.

May sat and had a quiet cup of tea with Ryan in the lobby after the tutu mob left. Then she went out to the porch to sit and work on her 'need to do' list. First, her resume, she could use the computer at the Inn for that. Second, she needed an attorney. The ladies had recommended, Bryce Robards, Sheil's brother. They had been curious, so she told them her divorce was pretty ugly and left it at that. The truth as far as it went. She would contact him and set up an appointment. She had to be sure that her baby would be safe from Derek, and Bryce could advise her.

Next, a doctor. The ladies suggested a GP who was in practice with a group of other doctors, pediatrician, obstetrician and another GP. They all went to him.

And lastly, she would open a bank account for her pay check and rent.

She watched the tourists walk by and the Saturday boaters drift by on their way back to the marina. After the sun set she went up to her room to get ready for her first day on the job.

Another night that May just fell into bed and was asleep as soon as her head hit the pillow.

Sunday

Both May and Sheil arrived at the door to Vintage together at 12:15. They were both laughing. May said, "I was so excited, I couldn't sleep. I have been up since five." She had been, too. Designing. She could always lose herself in designing. She had a great idea for Jesse that she was working on. Her own clothing had been packed away so long, it felt new to her and she really didn't need anything for herself.

May had on another pant set from her suitcase. Good thing she only sewed wash and wear clothing. She had used the iron she had found in the closet.

"I got up early too. We probably could have started at five and we would be done now. The shop is open from 10 to 7 Monday through Saturday and 12:30 to 5 on Sunday this time of year. Shorter hours off season. And we have longer hours in season, 10 to 9 weekdays, and Saturday, and 12:30 to 7 on Sunday. As the newest full time employee, I would want you to cover Friday and Saturday night because my part time help like to date. Until season, I will pay you for a 45 hour week. You get a one hour lunch or supper break, however you want to work it out. For now, take Wednesday and Thursday off. I wander in and out. I have a crew of part timers from the high school, the community college, and the retirement community. That includes my own 2 high school girls."

"You have high school girls? You're not old enough. Oh, I am sorry. I didn't say that," May said embarrassed.

"No, It's OK. My husband's girls. Mine now too," she said smugly. "You will love them. Twins and they are truly nice people. And so young and full of fun. You'll meet them; both of them will be in later today. The two together make the place crazy. Happy crazy." She said with a warm smile.

"I will get you a key so you can open and close. That can wait until Monday. Enter through the back door. Lock the front from inside. Turn on lights, boot up the computer, and point of sale register. Everything is digital, but we do have to make backups. Old fashioned hard copy receipts and log books. Sometimes power goes out. So you will have to learn both ways. OK?"

"Sure, I can manage. I'm computer literate and even have some accounting under my belt."

Sheil took her through opening procedures, then turned the sign to OPEN and unlocked the front door. Explained that during quiet times, May should make sure the racks are all straight and check the mail and open any deliveries. "It's OK with me if you read or write when there are no customers. Yesterday I got a delivery of vintage clothing from an estate sale, so we can open that now and you can learn how to sort through the clothing."

There were three large cartons in the back storeroom. Sheil opened the first and started taking out the garments, May thought it was a little like Christmas morning must be. They took the items out one by one, carefully examined them for wear or tear. Only the perfect or near perfect items would be sold. A card would be made, digitally, for each item describing the fabric, style, and approximate date of the piece. If they knew who owned it, or where or when, then those facts were also included for the purchaser. Cost, source, and date were added to the inventory. The selling price would be factored and also included. The near perfect would have the imperfection noted. Everything would be cleaned and pressed, if needed, before going out into the shop. They worked slowly through the boxes together. Both oohing and ahhing and expressing opinions as each piece was shaken out.

The articles which would be sold were hung together. There was another rack of items which might be profitable after cleaning. Cards were made up for each item.

And there was a discard pile.

They took a couple of breaks for Sheil to wait on customers. May helped and learned how to wrap the purchase in tissue paper and tie a special bow.

May looked at the discard pile longingly. Sheil saw her and said. "It's tough to discard a whole dress because of one stain on the skirt or a tear in the bodice, but it has to be done. We won't sell that and no one can wear it. You have to harden yourself, close your eyes and put it in the trash and not think about it anymore."

"But the rest of the dress, all that beautiful fabric."

"Trash," Sheil said firmly.

May couldn't bear it. Be brave, she told herself. "Sheil, I know I am just starting, but I can make lovely clothing from this fabric. Please? I am a seamstress. Give me a chance." She was stroking a soft yellow dress with lace trim. She could already see the top and skirt in her mind.

"OK, go for it. Take the whole pile of discards. We can put them in a shopping bag. If you can save any of that, we both will be happy. I hate to throw away anything also, but I can't sell it, it's just rags now." They folded the pieces neatly into one of the large shopping bags for May to take back to the Inn.

The bell over the door jingled and two voices could be heard laughing. "No, get out. She didn't," said one.

"It's true she did."

And then the girls saw Sheil and May.

"These are my daughters, Melanie in red with short blonde hair, and Kimberly in orange with the long hair," she told May and then looked at the girls. "Who did what? Tell us," she ordered. "We want to laugh too."

Melanie almost looked a little nervous. "OK, since you order it. Guess who learned how to make a tutu last night. And then guess who taught her."

May was mortified. She had no idea which way this was going to come down.

"My Lord, get out of here, what are you talking about. What do you mean tutu?" Sheil asked.

"You know, those little fluffed up skirts ballet dancers wear?" And demonstrated with her hands and a first position knee bend.

Sheil laughed, "You look so cute. I didn't know you could do that."

"We both took ballet and tap dance lessons. We could probably still do a few routines if you want to watch," Melanie threatened.

"Give. Just tell the story. Now, please."

"Carol made a tutu for Carly last night. And Carly helped."

"She didn't. Get out of here. No way she would do something domestic like sew. Did Marge do it for her?"

"Nope. Carol and Carly made it themselves. Marge set up a group session with Joan and Kit, Marla and Sabrina, and Jesse." She paused for effect. "At the Inn. And the new lady in town helped them all make tutus," she finished triumphantly.

And then she pointed at May. "And this is the new lady in town. And I saw Carly's tutu and it's great and Carol says she going to make more it's so easy."

"Well, I am speechless. Carol sewing." She looked at May and said, "May, you have done the impossible. How long have you been in town? How did you arrange all this? Why don't I know about it?" She took a breath and then said, "Tea time everyone. I want to hear the whole story."

"Me too, I'll boil the water." Melanie turned on the stove and Kimberly got the cups.

So May explained the whole story from the first tutu that Ryan thought had to be shot to the end. With multiple interruptions by customers.

May was surprised when Sheil said, "Time to close." The day had raced by. The shop was busy and exciting. May had even waited on her own customers and made some sales with Sheil nodding approvingly. May couldn't believe how much fun she was having. They had each taken a short break, over at The Fry Pan. She had gone with Melanie who was a kick and a half. May didn't know why that expression fit so well, but it did.

There was nothing about the shop, her fellow workers, or the customers May didn't like. Especially since she had the rejected clothing to work on this evening. She would start on that top and skirt this evening.

Sheil walked her through closeout procedures and sent her home with her shopping bag.

Ryan was waiting for her, anxious to hear how her first day went. She thought that was so silly but endearing. That he seemed to want to hear all about it. She told him everything. But he drew the line when she wanted to show him the clothing she had brought with her and sent her to her room. "Just not manly," he'd said.

In her room, she took out the yellow dress. She could see the skirt set. Her design would work. She carefully took out all the seams. Then took the pieces to the laundry room, hand washed them and put them through a light dry cycle. While they were drying, she set up her sewing machine on the desk and sketched, cut out her patterns, testing them for fit and made corrections. It had been a long time since she had designed, and it gave her both pleasure and comfort. Derek had convinced her that she was not very good. He was so wrong.

When she returned to the dryer, it was just binging the end of cycle. Back upstairs, she examined each piece as she pressed it. Perfect pieces, enough for her designs. The ironing finished the drying process.

She placed the fabric on the bed and positioned her patterns on top. Yup, she was good. This would work. After she pinned the patterns to the fabric she decided that would be a good stopping point. She could think about it in case she changed her mind, sometimes she got a better idea overnight. She laid the pieces neatly on the desk to finish the next day.

~

"Who do we have at that Vintage clothing shop? I don't recognize her," Nick spoke into his cell. He had seen her from his boat. Even from that distance, he felt a jolt through his body. Wondered what he would feel when he was up close to her. He'd watched her go into Vintage. Looked like she was working there. And the Help Wanted sign was gone. His people were supposed to let him know when they got an operative in there.

"What do you mean? They've hired someone?" his cell asked. "We couldn't find anyone who can qualify for the job."

"Qualify? It's a sales clerk. How do you qualify to be a sales clerk?" he demanded.

"Hold your horses. Vintage wanted someone who actually knew about old clothes and tailoring. Our gal didn't even have a chance. We all thought because she was a clothes horse she could do the job, but the owner didn't even want to talk to her. We don't have anyone who knows that stuff. I guess they hired someone else," the cell told him.

"You're not kidding? You don't know who she is? You promised me someone on the inside for backup. I thought we were going to get one of our own people into that position at Vintage."

"We don't know who she is or where she came from. We didn't even know she was there. Can you find anything out for us? Get a name and we'll do some checking."

Week 2: Monday

May arrived early, but Sheil was already there to supervise as May opened, nodding her approval when May did everything right. The day started early with a customer right after they opened and May found it just as much fun as her first day. She loved helping the customers find the perfect outfit. Still, she was tired and ready to stop when Sheil announced closing. She had thought all day about finishing the skirt and top tonight to wearing them tomorrow. She was ready to switch gears and sew.

She cut out the short skirt and the top. Might be enough for a little clutch purse with a fabric handle threaded thru the top. She cut the facings from remnants of the stained piece.

Seeing one of her designs take shape was always exciting. Sew, press, test for fit, sew, press, test for fit. It was all muscle memory. The design was a simple pattern and didn't take long. She pressed out both completed pieces and tried them on in front of the full length bathroom mirror. She was so excited, she would have gone to show Ryan, but it was one in the morning! And she had missed supper. Again. She could show Ryan in the morning.

Tuesday

May double-checked her appearance the next morning and walked to the front desk to twirl in front of Ryan. Pretty pleased with herself. (So there Derek, she thought.) She felt young, and feminine, and summery. "I made it last night from a cast off," she glowed. "Do you like it?"

"Well if you aren't a breath of spring," he said with a smile. He guessed he knew people made clothes. Certainly Marge did. But he had never actually seen a finished product and associated it with dressmaking.

"You made it? You made it?" Jesse asked. "You can make clothes? Can you make me something?"

"Jesse!" Ryan said. "That's not polite. And it's a little selfish too." Jesse immediately became crestfallen and said, "I'm sorry."

"That's OK," May said, bending down. "You bet I can make an outfit for you. But we might need to do some more fabric shopping. I made this from an old, old dress and yours should be new fabric like your tutu."

"Now, we're going to do it now?"

"Later, we can pick out the fabric tomorrow. You can be thinking about what you want. Then we'll have to schedule fittings around my job and your school. It will take time."

Jesse knew what she wanted, an outfit like May's.

When she walked into Vintage, Melanie said, "What are you wearing? What are you wearing? It looks Vintage. Well the fabric looks vintage, the style screams NOW!!"

"I made it. I made it last night. From the reject dress your Mom gave me. Do you like it? Do you like it?" she asked twirling gleefully, feeling a little like Jesse.

"Do I like it? Get out of here. I want it. I want it right now. Make me one. Where are the rejects? I want to pick out my own color and fabric. No wonder you have conned Carol into thinking she wants to sew. Me too." And then she hollered, "Come see what May did! I have dibs on the next one! Hurry!"

Kimberly came rushing out. Melanie announcing, "She made it! She made it from one of Mom's rejects! Can you believe it?"

Pandemonium broke out as the girls both squealed asking how she did it, how she knew what to do, what would look good, and when could they have an outfit of their own.

May was a little embarrassed at all the fuss and couldn't answer all the questions coming so quickly.

Sheil came in then. It took a while for everyone to calm down and explain. Sheil walked around May slowly. She remembered the dress, it had broken her heart to put it in the reject pile. It was the one May had been stroking yesterday. "This is the same fabric as that dress I put in the trash yesterday. The one you wanted. This is what you wanted to make."

Sheil had some thinking to do and she needed both her husband and her brother to discuss her plan. And get their approval.

"OK. Give me a few minutes to myself here. You both want May to make you outfits and Jesse wants one too? Right? Is that what you are saying? I need some time. I am going across the street and get some coffee. You guys finish jumping up and down and get ready to open."

Sheil sat with her coffee and smirked to herself. She had known May was a good idea the minute she saw her touching the fabrics. She just hadn't realized how good. A great employee who got along with people. One who had good ideas and lots of talent. Sheil had heard the tutu story from three different people last night. Now she had to figure out how to make May's sewing ability work for all of them. She was pretty sure she knew how it could work, but could she, should she, do it today? She would run it past her husband and her brother and if they liked it, then all of them could present the plan to May. She called them both to meet her in the coffee shop.

"Will you, will you, make us outfits? Can you?" pleaded Kimberly. She sounded a little like Jesse.

"I can design and sew them. But if you want updated vintage, you will have to get the materials from your mother."

"OK, no problem. Mom will let us take rejects I'm sure."

Melanie looked out the window and said, "There's Dad going into The Coffee Spot with Bryce. That's curious. Wonder what's going on over there?" May looked too; she hadn't met either of those men, yet. She was a little nervous. She hoped she hadn't done anything wrong. Sheil had looked concerned when she left.

Fifteen minutes later, the three walked over to the shop with coffees and muffins for everyone. "Let's go in the back room. Melanie put up the back in a half hour sign. We are going to have a business meeting." The twins looked at each other and at May and shrugged their shoulders.

It hadn't taken long for Sheil to convince her menfolk. She just told them the facts, and they agreed with her, she was a good business person and an excellent judge of character. And they agreed, the time was now.

Sheil introduced her husband Hal, and her brother, Bryce. Everyone sat down around the table, except Bryce, he preferred to stand and watch May. He trusted his sister's judgment and her plan, she was able to put complex ideas together. He was a little nervous because they knew nothing about May and he wanted to watch her reactions.

"OK May, here is what I know. Right now I am discarding about 22% of each purchase order due to staining, tears, whatever. I am proposing that you buy that waste from me at my cost." She held up her hand, "Don't say anything yet. Hear me out. You design any items you want and make them. We'll put them on a special rack and label them as Renewed Vintage Now styles in vintage fabrics. We'll work out some catchy wording. We will post signs for our new sideline and hang some samples in the front window and on the back wall. You sell them through the shop and pay me 25% of your profit. You can make clothes to order like you're planning to do for my daughters. Same deal with those, the shop gets 25%. We'll test it for a month and then we will readdress the percentages and draw up a new contract."

May was amazed. All she had done was make an outfit and Sheil was suggesting a partnership. An opportunity for her to sew and make money. "I don't need a contract. We can do that without a contract."

"Contract. My brother will write it and include the stipulation that we revisit in one month. I want it fair for everyone."

May was starting to nod but then remembered, "Oh, but I already told the twins I would make them outfits."

"Sell them the dresses after you make them."

"But I wasn't planning on selling them the dresses. I love designing and sewing. It's second nature for me. Besides, they are my Boss's daughters, how could I charge them? How will a contract affect that?"

Bryce liked that. He let out a breath. Sheil was right again and he gave her a nod.

Sheil looked at May with a crooked smile and a shake of her head. "Right, I am your boss and I say you can't charge my daughters this first time. Bryce, the first new vintage for each of my girls will be mentioned in the contract as prototypes. And the twins will get those vintage rejects for free."

Bryce agreed, "OK, that sounds good. For everyone. I will have the contract tomorrow."

"I'm off tomorrow," May said.

"You're off tomorrow, that's right. I want you to move in upstairs. No waiting period. Can you move in tomorrow? Move on my time. I'll put you on the clock for the move."

Wow. So much, so quick. May laughed. "Yes, I can move tomorrow. I don't have much with me. So, yes, I can move in tomorrow, nine o'clock?"

It was settled. May couldn't wait to move into her own place. Rent so cheap it was a steal. She couldn't wait to tell Ryan.

She told the twins she would also bring back the pieces she took home yesterday and they could see if there was something they wanted. She could show them some designs after they found their fabric. Yes, she was excited. This was another job she could do pregnant and with a baby. Life was looking good. She went to work.

That night she was almost too excited to sleep, again. She could hardly wait for morning. She was so excited, she packed her few possessions and then repacked. Showered and repacked. And finally made herself stop going crazy and go to bed. Grinning. She couldn't stop grinning.

Wednesday

Sheil saw her walking down the dock dragging one roll bag and carrying an old sewing machine. Her new employee had one suitcase and a sewing machine?

"Is this it? Do you have more?"

"No, this is it, a suitcase and a sewing machine. Everything I own."

There was a story here, Sheil thought. She grabbed the suitcase handle and climbed the outside stairs dragging it up. Unlocked the door, wheeled in the case, and gave the key to May.

"Get yourself settled. You can get some essentials at the marina grocery store. Or go back into town. I brought up a set of vintage linens, they are on the counter."

May just stood for a few minutes, looking around. Her own place. It had been so easy. Should that make her nervous? No. She had chosen to move, selected a location, found a job, and was ready when the opportunities presented themselves.

She put the sewing machine on the counter and took the linens to the bedroom. She loved the blue on green coverlet. The pale green sheets would be perfect. The percale sheets were soft, cool, and silky as she put them on and made the bed. She wondered if she could buy the sheets, maybe with an employee discount? She just wanted to bounce on the bed, so she did. Just once and rested a moment with her legs stretched out, then crossed her ankles and looked at the room. Her room. Jumped up and dragged in her suitcase. Hung her clothes on vintage hangers in the closet. She put her underwear and white cotton granny gown, and the green frog, and the pink sheep jammies in the drawers. The jammies still brought a smile to her face and she could remember laughing when she made them.

She took her toiletries to the bathroom. No makeup to worry about. Put the suitcase in the back of the closet.

Next, the sewing machine. She took it to the small den and set it up. With her first check she would buy some fabric. She would sew. She missed it. Because Derek disapproved, she had just packed her life away to please him. She couldn't believe she had done that.

She had a design in her head, could see it in a charcoal gauze. Top and skirt. Maybe a second, patterned top and a fabric belt. Well, soon.

She shook herself. Stop dreaming May. Go buy some food. Make a list. Get a new cell phone. Well maybe not, she didn't need one. There was no one to call her and she had no one to call. The land line in the apartment should be all she needed. She must ask Sheil about it.

She got her purse and her key. Her key! And set off for the marina store. She would have to explore the rest of the shops, later or perhaps tomorrow she thought. And the docks with the fishing boats and sight-seeing tours.

She gloried in picking out milk, bread, eggs, orange juice. Butter or margarine? Margarine for now. Peanut butter. Cheese for grilled cheese. Soup? A couple of cans. And coffee. Had to have coffee. Tea. She had seen the Bunn in the kitchen. Had forgotten to check for filters, so picked up generic. Oh, she could get muffins at The Coffee Spot on the way back. Lettuce, tomatoes, chicken for supper? Yes. Potatoes and salad dressing. She would have enough for a few days. And resupply would be easy. The marina was well stocked on necessities and seemed reasonably priced.

She asked the clerk if she could use her credit card, reminding herself to open a checking account and get some cash. She was happy she had kept her license. She'd never needed it with Derek. Couldn't she just stop thinking about Derek? She would make that a goal.

"Sure", the clerk said bringing her mind back to the present.

A short, kind of round man standing by the clerk said, "I didn't see a new boat pull in."

"Oh, I'm not on a boat. I'm working at Vintage, working for Sheil. I just moved in this morning. I'm May Johnson."

"Welcome aboard," he said smiling. "I'm Jeremy Michaels, I run the marina." He seemed like a cheerful guy. Short and stumpy with curly blonde hair.

"Thanks. I am excited to be here," she said with a bright smile.

Now she had to figure out how to transport her groceries back to her apartment. She said to the clerk, "Looks like I'm going to need a couple of those cloth shopping bags also. I forgot I had to get my groceries back." She was a little embarrassed. The bags would be full and heavy.

Jeremy said, "Wait a minute," and hollered at a man with a captain's cap. "Hey, Nick, you got a charter this morning?"

May was aware that Nick had been watching her. She had seen him a few times in the last two days. Always carefully not watching her, he had kept a close eye on her the whole time she was in the store. Somehow she always sensed when he was around and now he seemed bothered that Jeremy noticed him.

"No, no charter till this afternoon." At first, Nick was irritated at being singled out. Jeremy was a notorious matchmaker. But then he thought, this might be a good way to learn something about the new sales clerk. Maybe he should thank Jeremy. He had thought about asking Sheil or the twins about the new clerk. It wouldn't be out of line for him. Everyone thought he was a skirt chaser. And catcher. Now he was glad he hadn't asked.

"Well come on over here and help this little lady carry her groceries home."

"No, I can get them," May said. "It's only a short walk." And besides, Nick made her nervous. He looked right at her then, pinning her, and she felt her stomach drop. Oh, boy. Was he ever… not cute, all male. Whatever he was, her body was saying ooohhh, while her mind was still trying to sort him out. His face was square, strong. His smile didn't reach his green eyes. About her height, a tad taller, maybe 5' 10". Tough? Craggy? Dangerous, she thought. Dangerous, was the word she needed for him.

"Nick will carry your bags. Won't you Nick. Meet May Johnson; she just started with Sheil and has moved into the apartment." Looking at May he continued, "This is Captain Nick London, he owns London's Luck, docked over there, and takes out fishing and sightseeing charters."

"Pleased to meet you," Nick said to her with a smile. "Let me have that heavy sack."

When May hesitated he continued, "We're all family here and help each other out. And like you said, it's only a short walk, I can manage it."

Again she felt a little embarrassed and silly to be so nervous. "OK, great, I think I got carried away and overbought. Not used to carrying my food home."

"Oh," he said, "How do you get your groceries home?"

"With a car?" she said with the unvoiced 'Dah' at the end.

"Good point, we tend to forget that here. Sheil probably has a red wagon by the back entrance. That's the way most of us get our sacks home."

"Oh, I did see that. Just assumed it meant there were children around."

"That too."

"I can see that I'm going to have to learn new everyday habits if I am going to settle in here. It will be an adventure." She laughed, and said, "And it will be interesting to see how many more ways I can embarrass myself."

He liked her laugh. And that she could laugh at herself.

"Where are you from?"

"Back east," she replied. She had started out back east, that was the truth.

"Just back east?" he pushed.

"Yes, how about you, where are you from?" May said not budging.

"Here, actually."

"Oh." They came to her stairs. "I can get them from here. Thanks so much for your help, I don't know how to repay you."

"I can carry them up, you can pay me with lunch maybe," he said with a smile.

The suggestion and smile made her more than a little nervous. The smile was one she felt sure he used to catch his women. The one that didn't reach his eyes, his leer. But she said, carelessly she hoped, "I'm not settled yet and really don't have anything for lunch. Let me do it another day. OK?"

"I can help you put away groceries and unpack."

"I can manage that. I'm unpacked already and I think I can put away my own groceries."

'It would be fun. We could get acquainted." Pushing again.

"No, thank you Captain London. Not today." This time she put finality and a bit of anger into her voice. No one was going to push her around.

He didn't seem too happy with the idea, but other than being rude he would have to accept it. "OK, see you around May Johnson. Say hey to Sheil."

She watched him saunter back toward the marina for a minute and then carried her groceries upstairs. Probably a good thing she didn't have to carry them home after all. They were heavy and awkward.

She started the coffee, was glad she had bought filters, there weren't any. And toasted bread, she had forgotten the muffins. She wouldn't have stopped with Nick anyway She put everything away. Maybe tomorrow she would have time for muffins. She added some margarine to the toast and noticed for the first time that there was a deck off the kitchen overlooking the marina.

She went out and sat at the table and ate as she watched the boats and tourists. And Jeremy and Nick talking in front of the marina. Could she pick out his boat? She would have to watch and see where he went. She hoped that he'd not seen that she did have food for lunch in her sacks. She was not intentionally unfriendly. Just was not yet ready for company. Not ready for another controlling male.

She leaned back and thought that coffee on her deck could be habit forming. Baby will love this.

She cleaned up and went downstairs and signed the papers that Bryce had drawn up. Laughed at herself. Signing papers with an attorney, again. But such different circumstances. Laughed again when she realized it had almost been half a day since she had even thought of Derek.

She asked Bryce if she could make an appointment for some personal assistance and he told her to come in the next day. So that would be one item off her list.

Thursday

The next morning she was sitting under the umbrella at The Coffee Spot with a cappuccino. She had decided to come down here and watch people. She had met Janine, the owner. A large, solid, brisk woman with her gray hair in a bun. Not overly friendly.

May felt more like part of the dock activity here instead of a watcher from her deck. She had almost finished when she saw Nick. And saw when he spotted her and started toward her. She wondered if she could gather up her things: drink, book, purse, and leave, but quickly realized there wasn't time And she wasn't going to start running away. Besides she could handle one pushy man.

Nick got that stitch in his stomach again when he saw her. He couldn't figure that out. Only happened with her. She wasn't his type though, so why was he interested? He decided to go over and talk. Saw her anxious look and figured she didn't much want to talk to him. "Hi." That was original he thought.

She looked at him a minute and said. "Good morning."

"Thought I should apologize."

"Apologize?"

"Ya, I was a little pushy yesterday. I'm sorry."

"A little pushy?" she said raising her eyebrow. "Is that what you call it?"

"OK. A lot pushy. I'm sorry. I'm not generally that way. How can I make it right?" He said this with the smile he knew worked well on women.

"Just keep walking."

Shocked he looked at her considering and lost the seductive smile. He replaced it with a cold look and said. "OK. Sorry." And turned to walk away.

She was instantly sorry. That was rude. It was his leer that made her say it. She had never liked the smooth talking type. "Now, I am sorry," she said to his back. He turned his head to look at her.

"That was rude and I'm not generally rude. If you promise not to get pushy, I'll promise not to be rude."

"Done," he said. "Can I get you a refill? I was just going to take a break myself."

She hesitated and then agreed. She felt a little like company. "Cappuccino."

"Tell me what is happening over there?" she asked when he came back pointing across the marina.

"Well, the tour boat is loading for its trip up the shoreline. And that commotion with all the kids? That's a family, getting ready to rent a skiff for the day. They will all come back sunburned." He took a sip of his coffee and started on his muffin. He had brought her a muffin too.

"They rent skiffs? That might be fun."

"You don't need to rent a skiff; you can go out with me."

She just looked at him.

"Oh, too pushy again?" he laughed. "OK, you can rent a skiff. But I could show you a good time."

He knew that was a mistake because he could see her trying to decide how to react to that.

"I didn't mean that the way it came out. I meant that I could show you around, point out the landmarks, describe the birds. Feed you lunch. That's what I do when I take out sightseeing charters."

She hadn't been serious about going out in a small boat and didn't intend to go out with him. She decided to accept that as an apology and explanation and changed the subject. "Shouldn't you be out on a charter now?"

"No charter this morning, but I am taking out some folks this afternoon." He pointed out his boat tied up on a finger pier he called it. "That's my boat there."

"How did you get started in chartering? What type of qualifications do you need?"

He wondered who was interrogating whom. "I grew up here, on the water. I was guiding by the time I was 16. You have to meet U.S. Coast Guard requirements. And have a Captain's license. It also helps if you can find and catch fish, if you want to keep working. You need to be able to get along with all sorts of weird people. And keep the idiots safe on a boat."

"That must be where pushy comes in?" She was smiling.

He laughed again. She liked his laugh, a sound like a brook. And she liked his face when he laughed. It lit up.

"Ya, landlubbers can be pretty stupid."

"I can imagine, being one myself. No experience with boats or water."

"You really do need to come out with me."

"No, I don't think I am ready yet." She said it softly not sure if she meant ready for a boat ride or a boat ride with him. She was still married. Funny how she hadn't thought of herself that way. Still married. Had already put it behind. Put Derek behind. It must not have been love she thought again.

"Where did you go?"

"What?" She snapped back to look at the man across from her. "Sorry, my mind wandered and forgot to come back. No, I am not ready for a boat ride."

"Another time, then." And there was that smile again. The leer that she was sure all the women fell for.

Time for her to leave. "Thanks for the snacks and the conversation. I have a date." She stood and gathered her things.

"Maybe we can meet for coffee again," he suggested. This time with the nice smile.

"Maybe, bye." She smiled, and left for her meeting with Bryce and her date with Jesse thinking that she liked the Nick with the nice smile. And then stopped herself, she was still married. She told herself, "Yo, girl. Still married and pregnant." Not a good time or the right circumstances to be thinking about a nice guy. Maybe just a friend? A brother? No, that was not the way she was thinking of him.

Nick watched her walk away. The smile that always worked for him with women scared her away. That had happened twice. He liked her. Wondering. Who did she have a date with when she wouldn't even go out on the water with him? He shrugged it off and got ready for his charter.

She found Bryce's office easily. There was no secretary in the outer room, so she called, "Knock, knock. Anyone here?"

Bryce came to the inner office door and waved her inside. As he finished up on the phone he sat down and motioned her to a chair. "OK, what can I do for you May?"

She took a deep breath and told herself, just spit it out, again. You are well practiced with the story now. "My husband has thrown me out. He is divorcing me. I am pregnant and he doesn't believe the baby is his. Here are my copies of the documents he filed for a petition for divorce. And these are the forms where he relinquishes all rights to the baby. I need you to assure that the divorce goes through and that Derek has fully relinquished and waived all rights to my child."

Bryce felt his jaw drop. He had expected her to want more information on her new Vintage contract. He closed his mouth and took the documents. He took his time reading through them. And then read through them again, taking notes. He was calculating how this might affect Sheil and if he had read May wrong.

He was impressed that she didn't even fidget while she waited. "I will need to ask you some questions," he said looking at his notes.

"Before you begin, I told Sheil I was pregnant when she offered me the job. She doesn't know the circumstances. You can talk to her if you want. And you can tell her why I came to see you. I might tell her myself. I don't expect to be able to hide my condition, but I haven't told anyone else. Except Ryan."

"Why Ryan?"

"I don't know. Actually I have no idea why I told Ryan. It felt right at the time. He has been very supportive. Almost like a Dad." If she'd had a Dad, he would have been like Ryan.

"These papers indicate that you have made no claims against your husband in the divorce." He made that a statement.

"That's right; I don't want anything from him."

"What about child support?"

"No child support. I do not want Derek ever to be able to come back and want a role in raising my child."

"What about the child's father? Will he want a role?"

"The baby is his, Derek's. There is no one else. Derek claims he is sterile, but DNA would prove him the father. I don't want to pursue that. There is no way I would want him in my life now. He threw me out. Me and the baby."

"OK."

He thought some more. "The paperwork is excellent. I can't do anything better. You already did this job right based on what you say. It looks like you have about 3 ½ weeks more for the final decree. You are already using your maiden name. That is borderline legal in this time period. But you should be OK. I will get in touch, check the progress, and make sure you get copies of everything."

She paid him a minimal fee and then walked to the bank where she opened an account and transferred money. From there she went to the medical building and made an appointment with the obstetrician. She signed paperwork to have her file sent from her old doctor.

Finally, she walked to the Inn to meet Ryan to take Jesse to buy fabric. They were going to buy fabric for shorts with an elastic waist and a top which May would design. May explained that it would be a few days before she would have some completed designs. And then she would have to fit the patterns, cut the fabric, sew, and fit again. Jesse could help.

They went back to the fabric store and selected fabrics which were an easy care pink for the top and green for shorts. May was beginning to see a pattern here. Marge asked what they were making and if the tutu group would be working together again.

Jesse jumped right on that. "Can Sabrina have one too?" she asked May. "Can Sabrina make one like mine? Hers will be blue and green. She likes blue and green."

May couldn't refuse her. I guess we could, they wanted to do another project. Marge said she would contact the two other Moms and help them select their fabric. The kids were all pretty much the same size and there would be few alterations in the basic pattern. The tops could be different styles. Or the Mom's could add appliques made from the shorts fabric. Jesse was jumping up and down with excitement as they headed home.

May relaxed over tea with Ryan, laughing about her new sewing group. Ryan explained that his daughter-in-law wouldn't be back for another week, maybe two. So the sewing group, or tutu group, would be a good distraction for Jesse.

He was pleased that Marge had jumped right in to include the other Moms and that May was being treated as part of the town family. "You call on me if you ever need anything." He patted her hand.

She left with tears in her eyes and went home. Home she thought with a sigh. And sat on her balcony with a book. She felt edgy at one point and looked up to see Nick watching her. He was always watching her, she had meant to ask Ryan about him. Maybe Sheil would know something. She ignored Nick and went back to her book. At dark she went in to work on the designs for Jesse.

Friday

Nick looked for May at The Coffee Spot next morning. Invited himself over again to sit and talk. Brought her a cappuccino and a giant blueberry muffin with homemade jelly. Though May had planned on visiting a few more of the shops before work she stayed and listened to Nick tell fishing stories. She loved to watch his face. When he laughed she could see light shining out. Not at all like his leer. It was over too soon though because she had to go to work.

He came by with subs for her evening break. Melanie hollered, "Uncle Nick, you brought dinner. Hope you got my favorite."

Uncle? May thought. She really would have to find out about Nick.

"Got you meatballs, Nasty. Italian for me, American for the new girl," he said it with his warm smile looking at May.

At first she was going to refuse but decided that might not be polite. Besides, she didn't know if this might be a routine, between Uncle and niece. Three people, that would be OK, she thought. She wouldn't be alone with him. But then Melanie got a call and walked off to take it in private.

Nick moved close to her. "Let's go out in my boat tomorrow. Just you and me."

She looked at him trying to figure out if this was a simple invite or a date or would he be expecting more. She couldn't tell. "No, I have to work. Thank you."

"We'll make it a morning trip. Just a couple of hours."

"No, I don't think that would be a good idea."

"Sure it would, we could be alone. On the water. Nothing more beautiful than two people alone on the water. I insist." He added.

She still couldn't tell what was behind the words. But the I insist part struck a nerve. "No. I can't"

"Don't be a tease. You know you want to, all the girls want to." And there was that smile again. The Girl Killer leer. The one she hated.

She was saved when Melanie came back in.

She said, "No, Nick, I don't want to go out in the boat tomorrow. But thank you again for asking me." Stiffly polite. She could feel her teeth grinding. But she knew how to do the polite social refusal. This would be her last polite refusal.

Melanie looked at the both of them and said, "Good for you May. All the girls fall for that line." She pointed to the tourists looking in the window. "I bet they come in," Melanie said just as the door chimed.

"I have to go to work. How much do I owe you for my sub?" May asked Nick.

"Nothing," he growled. He left through the shop.

"What happened? He sure left in a huff," Melanie said.

"I don't know," she said shaking her head. Because she really didn't understand any of it. He had demanded she go on the boat with him and he hadn't liked that she refused. But that didn't explain his attitude. Surely some other woman, somewhere, had refused him.

Saturday

Nick found her the next morning at The Coffee Spot again.

She saw him coming and yes, she would leave if he tried to sit with her. But he just nodded as he walked inside. She relaxed with relief. All her preparation to be brave and then he just walked right by her. But her relief was short lived because there he was in front of her. Smiling the warm smile that melted her insides.

"Got you cappuccino and a blueberry." And, just like last night's nastiness hadn't happened, he put them in front of her and sat down.

She looked at him amazed. "That must be some other tease you bought those for. Excuse me I have to get to work." She started to get up.

He grabbed her arm. "Don't leave, what will people say? They expect you to be nice to me." Nodding his head toward the dock.

She looked and saw people watching. Dock people, shop people. He thought he was going to embarrass her? Into sitting with him? She didn't think so.

Quietly she said, "Let go of my arm. Or they will really have something to watch. Don't try to intimidate me with peer pressure."

He looked at her face and saw her determination, but didn't let go.

She was so angry. She stood tall and confronted him. "You think you are going to embarrass me in front of my neighbors? You think I am afraid of what they will say if I leave you here? Don't you dare try to back me into a corner. I will never do what you expect if you back me into a corner. Remember, I said I don't like pushy. You are the one who should be embarrassed. At the very least you owe me an apology for the way you treated me last night. And for what you are trying to do to me now. Stay away from me." And she backed up, smiled at her neighbors, and tossed the coffee at him. Missed mostly. She walked slowly away. She didn't dare turn to see the look on his face. But she saw her neighbors laughing.

She went toward Vintage and saw Sheil standing at the window. That figures, she thought. That's probably my job. And my apartment. And my future. Just because I lost my temper. She just shook her head and walked upstairs to her apartment. She left the door open. She knew Sheil would be up. Sat at the counter. All gone. Job, home, new friends. All gone because she couldn't let one stupid man boss her. She waited.

"Am I fired?" she asked when Sheil walked in. "How soon do I have to move out?"

"Fired? Move out? Are you crazy? Get out of here. Why would you be fired?"

"Oh, only because I rejected the golden boy in front of the whole town?"

"Hey girl, if you don't want to sit with a man, you don't sit with him. It shouldn't matter what the town thinks. Wait a minute. You thought you would lose your job and you still left him sitting there soaked in coffee?"

"Well, ya, that's the way it works doesn't it? He said you all expect me to be nice to him."

"No. No one expects you to be nice to Nick, not even Nick. We all love the idea that there appears to be a spark between the two of you. But don't you ever think that you have to make us happy to keep your job. In fact, I am tempted to give you a raise. You didn't give in to his threats, you dumped coffee on him, and you have the whole town laughing at him. He deserves it. No way are you fired. I am going to give you a raise."

May looked up at her hopefully. "Really? You're not going to fire me?"

"No way. Now come here and give me a hug. You need one too."

May whimpered on Sheil's shoulder. "I was so angry at him. And mad at me too."

"It's OK, now sit down and I'll get you a cup of tea." And then I am going to go over to that boat and kick him she thought. "Why are you mad at yourself?"

"I like him, I think. I shouldn't like him. I'm pregnant, Sheil. Remember. How can I like Nick when I am pregnant? And I'm married too." She wailed.

Sheil almost dropped the teapot. She had forgotten that May was pregnant. But married? "You're married? I just assumed it was a boyfriend."

"No. I'm married." She sniffed. "At least I am for another three weeks. My husband threw me out when I told him I was pregnant and he filed for divorce immediately."

"Then it was a boy friend?" she was shocked, May didn't seem to be that kind of person.

"Of course not. What type of person do you think I am?" She took a breath, hearing herself. "I'm sorry. You really don't know me well enough to know what kind of person I am. But I don't sleep around. The baby is my husband's. He says he's sterile and the baby isn't his. But he's wrong. And I don't want to talk about it." She fled to the bedroom.

Sheil followed and comforted her. "You don't have to talk about it. You don't have to say anything. Go wash your face and pull yourself together. Come down to work when you get ready. We have a new shipment of clothes to sort through."

It took May awhile to stop the hitches and get the red out of her eyes. When she thought she would be able to speak without crying, she went to work. Downstairs, she found Sheil talking to Nick. She didn't want to be here. But she stayed; she wasn't going to let his presence dictate her actions. The twins were with customers but May could tell they were all ears. She was sure that, even if they had not witnessed the scene, someone would have told them. She looked at Sheil, wondering if she had told Nick anything. Sheil shook her head and said, "Nick just walked in and wants to talk to you."

"I don't want to talk to him"

"Well just listen then," he growled and looked at Sheil and said, "This is private."

"No, Sheil, please don't leave. I don't want to be alone with him." When she saw that Sheil was going to stay, she looked at Nick and said, "Talk."

He looked uncomfortable. She saw some coffee stains on him, so she hadn't missed entirely.

"I'm sorry," he said and stopped.

She waited to see if there was more, but apparently not. "OK."

To Sheil she said," Let's go open that shipment."

He stalked toward her, "I'm not done." He looked to Sheil for help and only saw disapproval. Turned back to May and repeated, "I'm sorry, May."

"OK, I got that. You're sorry. I said OK."

"I'm sorry for being an ass. I'm sorry for what I said last night." He looked at Sheil again, but she was still just standing there. "I shouldn't have called you a tease. It wasn't true and I didn't mean it. I should have apologized to you this morning before I backed you into that corner. I am sorry I did that. I don't usually browbeat and threaten women." He didn't either. Had not ever done that before. Something about her made him push for a reaction. She was driving him crazy. He generally knew exactly what to do and say around women. None had ever made him this confused. Or angry. Or aggressive. "I deserved what I got." He motioned to the coffee stains and didn't make any excuses.

"Please accept my apology." He was almost begging now.

She looked at him a moment longer and then said, "Apology accepted. Now I have to get to work."

He didn't know what else to say. Tongue tied? Him? So he turned and walked out.

May took a deep breath and held up a hand and took a couple of more breaths and said, "OK, I don't want to talk about it. Let's open the packages."

This time they were all hoping for some damaged goods. That was a twist. And they were not disappointed to find three dresses that were not good enough quality for sale. They readied the rest for sale or dry cleaning and entered the appropriate information into the computer for tags. Finally, May worked up the courage to ask Sheil about 'Uncle' Nick.

"Nick really is their Uncle. He is their Mother's baby brother. He left town before she died and just came back a month ago. He lives on his boat, even though he still has the family home here. Hal takes care of it for him, rents it, puts the money in Nick's account."

The twins were between customers and each selected a dress for redesign; the third item would be redesigned for sale. Melanie picked the long, maxi, blue with lace trim. The trim was discolored and torn. Kimberly the plain yellow. The yellow had elasticized sides where the elastic was stretched out and rotted but the full skirt contained sufficient fabric for an outfit. May would work on designs. Designs that would complement the fabrics, the colors, and the twins. They both wanted dresses which would require some extensive preplanning and measurement.

The day was busy in the shop and May soon forgot the ugly scene and later apology. But every once in a while one of the twins would giggle and say, "Wish I had seen that." And then immediately look chagrinned. "Well he was a jerk to put you in a position like that. Did you really throw coffee at him?" And more giggles.

May just laughed it off and tried to put them at ease. After all he was their uncle. "Well, I missed with the coffee, mostly. Maybe next time I will have better aim. And a chocolate milkshake." So they spent the evening laughing about the best type of drink to throw at a jerk. Not Nick, some other jerk.

The shop stayed busy for the rest of the night and by the time she got back upstairs she was exhausted. She collapsed on her deck for an hour before going to bed.

Sunday

She worked up her courage and went back to The Coffee Spot. She had to face her neighbors. She cringed inside but walked over and sat at her table. She sat and ordered a veggie omelet and home fries.

She was not so brave really; she knew that Nick was out on a charter. She thought his boat was gone. She had not yet figured out a way to identify which boat it was, but his parking space at the dock was empty. The boats all looked the same to her.

Janine came out with a huge muffin. "You deserve this. We all love Nick, but that doesn't mean he gets to be a bully. I heard what he said to you. Your breakfast will be out in a minute. On the house."

May's felt her jaw drop. Janine was being nice to her? May had never seen Janine be nice to anyone. Three people stopped by and patted her shoulder. She almost cried. She almost felt sorry for Nick. Wondered what type of treatment he was getting. When she thought about it, she realized it was women who were comforting her so she supposed that the men were doing the same to Nick.

She ate everything. Left a nice tip, enough to cover most of her breakfast. Everyone had to earn a living here.

She went to the Inn to meet with the tutu group. The kids were at church school, it was just the Moms this morning. And of course they all wanted the inside scoop on Nick and The Coffee Spot scene. She just said Nick had gotten too pushy and she had lost her temper and before she knew it she had thrown her coffee in his face, sort of. She was sorry about that. She was fair. She told them that he had apologized. A sincere apology.

Carol said, "But you two look so good together. And we would love to see Nick with someone nice. Can't you two work it out? I know he likes you and you seem to like him. Even now you are not telling the whole story. And you didn't have to tell us he apologized."

"I can't go out with Nick." Lately it seemed she was always taking chances. "Remember, I'm married."

"Where's your ring? Why aren't you wearing a ring? Have you told Nick?"

May looked at Carol sadly, she took a breath and said, "My husband threw me out. He is divorcing me. I don't want to be reminded, so I don't wear a ring. That's my right, not to wear a ring. Why should I tell Nick? I'm not seeing him. I'm not dating him. I am not anything to Nick. I don't need to tell him anything. I thought he might be a friend. A guy friend. I never led him on." She stopped herself, she was whining.

"Why did your husband throw you out? How does a man throw out his wife?"

"I am not ready to talk about that yet. Soon, I'll explain soon. And it is simple to throw out a wife if you are angry and powerful. And my soon-to-be ex is both those things. Any other questions? Let's get them all out of the way. And if you want me to leave, we don't have to sew. I'll understand."

They all looked at her as if she were crazy. Then at each other. "We're not judging. We came to sew and get the gossip. You have the inside scoop. We're staying. The kids need their shorts and tops. You promised we could make them today. Or at least get started. How you and Nick treat each other is between the two of you. What your jerk of a husband does is on him."

May sighed with relief and put them to work pinning patterns to fabric and cutting out. They gossiped about other people, thank goodness.

Work at Vintage was a repeat of Saturday. Steady customer walk ins. Some buying. Some, locals, came to see the woman who threw the coffee at Nick. May let them look and helped them with clothing, but had nothing to say about her activities yesterday.

A couple of shop owners came to talk to Sheil about their meeting in the morning and to see if she had any ideas about the Cove Dock advertising. When they left, Sheil said, "I don't know what we're going to do. We really wanted something different this year, but no one has any ideas. And the first weekend is soon."

"What are you talking about?"

"How to get tourists and visitors here at the Cove Dock Shops."

"Can I help? I volunteered with some promotions before I came here."

"Please, please do"

"Simplest and least expensive type of promotion, Vintage can have pairs of students walk up and down the dock modeling Vintage clothing. Each student would carry the card detailing the origin of their outfits. The students would approach and share this information with the public. And if the chocolate shop and muffin shop are agreeable, the kids could handout small bites as they stroll up and down the dock in and out of shops. You already have the employees and with the snacks you could share the costs. Vintage could have models anyhow each weekend. They could also carry colorful balloons and streamers with shop names. And there are lots of other things too."

"That's great. Get out of here. That's great. Why didn't I ever think of that? You're great. You're coming with me tomorrow. Get more ideas together to present to the owners. OK?"

"Sure," she said that a little nervously. She knew she had more good ideas, she wasn't sure of presenting them, but she could do it. This was a new chapter in her life. More doors opening. More chances to become part of the community.

Week 3: Monday

She was ready when Sheil came for her the next day and they walked together to the restaurant for the meeting.

As Nick gassed up his boat after an early morning birding charter, he saw the group of shop owners going into the restaurant. "What's going on in there?" he asked Billy, the marina assistant manager who was acting as dock boy.

"The shop owners are having sandwiches and deciding on a season advertisement plan. Everyone's invited. Charter captains too. You should go on over. They will be starting soon."

Nick was shaking his head, "Meeting, no way." Though he wondered if maybe he would learn something about the people he was after.

"That little chica you been watching is in there."

"What? What little chica? What do you mean? Who have I been watching.?"

"That one that lives over Vintage. You watch her all the time. Her deck is the first place you look whenever you come in off the water. And you always notice her. And there was that thing the other day at The Coffee Spot." He said that last one with a smile.

Nick had gotten a lot of good natured ribbing about that. Everyone might not have seen it, but everyone made it a point to mention it to him. A couple even asked for lessons on how to pick up a girl. He just walked away, disgusted with himself.

"Do not watch her," he grumbled. "Am not interested in her." Had he been that obvious? Even before the coffee scene? Well probably the coffee scene hurt him a little and brought them both some notoriety.

Laughing. "Ya. You're not interested in her and I'm not an assistant marina manager. Why don't you just throw a move on her and get over it?"

"Already tried that."

"Got shot down good, too I'll bet. Always makes the chase more fun."

"You know, maybe I do need to be in there. OK if I tie the boat here for 1/2 hour?"

He got inside and sat down in time to hear Sheil say, "May has suggested that I have a couple of sales girls dress up in vintage clothes and walk along the dock talking to tourists. I like the idea. She has more ideas for an event to open the season and I'm going to let her explain.

May started slowly. She had made and reviewed her notes and was used to speaking to groups. Just not this group. "You could start the season with a one day event or a weekend event. The three day, Friday through Sunday, time would work best for my ideas. And the activities during The Event could be used any time during the season, either as a group or for single shops.

Each shop could have the girls carry or wear samples. The shops might want to have their own clerks wear their products. Like Sheil will be doing. But the models should always travel in pairs. The teams could also wear some article from Cougars Cove Fibers, or the Jewelry Indulgence Shop or T-Shirts. They could also carry samples of lotion from Soaps to share with visitors, bites of chocolates or muffins. Maybe The Fry Pan would have an appropriate tidbit. They could dangle glass birds, or cranes, or Whimsy designs.

Some shops could offer an activity for the tourists during The Event. Dainty Bits Chocolate, you could put on a special display trimming candies or dipping strawberries. And then you could work with a group of customers helping them dip candies that they purchased. Or give a demonstration of how to make truffles. Or give away the truffles. Or sell them, for a minimal, at cost amount. And that should be our only rule. No samples above cost.

Back to chocolates. Can the tourists help make them? Can they make and eat their own truffle? Can they frost muffins? That would probably be cupcakes, not muffins." She got a laugh on that one. And watched the chocolate and muffin folks jotting down ideas, she hoped.

You could sell dollar chances, for a $20.00 basket of chocolates or muffins. Or you might consider if you can do the basket for free. Get a crowd together. And pick 3 or 4 lucky customers. Do that 3 or 4 times a day. Advertise the times so folks will know when to show up."

The Artists' Shop. Have 8 or 10 canvasses set up for a lesson. With brushes and paints, water color or acrylic something fast drying because the 'new artists' will want to take them home. Lead them thru a simple scene. One everyone and anyone can do. There could be a very minimal charge, not more than five dollars. Have them all go home feeling like winners. They'll be back. This can be a short art lesson. Maybe have a winner who receives their lessons free or half price. Advertise your lessons.

Origami? You could give a simple demonstration. Something with only a few folds using plain copy paper. Let the public make some that they could keep. I guess you could set a goal for one thousand cranes made during 'The Event'.

Cove Photography? The new digital Polaroid sounds like a great tool to me. Walk around and snap shots of the public with the digital Polaroid. Hand out the pictures. Or sell them. But they have to be cheap. Your cost only. You could offer enlargements too, and charge for those, like they do on cruise ships. And everything would be digital.

Glass Bird? Earth Pottery? Whimsy Metal? Soaps? Jewelry Indulgence? I can't think of any activities. I don't know enough. And I left out the restaurant because I'm out of my depth there also. Maybe we can get together and see if you have ideas?"

"Each shop could have its own flyer. I have some samples here that include some of the ideas I just mentioned." She passed them around. "I think some could have coupons or chances for special items or for the activities. If we have a huge turnout we may need to use chances for the activities. I don't know how you do your print advertisements. But we could publish online."

"We need to set up a schedule for the activities. Do we want each one in its own time slot? Could they overlap?"

Jeremy said, "We could also put out glass donation jars in each shop for Amy Sutton. You all know that she is in the hospital in Texas. We really want her home. Medical transportation is expensive. And she has lots of bills. We won't make it a theme or even advertise it. Just have the jars sitting there available for donations."

May continued, "We need to decide who will participate and in what manner and if you want flyers. There is not much time for that, so Vintage will be selecting models and clothing today. If anyone wants us to demonstrate their wares, let us know."

All during her speech the shop owners or managers were nodding and whispering to each other and, like Chocolates owner, they were jotting down notes. Everyone seemed enthusiastic.

Jeremy put May in charge. He looked at her and said, "May, you go around to the shops, see what they are selling, and help with ideas and promotions." He looked around and got agreement from everyone.

"What about charter boats?" Nick asked.

It was suddenly quiet. Of course they all knew about 'the scene' which was how May thought of it. She finally said, "I don't know anything about boats, or charters, or the water. Maybe someone else can handle that."

Nick said, "Well I know about it, that's what I do. Take people out on the water to fish or sightsee or bird. I'll take you out and you can see it all first hand and put together something for us and the tour boats."

She didn't want to be in a boat, or out on the water, or in a boat out on the water with Nick, but before she could say anything, the others were agreeing with Nick. "Yeah, most of the people who charter, also shop. So that's a good idea, Nick. And sometimes the men go out and leave the wives on the dock. May can go out with you and research the shops," Jeremy decided.

Sheil spoke up, "It's settled. May and I will visit the shops on the dock and explore each shop for ideas for 'The Event'. Today, tomorrow and Wednesday. If you want May to give you individual ideas, she'll do that as we walk through. Then we'll work out a design for flyers. And a schedule. And take those around for approval. We will distribute finalized flyers as we have them completed. Get the community interested and talking. This will be a practice run. We don't have time to do a full advertising campaign. We can do a simple 'The Event, Come and Play'. For newspapers and print. The flyers can go online as they are completed. Don't forget the Pot Luck Sunday, we might be talking to some owners there. Let's eat now."

Nick came over to sit in the empty spot by May. She cringed inside, but just smiled at him.

"When do you want to go out?" he asked.

Never she thought. "I'm off Wednesday, Sheil and I could go Wednesday."

She looked at Sheil for confirmation and got a nod, and then a shake of her head. "No you're off Wednesday and this is work. Tomorrow. We'll go tomorrow morning. And then work a few hours in the evening."

May looked at Nick, "Do you have a charter?" she hoped.

"No, we'll go out Tuesday. Bring some snacks, we can see as much as you need to in a couple of hours."

"Great," she managed to say that with a smile but wasn't looking forward to it. She was thrilled she'd get to visit all the shops and learn how the shops were managed. She was getting paid to shop. Of course she wouldn't be able to buy. And she loved that she would get to design the flyers and share promotional ideas.

She and Sheil spent the rest of the day walking up the dock, stopping in at each shop. Talking to owners and employees. Sheil told May what she knew about each shop and owner. Who they were, where they came from. Local or a mystery. Once May got Sheil started she came up with great concepts and they ran their ideas by the owners. They made copious notes covering what they saw and heard. It was exhausting but fun. Everything they suggested met with approval.

They could draw up flyers for many of the shops with what they had learned. A couple of owners had added some of their own ideas. The pottery, metal, and glass shops wanted more time. As did the T-shirts. Soaps manager, Paul, needed to contact the owner. Only the antique shop owner was not sure he wanted to participate. Liked to think of himself as above the crowd, Sheil said. May decided she would go back to those shops to discuss special campaign ideas.

Sheil spent the afternoon, in between customers, inputting the data and setting up a tentative schedule of activities. May would design flyers and have drafts printed for approval. They had enough participants now for The Event, but May wanted everyone to join. It would be good for each shop to have its own advertisement, with a coupon or chance. They really needed to know if more shops would have activities before they finalized the schedule.

May would touch base with the other shop owners tomorrow afternoon. To hand deliver the draft flyers and to ascertain who else wanted to be on the schedule for activities. After the boat ride.

She visited with Ryan in the evening and fitted Jesse's outfit. She didn't need to fit her, all little kids shorts fit about the same. But she knew Jesse would love the attention and Jesse did love the idea of a fitting.

Tuesday

She was both dreading the boat ride and excited by the idea. She had never been on a small boat before. Sheil would be going and Nick could be fun. May picked up muffins, Danish, and coffee. She wouldn't need a bathing suit, didn't own one. She wore her new shorts and top which should be OK to stay in the boat and just rest and sun. She piled a hat and a long sleeve shirt and sun lotion in the wagon with the food and walked across to the dock. Nick smiled at her when he saw her coming. The nice smile. It warmed her all over.

"Hi. I'm ready and brought coffee and muffins."

"I will kill for coffee, let me give you a hand."

"Thought I would do my share, since you are doing the guiding and gas. And maybe Sheil will be taking pictures. Where is she?"

"She just called and said she couldn't make it. Had a conflict." Before May could say anything, he hit her with that smile and said. "I promise not to make you walk the plank. And I already apologized for being an ogre."

"OK," she wasn't sure. But she put on a brave face. "Fine."

They drifted down the shoreline and into a cove. He explained the landmarks and trees and pointed out birds. They anchored in the cove and he gave her a lesson in fishing. She was pretty good at casting. But not catching. He caught 3 or 4 small fish which he brought alongside and showed her and then released.

After an hour or so, they set their poles in holders and broke out the snacks he had. She told him some funny tales about customers the night before. She could mimic pretty good and her facial expressions had him roaring. He told some stories about guiding.

The good conversation, sun, and food worked their magic and she stretched out on the bow and closed her eyes, listening to the lap of water. She was half asleep taking in the sun.

He watched her. She was just sitting there. Her eyes closed. Her lips slightly open. He bet they would be soft, warm. They lured him and he leaned over and laid a gentle kiss on her lips.

Dreamy she touched her lips with her fingers, as if holding the kiss on. She opened her eyes and looked right at him, dreamily. Sweet. The simple kiss warmed her all over inside like the sun and air had done the outside. She wanted to hold onto the sensation. An instant later reality hit her. She was horrified at her reaction. She sat up so quick she almost knocked him over. Shocked and dismayed, she backed away. "Oh, no," she said. "Oh, no." I'm still married and pregnant and kissing another man.

He didn't understand. That simple kiss jolted all the way though him. At first she almost responded. He had smiled to himself. He wanted more and had reached out for her. But she jumped up and away. He saw the horror in her eyes. That angered him.

"Come on, you liked that," he growled. The kiss had rocked him to his core and she had reacted to it at first. "You did like that kiss. You enjoyed it."

"Yes, it was nice," she whispered. She touched her lips again. She could still feel the kiss, like honey. Gentle, sweet. She wanted more. But she couldn't. She opened her mouth to tell him, but he cut her off.

"Sure it was. Why are you suddenly playing all innocent and hard to get? Why else come out on the boat with me?" He didn't mean that. Anger made him say that.

"I thought you asked me as a friend. To come out for a boat ride and fish and to show me around for The Event," she said weakly, puzzled by his hostility.

"We are friends," he sneered. "We can be friends with benefits." Where did that come from?

Now it wasn't just her body's response to the kiss that scared her, it was his attitude. Went bad so fast. From sweet to hostile. In an instant. He wasn't going to scare her. Now she was angry. "I guess it is time for me to be embarrassed again. By not knowing the rules. I thought an invitation for a boat ride was just that. I didn't know it meant friends with benefits. You mean the sexual kind I take it?" she tried to appear calm.

"Well, honey, what other kinds are there?" He was acting like a jerk and he knew it, but he didn't seem to be able to stop himself. That look of horror on her face really ticked him off.

She closed her eyes. She did like the kiss, but a kiss didn't translate into benefits. And why was he so angry? This was that pushy guy she had first met. Not the nice guy telling stories earlier. "I never meant for you to think that. This, what you are saying now, is ugly and mean. Take me back please."

"Take you back?"

"Yes, please take me back to the dock now. I don't believe, even in this town, that an invite for a boat ride means let's have sex. And we both know you aren't going to force me, in spite of how you are acting now. So let's call it a major misunderstanding on both our parts and you dump me back on the dock."

He went absolutely still. Force her? She thought he might force her? How could she think that? It was obvious that she wasn't totally sure he wasn't going to force her. He had really screwed up if she was afraid of him. Abruptly he turned, brought in the poles. Pulled the anchor started the engine and headed back. It was a quick ride. Fortunately, it was too noisy for conversation. He pulled up to the pier. Threw one line over a piling, leaving the engine idling. Grabbed her stuff and dumped it on the dock. She stumbled over the side by herself. As soon as she had both feet on the pier, he released the line and took off.

She knew that half the town was watching. And the other half would know about it by noontime. She wasn't going to cry in front of them and give them more to talk about. She was lucky he had brought her back to her wagon she thought. He could have left her at the marina entrance and made her walk back. She was gathering her stuff when Jeremy walked up. She should have realized someone would come over.

"Are you all right? Where did Nick go?" He sounded concerned. The whole dock was probably concerned. What was she going to say? She couldn't actually tell them what happened because it still hurt too badly and she probably couldn't tell the story without a crying jag.

"I got seasick. I mean all over his boat. It never occurred to me to throw up over the side. I've never been on a fishing boat before." That was true. She had been on yachts, never small boats. She made up a joke. "Then he said the wedding is off. Couldn't marry a landlubber like me. Broke my heart. I think he went back out to hose down the boat." She got a laugh out of that. It sounded reasonable. She finished putting her stuff in the wagon. "Now I am going home to bed or the bathroom, depending, though I hear seasickness ends when you're on dry land. After that I will work on the charter and tour boat flyer."

As soon as she was in the apartment she threw herself down on the bed. She thought she was going to cry but found that she was just disgusted. With herself a little. More with him for being such a jerk. So much for being friends. She was a jerk too. To let his attitude upset her so. If she were a different type of person, more than friends could have been fun. The kiss was so sweet. How had he gone from a sweet gentle kiss to expectations and demands? Was she that innocent and naïve? Obviously, she was.

She wasn't going to sulk and feel sorry for herself, so she finished up the schedule and drafts for the flyers, including a very nice one for the Charter and tour boats. She took them to the Artists' Shop for printing. They were enthusiastic, added some ideas and designs, and ran off hard copies for her to take around to the shops.

The Glass Bird decided that they would give small 1 inch glass birds in many colors for the models to carry. And would sell them at cost. Earth Pottery would give a clay demonstration. How to make a luminary. May thought that was a great idea. They would also give a class for a nominal fee to cover the supplies. The participants could make a simple flat design, with clay flowers which they would paint. Metal Whimsy thought maybe he could have small leaves cut out for painting. May would get back to them for their final decision. Meanwhile she would work on fliers for the other shops.

Soaps and Jewelry still needed more time, but The Antique Cabinet owner had finally given the manager permission to participate. He asked her to look around for ideas for a flyer and an activity. The shop had interesting things, mostly junk though, or very well used antiques. She touched almost everything making notes and moving a few things to the front desk.

"I think the marbles might be good. The bag is marked $5.00 and there are about 100 marbles. I think you could add them as a bonus to some of the sales for someone who had kids with them. And I love these 'artificial crystals' they're labeled. Any of these would be nice for the chance or $1 sales. And I found this scene of a marina, marked for $40.00. This could be your main entry item. But it needs a really great frame."

The manager sent her to the back room to look at his stock of paintings and frames. "Some of the paintings are sold and waiting for pickup though," he warned.

She saw racks of paintings and frames and a large crate in the corner. She found some really nice reproductions by an artist she didn't recognize. And a really ugly frame. Then saw the perfect ornate frame. As she tilted the paintings forward to get to it, she stopped. She was looking at "The Grange". And not a reproduction of "The Grange". But the original. Surely it couldn't be. Not here. It should still be with Kathy in restoration or hung back on the wall in the museum. But it was here. There was no mistaking it. Here in the middle of cheap reproductions. She let the pile tilt back to the wall. Took a deep breath. This was wrong. She had an urge to run. But walked back out and said, "I'm running a little late. There is a wonderful ornate frame back there for this painting. And I have an idea for that really ugly frame. I will come back later."

She went back to Vintage to think and she worked a few hours in the back room on flyers and schedules. It helped settle her. She supposed the painting could have been sold. But surely she would know about that. Wouldn't she have read about it? Or heard it on the news? She laughed at herself. Well no. She hadn't been reading newspapers or listening to the news since she moved here. It was too late to call Kathy tonight; she would wait until the morning.

That evening, she started on designs for the twins. Designs to match the fabric to their personalities.

Wednesday

In the morning May still was uneasy. There was no way that the museum would sell that painting. Even if they had sold it, it wouldn't be in the backroom of the antique shop. The more she thought about it, the more she wanted to know. And it was a good excuse to call Kathy and catch up. It took a while, there seemed to be some delay with the switch board. But finally Kathy answered. "Hi, Kathy, this is May, ah, Elizabeth." There was silence at the other end of the line and May held her breath. Was Kathy going to speak to her?

"Where are you?" Kathy demanded. "Are you OK? What happened? How could you leave town and not say goodbye. Not call all this time? Are you OK? Talk to me."

May laughed with relief. "I'll talk, but you have to be quiet first and give me a chance. I'm fine. I'm sorry I didn't get to say goodbye. But I couldn't. And I felt that I should be settled in a little before I did call. And I didn't know what Derek would do if he thought you were talking to me."

"Derek, what an ass. I never did like him. So pompous and full of himself. What did you ever see in him Elizabeth?"

"Not Elizabeth, not any longer, I am back to May. Call me May."

"May then, we need to get together so you can tell me what happened. Are you sure you're OK? Do you need anything? Where are you?"

"Getting together will not be easy, I don't have a car, but we can talk on the phone. And email. Take down my landline. I don't have a cell. Derek cut it off. And I haven't opened a new account yet." She read off the phone number. "I'm on the west coast, south of Ft. Meyers. A great little community called Cougars Cove. I love it and I'm fine. I have a great job and I'm making new friends."

"Look, Kathy one of the reasons I'm calling. I just saw "The Grange" in a store room here. In a junky antique shop. Did the museum sell it? I haven't been paying attention to any news. Too self-centered lately. But I think I would have heard that."

"What? What did you say? You just saw "The Grange? You can't have. Where?"

"Right here in the Cougars Cove Antique Cabinet."

"Are you serious? Are you sure? Never mind, of course you are. Wait a minute let me get my breath. Hold on a minute."

May waited. After a few minutes, she said, "Are you still there, Kathy?"

"Yes, I am. Hold on another minute. I'm thinking. Don't say anything more. I have your number. I'm going to have Marty call you. Stay where you are. He will explain. Do whatever he says. OK?"

"I don't understand. Who's Marty?"

"Just stay right where you are. He'll call you back soon. Promise me you'll wait?"

"OK." What else could she say? She had nothing scheduled. Nowhere to go. She sat nervously waiting for the phone to ring. Why couldn't Kathy talk and who was Marty? The painting didn't belong in the Cabinet that was pretty obvious.

Even though she was expecting it, she jumped when the phone rang almost knocking it over. She grabbed it and said, "Yes?"

A deep voice said, "Mrs. Stratton?"

"No."

"This is not Elizabeth Stratton? I was told Mrs. Stratton would answer the phone. Could I please speak with Mrs. Stratton?" the voice was stilted and officious now. And a little disgusted.

"Yes, yes, you are speaking to her. I'm sorry. I'm a little confused and nervous."

He sighed, what kind of a kook was he talking to? Kathy had insisted this woman was level headed and knew her art. But she apparently didn't know her own name.

Before he could say anything she continued, "Call me May, I'm using my maiden name, May, May Johnson. My divorce from Derek Stratton will be final shortly and I don't use Stratton anymore." For all of 2 weeks anyhow. "Is this Marty?"

Maybe she wasn't a kook, Kathy had said Mrs. Stratton, but had also called her May. His mistake, he should have checked. "Yes, Marty. Are you alone right now, can we talk?"

"I'm alone, go ahead."

"It's about the painting, The Grange. Kathy says you saw it and that you wouldn't make a mistake about that. Tell me about how that happened."

"Yes, I saw it last night. But could you please tell me who you are and why you want to know and what the painting is doing here?"

"Special Agent Marty Martinson, Art Crime Team, FBI. And as you may have guessed, The Grange was stolen. Two days ago, while it was still in restoration. We have managed to keep it quiet. I need to talk with you, meet in person. Can you be here about 10 o'clock tomorrow morning? Can you meet with me?"

"OK. But not there. I can't get there. You will have to come here."

"Is that Cougars Cove?"

"Yes. Can you come here?"

"Yes," he could drive it in about an hour.

"You can't come to my apartment though if you want to keep it quiet. I'm in a very small community; people will see, they see everything and they talk about everything they see and they ask questions. And I would rather not answer any more questions right now."

"Where then?"

"The Inn, meet me at The Inn on Main Street, in the lobby. How will I know you?"

"About 6 foot, medium build, longish dark hair. Oh, and I will have a red box."

"Oh, thank goodness, I was so afraid you were going to say that you would be the guy with the hat, reading the newspaper." She was instantly contrite. Sorry, sometimes I joke inappropriately."

He laughed, "That's fine, and I will see you about ten. And I know I don't have to say that you shouldn't talk to anyone about this."

"Oh, no one."

"See you at ten." He hung up feeling relieved, if she could joke about this, she would probably be able to handle herself pretty well.

May wondered about the theft, and how the painting got here. She'd find out tomorrow. She distracted herself by finishing up the flyers and then turned to her sewing. She could see in her mind the dresses she wanted for the twins and spent the day working on her designs.

Thursday

She had two hours to kill and she was a nervous wreck. She needed to be busy. The designs had changed overnight. She'd had a new thought and decided that the fabric would work better this way. She became lost in the redesining process. Every once in a while she would touch the fabric to get a better 'feel' for the design. She almost missed the time.

She hurried to the Inn, looking around as she entered. She saw one person in the lobby and he was carrying the red box. First she walked to the desk clerk and asked if she could use the conference room. With his nod she went over to the man and said, "Hello, Marty?"

"Yes, May?" Gosh, not just smart, but pretty he thought. Kathy hadn't mentioned pretty.

"Yes. Maybe you should show me some ID?" she asked a little embarrassed.

He pulled out his wallet with his ID and held it out for her. Smiling, that she would be embarrassed to ask.

"OK. Thanks. I got us the conference room; we can go talk in there." She turned and led the way past the elevator.

He followed her and started by saying that Kathy had given May excellent references, but that he had to have her look at some pictures. He opened the box and laid the pictures out on the conference table. "This is sort of a test. I need you to look at each of these for me please." There were twelve of them. Color 8x10s of paintings.

She looked at each one, some a little longer than others. Three she barely even glanced at. "OK, what do you want to know?"

"Tell me what they are."

"I can tell you what I see in each photo. There's a lot in the actual painting that helps to classify it. And sometimes microscopic, or infrared, or other in depth test is needed for authenticity." She waited for his nod and then she lifted the photos one at a time, identifying artist, date, value, and location of each painting, whether museum, or private collector. She passed each one to him. She left four on the table. The first one of the four, "I don't recognize it at all, but it looks like the same technique used by an early American artist." She pointed to the last three and simply said, "Forgeries."

"I'm impressed. I didn't even do that well and I'm supposed to be an expert too. OK. Tell me how you discovered the painting."

He had her repeat the story three times, asking questions. And then just sat and thought. Finally, "Is it possible that there might be another painting hidden there?"

"Yes, I didn't see, but I didn't look through everything. I got scared and got out of there."

He thought some more. "OK, tell me about the dock and the shop." He would need to coordinate with the locals, maybe. They were going to have to keep an eye on the shop. That would be a problem he supposed when she described the Cove and then gave him copies of the flyers for The Event.

"What's your cell number?"

"I don't have one. The land line works for the few calls I make. You have that number."

"OK, we can get in touch with you that way if we need to. For now."

"You shouldn't need me for anything else. You really didn't need to see me today at all. And you know everything I know."

"And we appreciate you taking time to meet with us. We will try not to bother you again. I would appreciate it if you would keep all this quiet. We don't need word leaking out that a multimillion dollar painting is in a backroom here."

"Not a problem. I won't even tell Kathy anything else."

"Good. Here is my card with my cell number in case you need to contact me."

"Hope not. I mean it was nice to meet you, but I don't need to be involved with the FBI." She shook hands and left. She was thinking that this was not a door she wanted to walk through in her new life. Thought it with a smile. Felt his card in her pocket and headed for the front entrance. Nope, didn't want to be involved in police work.

"Just what the hell do you think you are doing?" Nick bellowed at her. He had been just leaving the boat supply shop with a part he needed when he saw May in front of the Inn looking around furtively before she walked in. Curious, he crossed the street and followed her. He had seen her go into the Inn a few times and stay about an hour each time. And yes, he was watching her to try to determine where she fit into the picture, not because of anything personal or the way he felt about her. Yes, he did enjoy watching her. But he had to watch her because she was an unknown.

He had seen her go to the desk clerk and then she had approached a man with a red box sitting in the lobby. Nick only saw him from the back through the window. They exchanged greetings, the man stood and took out his wallet and showed it to her. May then led him to the elevators. Nick was too shocked to move.

What was that? That couldn't be what it looked like. Could it? She was going to a room with the man? He should just leave now, he was too angry. But he knew he would wait for her to come back down and ask her. The longer he waited the angrier he got. And when she showed up about 45 minutes later he was furious. He'd stomped over and screamed at her.

"What?" she stammered and looked a little uncomfortable.

At least she had the grace to look embarrassed he thought. "You went to a room with a man you picked up in the lobby. I saw you. You can't deny it. Admit you took him to a room."

"You were watching me? Wh why are you watching me?" Still stammering.

"What was that all about? Why did you take a man up to a room? What did you do up there?" He was furious.

Slowly she realized what he was suggesting. How could he? And that thought got through her confusion. And now she was furious.

"Wait a minute. Wait a minute. You think we went to a private room for sex?" she was so shocked at the idea, she was almost speechless.

"Ya, I think that little miss innocent earns her living on her back. Maybe that's why you wouldn't give me the time of day. I didn't offer you any money. How much money do you need before you fuck?"

Another man, another place, almost the same charge. Why was she even surprised?

She slapped him, she couldn't help it. He grabbed her arm.

"You're hurting me. Let go of me," she said between her teeth. "Let go of me right now or I will scream for the cops."

"Oh, ya, and tell them what? That you just got through turning tricks?"

That stopped her. He was right of course. No way that would work. Not that she would have screamed for help anyhow. She had never had to scream for help. She couldn't tell him the truth about Marty. At this point she sure didn't think begging or crying or lying would work either.

"What will it take to make you let me go? You want me to say I took him to a room. OK. I did take him to a room, so what." She said flippantly.

Even though he had seen her do it, he didn't expect her to confess to it. He had hoped she would come up with an explanation he could accept. However outrageous. He just looked at her with disgust

"Will you let go of me now?" she asked.

When he didn't, she said what he apparently wanted to hear. "You want a freebie? Honey?" May said turning on her sultry, sexy voice. She couldn't believe those words came out of mouth. But they worked.

He let her go so quick she stumbled back. As she regained her balance he gave her one loathing look and left.

She was shaking so badly she had to sit for a minute and calm down. Now what did she do? Would Nick go directly to Sheil and tell her what he saw? Correction, what he thought he saw. And she sort of confirmed? She wouldn't have said that if he hadn't made her so angry.

What would Sheil do? First things first, she better go back and tell Marty.

He was on the phone, surprised to see her back, motioned her in. Told whoever it was that he would get back to him. And then she had to explain Nick and her relationship, or non-relationship. Together she and Marty considered the different possibilities and decided they could only play it by ear. They couldn't tell Nick what was going on because they didn't yet know if he was part of the art thefts. Well, she knew he wasn't, but Marty didn't. She would just have to deal with the situation until Marty came up with a solution.

Sheil was waiting for her when she got back. Her heart dropped. Nick had told Sheil. And now May would have to leave and she loved this dock and its inhabitants. Thank you, Nick, she thought. This is the second time you have messed me up. No she had done that herself. Better face the music.

"What happened in town?" Sheil asked. "Nick just came stomping by here like a mad man. And you look like your dog was just run over in front of you."

"He didn't stop and tell you?"

"No. Come on in and I'll make you some tea."

May followed her in and sat in the bright back room, holding back tears. Hot tea in this room should help calm her. And what could she tell Sheil?

Sheil put the cup in front of her and sat down with her own cup. May took a sip and said, "I can't tell you. It's pretty personal. He saw something, well he thought he saw something. He thought he saw me do something pretty despicable. And I let him, no encouraged him, to believe it. I was so angry, I didn't think. I just lashed out and slapped him. Yes, I hit him. With my hand. And then I slashed at him with my words. Who knew that I could say such hateful things?"

"Oh, Sheil, I have made such a mess."

"If you hit him, he needed it. Tell me what happened. What exactly did you say?"

"Nick saw me meet a man at the Inn. He accused me of turning tricks and I was so angry, I hit him. And then," she got all clogged up and held up her hand for a minute. "And then I offered to do him. For free."

Sheil busted out laughing. "And you didn't invite me to see that? I'd give a million dollars to see his face. And to hear you make an offer like that."

"You think it's funny?" May asked aghast.

"Honey, I barely know you and I know you're not turning tricks. There are probably 100 different innocent reasons for you to be at the Inn. For you to meet a man there. The funny thing is, Nick really likes you. I can tell. But he's fighting it and looking for reasons to hate you. Thinking you're turning tricks would be a good reason. The whole dock knows he likes you. Don't give him another thought. He'll either come around or not. Give him time."

She sent May upstairs to calm down and wash her face. Again.

The twins were downstairs working so May returned with the designs. She had two designs for each dress and she laid the patterns on the fabric to help the twins envision the finished product. They each made a quick decision and May fit the patterns. That took time and the twins were worse than Jesse. Fidgeting and bouncing around.

She spent the day and evening pinning patterns, cutting and pressing, and sewing and pressing. She was delighted with the way her designs were emerging.

Friday

Nick couldn't leave it alone. And the next morning he stomped into the Inn and walked into the office, slamming the door behind him.

Ryan looked up and said, "Well good morning to you too."

"I don't understand why you are letting that piece of trash hustle johns in your Inn," he snarled furiously.

"Whoa, now boy. That's a lot of accusations in one sentence. Why don't you sit down and take some deep breaths and explain to me just exactly what you are talking about. No one is hustling johns in my Inn. And what piece of trash are you talking about?"

"May, that's who, why are you letting her take johns upstairs?"

"Hunh? May's doing what? In my Inn? Have you lost your mind? It's too early in the morning for you to be drunk. Did you fall and hit your head?"

"Don't give me that. You got to know about it. Nothing happens in this Inn you don't know about."

"You think that I'm letting May   ? I can't even finish that statement. How can you even think that? You know me better than that. And I thought you knew May too. What's wrong with you boy?"

"I saw it myself. She comes in here 2 or 3 times a week and stays for about an hour. And yesterday I saw her go upstairs with a john."

"Oh, no you didn't see that."

"Don't tell me what I saw. I know what I saw." He said it dangerously.

"You are seeing her come into the Inn two or three times a week. That's true." Ryan said it quietly. "What could possibly make you assume those visits are sexual?"

"You think I'm stupid. There is no other explanation. She even admitted it to me."

"She told you she was turning tricks in my Inn? I find that seriously hard to believe."

"Well she didn't deny it when I accused her. Even offered me a freebie."

"You have got to be dumber than a rock. The underside of a rock. You accused her of turning tricks? How can you even say such a thing?"

"Oh, all you people think she is so sweet and innocent. But I am here to tell you she's a slut. A whore"

"Get out; get out of my office right now." Ryan stood, glowering at Nick. "I am not going to listen to you insult a very decent woman. So leave or sit down and shut up. Give me a minute to decide if I should explain to you what is actually happening." He was angry and disgusted with Nick. He wasn't sure if he should tell him anything. May hadn't, apparently. He could see Nick was suffering. But maybe Nick deserved to suffer. On the other hand, May didn't need to be slandered like this.

Nick crossed his arms, shut his mouth, and sat, daring Ryan to explain.

"OK, this is no secret, so I can tell you that May comes every few days because I ask her to."

"You're pimping her?"

"Get out. Just get out." Ryan said with disgust. "Don't bother to come back until you can be civil. And don't be spreading stories around town which have no basis in fact. Don't hurt her any more than you already have. What's wrong with you anyway?"

Nick just sat, the woman made him crazy. Was Ryan right? Had he read it all wrong? But there was that guy and she did admit it.

"Nothing's wrong with me. If I'm wrong, than you should explain."

"She's making, designing and sewing, an outfit for Jesse. She's visiting Jesse. She's fitting Jesse for the outfit."

"What about that guy? I saw her meet him. Why did she tell me she was with him?" he demanded.

"That's her personal business. No, not monkey business. Something else. Not your business. Not mine. And she wasn't upstairs. She was in my conference room. You apparently didn't see her go in there. And as for her telling you she was turning tricks." He stopped.

"She admitted it damn it," Nick interrupted.

"Did you really call her a whore to her face? What would you expect her to say? Maybe you should reexamine that conversation," Ryan suggested evenly.

Nick played the conversation back to himself. His ugly accusation. Her shock. And then her calculated decision, he had watched her make it. Saying the only thing that would have stopped him.

He groaned. Ryan might be right. It could have played that way. What he knew about her and she had promised never to do what he expected if he backed her into a corner. She would hit him back by agreeing with him. He had surely screwed up.

"Yeah, I can see you have figured out that you're a real asshole Nick. Get out of here."

She just made it to work after her doctor's appointment. She liked her new doctor and was relieved that everything was fine. With both her and the baby. The doctor said she didn't need a GP yet. That was good news for her bank account. Of course, after the baby was born she would need both a GP and a pediatrician.

She worked with one of the retired women, Doris. Doris never stopped talking. She didn't seem to care if anyone was listening or not. Though May did try to listen. But, mercy, the woman never took a breath and didn't actually have anything to say. Though Doris was a good worker and didn't seem to ever slow down. Put May to shame. Sheil really knew how to pick her employees. Doris explained the Dock Pot Luck on Sunday. May had forgotten all about it. She didn't think she could go because she was working, which should be a good excuse. But Doris explained that she was not only expected to go but also she would have to bring something. And the restaurants would have snacks at cost. The public would also be there. It was an annual preseason party.

They worked together and Doris helped her close. May put the finishing touches on Melanie's dress. She could work on Kimberly's tomorrow. And she needed to think of something tasty and easy to make for Sunday.

Saturday

Marty called early. He was coming Sunday. He wanted her to set up cameras in the Cabinet. "Me?" she said. "I don't know how to do that. I'm not a cop. You need to get someone else."

"You're there. You can get in the backroom. Anybody we send will be suspicious and we need you to help us out. I'll bring the cameras and show you how to use them." He told her that if she could hide the camera and a GPS tracker in the storeroom, no one would need to physically watch the shop. That made sense. She had been a little concerned that they might want her to spy for them. Not something she wanted to get involved in. But he made hiding the gadgets sound simple. Then he wanted to know where she wanted to meet. Probably not the Inn again. She suggested the party. They could blend in and he could come to the shop and give her the cameras. They arranged a time and he hung up.

May saw that Nick's boat was still in. She had seen him come in from town. She knew she had to talk to him. She had to explain why she had said what she did. And she should explain her circumstances to help him understand her actions. Maybe get him to leave her alone. Was it the right thing to do? Was it the right time? Or even the right place? She was not sure but it didn't feel right to put it off any longer. She put her head high and walked across to the dock and down the pier. She knew the whole dock was watching. Nick was out of sight, inside. "Hello aboard the Lucky London," she called. She had seen people do that on TV. She waited. She was just getting ready to call out again when he came out. Angry still, she saw.

Before he spoke she said, "Don't say anything. Let me talk. It's my turn to apologize. And I want to explain, too,"

"You have already said everything I need to hear." He was still angry, but not sure who he was angry at.

"No, I haven't. I gave you a chance to apologize, you owe me my chance."

He got an ugly smile, "Come aboard."

"No. I will not come aboard. You will misjudge. You already are. Misjudging. I can see it." She could just tell from the look on his face that if she stepped aboard he would revert to the friend with benefits. She didn't need that attitude. "So either stay there and listen or come here and sit on the dock box with me."

He considered and then climbed down to the dock and sat. She put the whole bench between them and turned to look him in the eye.

"I never intended to deceive you or mislead you. Well, maybe when I agreed I was a whore. That is't true, but you made me angry with your accusation. I am not now nor have I ever turned tricks. I don't even sleep around. I go to the Inn to visit Ryan and Jesse, and, no I am not sleeping with Ryan either. He is more like a Dad to me. I am a seamstress and I am making an outfit for Jesse. I need to measure and fit her for the shorts and top I'm making and it has taken multiple visits. You can believe that or not. I can't prove any of it."

She saw him nod and continued, "What you saw yesterday was something else. I can't talk about it, but it was nothing like you imagined or suggested. It was part of my life before I came here." She held up her hand when it looked like he was going to interrupt. "Don't say anything yet. Let me finish."

"I'm married." She saw the shock on his face as he stood up.

"You're married? You're married and fooling around with me?" He said it quietly. His tone chilled her but she had to get the rest out.

She looked around, people were watching them of course, but probably couldn't hear. "No, I was not fooling around with you. I thought we could be friends. You acted like a friend. I liked you. As a friend. Not as a boyfriend. Not as a friend with benefits. It never occurred to me that you were thinking that or I never would have gone out in the boat with you alone."

She took a breath. "Wait, I'm still not done. I'm sorry that you got the wrong impression. I still don't know you well enough to tell you my personal business, but you need to know. My husband is divorcing me. I will be single in 2 more weeks. That's not an invitation. It is simply a statement of fact. I will be single, but, not available," she paused here and drew a breath. "My husband kicked me out because I'm expecting." She stopped.

"Expecting what?"

"I'm two months pregnant. My soon to be ex-husband does not believe my baby is his. He kicked me out. And before you say anything, the baby is his." There, she had finally said it.

He stopped pacing. Looked at her. "You let me kiss you? And you knew?" Bewilderment and disgust now.

"I didn't ask you to kiss me. The kiss was beautiful." She put her hand to her lips to feel it again. "But, I was horrified because I had let it happen. I would have told you then, but you wouldn't listen. And I didn't know you well enough to explain my personal circumstances. Or air my dirty laundry."

"Where do you dream this stuff up? Is any of it even true? You just keep on coming up with them lady, don't you? Pregnant? Now you are saying you are pregnant? You led me on. What are you really doing here now? What do you expect to get out of this confession? Is that what it is? Or another story?"

She didn't know what buttons he pushed with her. "Don't worry, the baby isn't yours."

He choked on that. "Goddam right it's not mine. If there even is an it. With you, one never knows what the truth is."

"With me, the truth has always been there. I have never lied to you. And I suppose, if my own husband doesn't believe me, I can't expect a near stranger to either. So I don't fault you. And I can't make you believe. I don't really care if you do. I felt you had a right to know. You have always chosen to see something that isn't there when it comes to me. It seems to be that you want to always believe the worst, expect the worst of me. But that is your problem, not mine. My problem was to tell you. About me. About my circumstances. Try to apologize. Try to explain."

"So what do I believe now? You are either pregnant and there is only one way to get pregnant. Or you're lying about being pregnant for whatever reason. Either way, it doesn't fit your goody two shoes image."

"I can't be worried about how you see me. That's your problem. Why do you feel that it is your duty to be my moral judge? And why do you always have to make sure to share that judgment with me? Do you think I can't see it in your face? Or does it just make you feel good to call me a whore? I can see you're not listening now. You are still mis-interpreting everything I say. Looking for an ulterior motive. So, one more time. I am a pregnant, soon to be divorced woman, who never intended to mislead you. I am sorry for any embarrassment and confusion I have caused you."

"You are some sick creature." He turned and climbed back on his boat.

She watched him leave and then she got up and walked away. She was trembling. That had been really ugly. But at least it was over. He knew the truth now. What he did with it was his problem. She went back to her apartment and just sat with her head in her hands. Why did she always leave him crying or shaking? How did he have so much power over her? She liked him, didn't have any right to like him. She was attracted to him and wanted him to like her. That was why it hurt. If she didn't care about him, he wouldn't be able to hurt her. She looked at herself and was proud that she'd had the courage to face him. His reaction, well that was his choice. Her actions were the only ones she could control. She realized she had taken an important step facing him. She got up and went to work.

~

He was furious. Who did she think she was? What was she trying to do? He sat. He remembered that kiss. She had looked so sweet. So innocent. Ya, sure, innocent, he laughed at himself. Innocent? Pregnant. Boy, he was a fool. He had watched her laying there in the sun and had just wanted to feel her lips. Had leaned over and tasted them gently. Had not expected the fire that ran through him. And then she had been so horrified it had angered him. Not horrified at him, he realized now. Horrified at herself. And she was right. He had not given her a chance to say anything. He had condemned her for his actions. She hadn't led him on. It was all him. When he had brought the subs, he had expected, wanted more. Had backed her into a corner and demanded. She had admitted she liked him and that was what he had seen in her face. Like, not desire. And the next day, at The Coffee Spot, he had been an ass. Well he already knew that. Already apologized for those two incidents.

And at the hotel? Ryan had started to explain. And Nick had heard only what he had wanted to hear. What kind of man had he become? To immediately think the worst? That's what Ryan had asked him. And now he was asking himself. Because all this was on him. May had never done anything inappropriate. There was no reason for her to tell him anything about her personal life. They were barely acquaintanced. It wasn't any of his business if she visited with Ryan. Sewed for Jesse. Met with a strange man in the hotel. Not any of his business. So why did he want to know. Why did he feel like it was his business? She wasn't anything to him. Was she?

He knew he was fooling only himself. He liked her. More than liked her. The kiss had been special. That was why he had gotten so angry at her horror. That kiss had moved him. He had felt it all the way through his body. For a moment he had felt longing and peace. Like he was exactly where he belonged when he was with her. He could feel the heat now and she wasn't even here. And she knew it on some level too. Otherwise, how would you explain the way she had touched her lips except to feel that kiss again?

And the whole dock knew. The whole dock knew. They could see there was something between them.

Suddenly, he remembered the dream. He had woken up feeling warm and happy. Yes, happy and content. Satisfied. Fulfilled. And at peace. It had been a long time since he had felt any of those emotions, let alone felt them all together. In the dream, he had been walking to Hal's. Leaving his own house, which was blue? He was holding a baby, a boy. A boy which looked just like him. Gooing up at him. He was gooing back. Silly. And he was leading a toddler by the hand. A pretty little brown haired girl, who looked like May. And May, with short, saucy, brown hair, not blonde, was holding the child's other hand. May was leading a yellow dog on a leash. He was looking at the three of them with so much love it almost hurt. The little girl was giggling and laughing. May was singing a silly song. He felt such love.

Hunh? A dream? He was thinking about a dream? Well, yes, he was. That was pretty stupid. But the dream felt so real. The emotions so right. He was surprisedd. And gave the situation more thought. Finally, for the first time he was looking at his attitude toward her. His feelings.

He had liked her! More than liked her. From the very first time he saw her he had felt an attraction. That was his problem. That explained everything he had done. He, not her. He was afraid of that attraction. That attraction meant forever. He was afraid of forever. That was the problem. His feelings for her were for long term. He wanted forever, with her. Was that why he was so angry? Why she always put him on edge? Because he had fallen for her? And he had been fighting it with meanness?

He knew she liked him too or she would not have bothered to come here today to talk. That took guts. And he had treated her exactly the way she had learned to expect. Like scum. He had screwed up again. But now he knew the problem and he could fix it.

First though, he had to get his mind back on the job. He was undercover. Though, now that he thought about it, this 'affair' was really good cover. He might be able to use that. And now he had something to work with to find out who she really was. Because he did need to eliminate her as a suspect. At least that was the excuse he would use to look into her background. He would find out about her 'story'. Though he didn't doubt what she had told him. And why hadn't his people called him with her background?

The job, though. The job was what was important. And in all the time he had been here, he hadn't found a thing. Their source was impeccable. The drugs were coming from the Cove Dock. He hadn't found anything suspicious. Nothing was moving through the marina during the day. The only things moving at night were the turtle researchers. And a few lovers. He almost got caught one night following them. That would have been embarrassing. He wasn't sure what to do next, but he would give it another week at least.

Meanwhile he went to see Hal. Hal, his sister's widower. Hal, the man who had become his big brother, his confidant. He went to see Hal. Hal would be able to help. Hal had fallen in love twice. Not once, but twice. Successfully. He should be an expert. Yes, Hal was the person to help him with May. That's what he wanted. May and that future he saw in his dream. He would pick up a couple of six packs and go visit.

Sunday

The morning sewing and gossip group, AKA tutu bash group, wanted a first-hand detailed description of May's meeting with Nick. Everyone seemed to know that she had met him by his boat. It was time to tell them the horrid details. Would they hate her? Everyone would know soon enough when she started to show. And some people had seen her go into the obstetrician's office. You only did that for one reason. Sheil knew because May had to tell her before accepting the job. Ryan knew because, well, she was not sure why she had told him. And Nick knew, so no one would be blindsiding him

She started slowly as they pinned and sewed. Stumbling at first. Nervous. They listened attentively. When she told them she was pregnant. There was a pause. Is that a pregnant pause? She asked herself. Carol could always be depended upon to jump in where others might try to find the most appropriate comment.

"You're pregnant? You're pregnant? When are you due? Can we have our babies together? Will they be twins? Will it be a boy or a girl? Who's the Dad?" she trailed off on that one. Took a breath and before anyone else could say anything "I didn't mean that last. The Dad is not important. I wouldn't even know him. Tell me the rest, tell us the rest."

May laughed and the others sighed.

"OK, me too. But I want to know everything. All the gossip." Marla agreed.

May told them the same as she had told Nick. Told them about Derek. "You don't need to believe me. My own husband didn't believe me. So I don't expect that anyone else should either. And that's OK. I'm not going to explain to anyone else. They can just make their own assumptions. Everyone will anyhow. I'm realistic. And if I heard this story, I would wonder also."

Carol said, "Oh I believe you. I know there are assholes like Derek out there. Did you tell Nick? I know you told Nick. How did he take it?"

"He wasn't happy. He didn't believe me. How do you know I told him?"

"Because that's the kind of person you are. You wouldn't tell us unless you had already told him. And he needed to know before your relationship could move forward."

"We don't have a relationship," May said.

"You keep on telling yourself that."

Carol added, "I want you to be my baby's aunt. And I'm going to be your baby's aunt." And she hugged her. They had a group hug.

May wiped a few tears from her eyes and said, "Let's finish here. I still need to make something for the Pot Luck. Are any of you going?"

"Oh, we'll all be there. It is a great excuse for a party. The guys act so manly, drinking beers on the dock. They are fun to watch. The kids all eat and play, and we gossip and shop. And there will be lots of gossip about the new girl and how nice she is."

"What do you bring?" May asked.

"Any kind of finger food or drinks. Though the single guys generally bring the drinks and potato chips, or paper plates and napkins. No one really coordinates any of it. We each chip in a couple of dollars for the paper goods. And the rest takes care of itself."

"OK, I guess I will think of something."

They got back to the sewing. Joan and May had both brought their sewing machines. May helped them with the pinning and watched as they sewed. Giving them pointers. "If you sew too fast the sides become uneven and gather. A medium speed does best. It also lets you guide the fabric through." She was able to demonstrate the gathering where one of the Moms had been in a hurry. She showed them how to press out each seem as they sewed pieces together. And some methods to rip out a seam and pin and re-sew. They finished the shorts and tops. Next week would be quilts. The ladies would bring all their scraps.

~

Nick found that he was actually enjoying himself at the pot luck. He knew a lot of the people and it was interesting to see who was with whom and how many kids they had. He had been gone a long time. Even though he had been back in town for a month, he had not left the marina area much or bothered to look anyone up who wasn't family. Except Ryan and the Sheriff.

May was there. She seemed to know many of the people too. Talking and laughing. A happy person with a bright smile that started inside and lit up those around her. He watched her stand on her toes and kiss Ryan on the cheek. Saw him turn a little red and bluster at her. She just ginned at him. Nick wasn't sure he liked that. She was his girl. He wandered over and finally caught her alone. She watched nervously as he approached and he saw the exact moment she decided to tough it out and not run away.

"Brought you a cold water," he said handing over the iced bottle. "I see that's what you're drinking."

"That's sweet, thanks." May thought it's the nice Nick, for a little while anyhow. He didn't say anything, just stood there so she asked him about some of the people.

He pointed out Marla and her husband, David, a really good looking guy she thought. Did she say that out loud? She could tell she did from Nick's expression. "So I'm still acting like I'm in high school, get over it. You would say the same thing if you saw a pretty girl. Except that you would use girl not guy. Admit it."

"Maybe not the word girl," he gave her that killer grin, the one she liked. "What did you bring to the pot luck? I want to go try it out."

"The stuffed potatoes." And when he looked puzzled, added, "They're on the big table. Look like a potato half, they are a potato half. Some are stuffed with sausage, onion, and pepper and others with tomato, peperoni, and cheese."

"Those are yours? I ate five already. You've got to marry me. They taste great but they are all gone. They only lasted about eight seconds."

"I don't wonder if some pigs gulp them down five at a time. Where did you find the room for them anyhow?" She ignored the married comment even if it did make her inside mushy.

"Oh, I just washed them down with beer."

May laughed at him and slapped his arm.

And then he said, "Saw you kiss Ryan." He said it as a statement, not an accusation, but idle curiosity. Looking for an explanation.

So she treated it that way. She would be nice as long as he was, and there were people watching. Hoping for another scene? "He just makes me want to hug and kiss him all the time," she said with a warm grin.

"Now you really do need to explain," he said it seriously.

"I hope whenever you ever catch me in a compromising position, you will give me the benefit of the doubt and let me explain. I like this Nick that asks politely, so much better than that one that accuses angrily."

He laughed, pushed a strand of hair out of her face, and promised.

"So tell me, why were you kissing Ryan?" he repeated.

"He said that Jesse wanted to call me Aunty and he wanted to know if he could tell her yes, after he OKs it with his daughter. Whom I get to meet next week. It just made me so happy. Made me feel like, well almost like, family. He earned a kiss."

"OK. Pretty soon I might do something to earn a kiss too," he joked.

She looked at him somberly. "I'm still married, and don't forget my condition. I don't do one night stands. And I don't do for a whiles. I do long term. When I'm single again, maybe I'll call you. If you still feel the same way. If you can deal with my condition. If you stay the nice Nick. I don't like that other guy at all. And now I'm done with my condition and ifs." She was a little uncomfortable, but at least he knew now she was interested and what she wanted.

"Well that's too bad. I do do one night stands and for a whiles. We would be perfect for 2 or 3 months," he drawled. What? Hadn't he decided he could do long term with her? Must be a reflex statement when he was talking to a woman?

"You probably won't be the one I call when the divorce is finalized then. Too bad. But we can still be acquaintances. Not friends. I don't think we could be just friends. But acquaintances could be OK. Maybe."

"I can change," he told her. Why had he said he only did for a whiles. Wasn't he looking for long term with her? "We can be friends; I do like what I see."

She looked at him and finally said, "I don't think so. I need to visit some more people and go back to work."

He watched her walk away. He was always watching her when she was around. He thought about her condition and her ifs. Didn't know if he could handle all of them, let alone her physical condition. But that one kiss. That one kiss. Another one like that and he was pretty sure he would be begging. She had made sure that he knew up front what he would be getting into, if he was interested. And had let him know that she was interested.

Later he saw her talking to a man. Nick could only see him from the back, tall, gangly, curly red hair. There was something faintly familiar about him. The man headed inside Vintage and a few minutes later May followed. Hunh? Now what? Now what was she doing? He waited a few more minutes; no one else seemed to notice that they were gone. He followed, into the shop. He could hear voices from the second dressing room and silently looked in the door. May was facing away from him and bending forward, both arms up. Looked like holding the man's head as he bent down over her chest, telling her to stop fidgeting.

"How can I? When I don't know who might come in the door and see us doing this?" she complained.

"Ya, how can you, May? God dam it, how can I give you the benefit of the doubt when I walk in and you're doing this?" Nick bellowed. How could she be with another man?

May jumped back and turned around so quickly she hit the guy in the head with her elbow with a slunk sound.

"Ow. Be careful. That's my nose," he howled.

Even the voice was familiar to Nick, but he couldn't quite place it.

"This is not what you are thinking, Nick London. Remember your promise, not to always think the worst." She spit out quickly, trying to think of an explanation.

"I am giving you the benefit of the doubt. I am not punching this guy out and it looks like you hit him for me anyhow." He paused, and looked at the man again because Nick did know him. "Peter? Peter Hanson? Why I'll be. What are you doing here? What are you doing with my girl?" he asked angrily. Oops, 'my girl'? That sure slipped out of somewhere.

Both Peter and May said, "Your girl?" at the same time with the same amount of amazement.

They were all speaking loudly at once, when Ryan stomped in with Sheriff Rogers. "Hold it down. Hold it down. All of you be quiet and calm down. People outside can hear the shouting."

Nick looked angry, Peter was holding his nose, and May was thinking of panicking.

Ryan looked at Nick and said, "Nick, not another word from you. Go over and sit in the chair. Just stay there. No, you aren't leaving," he continued when it looked like Nick would push his way past and out the door. "I need you here."

Nick looked at all three of those men together and realized more was going on then he knew. Ryan, Sheriff Rogers, and Peter Hanson, the FBI tech? What was going on? He had never seen Ryan this angry. Well when he had been accusing May, Ryan had been this angry. Nick decided that he needed to be here too. Needed to know what was going on. He sat down and watched. This should be interesting.

Ryan told the Sheriff to look at Peter's nose.

" May," Ryan put a hand on her; "Calm down. Take a breath. Let me take care of this. You can trust me to fix it. It will be alright." He watched her until he was sure she was OK.

Marty came in at that point. "What a mess. What a cluster fuck."

Ryan turned to him and stared him down. "Well it's your fault Marty. I can't believe you left me and Nick out of the loop." Ryan said. "And Rogers, you should have known better and not let Marty talk you into it."

"I didn't know anything until just before you came over," Rogers said disgusted. "And I was looking for you Ryan, to give you a heads up when the shouting started."

Ryan looked at Marty. "Christ, I leave you guys alone for one month and look what you do. Mess up two undercover operations. Two operations! Two stings, at risk now! Because you couldn't share information."

"I didn't even know you were in town," Marty complained.

"Doesn't matter, you knew David was here. You should have brought the locals into the loop. And Nick too." Ryan took a breath, "OK. OK it's done. Let's fix it. Marty, was there much attention out there? Did anyone notice anything?"

"No, I don't think anyone heard the shouting. I don't think anyone even noticed. You guys heard it because you were near the door."

"Well that's good, though from what I did hear, it could fit into a way to salvage this mess. You all be quiet while I think."

They were all quiet. Watching him.

May was speechless. She felt like she was at a tennis match turning to look at first one of the men and then the other. Ryan? Ryan was acting like he was in charge? In charge of what? How could he be? He was an innkeeper and a grampa. The other men were letting him take charge. And Nick. Marty left Nick out of the loop? What loop? The art theft? Why did Nick need to know about the art theft? Who was Ryan? Who was Nick? How was Nick involved? Involved in what? Why didn't Ryan say anything when she met with Marty? How did Nick know Peter? My girl? What did 'my girl' mean? She sat there, maybe with her mouth still hanging open. She didn't care. 'My girl'?

"OK, this can be a simple fight over a girl, if anyone even noticed. We don't need to say anything. That can be the backup story. Nick, everyone in town knows you're chasing May. And she isn't running away too fast." Both of them started to comment, Ryan just looked at them and they hushed.

"That will explain Peter. Maybe he got drunk and cornered her in this room and Nick rescued her. Punched Peter in the nose. Yeah, I like that. That should work. And Peter will have an ignominious departure in a few minutes."

"Aw heck, why do I have to be the drunk?" Peter whined.

"Shut up. Peter can finish showing May how to wire that stuff up and then there will be his ignominious departure. We have time. Marty, do you at least have warrants for that equipment? Please say yes."

"Yes, we got them based on May's information, her background and expertise and a visual test too."

"Good. At least you did that right. Does Peter need a Doc, Rogers? We could call in Doc to fix his nose. But that would be one more person in the loop."

"No. Not even a little bloody. We can say he was just here with Marty, as tourists, if anyone asks. We can say they heard about the potluck and came to see what it was like and he drank too much. That will work. Where did you ever get that word ignominious? How about we use stupid and drunk?" Rogers' humor took the edge off.

"That will work too, if we need it. Introductions first so we all know who everyone is. Nick, you apparently know Peter our FBI technician specialist. Marty brought him in. You saw Marty the other day. He was the man you saw with May at the Inn. I didn't see him and he didn't know I was there or I would have told you then. Meet Special Agent Marty Martinson, Art Crime Team, FBI. Marty and Peter are here because May spotted a stolen painting and probably has uncovered a long term art theft ring. Marty's plan was, and can still be, for her to go into the Antique Cabinet and take videos from that camera Peter was showing her how to put on. And then she was going to hide another camera in the storeroom and put a GPS tracking device on the stolen painting. Marty can track and follow the painting electronically from anywhere by phone."

Nick was on his feet. "They were going to run an operation under my nose and not tell me? They were only telling David? Now? While they're wiring up May? I've been here a month now undercover and them showing up could blow my operation. How long have they known this? And why didn't they contact David sooner? "May is not going to do that. I don't want her involved. Find another way."

May got a word in edgewise. "I'm right here; someone needs to tell me what is going on. I think you have some explaining to do Grampa," she said looking at Ryan. "And you too Nick."

Ryan had the grace to look a little embarrassed. "I am exactly what you think I am. A grampa, a temporary Inn keeper. I am also FBI, but I'm on 3 months leave to help out my daughter-in-law. I knew about Nick, David told me. We've worked together before and he thought an extra pair of eyes and ears wouldn't hurt. Nick agreed. But I didn't know you were involved in anything until I bumped into this idiot," he pointed at Marty, "talking to the Sheriff. By the time I got there both you and Peter were gone and it took me this long to get the story. I'll get to Nick later. Let's get moving with Marty's cameras before someone comes in. "Peter, show her how to work that camera."

"No, May isn't doing that. It's too dangerous," Nick said.

Ryan looked at Nick, "She is the only one who can do the job."

"No," Nick repeated.

"Nick, she has already agreed."

"Well than, I'm going with her."

Ryan looked at him, and then at May, who nodded her head. He sighed and said, "Peter, I guess you better show Nick how to work the camera too, as he seems to think he has a responsibility here. They can do it together. Explain how to hide that miniature camera in the Cabinet storeroom. And shut up Nick. Pay attention. We'll deal with your sting after Peter gets done."

Peter walked them through the instructions two times. "Don't forget to turn it on and turn it to record and test it first. Same with the GPS on the painting," he said one last time.

Then he made them do it themselves, twice. When they had it down, Ryan said, "Marty you and Peter go back to the Inn. David, go along with them. Nick and I will meet you there later." The three men walked out.

Nick was a professional. He knew they had to do the practice run throughs, so he had kept his mouth shut. But as soon as Marty and Peter were gone, he demanded answers. "Just what's going on? What kind of an operation are they running here? How could you not tell me? You can't be running two stings here at the same time."

"No choice Nick. Once May found that painting, no one had a choice. And yes, Marty should have gone to David immediately. I'll deal with Marty."

Somewhat mollified, Nick turned to May. "May, how could you not tell me? You're always saying you have been honest with me. But you are in the middle of an FBI sting and you just forget to mention it?"

She wasn't going to let him do that. Wouldn't let that accusation fly. "The same reason, you haven't said anything about whatever it is that you are involved in here. The whatever that explains how come all these men know you and accept you as one of them. The whatever that almost gives you a voice in what I can do," she finished quietly.

"I was under orders," he trailed off as she nodded her head. "Shit I guess we are even on that score. Even though I am not the one claiming to tell all." He put his hands up. "You're right, you're right, I just had to say that one time and get it off my chest. We're even."

He changed the subject. "We'll do this tomorrow morning. When you go over to talk about the flyer. What time? I don't have a charter, why don't I come up to your place? No? I guess not, I won't come to your place," he ended when he saw her face. "I'll meet you at The Coffee Spot around nine. That OK?" he added. He figured she would agree to that.

She nodded. Nick turned to Ryan and said, "Come on Ryan, we have some talking to do and some asses to whip."

They left together as May wondered again how things could change so quickly. She sat down and took a deep breath, and played it back. Who would have thought so much could happen in so few days. And Nick with my girl. My girl? Hadn't he just cut her off at the knees an hour earlier with his 'only do awhile, not long term'? She shook herself. How come my girl was the only thing she was worried about? All that was going on around her, the FBI, her involvement with an undercover sting, art theft rings, and whatever Nick was working on, and she thinks about my girl? Her head was really messed up.

She started straightening clothes and was thankful when the bell chimed announcing shoppers. She was almost afraid it would be Sheil and she didn't feel she could explain anything to anyone right now. So she breathed a sigh of relief when tourists walked in all excited about the potluck and ready to buy some Vintage clothing.

She made three sales before closing and was thinking about going back to the party when Nick knocked on the locked door.

She opened it, looking a question. "Come on, I'll buy you dinner." He tried the nice smile again, the one she seemed to like. He had given this a lot of thought and decided he wanted to have dinner with her. He would deal with the one night stands and a whiles later.

"We need to discuss tomorrow," he added when it looked like she was not going to accept his invitation.

His meeting with Ryan and the FBI guys had been informative. Marty was pretty impressed with May's credentials. "Smart. Sharp. Knows her stuff," he said. "Derek Stratton, her soon-to-be ex, is a big name among the Tallahassee elite, runs a very successful investment company. Rumor says he is already shepherding around a blonde replacement for May. Don't know if May knows."

"This is the third painting to disappear in the last six months. May spotted it about two days after it went missing and called her friend Kathy at the museum. This is the first time we have even come close to finding one of the paintings. The plan is pretty simple, we are just going to watch and listen. We want to know who set up the theft, who did it, who is buying, and who is selling. Knowing where the painting is gives us a big leg up. We didn't know about your drug operation."

Ryan just shook his head. "Dumb and dumber. No way a takedown of the art thieves won't conflict with the drug operation. You people need to keep in communication. Idiots. Keep the channels open from now on and keep Nick in the loop. Send the video feed here, to my place, and to each cell phone. This will be the base for both operations." He looked around for agreement.

"OK, I'll tell them at the office, both offices. Anything else Marty?"

"No, you know everything we know. One of the paintings is in that shop and May and Nick will put in the cameras and the GPS locator. All the audio and video will show up here and on your cells."

"That's it then. Get going," Ryan told Marty. "Nick you and David stay. I need to know more about your end, if I am going to try to coordinate. David, OK with you?"

"Ya. We were going to set up in my house, but this is better. We can't use my office."

Ryan had decided that May and Nick should be seen together starting now. He wanted the community to get used to seeing them together. As friends or more. Ryan had said to Nick, "My girl? Did I hear that? Did I hear you say that?" Nick gave him the finger. Ryan had admonished, "I like that girl. You be careful with her."

May brought him back to the present, "I thought we were going to do that tomorrow at nine. And you can't be hungry," she asserted, "You ate five stuffed potatoes."

Couldn't the woman even agree to dinner without a battle? "Things have changed. We can go to The Fry Pan. We need to talk over what to do." He waited while she turned that over and saw her decide not to ask questions. She finished locking up and they walked to The Fry Pan and got a booth in the back. He noticed that people were watching. Hoping for another coffee scene?

"People are watching. They think we are having dinner together," she said nervously.

"We are having dinner together," he said reasonably.

"You know what I mean." She said it crossly just loud enough for him to hear. She kept a smile on her face. Not a pleasant one. "And you know what they're thinking. Just a few hours ago we decided we were not going to be friends or more. And now the whole town will believe we are dating," she complained. She heard the whine in her voice and hated it. But she was frustrated with the situation and there was no way to change it now. "Talk now or I am leaving."

"You don't have any coffee to throw at me," he thought he was safe.

"I can do the same with the salt shaker. Talk. Now," she told him sweetly.

"OK, OK, don't get angry. Calm down."

"I am calm." She reached for the shaker as she started to stand. Well no she wasn't calm. He did that to her.

"Ryan wants us to be seen together." He said it quickly, before another ignominious incident happened. Ignominious? Was that the word of the day? He had used Ryan's name, it was the only thing he could think of to make her sit. And it worked.

"Explain." She was doing short sentences now.

"He thinks, and I agree, that you will be safer if we are seen together and I can better help with the camera and GPS if folks think we are together. Or I can provide a distraction if you need it. Whichever. We won't know the circumstances until we go in the shop. We might not get another chance. If people see us having dinner together tonight, they won't question me helping with The Event tomorrow."

She had time to think that over since the waiter chose that moment to take their order.

"Grilled cheese with tomato and a glass of milk, please," she said.

Nick looked at her like she was crazy. She stared him down. What the hell, "Give me the same," he said. The Tallahassee socialite eating grilled cheese?

"Grilled cheese on our first date." He knew it was a mistake as soon as he said it and waited for her explosion.

"Not a date and it wouldn't be the first anyhow. The previous dates have been disasters as I recall. Let's not even go there. I am not dating you Nick. So tell me your plans for tomorrow."

"I go with you; you do whatever you have planned for the Event. When we get to The Cabinet we play it by ear. You show them what you have planned and go to the backroom for something you want. I will try to go and help. We put up the camera, test it, and place the GPS. Let me take charge if we run into any problems. You follow my lead. Simple."

She was thinking about that when their meal came. Made sense except for one thing. "What makes you the expert? The protector? Why are you doing what Ryan wants, and who is Ryan by the way? Why does he want you with me? Who are you for that matter?"

He was going to try to tell her as little as possible, even though Ryan had recommended full disclosure. "I'm in law enforcement. I know what I'm doing. That makes me the expert."

She waited for more, but he just sat there. So he wasn't going to tell her. "That's not enough. And I don't believe it."

"Which part don't you believe?"

"Stop treating me like an idiot. What are you doing here? How do you know Ryan? Why does he trust you to protect me?"

"Can't you just accept that I am here on an assignment, under-cover, and I would rather not go into that? There is too much at stake if there is a leak. I'm not saying you might leak it. Just that I want to keep it close. Here's what I can say. I grew up here. I left eight years ago. Joined the army, MPs, and then FDLE, Florida Department of Law enforcement, when I got out. Before last month I only came back for my sister's funeral and Hal's wedding. I kept in touch with the twins, or they kept in touch with me. I never intended to come back. I have the family home still. Hal, is keeping it rented for me. No one notices that I am back. I don't own Lucky London, the Feds do, but I do have a charter license."

"Ryan trusts me. We have worked together before. And I worked with Peter. I'm a good cop, and I need to guard my assignment and make sure you don't inadvertently stumble into it. That could be dangerous for both of us."

She considered that. It sounded like the truth. And it did match up with what she already knew or guessed. "OK, I will accept that and not ask more about your assignment."

"That was quick. You are not going to demand more?" he asked a little puzzled.

"No, that lets me know enough so I don't get in your way and I can understand where you are coming from. Remember I don't like pushy. From anyone. I truly think you would tell me all of it if you thought I needed to know to be safe. This is enough for now. And it is nice to know I will have help if I need it tomorrow."

She ate her dinner without another word. He watched for a minute and then followed her example.

"I'll walk you home. Only to keep up appearances." he added when he saw her hesitate. And then he did walk her to her apartment and watched her go up and inside safely. It killed him to do that. He really wanted to go up with her. Kiss her goodnight. But she had been clear about the boundaries. And Ryan would expect him to act profession-ally.

As she was lying in bed that night she thought, "My girl? What did my girl mean?" she fell asleep with a smile.

Week 4: Monday

The next morning she had coffee and toast on her deck. She admitted to herself she was nervous. About spending time with Nick. About hiding the cameras. The sting. She laughed to herself over the word. Her and sting in the same sentence. But she was most nervous about spending time with Nick. She was tough, she could resist Nick. The sooner she got the camera and GPS placed the sooner she could get away from Nick.

She gathered her files and went down to talk to Sheil only to find Nick already there. Deja vu. At least he had already told Sheil he was going with her this morning so May didn't have to try to explain. Apparently whenever Nick decided to do something it was done without any questions. Hadn't he said last night they would meet at The Coffee Spot?

"Are you alright with Nick helping?" Sheil asked May. Sheil had heard about some sort of problem at Vintage last night and that May and Nick had dinner together. Sheil was not totally surprised, but she wanted to make sure May was OK.

"Yes, Nick offered last night to go with me and I accepted his help. I'll pick up the proofs and drafts and then we'll hit all the shops again. We'll come back here when we're done and go over everything with you."

Nick took her files and they went out the door. "Where do you want to start? The Cabinet?" she asked hopefully.

"No let's start here and work our way down and then back over. That would be more natural. It's what you both did the other day, right?"

"Yes, OK." She had been kind of hoping they could get the Cabinet out of the way first. Then the really tough part would be done and perhaps she could have gotten rid of Nick. This way the Cabinet would be last. She resigned herself to being around him.

He laughed and said, "I'm with you for the whole thing kid. You're stuck with me for today at least."

She decided to enjoy the moment. He would probably be the nice, fun Nick today. The one she did like to be with.

She gave the shop owners their drafts and got approval from each of them. They liked her suggestions and picked times for their events. The three day event, called 'The Event' was growing. She left copies of the draft flyers and promised the final documents soon. She was so wrapped up in what she doing that she forgot about the sting. She loved this three day idea and couldn't wait to see how it would work out.

Nick watched her with a new respect. She was good, he thought. She really knew what she was doing and was able to inspire the owners. He jumped in once and convinced a shop owner to do it her way. She had looked at him in surprise and he shrugged his shoulders at her. He was just helping.

He almost balked at visiting the soap shop and she chided him for being nothing but a timid man. "It should be interesting for a smart guy like you. Homemade soap is becoming very chic and olive oil lotions and soaps are becoming popular." She paused as if done and then continued thoughtfully almost to herself, "And I haven't really figured out what is going on here."

"What do you mean?"

"Well, they work some nights."

"You all work nights."

"That's not what I mean. They come in around one in the morning and work, making soap, I guess, until about three. It's strange."

He jumped on that. "Hey I'm here every night. I haven't seen that."

"They don't come in the front. They come in the back and only stay in the back rooms. I see them sometimes when I can't sleep. Hear them first. You wouldn't see them from your boat. They're out of your line of sight. Anyhow, Soaps haven't decided to join in The Event yet. These are the last guys we need to sell, though it should be easy because they are the only ones not participating."

Nick was thinking about what May had said about late night work. This could be it; this could be what he had been looking for. His gut knew this was it.

The bell chimed over the door as they walked in. The place smelled like a flower and incense shop. "Hi. We're back. Today, Mr. London, the charter captain, is helping. I have a draft of a flyer for Soaps you can look at. I based it on your descriptions in the brochure. But it would be better if I could include some information on how you make the soaps in the backroom. Even better if you would let customers back there to watch you make a batch. Or maybe you have a lotion they could all get a sample to rub on. Here are activities some of the other shops have approved so you can see what they're doing." She took the documents over to the clerk.

He took them saying, "I finally got the owner, and she said that I could make the decisions. I'm Paul, the assistant manager. I really want us to be an active part of The Event and I can't wait to see what you have for us so far and what the others have done too. You go ahead and wander around the shop. And the back is open."

Nick and May wandered together, sniffing different fragrances. Nick got a squirt of Angel Trumpet calming salve and rubbed it on May's hand. They both focused on her hand. She felt that massage all the way to her toes. Her mouth went dry. She finally pulled her hand away. "It does feel calming," she said even though her heart was racing. She turned away and walked into the back room.

"Can you walk us through the steps?" he asked Paul.

"It's actually very simple and very safe since we don't use lye. Well, we do use lye for the block soap. The lye is completely gone by the time we finish these steps. Then we use shavings or chunks of the block soap. We start with the glycerin, that's here." He showed them and demonstrated. We cut the amount we will need for the run. We melt it here in our double boilers. This is actually the only dangerous part, like boiling water or candy. We add one of these food dyes, or a pre-determined mixture of colors, for the type of soap we are making. We might want a yellow for lemon or orange for orange. Then we add our essential oil or fragrance - lemon or orange from my previous example. And then we pour the mixture into our molds. My sister actually designed some of the molds. We sometime add objects, embellishments, at this point. We like marbles and crystals. Items that match the color or scent - might even be oatmeal. Some fun thing for the customer to find that identifies us. We have a huge selection of molds and embellishments. When the soap firms up, we slip it from the mold, wrap the bars in a simple wrapper, stick on a label, and price."

He went through it slowly going to each piece of equipment and explaining what and how it was used.

"How about for lotion? Is it the same procedure?" Nick asked, just to show interest in the other process.

"Yes pretty much. Except there is no cooling mold stage. Lotions are about the same except we start with natural beeswax, which nourishes the skin. That's melted in the double boiler. Add the oil, maybe it would be extra virgin coconut oil which gives a rich creamy texture, and a wonderful fragrance. There is an extra step where we heat distilled water to the same boiling temperature as the wax and blend them together in the blenders over there on low for about 1 minute. Add Aloe Vera and any essential oil and continue blending for 2 minutes on high. The Aloe is a succulent plant closely related to the aloe we have here. It is frequently used in herbal medicines. We pour those into glass containers and bottles. Add labels and price."

May was taking notes and drawing diagrams as fast as she could. "This is great. You wouldn't even need to do a demonstration, just walk through the process like you just did for us would be terrific. The public would love that. And then pass around the samples. But just in case how long would it take to make a complete run-through. Or we might think of you having most of one boiler done and then finish it for the tourists." May and the manager got together and talked over her notes.

And Nick was thinking. Of course, this is where they're doing it. He could see it. Put the dope in the plastic baubles or baggies. Put the baubles and baggies in the soap, while it cooled before it hardened. The empty baubles were right there by the baggies. Right here in the shop backroom. No wonder he hadn't seen them. He was out and about most nights, but not in back of the soap shop when the drug dealers were here.

And then they could take the soaps to their high end market and no one ever paid cash for drugs. They bought soap.

While May and Paul were busy, he took pictures and sent them to Ryan and David. No text, just pictures.

Nick wandered back out to the sales area as May finished up. Paul thought they could do one maybe two runs a day for the event. That way they would even have extra product to sell. May said she would get with him on scheduling.

When they were back outside, May said, "Lost you for a while there. What did you find?"

"Nothing, just looking around. This making soap is real interesting."

"Don't give me that. You are on a high. I can feel the energy coming off you. You learned something and it is not about soap. What did you find?" she asked again.

"You can feel energy coming off me?" he asked incredulously.

"Yes, dummy. As soon as he showed you the embellishments, your whole body jacked up. But don't worry, I covered for you. He didn't notice." She looked at him a moment and then said. "Oh, I get it. It has to do with your assignment. You found what you were looking for. Well, congratulations. You don't have to tell me. I won't push. I don't want to know." She changed the subject. She really didn't want to know.

"Now we need to go to the Cabinet. Want to work it the same way? That went well in there." She flashed on him gently rubbing her hand and turned and went into The Cabinet.

The owner, George Dunning, was in the shop. May tried the same opening with him, introducing themselves, and passing him the flyer based on her previous visit. "This is of course just a draft, but it includes the marbles and 'gems' and the ugly frame in the back room. I took the liberty of making that your auction item. Your clerk said it had been around forever and even with the price almost nothing, you can't sell it. I decided we should call it "The Ugly Frame No One Wants" and let people take chances on winning it. The committee will buy it from you and auction it off." She placed the papers in front of him "You can hand out marbles to kids who are old enough not to swallow them. And crystals to some of the ladies. Or the models could do that for you. Let me show Mr. London the frame and he can bring it out for us while you look these flyers over. And that painting with the ornate frame will be your attraction."

As they discussed the marbles and 'gems' Nick had wandered around the shop. Touching things. He noted the surveillance cameras. Strange in an antique shop that did not seem to have anything of value. Most of the stock looked like junk. Of, course he didn't know much about antiques. He would have to ask May when they left.

She headed toward the back room with Nick following her. "The frame is right over there on that flat." And as she pointed it out, she reached in her bag for the GPS. He grabbed her by the arm and backed her up against the wall by the door. And leaned down as if for a kiss. She was shocked, motionless. He missed her lips though and whispered in her ear. "There are cameras in here. I see two. Wait for me to block them before you attach the GPS. I'll give you a nod. First give me the camera. I'll put it behind your head on this shelf." God, he hoped there were only two surveillance cameras. Seemed reasonable. More than that would be overkill. Two was overkill.

She fumbled her hands between them into her purse and he put a hand on the back of her head and kissed her. He couldn't help himself. It started as just a kiss, but her lips parted and he invaded. He kissed her deeply. And she kissed him back. It seemed to go on a long time. She whimpered. Turned her head and whispered, "Nick." And then "Nick. Stop." Tried to push him away. And jabbed him with the camera.

"Ugh. What? Oh." He couldn't believe he had lost control like that. But she was so close and smelled so good. He had thought he would just have a quick taste. And lost it. The woman drove him crazy. He looked at her hungrily. He didn't want to stop. He could still taste her and was thinking of settling back into another long kiss.

"The cameras," she said urgently. "The cameras."

"Oh. God. The cameras. They're recording this." he said and took a deep breath. "OK, good." He reached down and grabbed the camera away from her, made sure it was on and put it on the shelf behind her as he wrapped that arm around her. He could get one more kiss. But she saw his intention and turned her head. He groaned. Whispered in her ear. "OK, When I'm getting the frame, I'll nod for you to put on the GPS. As soon as I block the camera. Can you do it? Just nod."

She nodded.

They moved over to the rack and she started sliding the paintings forward. She didn't even pause when she got to the painting, but breathed a sigh of relief that it was still there. The frame was behind it, so as Nick twisted to lift it out he blocked the camera and nodded to her. She pushed the GPS onto the frame and it fell off.

She froze and her eyes met Nick's in horror. He shrugged his shoulders and motioned his head for her to get it. She still didn't move. He winked. Winked! The wink sent an electric shock through her and jump-started her system. He smiled at her and continued to make believe he was having trouble getting a grip on the frame. Giving her time and cover. He kept twisting the frame to get it out of the rack while she finally located the GPS and stuck it on the inside of the frame near the painting. Now she smiled and said, "Let me help you with that ugly thing." At the same time as he pulled it out and said, "I got it". Just as the owner came in.

"What are you doing there?" he hollered at them. "Leave those paintings alone. They're very valuable."

"OK, OK, we're just pulling out this frame for the drawing. But we need to dust it off. Maybe even wipe it down," Nick said, as he put it down in front of the owner. May slowly pushed all the paintings back in place gushing at the owner. "This is the frame your assistant manager said we could use. It is truly ugly. It will be fun to see if people will buy chances on it. The winner might even refuse to take it. It will be great fun. I can't wait to see it. Don't you just love the idea? But I don't think we should dust it off or wipe it down," she prattled on, mimicking Doris, and finished up breathlessly. "I can't wait to see how much money we raise. And this is the frame for the painting. You can carry that one for me, lease." They followed Nick out of the back room. Leaving a cloud of dust behind them.

George was dumbfounded by May's speech and just nodded his head, looking at the frames. He couldn't get a word in edgewise. May kept talking like Doris.

"Do you think we should clean it?" she asked. "Or will it be better to leave it the way it is? Should it be ugly and dirty? Or just ugly?" she babbled some more breathlessly. "We'll leave it up to you. You're the expert. Either way will work with the flyer."

Nick smiled to himself. That woman had a quick mouth. And the breathlessness might actually be from the circumstances. She had sounded perfect. She had snowed George completely. He had probably been watching them from the monitor behind the counter. Nick could see it was a split screen. Four pictures, from four different feeds. He had spotted the two out front here and then the two in the backroom. He had been afraid he might have missed some in the backroom. So he took a breath and stopped worrying. He would like to have a copy of those kisses. He wondered what George would do if he asked? Right, a charter captain can spot hidden cameras. And May might take exception too. But the idea gave him a smile.

As soon as they were a few steps out the door, she whooped and grabbed him by the shoulders. She was exuberant and laughing. "Oh, God. Oh. God I thought we were dead." She was laughing with relief. "I was so scared when I dropped it."

"You were great. You were beautiful!" He took a breath and then mimicked, "It is going to be such fun. I can't wait." He held both her hands, facing her. "You can have my back any time lady. That was a great save, a great save. And he was watching us. He was watching us on the monitor. Bet he got an eyeful too. I'd like to see that feed myself. He didn't come in until he saw us by the painting."

They walked back to Vintage. She fell into a chair in the back room after she told Doris she would be out to help in a few minutes. She felt weak and exhausted. He said, "It's normal after an adrenalin high." He put water on for tea to calm her and while it was boiling he called Ryan. "We're back. You getting video?"

"Everything is working, David is here. Come on over and explain the pictures you sent from the soap shop."

"I'm making May some tea. Things got a little scary for her. I'll head over when she has calmed down. You'll like what I have."

He loaded her tea with sugar and held it out to her. "Drink this; it will help with the weakness."

He watched the color come back into her face. That had been a close call. Two close calls. Both the cameras in the back room and the dropped GPS. "Ryan says the camera is up and running."

"Great. Nancy Drew, I am not. I almost fainted. My heart stopped when I dropped that GPS." It had already stopped once when he kissed her she remembered. It stopped for an instant. Her insides melted, and then her heart started again and she was lost in the kiss. She licked her lips. She needed to remember that he was for now, for today, for to-night. She was forever. "I am all done with adventure and undercover work. It's all yours. My part in this operation is officially over. I go back to sales clerk and Event promotion. A normal quiet life. Thank you very much." A long speech, but she got it all out.

"No sweetheart. We still have to keep to our cover story. We still need to be seen together. You don't get rid of me that easy. Sorry." He didn't look sorry. He wasn't sure that was true, but it was working for him. "Tell me about that antique shop. You've been through it. Is that stuff any good? It looks like junk to me."

"It is junk. I didn't see anything of value there except the painting."

"Will you be OK while I go meet with Ryan and fill him in on our day?"

"Yes, I'll be fine," she said grumpily. Good, he was going. She didn't know if she could bear to be near him much longer. He was being so sweet and concerned. Just need to tough it out. "Take my camera. No reason for me to have it anymore." She took it off and handed it to him. "I got really good shots of the paintings in that rack. There may be more than one there that was stolen. And Marty can verify The Grange. The camera was running all the time I was attaching the GPS. You should have Marty check those other paintings. I was too nervous to look."

She took his breath away. He couldn't believe that as scared as she was, she had enough self-control and resilience to take pictures. She kept surprising him. He wondered what she would be like in bed. Would she…? What was he thinking? She didn't do a whiles. She had been upfront about that. He only did a whiles. They were not going to be getting together. He had to get his mind back on work. And later go find him a woman, any woman in town.

"You think there is another stolen painting there?"

"Yes, I got good pictures of it. Tell Marty to look. I'm just going to sit here for about 5 hours to get my breathing back to normal and then I need to work on these schedules and flyers and get out on the floor. Being busy will help me settle."

~

The men were waiting for him in Ryan's house. The video of the unoccupied backroom was on the monitor.

He handed over May's camera and said, "May says she has the painting on there and Marty should check the others on that rack too. She thinks there might be another stolen one there."

"We saw. And we are already running comparisons with the Grange. But the pictures are good enough to confirm it is the stolen painting." Marty was ecstatic. "Yes, I saw two other stolen items in that rack. We will do comparisons on those too. Makes sense that they all should be in one place. That warrant sure paid off."

"May, she's good. You know she dropped that GPS? When she first tried to put it on, and I thought she would die. Right there. She looked so frightened. But she sucked it up and did the job. And she had the forethought to make sure we got images of the painting. The others too. That is some lady." Nick was shaking his head.

"The shop looks more like junk then antiques. And May agrees. So George is probably making his money fencing or as middle man." He told them what happened in the shop and the backroom. Told them about the surveillance cameras.

"They didn't catch you did they?" Marty asked.

'No. We did OK." He didn't tell them about the kiss. Hot. He could still feel the aftershocks. Didn't want to think about it. She wanted long term only.

Then he said, "I think I found the drugs."

That made them all look up. "The cell pictures? The soap shop?" Ryan asked.

"Ya. I think they're putting the drugs in empty charms or capsules and then putting the charms in the soaps and lotions. Then they can just carry them out. May says they're working there some nights. She doesn't know who, but can see the activity from her windows." May again. May finding the drug runners when he couldn't. "I tried to get the whole process. Throw the picture on the screen and I'll explain."

They all examined the pictures. Was this really what they were looking for? How would they find out?

"You're going to have to move in with May." Marty said.

"Oh no, not going to happen. I am not moving in there. She can call me if she sees them. I can walk over."

They tossed that around some. Threw out more ideas. "Why not more surveillance cameras. On the Soap Shop. Outside. Feed the video to cells, same as the Cabinet? Get another warrant."

"OK. But I think I will ask May about moving in," he said with a smile and he went out to try that.

He found her in the shop helping customers. He nodded to her and went in back to wait.

"No." she said. "No. You are not moving in. I don't care about your operation. I am setting down roots here. I'm making friends. I have been honest with them and they accept my past. They accept me. And before you start. It's not so much my reputation with them. I could handle having people thinking that I came to town and immediately shacked with the local bad boy. But what happens when I start to show? The timing will look like the baby could be yours. You'll be gone, Nick. You won't have to handle the fallout. What do I tell my baby about her father? Nick's name will follow us forever. I don't want that and I won't do that. Find another way"

She took an angry breath. "Put up a motion camera for God's sake. You know, like the one we just put in the Cabinet. It can alert you when someone drives in the alley. It can get pictures of the vehicles and their tags. It can get pictures of the people. Then you can sneak over and watch. You don't need to be in my apartment. What's wrong with you people anyhow? This is your profession. Your business. And the best you can come up with is Nick shacking up with me? Did you forget all about technology? Four big strong men. Cops. Spies. And all you can come up with is sex. Ask me if I'm surprised? Men!!!" She finished with a disgusted shake of her head.

"And what about the empty apartment over Soaps? Or the vacant shop two doors down? What is Marty's cover? And Peter's? Maybe they should be looking for a location for an outlet store? Go rent the empty shop. Stay at the Inn. Spy from there. You are not staying with me."

He listened to the whole tirade. Agreeing with her all the way. But moving in was the easiest solution for them. And they had discussed cameras and rentals. He was surprised she came up with them on her own. On the spur of the moment. Smart. Quick thinker. But then she proved that with the videos of the painting. Of the whole rack of paintings. Marty's people had identified the other two stolen canvases in the bunch. So why were all the paintings in that one spot? They should have been sold and moved out by now.

"Go away", she said. "Just go away. I have work to do. And you were supposed to help me with The Event schedule today."

"I'm not done yet. Moving in was the easiest plan for us. But we also looked at your suggestions. We are professionals. We can't get a warrant for cameras based on my gut. But you could ask us to put a surveillance camera, video only, outside your back door. Motion sensors. One could overlook your back door and the alley. Put another downstairs which might be able to catch license plates. They would chime whenever they sensed motion and record whatever happens, while sending it to our cells. Then I can mosey over and watch. And Marty and Peter are going to a local real estate agent as we speak."

Now she was angry. "How dare you? How dare you? You rotten SOB. You vile fiend. You despicable beast. As if you haven't put me through enough today, you come back here with that crazy suggestion. To what? Just to see my reaction? Get out. Go talk to Sheil if you want a camera. I don't want to see you. Put it up when I'm at work."

"We're going to have to do it after dark. After the shop closes," he said it quietly, anxiously. "And all we need is your permission."

"Sure, go ahead. But you should talk to Sheil. It's her place. And do you really want to have it done after dark? Doesn't that make it 'secret'? Will that work in court?" What was she doing? His job now? Frustrated with herself, she turned and walked away.

He could have handled that better he thought. He should have told her up front that moving in was not their only option, just their best solution. But he had wanted to see what she would say. Maybe she would have fallen for it. But now he had really alienated her. He followed her out to the shop saying, "I still want to help with the schedule and data entry."

"No. I don't think so. I don't want you anywhere around me. You make me so angry. And I hate that. I hate being angry. And I hate being treated like a simpleton. I seem to always be saying 'no' to you. Go away."

"Our cover," he prompted her gently.

"I can fix our cover. We can have another really conspicuous fight. I will be happy to push you out the front door and continue calling you vile names for all the locals to hear. It will put the 'coffee scene' to shame. Do you want that? Because I will start if you are not out that door in 5 seconds."

He spent 4 of those seconds trying to decide if she would really do it. And the last second getting out the door before she followed through on the threat.

He would call Ryan and have him make the arrangements to install the cameras.

May gathered her papers and file from the sales counter and told Doris she was going upstairs to work. The schedule was almost perfect. Just one problem. She was going to have to cancel the 'Get your Hands Dirty' session for Earth Pottery. The potter had decided that it would take at least 24 hours for the clay to dry before painting. And then the paint needed to dry. It was too bad because she was already thinking of ways to tie it to the soap making. But there would still be a demonstration. He would demonstrate a simple luminary. May wanted to be present for that. Observers would be chosen from all the chances. There would only be room for 15 people.

She put everything in order for Sheil to proof. Then she finished the hems on the twins' dresses and finally settled into a long hot soak. Wondering if she should buy some bath soaps. Probably not until Nick got done with whatever he was going to do there. What was she going to do tonight? She didn't want to go out. Couldn't face anyone. She wanted to stay home and crash. Maybe sew some more? Read a book? She didn't have a book. But she did have scraps of fabric. She could start a quilt for baby.

Nick wouldn't need to come into her apartment to place the cameras. She could stay home, inside with the door locked. That was a plan.

The phone was ringing when she got out of the tub. Who knew the number?

Answer it and find out, silly.

It was Sheil. "I know you've already put in a long day. Come on over. Hal is cooking, BBQ. The twins will input all the data you collected and help with the coupons and chances on line. We can sit back and point and kibitz. Let them do all the work. We'll drink lemonade or iced tea and snack and tell stories. Just have a lazy evening. How about it?"

May hesitated, then, "Sounds like fun and I have everything in the file in order. I was going to stay in and sew, but I can bring it with me and it will be nice to be with people." Just as long as the people weren't Nick. "Where and when?"

"Come on over now. And you can bring your hand stitching and sew while we tell the twins what to do. Best of both worlds."

May followed the directions, turned right after the Inn onto Brackett and then left onto Wren. The houses were just what she pictured whenever she thought, 'little white house with a picket fence and 2.5 kids'. She always added a dog to that. She walked past the second house down. A badly weathered pink. But it should be blue she thought. She could hear the voices and laughter from the street and walked through the gate to the backyard.

Turned out to be a great time. The twins put on their new dresses. Excitedly modeling. And Sheil had three more garments for May. All three were shades of rose and mauve. May just knew she could blend them together. Could envision something two tone, mauve and rose. Maybe with a pretty trim down the seam. A top and a matching gored skirt. She might be able to make two outfits from the three garments.

They laughed and giggled and worked. The twins had more ideas for the coupons and put them all on one printable page. Another page would have the schedule of events. Each shop had its own page with a coupon. A customer could print the page and tear off the coupons and chances, then drop it in a box in the shop. The shop would have the box right on the counter. Then at the scheduled time there would be a drawing and the lucky winners announced. May said she wanted to see the pottery demonstration and she wanted to see who won the 'ugly frame'. Would she need a chance for that? They decided the pottery chances should all go to the public, but there would be plenty of room for the ugly frame drawing. The twins finished the flyers and printed out samples. Sheil would take them around in the morning.

Hal came out then to start the BBQ cooking ceremony. More tea was poured and May brought out her sewing. Explained how it would be a receiving blanket for her baby. The twins talked about their college plans; they wanted to stay local they were planning on the community college and the Vo Tec.

Then Nick walked in. The twins jumped up to greet him and ask for presents. Which he handed out. Apparently it was a tradition of sorts. The twins got free music downloads, Sheil got flowers. Wasn't that sweet, May thought. He looked at May and said, nervously, "I didn't know you were here or I would have brought you something also. Hal just said come on over for BBQ." He grinned and said, "How about a kiss?"

May put on her proper pleased to see you social face. "Not a problem Nick. I don't need a gift. Just seeing you is enough to make my day." Sarcasm. Wonder if he recognizes sarcasm? And she could see that he did. But she wasn't going to feel guilty, he started it.

"No, the kiss would be for me," he laughed at her.

Sheil laughed also and said, "Get out of here. Give me a kiss," she ordered and went in to put the flowers in water.

Nick told Sheil that he had purchased some remote control video cameras for the shop to take pictures of The Event he explained. He wanted to try them out and thought that Hal could help him put them up later. "You're supposed to be able to pick up the feed on cells or iPads," he said. The twins were excited and wanted to rush over immediately and help install them. But it was agreed that after dinner they would all troop over. Nick watched Hal cook for a while and helped carry food. Then he sat beside May. Right beside her, thighs touching. Even though there was plenty of room on his other side. He knew it made her uncomfortable.

She didn't cringe. "That was a pretty smart performance. No one even asked why you have cameras or why you want them outside the shop. Slick. Sometimes you don't act so stupid. How many cameras do you have?"

He decided to take that as a compliment and told her, "Four. Two for the front door area, one at the back door down the alley and one upstairs pointing down the steps and into the alley. You can use the one out front for promotion for The Event."

She didn't have anything else to say to him and ate silently listening to the others. Seemed like a happy family gathering. If you didn't notice the tension between her and Nick. May could tell that Sheil noticed.

Everyone helped clean up and then they all trouped over to Vintage. There were still enough people around that they soon had a large audience. The Event coverage explanation satisfied everyone.

They tested the cameras from inside on their cells. One of the twins would walk out and around and back and up the stairs, and then the other would repeat the action. It was really cool how well the feeds worked. And with the twins' help installing them, the cameras worked on the first run. Nick had thought that Peter would have to sneak over later and fix them. As it was, Marty and Peter were watching from the Inn. Everything was ready for tonight.

They were done playing with the technology by ten and Hal, Sheil and the twins headed home. Nick started to go upstairs with May. "I'll come up and visit. Maybe get that kiss."

"One more time Nick. No. You are not coming upstairs with me. Don't push your luck. I can still make a scene. Go home and set up your camera receivers. Leave me alone. We are not friends. And we are not acquaintances either." She said it between teeth clenched. She went upstairs, inside, and locked her door. Leaned against it and took a deep breath. Why did things have to be so complicated? She really liked the nice Nick. More than liked him, if she was truthful but she couldn't stand the Nick this afternoon and tonight. Pushy. Always too close, watching. She wanted to stay in this town. She would see Nick every day. Maybe he would get tired of annoying her. She would hang on to the thought that he would be gone as soon as he finished his assignment. And she hoped that would be soon.

Nick had hoped she would let him visit and then he could set up the rest of the cameras on his way home. And maybe get that kiss. Or a couple of them. Now he would have to come back later and put them up. Those he had set up already were for show. The ones he would set up out back would capture faces.

Tuesday

Next morning, she gathered her sewing, the pieces, and scraps for the baby quilt, and stuffed them into her black polka dot purse. She loved that purse. Even the silly bow. Generally she took that type of useless decoration off immediately. But this bow made her grin. She headed to The Coffee Spot. Slowed down when she saw Nick was already at her table with two coffees and sticky buns. He stood and pulled out a chair for her. "Please? I saw you coming and got you coffee and a bun," he said.

"Only because you said please. And I want that bun. Gimme." She grabbed it and took a sip of her coffee. Ah, perfect, almost. "And I want to know what you saw last night. Who was outside my place?"

"That was me," he admitted.

"You? What were you doing on my back deck? You scared me to death."

"I didn't mean to scare you. I thought everyone was asleep. And what I was doing, is need to know." He tried that.

"Yes, I need to know. You are supposed to stay away from me. You dragged me into this with your little escapade. And I need to know and deserve to know, now."

"I was putting up cameras."

"You put up cameras yesterday. The whole dock saw you."

"They did and that's the problem. Everyone knows where they are. It will be easy to disable them. So I put up hidden remote controlled ones with motion sensors and night vision. You don't need to worry, because Ryan and Marty and I will all know if anyone is outside your apartment. Why didn't you call me?"

"And tell you what? I was pretty sure one of you would be checking your monitors. Anyhow, I don't have your number."

He gave it to her and when she wrote it down he asked why she didn't just enter it in her cell.

"I don't have a cell. Well I do, but I don't have service. My husband cut it off and I don't really have anyone to talk to so…" she left it at that, none of his business.

He wondered at that. No friends? Family? "I'll get you a cell with the video feeds link set up and all the numbers you need on speed dial. You should be able to communicate with any of us."

"Thanks. You'd let me check the cameras? Really? That's nice, but no, I don't want you giving me a cell. The land line will work for me. And I don't need to watch your video feeds."

"What you want is not going to matter too much anymore. You are part of the operation now. For better or worse. Have a bite of your sticky bun. It's good." He watched her take a bite and got lost when she licked first her lips and then her fingers. Caught himself and continued. "The manager of Soaps, Paul, is a half owner. Set up the business with his sister, Wanda Norton. She is keeping her day job, a book-keeper, while he runs the place. Nothing bad on either of them. I have some history on George, though. George has a long record as a mover or go between. Doesn't buy or sell but holds goods while the buyer and seller negotiate. He is shady but smart enough not to ever have been caught. Yet."

"Marty wants to just watch until the buyer shows up. He probably isn't going to rent the empty shop. He can do his job from the Inn or downtown. It will be sit and wait. I don't know what his timeline is."

"Why are you telling me all this and being so nice?"

"Ryan told me to put you in the loop. And the more you know the safer you'll be. What are your plans for today?"

"Open the shop and then, when Sheil comes in with the flyers, one of us will take those around to the shops. Then I'll work on the floor."

"I'll go with you. I want another look at Soaps and The Cabinet. I'll come by for you at ten."

They finished and went their separate ways. She with a shake of her head. I'm going to be in the loop, Yippee! It was a little exciting and she trusted that she wouldn't be asked to do anything more.

When he came to the shop, he gave her the phone and made sure she knew how to use it. Then they went to the shops.

Soaps owner, Wanda, was there and excited about the weekend Event. May introduced herself and Nick, who wandered around while May showed Wanda the flyers and looked at the special delicate lotion jars Wanda had ready for the winners of the drawing.

"These are wonderful. I love them. The shapes and colors are delightful. Do the colors match a fragrance?" she asked.

"Orange for orange? Yes, of course. You really like them?" Wanda asked looking for approval it seemed.

"You should add them to your inventory. They would make excellent gifts and favors. I'll make a note for Wayne to send someone to take pictures; maybe we can put them in the next flyer. At the very least you need a display in the window. After The Event, I want to buy some." They talked some more and May thought Wanda would be another new friend.

"Come by Vintage some time and I'll show you around. Maybe we could do lunch," May suggested.

"Yes, I will. I would like that. I don't have many friends. Always working."

George was not at the Cabinet, so Nick poked around while the assistant manager, Neal, talked with May. He poked his head in the backroom and went in to check the camera placements. Satisfied, he went back to find May and Neal looking at an old, discolored cradle. May was stroking it. A look of longing on her face. He could feel that touch. Wanted to feel her touching him that way, looking at him like that. "What's up?" he asked as he came to stand with them, near the piece of junk.

"Oh, I want this cradle," she said it so lovingly that he looked again. And still, all he saw was a dirty, wooden piece of junk. He looked at her again and saw she was serious. He shrugged his shoulders.

"OK, some day you can buy it. We should get going. You need to get to work and I have a charter."

Later, May and Sheil went over the flyers one more time. "Great, that's all done and I'm going back to sales clerk and seamstress," May announced.

After work she started sketches for the rose and mauve outfit. She would use parts of two dresses for the shell and skirt she had envisioned. There was more than enough fabric for them. Even enough for a second outfit but she didn't see that one yet.

She didn't have the right thread and she wanted a special trim for the shell. So a visit to the fabric shop was in order. She could catch the tram at the Inn. It would drop her close. And on the way back she could visit with Ryan. She hadn't seen him since Sunday and wondered if their relationship might have changed. She hoped not, she really liked him as a father figure. She'd find out. With her plans for tomorrow laid out, she went to bed.

Wednesday

She had coffee on her deck the next morning, was that because she saw that Nick's boat was out? She gathered her things and set out for the trolley. Breathing in the scenery along the trip and excited to be on her own. At the fabric store, Marge cornered her as she was picking out the trim.

"I have three customers who would like to learn how to sew. The ladies from the tutu gang have said you can teach. I can give classes here if you will teach. I'd charge them a nominal fee to cover fabric and patterns and pay you as instructor. We could schedule it around your work, at your convenience. I would love to be able to run classes and if it goes well, we could set up a schedule."

May was speechless.

"I don't expect you to make a decision now, you should think about it," Marge continued.

"I think it is a great idea. I would love to do that. It would be fun and I could use the extra money."

"It's a deal," Marge said. "I'll speak to the ladies and I'll call you and let you know when I set it up. What days are you off?"

"Wednesday and Thursday, so you could set it up for either day."

They exchanged phone numbers and May finished her purchases. She wanted to do a Jesse, jump up and down, and sing, and dance, but did it in her head.

On her way to the grocery store she passed by the beauty salon, Nicolle's, and caught a glimpse of herself in the window. Dragging, stringy, harsh, blonde hair with an inch of dark roots. She was a mess. On impulse she walked in. The woman behind the counter looked up and asked if she could help her. Hesitantly May asked, "You take walk ins? Any chance I can get a cut?"

"Cut, dye, and set?"

"No. Just cut off all the blonde. That's what I want. I want to go back to me." Suddenly she had to be rid of that long blonde style. She didn't really care what she looked like afterwards. Just wanted to be her old color for her new beginnings.

"You're May aren't you?"

"Uh, yes," hesitantly.

"Oh don't look so scared. This is a small town and I heard about you from Marge, she was in last week talking about you. Come on back; let's see what I can do for you. I'm Nicolle," she said leading her back to a chair and mirror. She ran her hands through May's hair, front to back and side to side. "Yes, we want to get rid of this. Your natural color is beautiful and shiny. I'm surprised you bleached it."

"My ex, well soon to be ex, wanted to be married to a blonde."

"Men, bah. They'll be the ruin of us," she said disgusted. "Your hair would look great in a pixie. It will fall naturally. No fuss, no perm, no curlers. Maybe, but not necessarily, a blow dry. Want to try?"

"Yes. Cut all the blonde off." May loved this town. Everyone made life and decisions so easy. And they were so friendly. Well, not Nick. But Nick should not be in her thoughts. Ya, right, I won't think of Nick. Or that kiss. She locked her lips and then, mentally slapped herself in the face. Stop it. Not thinking of Nick.

She closed her eyes as Nicolle shampooed her hair and then sighed with satisfaction as the long ugly strands were cut off. Nicolle talked up a stream about what she was doing and then Nicolle wanted to know more about The Event. They talked as she snipped and measured. Fluffing May's hair with her hands. "I was right," she said triumphantly. "Wash and fluff. That's all you need. This is great hair and this style suits what I have heard about you. Good riddance to the ex. Look." And she held up the mirror walking around May.

It is good May thought. "It's me! I love it. I am so glad I came in. Whatever you charge, it won't be enough." They laughed together. May shook her head to watch how nicely her hair fell. It was a perfect cut for her face. She loved her natural color too. "Why do I feel taller?"

"Because you got rid of all that mess that was dragging you down."

May paid her and thanked her again. Couldn't get the grin off her face. She picked up a few items at the grocery store and caught the tram back. She went to find Ryan and share her news.

"Ryan, Ryan, I got another job," she sang out and finally got to imitate the Jesse dance. She forgot all about how this meeting might be awkward after Sunday's activities.

And he responded excitedly, "Come in here girl and tell me all about it. I'll pour tea. What have you done to your head? You look beautiful. You look like a happy person. But first tell me about your job, you're not leaving Vintage are you?"

"No, I will be teaching a sewing class part time, sometimes," and she told him about Marge's offer.

He agreed that it was a great opportunity. They talked about it some more over tea. And then her hair. Finally he wanted to know if the tutu gang would still meet at the Inn and they decided to see how things worked out with season coming.

He pulled out a cell phone and handed it to her. "The government is paying for it. And you need to have it for my peace of mind. He showed her how it worked. Showed her the speed dial for himself and for Nick, David, and Marty. Showed her the app for the video feeds. She stopped him there and watched.

"I can't believe this. Modern technology. You could hide a camera anywhere and no one would ever know they were being watched."

"That's the idea. But we always go through a judge and have a warrant."

"Are you really with the FBI?"

"Twenty five years. Law school first. I really am on leave because Liz needed help while my son is gone. So I'm here. But as you heard on Sunday, I'm back on duty and in charge until Marty's operation is finished. David's is a local state matter. I'll just coordinate until we get our man or men."

He didn't appear to want to talk about his son and where he was or what he was doing, so May didn't ask.

Then he invited her to dinner. His daughter-in-law would be back and wanted to meet her. Tomorrow night, behind the Inn, in his house.

Thursday

She was awakened about 1 AM with activity next door. She turned on her cell, checked the video link, and saw a car in the alley. Whoever it was they were already in Soaps. She texted Nick and got an instant response. "bz tmw." She finally figured that meant busy talk to you tomorrow?

She probably should not have texted him. Would his phone have rung? Or did it light up? She hadn't thought of that and now she felt like a fool. Probably he had it on vibrate and was aware already of the activity. She watched for a while, but nothing happened and she didn't see anyone, not even Nick. She busied herself with the rose dress for an hour and finally went back to bed. Tomorrow, Nick had texted. She would find out tomorrow.

Meanwhile Nick was sitting in his car, parked, lights out, on Main near the turn toward the highway. Waiting for the men to finish in Soaps and leave. Two men had gone in. He had tried to see in the window, but it was blocked from the inside. The car in the alley was a Dodge van and he could watch the van on the video feed on his phone. Ryan was running the video of the men's faces through facial recognition. The plate had come back on a 2010 Buick sedan, so that was no help. Nick would follow the van and see where it went. Marty was parked by the highway, they would tag team the van.

They didn't have enough for a warrant. All they had was someone making soap in the middle of the night. Hopefully the van would lead them to something that would be enough for a warrant. He settled in. May had said the action lasted until about three AM.

The two men came out at 3:30, each carrying a heavy sack. Nick let them drive out and past him and down Main. He waited for them to make the turn toward the highway and then followed to the corner. He called Marty that they were coming. The Bluetooth was a handy tool. It let them keep up a running conversation detailing progress and turns. Marty would enter the highway ahead of them. He was going to head south. If he guessed wrong then Nick could speed up to take over the tail. Otherwise Nick would hang back.

Marty guessed correctly, the van turned south. He trailed from ahead and Nick followed slowly, far behind. It was a quiet road and it was hard to follow here since there was little traffic. The van would spot his headlights. But there was enough traffic that he would able to keep his distance and follow inconspicuously until the van turned off. It turned right after it went over a bridge. Nick turned right when he reached the turn only to see the van finish making a U turn and go back out to the highway and turn south. He told Marty who had pulled into a convenience store parking lot further along the main road. Marty waited for the van to continue south past him and let a pick up get between him and the van. Again, Nick stayed far behind. The procession continued for about a mile. Then Marty said, "He's turning off down a side street and looks like he's doing the same U turn maneuver. Wait up where you are."

Nick picked up the tail as the van came back onto the main street. "Guess he is a one trick pony. Make a turn, make a U turn, lose any tail," Nick said.

They followed the van through town. It turned left and Nick drove by as Marty picked up the van. It was turning into a condominium parking lot when Nick entered the street. Marty drove by and turned down a dead end side street and parked and killed his lights. "See if you can get the street number or see which building they go in when you drive by."

Nick saw the van parked in front of the third building and the two men were getting out. He turned down the side street and pulled in behind him and got into Marty's vehicle.

"Did you get the address?" Marty asked.

"Yeah, and they were parked in front of the third building. Some-one will have to go in later and check the mailboxes. See who lives there. What do you think, about eight or ten units in that building?"

"Yeah. And we need to follow the van when it leaves, see where it goes. Might lead us to a distribution center. Or at least a name we can use."

"I have a charter, half day, at seven. Why don't you call Ryan see if he can get a relief out here. Can you stay until the relief comes?" Marty nodded. "OK, I'm leaving. I have just enough time to get back. Have Ryan call the Sheriff. I'll give May a heads up later. She sent me a text about activity at the soap shop."

Nick took off. Finally, he thought, finally, after a long dry month, they were getting somewhere. And it was all because of May. Didn't hurt to have the FBI on site too. Nick didn't have enough, even now, for a court order for video and audio inside Soaps. Or a GPS on the van. They would have to continue doing it the hard way. He want-ed both sides of the distribution chain, where the drugs were coming from, how they were being dispersed and where they were going.

He called May with a quick update, just before boarding his clients.

Two out of the three fishermen on Nick's charter were sea sick. What a mess they made. Made him think of May, telling Jeremy she had been seasick. Protecting him, when he deserved a beating for what he had subjected her to on his boat that day. He shook his head. What a woman.

At least these guys knew enough to hang over the side. Nick brought them in early since they didn't have the strength to fish. He felt bad for them and refunded half the cost and then cleaned his boat.

Ryan wanted a meeting. He had sent a backup relief for Marty. The condo was on a dead end street so they could watch from a parking lot on the crossroad with a clear view of the van and could video it. There had been no activity around it and it hadn't moved yet. But as Nick was walking toward the Inn, he got a text saying the van was moving. He changed direction and headed for his car.

Marty called and said he would be right behind.

Then the cops following the van lost it.

"I'll see if it goes north on the highway," Nick said waiting to see if it would go by heading north. A few minutes later, "Here it comes, it's heading north. I'll fall in a few cars behind. Marty? You behind me?"

"Yeah, I'll be another few cars behind you."

A few minutes later Nick said, "Turning right, going east on 41."

"I have you in sight." Marty said.

"It turned into the Ochopee Post Office. I'll go by and make a U turn and come back. Marty you should be able to pull in and just act like a tourist visiting the country's smallest post office."

"No problem. I'll keep the phone open. The rest of you guys pull over for now. There is only one person in the van. He's taking boxes out and carrying them into the building."

Rogers dispatched the Naples K-9 to make a drug search in Ochopee. The dog would alert, if it found drugs in the packages and they would have probable cause.

Next thing Nick heard over the Bluetooth was the obnoxious tourist complaining about cheap rental cars, sputtering, that he was waiting for the rental agency to show up with a replacement car. Then "Can't believe the Post Office keeps this tiny building way out here. Going to need me a whole bunch of these post cards otherwise no one back home will believe this. I don't know, no wonder the government is broke keeping this place open. Can't possibly get any business. You actually mailing those boxes? What are they anyhow? Some of those one price no matter what you put in boxes? How does that work for you? They look pretty heavy; guess you'll get your money's worth. My taxes at work." Marty excelled as the chatty tourist. He leaned over a shoulder and tried to make out an address, but the Post Mistress moved the boxes through the window too quickly. Marty kept up his commentary. "When you are finished I'll get these cards. Gotta say though this is the smallest post office I've ever been in."

The man paid his bill, got his receipt, and walked out.

Marty picked out some cards and watched Nick follow the van back west. He turned off his phone said, "Hey honey," to the clerk, "How soon does your mail go out?"

"It goes with me at 4 PM. I take it downtown."

Marty paid for the postcards with a "Thank you sweetums." He went to the door and called Ryan. "Ryan we need that drug sniffing dog here. If we can get a hit on these priority packages, we can get a search warrant."

"Rogers has it coming. Stay there and keep an eye on the stuff. Nick and the backups are following the van."

"The Postmistress thinks I have car trouble. I'll wait inside until the dog gets here and keep an eye on the packages." He turned around and went back to the counter and transformed into curious tourist who wanted to know everything.

The Postmistress decided that she must have judged him wrong as he really was a nice guy. Asking her all about the building and its history and her job. How the mail was moved. She was thrilled to show off her knowledge. Even added a few tidbits about the last customer and his soap shipping business. Pointing to the boxes on the inside of her counter, she said that the man shipped a couple of times a week. Priority mail. Three day delivery. Sometimes just 2 or 3 boxes. Sometimes like today with 8 or 10. The customer thought the post office was so good he never even bothered with insurance, although she was sure the box contents were valuable. He did get return receipts though. Had to know when his packages arrived. Had them all made out for her ahead of time. The return address was not the same as his manufacturing business because it was a subsidiary.

Finally the K-9 unit pulled up in front.

"Never seen that K-9 unit here before," she said as the deputy got the dog out and walked it around outside.

"Hey, there," the deputy said at the door. "Me and Ghost were driving by and I decided I need some stamps. OK to bring him inside?" Ordinarily the deputy would just walk in; but now the Supreme Court was looking at rules for drug dogs. The Sheriff's Office always got a warrant before bringing the dogs into a private residence. So far public buildings were deemed OK and a search of mail did not require a warrant since a dog sniffing parcels was minimally invasive. There was no expectation to privacy here. But the Deputy wanted to be invited to bring the dog in.

"Sure," she said. "I love dogs. Can I pat him?"

"Yeah, he can come to the window. You should be able to reach his head if he puts his paws on the counter. Careful though, He's a drug dog. You don't have any drugs back there do you?"

She laughed at him. "Oh, you," she said giggling.

But Ghost gave a positive alert when he got to the counter. Pointing at the boxes and whining.

"What's wrong with him? Why is he acting so strange?"

"He smells drugs in those boxes. I better get a warrant and some back up."

He radioed in that Ghost had made a hit and he needed a warrant. "Just leave those parcels there until the warrant gets here. Then we'll want to look at them and open them."

"Oh, this is so exciting. But those boxes only have soap inside. And I was just telling this gentleman all about those packages."

"Well, please wait for the warrant and the detectives before we talk anymore about it."

He turned to Marty and said. "Let's move to the door and talk. I need to keep the packages in view."

"We have to keep this quiet," Marty told the deputy. "Is there any way you can convince that woman not to tell everything she knows?"

The Deputy thought they could get the Post Office to transfer her to Naples and send in a replacement. "The Sheriff can work something out."

Nick and his backup tag-teamed the van back toward town. He was relieved to hear that Marty had found drugs with the soap. "Yes," he said and right then the van ran a red light and he lost it.

May answered the knock on her door and found Nick there. He had on a bright Hawaiian shirt and looked sweet and innocent. She was curious how last night's activities turned out, but she wasn't sure she was happy to have him outside her door. "Hi, Nick. What can I do for you? I'm on my way out." She was heading over to Ryan's for dinner. She had spent a quiet day working on the rose and mauve ensemble which was nearly done, so she was feeling good and was satisfied with the results. She had also started a skirt with the leftover fabric.

He just looked at her with his mouth open. And then she remembered the hair and giggled. "Oh, do you like it? Isn't it great? I love it" and she shook her head to show him how it bounced.

"What did you do?"

"I had all the bleached blonde cut off. I only dyed it because my soon to be ex wanted to be married to a blonde. This is me. The real me, my real color."

Nick was stunned. She looked great. This was the woman in his dream. The one with the shiny brown hair. He was shaking himself again, lost in the memory, the feeling.

"It is you. Exactly you. Your ex is an idiot. To make you dye your hair, to let you go." Thank God the ex was an idiot, because now May could be his. "I know you're going to dinner. I'm invited also and I thought we could walk over together."

"Nick you know this isn't a good idea. Remember we have different goals."

"Right. You are forever and I am for a little while. This is a little while, dinner at the Inn. I'm invited because I grew up with Liz. And Ryan thought that he, you, and I could go over last night's activities. Liz will leave us alone to talk."

"Oh, I'm sorry. I jumped to the wrong conclusion. I apologize." She was a little chagrined to realize that she had assumed he wanted to go out with her.

But it wasn't the wrong conclusion he thought. He really would prefer to be going to dinner with May. Alone. A date. But he had already set the boundaries for any relationship they might have. "Just don't let it happen again," he said with a smile. "And if you're nice to me, I will forgive you."

He saw her expression change and said quickly, "By nice, I simply mean that you don't chew me out and hit me with that look that shrivels my…ah, my brain. Let's go." Her laugh made him think that she knew what he had been going to say.

They didn't speak on the walk over and Ryan opened the door when they knocked. He introduced Liz, as Jesse ran in and hung on Nick. Then pulled away and twirled around. "See, Unca Nick. See my pwetty new outfit? Aunt May heped me make it. She came almost every day." Nick looked at Jesse's clothes and was not sure what was expected of him. "It's great," he finally said and then added, "and very pretty." She twirled away.

Nick glanced over and saw Ryan looking at him meaningfully. And he knew just what Ryan was thinking. He felt slimier then a snake. He was afraid he would see the same smug, superior expression on May's face and braved himself to look at her. But she was talking with Liz. If there had been any doubt of her activities at the Inn, Jesse was listing all the times May had visited. May was working with Jesse those times he had seen her come into the Inn.

May was still at 'Unca Nick' and wondering if Nick was related to Jesse also. Until Jesse called her Aunt May and May realized that Liz was using the titles for adult friends.

Liz thanked May for her time with Jesse.

"We both had fun," May said. "You have a wonderful daughter."

They sat down to dinner, lasagna, Ryan's specialty, and salad. Liz made chocolate cake specifically for Jesse. But they all enjoyed it. Nick enjoyed it. He had three pieces. After dinner, Liz excused herself to get Jesse ready for bed.

Ryan recounted the previous night's activities and added a few pieces that Nick hadn't heard. The FBI was officially working with FDLE now that they knew the drugs were crossing state lines by mail. They had a list of residents in the condo where the van had parked but none had come up with a criminal record. So they still didn't know which occupant they were looking for. Nick lost the van with the stolen tag. "Not his fault," Ryan said. "It ran that red light and barely made it through the cross traffic without an accident."

"We have addresses from each of the packages. Ten packages, 8 addresses. All to P. O. boxes. FBI is getting names and addresses on those post office boxes. There were fingerprints on the boxes, labels and even on the soap. But none of those got a match in the system."

"We'll replace the soap with the real soap from the shop and put GPS bugs in packages. We'll reship the soap in 3 or 4 days and follow and arrest whoever picks up the packages. Hopefully we will have our men here before then. Meanwhile, the delay in delivery will put a little extra pressure on our soap makers.

"FDLE will be at the Florida mail boxes, FBI will be watching those out of state. But Sheriff Rogers and FDLE, Nick here, still want the soap makers and their suppliers."

"We now have warrants to put cameras in Soaps. That's where you two come in. Do you think you can get back in there, like you did in The Cabinet?"

May waited for Nick to answer. She didn't like the idea; she had been so scared the last time. She didn't think it was a good idea, but she wasn't the expert. And that's what Nick said. "No. We can't do that. We have no excuse and we don't know who might be part of the organization."

He actually looked at May for confirmation. She couldn't believe that Nick would consider her opinion? She nodded. Nick continued, "We probably can't do a break and enter. It's a big weekend, though, and we might get an opportunity during one of the activities." He looked at May again.

"That could work," she said. "They're having soap making demonstrations. "One on Friday and 2 each on Saturday and Sunday. Tourists will need to buy a chance to watch, but we might be able to get in because we set it up."

"OK," Ryan said. "You two work it out. I'd like to have it done sooner rather than later. And we can use the GPS when we find the van. If we find the van."

"Our biggest problem is the talkative post mistress. The Post Master told her that she would be going undercover to the downtown office for the next two weeks. He is giving her a secret assignment. He told her she would have to be real careful not to gossip to anyone and to maintain her cover." Ryan laughed. Then got serious again, "But she'll probably leak fairly soon."

"There has been no activity at The Cabinet. Wait and see there."

Liz came back in and she thanked May again for all the time she had spent with Jesse. And for teaching her how to sew. "Who would have thought that my little girl would want to sew clothes?"

"I love that she does," May answered. They talked about kids and sewing. The guys wandered off. Liz looked back and forth between May and Nick, but May stopped her from asking by saying, "We are not together. We are not going to be together. We are just barely acquaintances. Although I think your father-in-law may be trying to be a matchmaker."

Liz said, "I can't believe you don't like Nick. He's fantastic."

May looked at her and said, "I thought you were married to Ryan's son."

"Well just because I'm married doesn't mean I can't appreciate. He would be a great catch. We kind of grew up together. He's like a big brother. I would love to see him settled down and happy. He looks at you like you might be the one."

"I'm not. And anyhow, you will learn soon enough, if Ryan hasn't told you already. I'm married, and in the middle of a divorce, and I have a lot of baggage." She got that out and waited, apologizing, I'm sorry baby. You are not baggage.

Liz didn't appear shocked, "Does Nick know?"

"Yes. We already had that conversation. I want a forever relationship. He wants for a while. I screwed up this time with Derek, but I'm not making the same mistake again. Not even with Nick."

Nick walked May home, all the way expecting her to bring up his ugly accusation. Finally when they got to the stairs he said, "When are you going to say it?"

"Say what?" she asked him. "Thank you for walking me home? Now I guess."

"No. When are you going to remind me how wrong I was to call you a whore when in fact you were playing with Jesse?"

She looked at him considering. "Probably, I'm not going to. You might man up and apologize though. Or not. I don't need to say anything."

"I'm sorry. Very sorry that I called you that. I am sorry that I even considered it possible, I didn't really believe it. I was being a jerk." That was when I was still being an idiot he thought. Before the dream. Before I got smart. "Will you forgive me? Please?" he asked her.

"Apology accepted. Thank you for walking me home"

Nick left her at the foot of the stairs. He gave her a devious smile like he had a secret agenda and wished her goodnight. Never even tried to kiss her. A perfect gentleman. Then he walked to his boat. Just as Hal had suggested.

May was still wired and finished the ensemble. It looked even better then she had hoped. The front and back center of the shell was the rose fabric, the sides were the mauve. The trim separated the two colors. It was pretty and slimming. The gored skirt was both fabrics, again separated by the same trim. Now she had an idea for a dress made from the third garment. She knew it would take a while for the design to gel though. She could be patient and not force it.

Friday

There was a feeling of excitement in the air when May went to The Coffee Spot. Almost all the tables were filled. That was a good sign. Folks were buying coffee and sticky buns and dropping chances into the coffee pot that was being used as a collection box. How cool was that. "Janine, I love the coffee pot for the chances. What a great idea."

Janine basked in her admiration and said, "Works really well. Almost like people want to put chances in the pot more than they want to win. We are busy. I mean really busy. I already started more sticky buns. I love your hair. That looks like you."

May knew the first activity of the day wouldn't be until Soaps' demonstration, which would start at 1:00. She might be able to time her lunch to go and see how many people came.

"The charter captains, ALL of them, went out at 8 for an hour or so." Janine said when she saw May looking toward Nick's slip. "Back in and then out again at 12 and then again at 3. The boats are all chartered with the guests just paying for fuel. This is so much fun. Oops, gotta go and get my buns"

And Janine thinks I need to know about the charters, May thought. So I won't be disappointed that Nick isn't joining me now? Everyone thinks we are a couple. For a minute she thought of how nice it could be. Then shook herself. She needed a distraction. Times tables. She could practice times tables. That's a good idea. Just sit back, eat your bun, drink your coffee, watch the early tourists, and do multiplication tables. She told herself, enjoy now, enjoy today, life is good.

May went to Vintage early and hung the mauve top and two skirts on the wall. Pleased with how good they looked there. She had already entered their data in the computer and made tags which included pictures of the original garments.

Sheil came in and saw her new hair. "Get out of here. How did you get something so perfect for you? Wait, you went to Nicolle."

"Yes, and I love it.

"Me too. I'm jealous. I couldn't pull that off." And then Sheil saw the mauve outfit. She was ecstatic. "These are beautiful, but you priced them too low. You are not charging enough for your designs and for the hours of work you put into them. Wait," she said holding up her hand, "I'm not done. You are a designer. You are working with Vintage clothing and making beautiful fashions. You need to treat yourself as a 'name designer' starting right now. People will be paying for your name as well as your designs. Therefore you are not charging enough. You have been in promotions and advertising. Look at the people out there who came for your event. What would these cost from a new designer?"

May said, "Wow, I'm a designer. I should charge for my name?" Her mind hung up on that, "If we price them too high, they won't sell."

"We don't care if they don't sell. We can keep them on the wall. As advertisement. We can always mark them down. But I bet they will be gone by Monday. And you need to label these pieces as the designer. Before we open. Sit down right now and design your logo. And sew it into each piece. I will make a sign and we can add your logo to it. Something like New Vintage by May."

"You're serious, aren't you," May said. "You really think we can use my name as a selling point? You think these designs are that good?"

"Oh, honey, they are better than good. Trust me here. I know current fashion sales. Now get to it. You can change your logo later if you need to. You can have a special logo for your original designs, and another logo for your vintage designs. But for right now, we need your name on these designer fashions."

"I like New Vintage. But before I was married, I used Designs by May. Derek didn't like it. He didn't want me doing work that any illegal could do in a sweat shop."

"Did I mention that Derek was an ass? You have an extraordinary talent for designing. Use it. Do you, did you, have a logo too?"

"Yes, I even have some labels already made. I kept them."

"I knew you were a smart girl. Of course you kept them. Go get them."

While May was sewing them in, Sheil made a sign that replicated May's labels.

"You know, I never even think of Derek except to think that he wouldn't like this or approve of that. I can't believe I don't think of him with sadness, except to feel sad for him, not me. Do you think I ever really loved him? Why did I marry him? Was I just so enamored of his attention that I was carried away?" She didn't realize she had said all that out loud until she noticed that Sheil had stopped working and was looking at her.

"It happens, you know. He must be a real smooth worker though to have been able to convince you. How did he do that?"

"He sent me flowers every day. Called every hour. Took me out to lunch and dinner. To plays and shows. Bought me new clothes, because I needed them in order to go to those places. To be seen by the right people. Convinced me I should be blonde. I can't imagine now how it all happened. I had just lost my Mom and was dealing with her hospital bills. The whole world seemed to be plotting against me and this man came to the rescue. Wanted to help me, be with me. It's scary to know that I let that happen. But at least I was becoming aware of it. It took me a few months to realize I might have made a mistake. Another two to be sure."

"Honey, we all make mistakes. Fixing them is the important thing."

"But how will I know, Sheil? The next time? How will I know if love is real?"

"Get out of here. Of course you'll know. Your heart will beat faster when you see him. A smile will light up your face when you hear his name. What do you feel when I say Nick?"

"See, see," Sheil laughed continuing, "Fooled you. You already are in love girl. Don't try to deny it. I've seen the way you look at him. And the way he looks at you."

"I know," May said distressed. "I do like him. I like to be around him. He can be so nice. And I love his smile when he is happy. Not that mean leer. That girl killer leer. There are two Nicks and I like the one a lot. The other not at all. Mostly I get the other one, the Nick who is only looking for fun. One night, maybe two. I don't want that. I want forever. I want a lover for me, a daddy for my baby. That's a lot to ask. And more than Nick has to offer. But I do smile when I think of him. And I never did with Derek. I am such a mess, I am so confused."

"You are not a mess. And love confuses us all. Remind me some day to tell you about Hal and me. You are dealing with some very tough burdens now. And dealing with them brilliantly. Don't worry about Nick and love. Whatever happens there is beyond your control. Let it happen, it will all work itself out. Give me a hug here and let's get back to work."

Sheil wasn't really sure that she had said the right things. She didn't know. Just went with what felt right. She was so proud of May and everything she had done for herself. And Sheil was sure that May was wrong about Nick's feelings. Sheil knew Nick and this was the loving Nick she was seeing. He wasn't playing here. He was serious about May.

"Oh," Sheil continued, "Cove Photos will take pictures and video of the demonstrations, painting class, models. All of it. We can use the pictures all year for promotions."

The twins came in then excited. They were the first models of the day and had already chosen their outfits. They would carry small bites of muffins and sticky buns. With lots of napkins. They had handouts to go with the clothing and the food. May laughed at their vamping and Sheil shooed them off and then put out an open jewelry box for the flyers, a Vintage basket for the coupons, and unlocked the door. The Event was officially started for Vintage. Two customers walked right in, talking about The Event while checking the schedule. They had circled what they wanted to see and put address labels on their chances. And the women were buying!!

The morning went quickly. Sheil and May watched as a crowd gathered in front of Soaps. "Look at all the people," May was giddy. "It's working, it's working."

The twins came in chattering and laughing about the fun of posing and interacting with the tourists. The girls were trading off with a couple of guys from T-Shirts for the afternoon and the four were thinking that tomorrow they should all go together.

Melanie had to come over and touch May's new hair.

Just as May was thinking, supper time, Wanda came in and said to Sheil, "I'm Soaps owner, Wanda Norton. And I have to tell you, this was such a great idea. We had a full house and not only did they take the free mini lotions, they also made purchases. What a great day for us. Probably the best sales day yet and it isn't even over."

Sheil told her it was all May's idea and that May and Capt. London had done all the heavy lifting."

While thanking May, Wanda exclaimed, "Oh, here comes my boyfriend," as she beckoned him over.

May looked behind Wanda and put her hand on the counter to steady herself. It was one of the men from the video. She took a deep breath and put on her social face. Wanda went over and grabbed his hand to lead him back to Sheil and May when he hesitated in the doorway.

"Sheil, I want you to meet my boyfriend, Bobby Frances. Bobby this is Sheil Burke, she owns Vintage, and May Johnson. May thought up our soap demonstration and I was telling them both how terrific the sales were afterward. I am really looking forward to this whole weekend." She paused and then said, "Now I have to take a few minutes to see your clothes, Sheil. Bobby, come on with me, maybe I'll find something you can buy me. We'll be seeing you May. We still need to do lunch."

She took Bobby to the other side of the shop just as Nick came in. May walked quickly over to him.

"Oh, Nick, look over my shoulder." She said it sweetly. "Do you see Wanda?" she asked, and waited for his nod. She continued, "And beside Wanda is…"

She didn't get a chance to finish. "That's him. You got him," he said with a whoop, looked at her calculating, "And you deserve a reward." He grabbed her and kissed her. They were both laughing.

"His name is Bobby Frances," May finished still laughing. He kissed her again. Boy this was fun. She wished she had more for him. "Oh, he's Wanda's boyfriend."

May looked at him, waiting. He was looking at Wanda and Bobby. "Don't I get another reward?" she asked. He looked at her and his eyes were hot. For her? Or because he had a name for his video?

"Oh, ya." He kissed her again. This time he added a lick . Two. Stopped, but still held her close. Finally let her go and backed away.

"I love my reward," she said. "Wish I had more information for you. I recognized him from the video and the name was on that list you had of residents at the condo."

He looked at her with admiration. "You are amazing. I would have gotten there. Maybe. The video for sure. Probably, not the name. You're quick." And he pulled her close again and gave her another kiss. And was lost in it when she broke away.

"I do enjoy that. Too much. But I'm still married and a forever kind of girl." She looked at him and said, "Your turn to complete the speech."

"I am a for a while type of guy," he finished.

"Let me know if you ever change your mind. Oh, Wanda and Bobby are coming this way. Maybe you will get to ask some questions."

"Wanda, you remember Captain London. Nick this is Wanda's boyfriend Bobby Frances." She explained to Bobby, "Nick is a charter captain and he helped with Soaps' demonstration.

"Fiancé," Bobby said. "Not boyfriend. We are planning on being married."

"Oh, congratulations to you both. That's exciting. When's the date?" May asked. Interesting that Bobby was suddenly a fiancé. A few minutes ago he was just a boyfriend. May could see that Wanda was surprised.

"We haven't set a date yet," he said officiously. May thought he sounds just like Derek. I wonder if Wanda is making a mistake. And then she shook herself. Well of course she was making a mistake, the man was a crook. Unless Wanda was in it with him. But the fact that he made his soap in the middle of the night argued against that.

Wanda had some questions about May's shell and skirt. They went over to look at it. Nick and Bobby were left alone.

May heard Bobby say, "So you drive a boat here?" condescendingly.

Nick didn't take the bait. "Yup. But we call it run a boat. Or navigate if you feel real important. Drive works though. But that word makes you sound like a tyro. That's a greenhorn. I take out people to fish or bird watch. Or some just want to spend the day on the water. Means I don't need to get a real job. Can play all day and still get paid. What do you do for a living?"

"Investment counselor," he responded, haughtily.

Nick really needed to get close to this guy. But Bobby's arrogant attitude would make it difficult. Nick decided he could play on that. "I take out a lot of bankers and consultants, a couple of local venture capitalists. You wouldn't believe the stuff they talk about." Nick stopped to see if he was on the right track and saw he had Bobby's attention. He had guessed right. Bobby was interested in the movers and players. "I guess that makes me the equivalent of a caddy on the golf course. I wonder if there should be a non-disclosure agreement."

"You mean like they talk about what to buy, what to sell?" Bobby asked, interested.

Nick decided to back off and acted nervous, as if he might be hiding the truth. "No, more like what's hot. Like your fiancé, she's really hot." He knew that Bobby had seen his nervous act, but calling his fiancé hot distracted him for the moment. "She sure is. I can take her anywhere."

Nick wondered if that was a play on words. The man was a real scumbag.

"What about you. You and the shop girl got it on?" he asked with a leer.

"Not my type. I got shanghaied to do this event thing with her is all." He knew that no one had seen him kissing May a few minutes ago. He would have to get May aside and explain this conversation.

"So tell me about your charters. Maybe I need to go out with one of those groups."

Hooked and landed Nick thought and proceeded to bore Bobby with details. Let Bobby come back to what he wanted. Nick was pretty sure he would be taking Bobby out on the water for a practice session within a week.

Meanwhile, May was telling Wanda that the rose and mauve outfit was a size ten and not a six. Wanda was disappointed. Then she said, "I just realized, you're May, May the designer!!"

"Yes. I take vintage garments that are not in good enough condition for sale and redesign them into something contemporary."

"Do you take custom orders?"

"Hard to do when we don't know what is coming in. We don't know sizes or colors or fabrics. You could make a request with a selection of colors or fabrics or styles and I could let you know if anything comes in." She didn't mention that Wanda might find something in Vintage that could be updated. She would have to run that be Sheil first.

"OK. Let's do that." And they went to the counter to exchange information, and then wandered over to the men. Bobby it seemed was ready to leave.

"Wanda we need to leave, I have to get back."

"I thought we had planned to spend the day."

"No, I got a call and I have to get back to the office now."

May watched as Wanda, obviously disappointed, said goodbye and they both left.

"He got a call?" she asked Nick.

"Not while I was here."

"That was mean. And manipulative. Wanda obviously wanted to stay. He could have come back for her. It is all of what? 5 miles? 10 if they go all the way around? He didn't really care what she wanted." Thinking, Derek. That's what Derek would have done to me. There was that Derek thought again. No hurt feelings, no unhappiness, just relief to be free of him. She needed to have a talk with Wanda, even if it was none of her business. "What did you say to make him leave like that?"

"I just bored him to death about boats."

"You? You couldn't bore anyone." Oops, she shouldn't have said that. It just slipped out.

He looked at her a minute considering, but only said, "I worked hard at it. And I told him I thought his girl was hot and I might be interested there. I didn't mean that. Wanda's not my type," he paused and said, "She was pretty surprised to find out she was a fiancé wasn't she?"

So he had caught that too. "Yes, I think that was the first she had heard of that."

Nick went on cautiously, "Then, when he asked about you, I told him you were just the only game in town, not my girl. And I didn't mean that either. In case any of the conversation gets back to you." He paused a minute thinking. And then admitted, "You aren't my type, but you are under my skin so deep I might never get you out. So I'm sticking close. After all you enjoyed my kisses and just admitted that I'm not boring."

She didn't know what to make of that. Under his skin? Decided to take it at face value. But it ratcheted up her heart beat.

"Now I need to follow them and see what they're driving and I better get the cameras and GPS. I'll be back and we can make plans." He gave her a quick kiss. 'Cause he wanted to. Then he took off and called Ryan to update him on Bobby. "They're getting into a Mercedes convertible." He gave Ryan the make and color and the tag. "And do we need a warrant for the GPS on the Mercedes? I better come over and get the equipment. May and I will figure out a way to get it set up."

"It will have to be before or after the demo tomorrow morning. We can say we just want to see how the demo works? I need to get time off." May said when he came back. "And you know, I've been thinking. Do you think you might want a camera outside The Cabinet too? To get a license tag. I mean. If they don't use a stolen one, it might be a good thing to know."

He blinked. Again, it's May who comes up with an idea that should have occurred a long time ago to the professionals. "Ya. I'll get Marty on that." He pulled out his phone and passed on the suggestion. Only shook his head when Marty asked why none of them had thought of that.

Saturday

The twins planned to spend all day with the T-Shirt guys. Changing costumes whenever they changed shop products. May was working with Doris Fuller again. She really was a nice lady even if she never did stop talking. Or maybe because of it. It was rather endearing because Doris didn't care if anyone was listening. Mostly she talked to hear herself, it seemed. May tried to say 'yes' or 'I know' every once in a while just to appear to be listening, but Doris didn't really even notice. She just talked. Right now she was talking about the luminary demonstration and May was interested. Doris's description was so detailed that May felt as if she had witnessed it herself. Doris explained every step of the process, along with the audience reactions. Her demonstration of Gordon's facial expressions, as he made the luminary, had May laughing and now May really wanted to see the demonstration herself.

In between customers, May straightened garments putting them in their proper places on the racks. One of the women who came in had watched the clay demonstration and had purchased an orange luminary. She decided that a vintage orange dress would be a perfect accessory to it. "Oh, I hope this fits, it will be perfect. This is my favorite color and the luminary is sort of a vintage candle. I almost feel like I am back in a time when I was happy." Her friend encouraged her to buy the dress and said that the woman had just gone through a long and ugly divorce after thirty years of marriage. Bad marriage.

May could sympathize. But again wondered that she herself felt no pain. She felt sadness that the marriage didn't work out, sure, but almost a secret thrill that it had been short and would soon be over. Felt nothing for Derek.

When Nick walked in, Doris went right over and began her story of the luminary demo a third time. May had listened twice and she watched Nick listen politely. That was sweet of him she thought. Most thinking adults would have walked away, quickly. May noticed that Nick was watching her over Doris's shoulder. She just smiled at him, tilting her head, she shrugged him a question, and he rolled his eyes at her. Doris didn't notice. Doris never noticed that sort of thing when she was talking. When she paused for a breath, Nick said, "I came for May, we have a date."

That stopped Doris completely and left her with her mouth open. May too, and a look of distress replaced her smile. He laughed at them both. He was happy to see May distressed by his remark. He took it to mean that there was hope for him.

Doris found her voice first. "A date?" She looked at May, "You have a date with Nick?"

"No," May denied loudly. Too loudly she realized. "We don't have a date." She knew what Doris was thinking. She had heard the tales of Nick and women. They all ended up on his boat. She needed to dismiss any thought that she might be ending up there. She had to be calm. "No, we don't have a date. I don't date."

And then to Nick, "What do you want Nick?" As soon as she said it she knew it was the wrong thing to say. No one could misinterpret his smoldering expression. May felt herself turn red and Doris said, "Oh, oh my." And May felt herself get redder, if possible.

She went on the offensive. "Stop it, both of you," she ordered. She didn't stomp her foot, but not stomping took all her willpower. Nick laughed. Doris put her hand over her mouth and giggled.

He liked that May was flustered. And wasn't sorry that he was the cause. "Come on May," he pleaded. "We'll walk around and look at the tourists. There is this cute little chica I want to watch." He ducked as she threw a hat at him and laughed. "No, really, I thought we could go to Soaps and get you a scent and then I'll buy you a grilled cheese."

He gave her the sweet smile she liked that melted her insides. She really was a mess whenever she was around him she thought. Then she realized that he was probably ready to set up the cameras and reluctantly agreed.

"OK, we can walk, but I can buy my own sandwich and I don't need a scent, I have my own." He gave her a knowing look. Don't go there she thought. Why did you say that? She could tell where his mind went. For half a moment she thought he would wink and her heart missed a beat. Just hesitated. She shook herself. This seemed to be a new habit for her whenever she was near Nick. Nothing like this had ever happened around Derek.

She turned away. "Can I take my break now, Doris?" she asked.

"Sure I can manage, go have fun."

"Let's go in back so you can get your purse and I can drop my knapsack," Nick said. And only then did May notice he was carrying one. She looked into his face questioning and he nodded.

She led the way into the back room, but when she picked up her purse he said, "Not that one, the big one. Your sewing purse, the black one with the bow." Nodding significantly toward the knapsack.

"It's upstairs, I'll go fetch it. Wait here." And she escaped before he could suggest that he come along.

Upstairs she thought, get ahold of yourself, woman. After the look he had given her, she wasn't sure she trusted herself around him. She wouldn't have felt safe with him up here. She was finding him hard to resist and had a feeling he knew that. He seemed attuned to her feelings. So it was better that he stay out of her apartment. Away from her. So why didn't he follow her upstairs? Wasn't he interested? She didn't believe that. That look, it must have given him some flashback too. She shook her head, now what are you doing? Complaining because he didn't follow you upstairs? She didn't want him upstairs with her, did she? Or did she? She was so confused.

Remember, she told herself, you're a forever girl, he is a for a while boy.

She gave it up; she could stand here and dither all day. She grabbed her polka dot purse. He had noticed it had a bow she thought with a smile and then, stop it she told herself. But kept the smile. He liked that bow. She went back downstairs.

Nick quickly switched his equipment from his knapsack to her purse. They waved goodbye to Doris who was with a customer. May decided she needed to know, "Will Doris tell the whole town that I'm going out with you?"

"Would that be so bad?" he asked her with an innocent grin. "Everyone will see us having lunch together anyhow. And probably assume since we are together, we're probably going out together. Don't you think?"

She did. She knew that. It was really 'the look' he had given her that she wanted to know about. Would Doris tell everyone about that 'look'? But she couldn't ask because then Nick would know that she had seen it, felt it.

He could read all that on her face and took pity. "Doris talks all the time. But she never gossips and she has never said a mean word about anyone. At least not back when I lived here, and I doubt that has changed. You can rest easy on that score."

She changed the subject. "What are you planning? To walk into the shop and take my purse and walk into the back room." As she pictured that she smiled. "That will look just a little weird won't it? Maybe Paul will think you want him to join you back there." She laughed out loud as his nod was replaced by a look of panic. "If you could just see your face." She had to stop and hold her stomach until she finished laughing.

Nick even got a quirky grin. "That would not be funny. But I can almost see some humor in it. Stop laughing," he ordered. "That is almost exactly what I was planning. But I can see that won't work, we'll have to play it by ear."

There were a number of customers in Soaps. But Paul came right over to them. Shook their hands. Tried to hug Nick, who put his hands up and backed away. Paul was ecstatic about the demonstration and sales and hopeful about the upcoming demo. A little anxious, he asked if there was something else he could do or should do to make it even better than the first demonstration.

It was a good lead in for Nick to suggest that he and May go walk around the shop and the back room for inspiration. It was just that easy. He and May could duck into the back room alone.

Though May was still nervous, worried that Paul would come back and see them setting up the cameras. Or maybe it was like the Cabinet, and Soaps had cameras set up in the back room. She asked Nick if he had checked for them and he told her he didn't see any. And then he remembered their kiss in the Cabinet back room and could see she was thinking the same thing. She licked her lips. Saw him looking at her mouth and she forced herself to look at the floor. She just knew she was turning red again. He found he was copying each motion. Licking his own lips and looking at the floor. God dammit, she had him crazy. He shook his head. Get your mind back on the job he told himself. But he could still feel that kiss. Wanted to try it again. Thought, steady boy, back to work boy, get the job done first.

Nick got busy. Put up two cameras, on opposite sides of the room, high up on shelves. No one would notice them up there. Each pointed toward the back door to catch anyone coming in. And each one covered a different section of the work area. "We can also operate them remotely to scan. Let me call Ryan to test them. What's Paul doing?"

"Some more customers just came in, he's greeting them. Wait he's coming back here." She caught herself with her hands together and her thumb in her mouth. Get a grip, she thought. Paul came in, "We keep running out of soap on the counter and having to replenish from the back room. The citrus orange is a big seller today." He picked up boxes and said he would be back as soon as he made the sale. May just wanted to sit down, she took a breath.

Nick called Ryan to test the remote scan and the sound. He held the phone and told May to walk to the back door. "And give me commentary. Walk to the back door and around the assembly line and tell Ryan what you're doing." And then to Ryan, "OK, test them now."

May did as instructed. "I am at the back door and looking at both cameras and now I am touching the trinkets and baubles and soap supplies. Here is the cooker and over here is Nick." She spoke quietly because she was afraid Paul would hear, but apparently it was loud enough because Nick said great to Ryan and hung up. He came over and hugged her, started to tell her she did a good job and got side-tracked by her ear. He was just leaning over to nibble on it when Paul bustled in. They jumped apart. Paul didn't even notice.

It was anticlimactic after the scare at the Cabinet, this had gone smoothly, but May was still shaking. She wasn't sure if the shaking was caused by the stealthy stuff or Nick's breath on her ear.

"Did you think of anything for me?" Paul asked.

For a minute Nick was confused and then he heard May say, "I do have one suggestion. Engrave the shop name and date on the soaps you make. Then people will have a keepsake. They might even need to buy extra soap just to use."

Paul clapped his hands. "I love it," he said. "We'll do it. We might even make some ahead to have enough prepared. I'll work on it when it gets quiet in the shop and Wanda will be here to help. Alone. Bobby is too busy to help her." This last was said with dislike.

"He does seem to be a little bossy and inconsiderate," May said and then immediately put her hand over her mouth. "I didn't say that."

Paul laughed and said, "I didn't hear it. But if I had I would have responded with lots worse terms. I just keep hoping that Wanda will see what we see."

May was thinking that she really would have to say something to Wanda. Maybe someday, over girl talk and lunch she would tell Wanda about Derek.

Nick grabbed May's hand before she could say more. "Come on May, we still need to fit in lunch." He laced his fingers with hers. They fit perfectly, like they were made to fit together. And it felt right to walk her out the door that way. He realized that since he had accepted that he was silly in love with her, his life seemed easier. Better. It only remained that he convince her that he could do forever. Right now, though, she was struggling to pull her hand away. He lifted it to his lips and kissed her thumb, remembering how she had chewed on it in the backroom. She stopped, with big eyes looking up at him. At her thumb, by his lips. Her mouth open. He laughed. He felt good. It felt good.

"Nick!" she said shocked. Breathless. It was supposed to be an admonition, but it sounded more like encouragement. He just turned and walked down the dock, her hand still in his. She decided to enjoy the moment and walked beside him, hand in hand, contented.

They sat at the back booth in The Fry Pan. Nick motioned her to be seated and ordered a cup of fish chowder and tea and grilled cheese for both of them. With tomato for May he said, as she took a breath to ask for it.

May couldn't think of anything to say and she was worried that she would just sit and smile at him. She finally came up with "Can you get the cameras on your cell again? You didn't test them."

"Hold on a minute and we can look." And a moment later he showed her the split screen view on his cell. He said that Ryan could control the cameras from the main consol. "You can get it on your cell too," he said. "Hand it over And I'll set it up."

"I don't really want to. Don't need to. You're the professionals. I'm the seamstress. I don't want to be involved."

"Well it's here. You don't need to look. Just hit soaps if you change your mind." He handed her cell back to her.

He changed the subject. "What are you making now? Did you finish the baby quilt?" When she looked surprised, he said, "You said you wanted to make a baby quilt last time we were here. Did you finish it?"

"No, I am having so much fun making it that I am taking my time and enjoying every stitch"

"Your baby will be happy in it because it's made with so much love," he said, and then felt like an idiot. "How did you get started sewing?" he asked.

She looked at him a minute and then told him. "I started with a borrowed pattern and an old flowered sheet. It didn't turn out too good. And I wanted to know why. So I hung around the fabric store for a while. Looking, reading and listening. I learned that it was important to use the right fabric. The right fabric being the one that would drape and hang properly." He looked puzzled. "You wouldn't use jeans fabric for underwear. You know, chaffing?" He laughed thinking about chaffing. She went on to explain that she seemed to have an instinctive ability to know the perfect fabric. Then, when she had learned as much as she could by hanging around, she started asking simple questions. The sales help and the customers were happy to explain what they were doing. She made her own pattern and went back and took her original dress apart. The fabric was perfect for her new design, so she tailored it for her body and remade the dress. By hand. And she was hooked. It was fulfilling and exciting to be able to make nice things. Individual clothes, her own special style.

She took lessons at the store where she could use their sewing machines. And then got a part time job. Fabrics and patterns were half price and lessons were free for employees. More and more she was designing her own patterns and soon was giving sewing lessons. And that was extra income. "It wasn't work," she added, "It was fun. Teaching especially." And then she figured she had run on long enough. She stopped.

"Why did you go into art?" he asked.

How did he know that? Had she told him? She didn't think so but couldn't remember.

"That is a story for another day," she said. "It's now your turn to tell me how you became an FDLE officer. Is that the right term? Officer?"

She wasn't sure that he was going to tell her. And she could see that he wasn't sure either. She didn't know how she should feel about that. She shouldn't care. After all he was only for a little while. But she found that she did care and waited to see what he would decide. He had told her a little before. Would he tell her more?

"It's Officer. You already know most of that story. I was pretty good in school. I enjoyed learning. I was the cut up kid. Not a bad kid, just a cut up. Never got into real trouble. Well, once when one of the guys hurt my sister. Almost put him in the hospital. You know most of the rest of the story. Joined the military, ended up in the MPs and liked that and then went with FDLE, Florida Department of Law Enforcement. Who have now sent me back home, undercover.

He hadn't told her much more, but it was a beginning. "How does it feel to be back home?"

"I like it."

"What was your sister like?"

She saw pain cross his face and immediately said, "You don't have to answer that. I'm sorry."

"She was an angel. She was 10 years older, 19 when our folks died in a car crash. She raised me. The community helped too. Someone was always stopping by with food or time. That's why I was never really bad. Never had the chance because someone was always there, acting as a parent. I owe everyone here in this town. Sis had started college, but got a job and went part time. I helped out at home. So I can cook and clean with the best of them. She met Hal in one of her night classes. Turned out they were both interested in the same courses and started taking classes together. He was in his last semester and looking toward a master's degree in English and writing a book. They fell in love, got married. Storybook romance. I was 14 by then, and they took me in. I was a part of their storybook. Hal just treated me like a younger brother. The twins came and they were both ecstatic. Me too. Now I was the big brother. I loved them. It was fun helping with them. I can change a diaper in two seconds," he said bragging.

"Joined the military at 18, went into the MPs and got my degree in Criminal Justice & Law Enforcement. Every year, I spent my leave home with them. Always brought everyone some silly present. I enjoy being big brother still. Hal taught at the community college and published his first book. It was an erudite work on the politics behind Viet Nam. Meant for a small number of war buffs. Surprised everyone when it became a best seller."

"He's that Hal Burke?"

Nick stopped, "You didn't know that?"

"I never put the two names together."

"He is so quiet and reserved it's sometimes tough to remember that he is a well-respected author."

"The twins were 8 when Sis died. Hit all of us hard. I came back on emergency leave and stayed until Hal could pull himself back together. The town turned out again. Someone always wandering by with food or help. The twins shared the household duties. Each did the chores they liked. Only a couple of hated ones required real teamwork and some of those just didn't need to be done on a regular basis. By the time I left, they were all pulling together. Sis raised them right."

"Each time I came back they were stronger. Ryan wrote two more best sellers. And then Sheil came back to town. The twins decided that she would make a good Mom and became matchmakers. Turns out they were right. They all got lucky. I got lucky, they kept me." He couldn't believe he had told her that. He had never told anyone. He had been relieved when Hal asked him to be best man. And then excited to babysit during the honeymoon. He had almost cried when Sheil sat with him to make sure it was OK with him, Nick, that she move in. She said his room would always be there waiting for him. He'd been an adult, by God, 27, and he had been as scared as a foster kid that he would be asked to leave. Then she said she could be a friend and would nag him along with the twins."

"I grew up with Sheil and Bryce, Liz, and Rogers. Well, all of them really. It was a good town. People cared. Still do. I like it here. Its home I guess." He couldn't believe he had shared all that. Really had missed the community and never known. Now he didn't think he would leave. His roots were here. Family. He looked at May and thought, his new family maybe.

"Yes," May said, "The people have all welcomed me. No one has been bothered by a divorced, pregnant, single woman. I feel wanted and loved. Protected."

"And now I have to get back and help Doris."

"I'll walk you back and get my knapsack."

Sunday

Liz was just delivering coffee and muffins to the conference room when May arrived for the tutu sewing group.

"Can I join you this morning?" Liz asked.

"Sure. We're going to work on quilt designs and try to incorporate our fabric scraps. Is Jesse coming too?"

"No. Ryan will be watching her when she wakes up."

The women exclaimed over May's new hair. And her Vintage outfit. She was thrilled. Liz had never seen her as a blonde, but Carol had a picture of her with Jesse and the tutu. They all agreed that this style and color fit her personality. Then Carol said, "Why do you look taller? It's not fair. You get a haircut and come out taller and thinner." They all laughed over that.

Each of the women put their fabric scraps out on the table for everyone to select from. Considering the short amount of time they had been sewing there was quite a variety. May showed them the designs she was working on for her baby quilt. She had cut some calico into small three inch animal shapes. There were a couple of shapes she wasn't sure what they were and confessed that she might have to recut those. Probably should use a pattern. The bunny, kitten, and pig looked good though. She had put together an outline of a heart in multiple calico prints as the centerpiece, also about three inches wide.

They tossed around ideas while drawing and cutting. And gossiping. May wasn't really surprised when Carol said, "What new person is dating a local boat captain?" To forestall their comments May said "I am not dating Nick. I don't care if you did see us together. We are not dating. And I don't want to talk about that. Have any of you been to the demonstrations or submitted chances at the shops?"

They let her change the subject and as the conversation turned to The Event May breathed a sigh of relief.

They broke up around ten as the women headed home to go to church with their families. May was talking with Liz in the corridor when she heard a shocked male voice ask, "Elizabeth, is that you?" May hadn't been called Elizabeth for almost five weeks and it took a while for the question to register. Both she and Liz turned toward the voice at the same time. "Elizabeth Stratton!" it said in triumph. "I thought that was you. Where is Derek?" And she could see surprise on his face, both at her being there and at her clothing as the man gave her a disapproving look. And May saw puzzlement on Liz's face beside her.

May found her voice, "Well Dominick Russon. What a surprise to see you."

He said what he was obviously thinking, "Elizabeth, I didn't know Derek was in this neck of the woods." He looked around as if Derek would appear out of the wall. May had never been allowed to be too far away from Derek and she could tell Dominick was baffled. He was checking out her yellow outfit. "You have cut off all your hair and it's a different color. And I almost didn't recognize you in that outfit. Where is Derek?" As if he couldn't believe that Derek could have approved the transformation. So unlike what Derek would expect from his wife.

"How nice to see you Dominick. Are you on vacation? Are you staying here?" Not responding to his question. She didn't want to discuss her divorce with Dominick. Let Derek tell him. She knew the suggestion that he would stay at an inn would distract him. He never stayed anywhere that didn't have five stars and he would be aghast for anyone to think that he would be at a quaint inn. "Isn't this just a quaint place," she continued innocently.

As she expected he addressed the fact that, of course he wouldn't stay at an inn. "No, no, of course I could never stay in such a place." She could see the excuse coming. "I have a meeting shortly and I'm just passing through."

"A meeting? On Sunday morning?" she asked. Why was he uncomfortable explaining? Generally he was bragging about whatever he was doing. She wondered if he was with a woman, though why that would make him uncomfortable she didn't know. He immediately followed up with, "You know us collectors. Meet anywhere, anytime for a new treasure." Laughing nervously.

She laughed with him, "Are you buying, or selling?"

"We'll see," he said enigmatically.

"Well, we won't keep you then. We wouldn't want to make you late for your appointment."

"Yes, well say hello to Derek for me." He hurried away. Almost looked like an escape. She disliked Dominick. Sleazy. Wealthy sleazy. With a bad reputation in the art world. It was reputed that he did not worry too much about provenance. He had always made her feel a little dirty when he came to the museum. As if he might be picking out his next acquisition. Her or a painting. She wondered what might have brought him to The Cove, which he certainly must consider a backwater.

And then she knew. He was involved with the art thefts. Knowing his reputation, he could be buying or selling. Either would fit.

May must have turned pale because Liz put a hand on her arm and asked if she was alright. May imagined that Liz must be confused since Derek had called her Elizabeth Stratton. And May needed to talk to Ryan. "I need to sit. Can we go to your house? I know it's an imposition. If I can just sit, I'll explain. Please?"

Liz held May's hand as they walked to the house. Ryan was in the kitchen drinking coffee when they entered. He jumped up when he saw them asking, "What's wrong?"

"Nothing, nothing, I just saw an old acquaintance and it distressed me," May said as she sat. "And Liz doesn't know my married name, so she's confused. And I just needed to sit down and have a cup of tea."

She looked at Liz. "That was a man from my past, Dominick Russon. He called me by my married name. My maiden name is Elizabeth May Johnson. I've always been May. My husband, soon to be ex-husband, Derek Stratton, preferred that I be called Elizabeth. He is divorcing me because I am pregnant and he does not believe my baby is his. That's my sad tale condensed to 3 or 4 sentences. 10 months of my life. Three or four sentences. But I am so lucky that God is giving me a beautiful baby."

She paused and Liz leaned down and gave her a hug. "A baby" she sighed, "How exciting. That's why you're making the baby quilt. None of the girls told me. Neither did Ryan. I am going to have to chew them out. I am so happy for you. It will be a joy. But why did that man upset you?"

"That man is a friend of my husband's and he was a frequent visitor to the museum where I worked. He always treats me as available, empty headed, arm candy. He's a sleaze and an art collector who is reputed not to look too closely to provenance." She said this last looking at Ryan and saw that he understood. "He hung around the museum a lot. He especially liked a painting called The Grange. I think he is staying at the Inn, even though he would never stay in any hotel but a five star one. And only the best suite. He's a snob and very worried about his image. I can't imagine what he would be doing here at the Inn, let alone in this town."

Ryan put the tea down in front of her and she picked it up and sipped watching him to see if he understood what she was trying to tell him.

He shrugged and said, "I got all that. And Liz knows about the cases we're working, the art thefts. Her husband, my son, is also law enforcement."

May was speechless. After she had figured out how to tell him what was happening without leaking anything to Liz, Liz knew everything?

"It's almost impossible to keep anything from her," he continued.

Liz said, "None of you guys mentioned that May was involved in the art sting. Or married. Or pregnant. Don't I have any friends? Oh, May, both the women and the men protected you. I can't believe that. I didn't even suspect. And you did a fabulous job of getting the information to Ryan. I'm terribly impressed. I almost missed what you were telling him." She hugged May again.

Ryan broke them up by asking if May was sure that Dominick was staying at the Inn or if she knew where Dominick was going.

May didn't know, but Liz said she recognized Dominick's name as a guest and he was in The Pelican suite. She had seen him head back upstairs.

"Good. Let me get some background on him. Liz, call Marty and have him come down for an update." He paused and looked at May. "You did really good. This will really help us. If you hadn't bumped into him, we would still be lost. And there was another theft yesterday."

"From my museum?" May asked.

No, this time, an art museum in southern Texas."

"So you think that painting is coming here? And that Dominick might be the buyer?"

"It is a good possibility, but we'll wait for Marty to come down. We also need to keep Nick and the Sheriff in the loop."

Marty came in a few minutes later with the Sheriff and Nick right behind him. Nick came over and touched her shoulder, "Are you OK?" he asked gently. He really wanted to stand her up and wrap his arms around her and kiss her hard. She still looked a little shaken. Ryan had updated him on the phone.

"Yes, of course. Why wouldn't I be OK? He's just a sleaze and I've dealt with him numerous times. He's a good friend of Derek's. It just shocked me to see him here. And then when I realized why he might be here, I was a little nervous." And why do you care she thought. Which was rather small of her. She knew Nick would be concerned about anyone.

Ryan described the situation. "Now we don't know that there is any connection between him and the art thefts, but it appears to be a good assumption, based on May's description of him. I'm running a check on him now. Getting known associates also. That will be coming in soon."

May wondered if any of Dominick's associates might also be at the Inn. It was the only hotel in town. "Maybe he checked in with someone else."

Liz went for the Inn register. Meanwhile they waited for wants, warrants and associates.

May was amazed at the extent of Dominick's record. Although never charged or prosecuted he had been suspected of involvement in a large number of thefts. Both as a seller and a buyer. He was associated with some clever thieves and a number of middle men. George's name was listed as one of those.

"Wow. All this time I have felt a little guilty judging him. He really must be a bad guy," May said in wonder. "Look, you men can do what you do. I'm the civilian here and this civilian needs to get back to Vintage. Sheil and I are modeling this morning and though I am already dressed there is still a lot for me to do. So if you think you can get along without me, I have to go."

Nick looked at Ryan who nodded his head. "Nick will walk you back. AND, before you object, he will pick your brain on the way."

May had nothing new for Nick and she sent him off when she got to Vintage. Sheil was waiting and watching, hovering. "Was that Nick? The man whom you are not dating?"

"Yes. You know it was. Don't ask. He was just walking me home from the sewing group. Don't ask me, I don't know why. Can we just get ready to model? I'm kind of edgy. I know it was my idea, but it was my idea for someone else to do it. Not me. And not me in my new vintage design." She was a little nervous. She should just treat this as acting like a model instead of acting as an important society matron. "I'm ready. The sewing group approved the outfit. Of course. What are you going to wear?"

Sheil showed her the new pink top and gray poodle skirt with the matching purse.

"Oh that's great. That is so Vintage. It is perfect. Go change."

"What are we carrying this morning, Sheil? I hope it is muffins. I'm starving."

They set off for The Coffee Spot as soon as the day sales clerk came on duty. Janine set them down with fresh brewed coffee with cream and sugar. Sheil preferred the real stuff. But then she didn't seem to have any kind of a weight problem. May had to admit, coffee was better with cream. She liked her first cup to be black and hot. Then added cream to the second cup. Felt so decadent. They were served hot muffins with homemade jellies. Janine approved the outfits and put down 2 muffin shaped baskets with individually wrapped miniature muffins inside for them to distribute. Some Coffee Spot customers came to their table and were encouraged to touch and feel the fabrics and read the tags. May handed out chances for Vintage and Sheil did the same for The Coffee Spot.

Already May was having fun. She and Sheil walked slowly up the dock, stepping into the shops, and sharing the muffins and news. Then they picked up chocolates from Dainty Bits. These would be carried in woven clay baskets from Earth Pottery. Along with chances for a smaller version of the basket filled with bits of chocolate. Sheil and May were giggling. Sheil said it was definitely a sugar high because, of course, they had been sampling.

Everyone seemed to be having fun and they went to the first drawing at The Coffee Spot and cheered the winners of several baker's dozen muffins, giftwrapped in paper baskets. The winners got to choose their own flavors and that seemed to excite them. May heard one say, "We get to choose the flavors? That's the best part."

May and Sheil met up with the two guys modeling T-Shirts. The T-Shirts were specially made for today. One said 'The Event' under which was 'Save the Ugly Frame' with a picture of the frame on an easel. The other said "The Event – Bid on Me Today". May figured that was purposely ambiguous as to whether you could bid on the T-shirt or the model, or maybe both. That was definitely the impression the wearer was trying to convey to a very buxom blonde anyway. The back showed the frame on a boat, with a happy face. The guys were handing out bracelets that looked suspiciously like Hospital ID wrist bands. They had what appeared to be the ugly frame with "The Event" and the date stamped on them. Some had the frame on a bike; others had the frame on the boat. The bracelets came in an assortment of colors.

May thought they were kind of cute. The tourists were lapping them up. The boys were also attracting a lot of teen shoppers, female teens. They, in turn, attracted the male teens. It was kind of fun to watch them all interact and listen to the pickup lines. No wonder the twins had volunteered for more hours.

The T-Shirt shop drawing was announced and they all headed over.

People were already gathering and milling around inside the shop. T-Man, as the owner called himself, came over and said, "I don't believe that people are buying this 'Event' stuff! 'The Event' caps are selling like hot cakes. Especially the ones with the ugly frame on a bike. I can understand the headbands with the frame; those are cheap and kind of hot. But the caps are priced high. I didn't expect to sell many of those. See those ugly frame wrist bands? Even though we're giving those away, people are buying extras for friends. What kind of sense does that make?" There were more cute and silly frame phrases. 'Adopt the Ugly Frame' and 'Let the ugly frame cook your gourmet dinner' being her favorites.

T-man had 2 big signs with arrows; one said 'get chances here' pointing inside blue T-shirt, the other, pointed to a red T- shirt with an ugly frame, said 'drop your T-shirt chance here'. That was cute too. May was impressed with the level of innovation or just plain silly. She peeked into a third basket and saw it was nearly full. This T-shirt said 'enter to win a free T-shirt of your own design'.

"I put out extra blank chances in case customers came in without them, but most people are using the ones from the flyers, already filled in. Come on, the photographers are here and we're ready for the drawing."

He dragged them to the counter with him and hollered above the noise, "Folks? Folks, can I have your attention?" He got out a referee whistle and blew loud and long. That had everyone covering their ears. "Time for the drawing for a free T-shirt with your own design. And because you folks look so happy and are having so much fun, we're going to have five T-shirt winners." A cheer went up. He waited for the noise to die down and then said, "The four models will pick the first four winners and the first winner will pick the fifth. And these guys over here will take pictures of everything. So let's get started. Guys shake up this T-shirt basket."

He did a drum roll on the counter with his knuckles as the two T-shirt models swaggered over, eating up the attention and cat calls. They shook the basket and Dennis reached in and pulled out a chance and looked at T-man for permission to continue. "Elisa. Elisa is our first winner."

Another cheer from the crowd as a pretty blonde teenager made her way up. May had seen her at The Coffee Spot that morning. "I want a pink one. A pink one with my Westie on it," she said.

T-man said, "Done. Just bring in his picture."

"Have it on my cell phone," she said holding it up. Everyone laughed as the photographers snapped pictures. The next two chances were drawn quickly. And then it was May's turn. She wasn't sure she had signed up for this but it was easy enough. Then it was Elisa's turn. She picked the last winner, an elderly grandfather with a little girl.

"T-shirts for both of you," T-man shouted. And the whole crowd shouted and applauded again.

"One more drawing for the ugly frame T-shirt." T-Man announced. He picked that winner and finished up by saying, "OK, the next event is 'I Can Paint' at The Artists' Shop. After that, don't miss your chance to bid on the ugly frame, save it and give it a good home. So shop here for an hour and then head over to I Can Paint and then the Antique Cabinet."

It's like a big party, May was thinking when T-man hugged her and said, "Man, you really know how to throw a party."

"You did it," she said. "You added prizes and let the winners pick what they wanted. It was your party. Look at these really cool 'Event' items you have. And you made it so much fun."

One of the photographers came over and gave May a picture of her holding up the winning chance. "I have a bunch more if you want to come and look. We are going to run them through a slide show on the big screen back at the shop. We're passing out pictures and business cards with all the information. People can watch and pick the pictures they want for a small fee." May had forgotten they were doing that. She watched as people gathered around the pictures that had been handed out already. She heard a number of people saying they would head to Cougars Dock Photos for pictures. The idea seemed a great success.

May suggested that she and Sheil watch the painting and then go to the ugly frame auction. "I really want to see that. I have to see if my off-the-wall idea works. This has been so much fun and everyone seems to be enjoying it."

Sheil agreed, "Both activities are on our agenda. We need to be there to pass out samples and help with the auction. That means we have to go." Smiling.

As they approached, they saw that Joan and the manager, Arnold, had everything set up ready for the drawing. Five lucky winners would paint a scene. This time the coupons were in a paint tin. Five easels were set up with stools in front of them. Palettes with an assortment of colors were waiting on the stools. A tourist drew five names and the winners each went to an easel.

Arnold explained, "We'll be making this simple Florida scene. Sky, water and trees." He pointed at a large sample painting. "We are using acrylics because they dry quickly. The colors you will use are on your palettes. You will also be mixing some of your own shades. You have water to clean your brush when we change colors. Paper towels to dry your brush, wipe spills, clean your hands. The canvases have been primed for you, that means they are ready to paint. We will all work together, one step at a time. You'll find a list of the supplies we are using and the paints on your stool."

"The sky is blue with a dash of red, darker at the top becoming paler as it joins the water at the horizon. The water is a green blue which is lighter at the horizon and darker near the bottom which is closer to you. The dark and light tones give the painting depth and perspective. There are some mangroves for a shoreline. We can go back and put in some light clouds and shadows when we are done."

"Are we ready?" he asked and got nods. The crowd was ready too. May wanted to paint but settled for watching.

Arnold led the group through the steps, explaining each as they went along. "Mix a little bit of red in with the blue and start by stroking across. Add a little water to make your color lighter and stroke below. Keep on going to about half way down. Now stroke from the top down over what you just did. And end by brushing across. It should be smooth with no streaks." It did look simple. He and Joan walked around the group, giving individual attention where it was needed.

"Now this is the hardest step. You are going to sketch in a horizontal line about 2 or 3 inches below your sky, across the canvas. Not all the way across. This is for the mangrove forest in the foreground. You will leave about 2 or 3 inches blank somewhere near the middle, but not directly in the middle, for a double S curve for your river. Just look at your sample."

"Wash your brush and mix a tad, that's a little bit," he explained laughing, "of green with the blue. And add a touch of white. This is for the water. Lighter at the horizon. Stroke across only. Streaking is good, makes your water look more fluid. The water will be about 2 inches on your canvas. Add a little color as you move to each stroke down. Darker as the water is nearer to you. Fill in your double S curve, stroking across, increasing pigment as you move down to the bottom of the canvas. If it gets too dark, you can add white to the color and lighten near the horizon. Always stroke water across."

"Wash your brushes. We are going to put splotches on the canvas for trees. These splotches will be different shades of green, but the splotches will be lighter in the background. You get to decide where you put them. The splotches will be the background for our mangrove forest. First lets mix green, yellow, and white. Pick a spot and blob it on the canvas and spread it around smoothly. Second, mix green, a tad, remember a tad is a little bit, of brown and white and repeat. Third try green white and a tad of blue and repeat again."

"Mix your colors again, without the white and dab spots on the canvas. These will be a little darker and stand out looking like leaves. Put a few on the water around your forest." He demonstrated.

"Paint an island just below your horizon. This will be almost white, with just a touch of blue. Blue because it is far away."

"Pick a spot for a dead tree near a shoreline. Make sure that it reaches over the water, for three dimensional depths."

"Now, see where the water is below your forest in the curves? Put in some shadows, under your forest on the water. This puts some more depth into your painting.'

"If you want you can put a dab of blue white in the sky for a cloud."

"Sign your painting and you're done. Step back. Step away from it and look. Look at them all. Take them home and frame them. They will look even better."

All the paintings looked wonderful. They looked similar yet each had its own distinct variation on the theme. It was amazing. People walked around looking at the paintings and commenting. Positive comments. Some of the new artists were giggling with embarrassment and pride. May heard people say they were going to sign up for lessons and others wanted a list of supplies to create their own mangrove scene.

"You know he's right, these all look good enough to hang. Almost seems as if anyone can be an artist," Sheil said. "These folks are really happy with what they've created. I like this one best," she said pointing out one, "Even better than the sample."

May agreed and suggested they get refills of sample muffins and chocolate and head to the auction.

They found a large crowd of excited bidders waiting in front of The Antique Cabinet and mingled with the crowd sharing candy and muffins and modeling their outfits.

Then they went inside. May was having a great time; it was like a country fair. She stopped to talk with Neal for a minute. He had the ugly frame on a beautiful tripod, thus emphasizing its ugliness. He was a nervous wreck. "George Dunning is in back, with a buyer and they're waiting for, I don't know, a couple of buyers, sellers? Dunning is furious about the auction. The one buyer inside is screaming about all the people." Neal wiped sweat off his forehead. "And I'm just going to stay out of his way. George OK'd the auction, so I shouldn't worry. But boy is he ever mad. In there, swearing and cursing. And I don't even know which painting he's selling. Don't know why they're upset about all the people here. You'd think he would be pleased to have people buying his junk. Instead he acts like their private sale should be some kind of big secret. Anyhow, the auction starts in 10 minutes and then all the people will be gone. Geesh, you'd think George would be happy at all the prospective customers."

May just nodded as all this came gushing out. So Dunning had a buyer and seller? She wondered if Marty knew and decided she'd better call Nick. She started to back away and was pulling out her phone when she turned and was looking at Aubrey. Aubrey, the secretary for the fine art conservation and restoration department. Aubrey, the holder of the keys. Why was she here? Aubrey was looking at her in shock. "Aubrey, what a surprise," May managed.

"Elizabeth Stratton. I thought that was you. But you look so, ah, different. I just had to come over here to make sure it was you."

Aubrey's never liked me, May thought, why has she sought me out?

"What are you doing here? Is Derek here?" From her tone, smug, it was obvious that Aubrey already knew the answer. She didn't even look around for Derek; she was busy watching May's reaction.

"No. I guess you didn't hear?" May could handle a snub. No problem. She could do this. She put on a smile, "Guess you didn't hear. Derek kicked me out." There, she'd said it. It was easy. Didn't hurt. In fact, she had to stop herself from smiling. And she hit a nerve by declaring it before Aubrey could. May watched Aubrey deflate. Aubrey already knew.

"Oh, that's right, I did hear about you and Derek. I just forgot." As if it was beneath her interest. "You know he's going out with this really nice woman now. Very high society. They make a beautiful couple. Sorry it didn't work out for you. It's too bad. There are even rumors that the two might be serious," she said as if confiding in May.

The information confirmed that Aubrey knew about her and Derek. And just had to be the first to tell May about her replacement. There wasn't much May could say to that, so she ignored it and changed the subject

"So what are you doing here Aubrey?"

"I'm here with my fiancé, nodding to a smooth looking man waiting by the entrance to the back room. We have an important meeting with Mr. Dunning." Superior and condescending now. And then annoyed she added, "What on earth is going on here? This place is usually dead at this time on Sunday."

"Oh, there's an auction here in a few minutes. The main highlight of 'The Event' promotion. Kicking off the beginning of the season."

"Well, I can't believe all the people. What are they auctioning?" she asked suddenly suspicious and concerned.

"Just an ugly frame." Not any stolen fine art, May thought. Because that could be the only reason for Aubrey to be here.

"Well, nice seeing you Elizabeth." And with a final dig, "Too bad about Derek. He was such a nice catch for you. My fiancé is waiting." She headed for the man standing by the door watching them. It was obvious that he was listening to the yelling in the back room and not very happy.

May watched the two of them talk angrily and again turned her back to reach for her phone but Sheil came up and distracted her.

"Get out of here. What a dreadful person. I heard her talking to you. Sorry, I couldn't help it. She's not a friend is she? Of course not. You wouldn't have a friend like her." She waited, giving May an opportunity to fill her in.

"No, not a friend. She is the secretary at the museum where I worked. And she has never liked me. Her derisive attitude is nothing new." And that was the truth.

May really needed to call Nick.

"Of course she didn't and I can tell you why."

"Why?"

"Because she's jealous. She will never have the self-confidence, ability, and natural charm that you have."

"Could be," May said but didn't believe it.

"Oh, oh. Looks like the boyfriend is leaving. And she's going into the back room by herself." Giving May a running commentary of the action. "Wonder what she's doing with George back there?" Sheil started for the door. "Let's peek."

May grabbed her and said, "We are supposed to be modeling. Not spying. And we have to help Neal with the auction. It should start in a few minutes." May thought quickly and said, "I'll call and see what's keeping Jeremy." Jeremy was going to be the auctioneer.

"Darn, OK. I see a group over there I missed earlier," and Sheil headed over to give out samples of appetizers.

May hit the speed dial. She was tapping her toe and murmuring, "Pick up. Pick up." Finally after three rings, seemed like it had been ringing an hour, Nick said, "What sweetheart?"

The endearment stopped her, embarrassed her, "Where are you? I just bumped into an old acquaintance from the museum, a secretary, Aubrey, she has a meeting in the back room at The Cabinet. Right now. There are already people back there and a lot of yelling." She thought he would understand. Hoped so. Was anyone watching the video from the backroom? Maybe she hadn't needed to call. She didn't wait to see if he understood. She hung up because Sheil was waving her over.

Her cell was ringing by the time she got there. Sheil looked at her questioningly and May shrugged her shoulders and answered.

"Hi."

Nick said, "You OK?"

"Um, yah. Are you coming for the auction?"

"I'm on my way, sorry. Everything is under control. See you in a bit."

He did understand, thank goodness. May really wanted to look at the security video on her cell, but there were too many people around. Then Sheil was shouting, "Jeremy, Nick, over here."

Nick had come in with Jeremy. May thought he looked calm and unfazed. She was amazed at how relaxed he seemed. Didn't act like a big art theft bust was about to go down. Guess he did this sort of thing all the time. She was a bundle of nerves, shaking, she was so nervous. Nick hugged Sheil and winked at May.

Oh my god, she thought. Does he know my insides turn to mush when he does that? And why if my insides are mush does the wink give me courage and strength? It does make me feel calm, safe, protected, and loved. Loved? Where did that come from? Does he know that too?

Jeremy said, "Let's get started. Hey folks. You ready to save the ugly frame?"

There were cheers and jeers.

"We're starting the bidding high. Check your billfolds. All proceeds go to Amy Sutton's hospital bills. And I'll start the bidding at 25 cents. Anyone?"

The audience was a little stunned.

"25 cents? Is that too steep for such a nice item. Anyone?"

"OK. Over there on the right, a quarter."

"50 cents," was hollered.

"75", "one dollar,"

The bidding took off and slowly rose to $10.00 in increments of 10 cents to 25 cents. At that point it slowed down and Jeremy stepped back up and said, "Is that my last bid?"

"Heck no," one guy hollered, "20.00"

And $25, $30, $40, was quickly bid by other men in the audience.

No one needed Jeremy. They were bidding against each other. The Dock committee just stood back and watched. The bidding was up to $50.00, when Jeremy stepped forward again and raised his hands to call a halt. "Wait now. Wait now. Take another look. This is an ugly frame. And it's not going to ride any bike or cook your dinner. Don't you all get carried away by the advertising." In an effort to keep the auction down to a fair price, he continued, "Now, going once at $40, going twice"

"Seventy five. Seventy five dollars," was hollered from the group.

"One hundred"

And Jeremy went to step forward again and someone yelled. "Be quiet Jeremy, we're having ourselves a bidding war here."

$125, then $150, and then $200

A moment of quiet and 300, 350, 500.

May watched in amazement as the bidding lobs were coming from all over the room. It looked like six or eight men bidding. At first, she thought the women beside the men were hitting the men to get them to stop bidding. But then she realized they were nudging the men to bid higher. And all the men sort of looked the same.

The bidding went all the way to $2,200 where it finally stopped. $2,200 dollars for a frame that was going to be thrown out?

Jeremy took a chance and crept to the podium, asked quietly, "You done out there?"

"Ya, till next year. I'm donating this ugly frame back then. Meanwhile it's going home with me to cook supper. Maybe teach my wife how to cook." The man laughed as his wife punched his arm smiling.

A cheer went up. "Let's hear it for the ugly frame".

"Hip, hip, hooray for the ugly frame!" and two guys grabbed the frame and walked it around the room.

May laughed, it was so ridiculous.

"I'll buy you dinner. Get your frame and let's go," said another man who looked almost like the winning bidder.

May looked at Sheil, "What just happened here?"

"Small town. That's what happened. People want to help. But no one wants charity. We let everyone do what they feel they can.

$2,200.00 will pay for air transport for Amy to come home. Did you notice the glass jars in the shops?"

"No. Wait, yes. They looked full and not just change, but bills. I forgot all about them."

"Those jars were filled every day. Some of them twice a day. Jeremy collected them. And he says there is a lot more than $1,500.00 dollars so far. Everyone does what they can."

May hugged Sheil. "I am so glad I moved here. I need to put money in a jar."

"No, you don't. I said everyone does what they can. You organized The Event. You have worked hard on it. You have done your share. There would be no Event without you. Everyone does what they can and you have done what you can. No one expects you to donate money too. Besides, you're poor."

May laughed. Not with friends like these she thought. Then she noticed Nick coming over. He put an arm around Sheil and said, "Those Jones boys are something aren't they?" He looked at May who didn't understand and said, "They were doing all that bidding. There are eight of them, the Jones', and they'll probably split that bid. They bid the frame up to what the Suttons needed and then they stopped," he explained. "Sheil, I need to borrow May. Can she take her break now?"

"Sure, have fun, in fact May, take the rest of the day off. You have worked a whole day already. I need to start the music for dancing now and bring in the snacks, Neal will help."

"That was wonderful. That was so great. I love this town and the people." May was on a high. Better then drugs she bet. Not that she had ever tried them. These people made her feel so good.

Then she suddenly realized that Nick had her hand and their fingers were laced together again and he was leading her out of the building. People were looking at them and smiling.

She tried to pull her hand away but he held fast. "What are you doing? Where are you taking me? People are looking. Let go of my hand."

He stopped and put his face by her ear and said, "Don't you want to know about the back room?" And he realized he should never have gotten this close because now he wanted to lick her ear. He breathed on it.

It took a while for the words to register in May's brain because her heart stopped when she felt his breath on her ear. And her brain jumped ahead with visions of them naked, in a back room.

Fortunately, he moved away.

"Back room?" she said shakily.

He laughed; he bet they both had the same vision. And he jerked his own brain back. "Back room, art theft, remember?" Still looking and tempted to nuzzle that ear again.

"Art theft? Oh, my God I forgot. I was going to tell you. I need to tell you."

"Hold it; hold it till we're outside."

They had to stop and talk to a few people who wanted to congratulate May. For the great 'auction'. Wink, Wink. And for the success of The Event. She was embarrassed. She hadn't really done that much.

When they got outside, he continued leading her. "Where are we going?" she asked again.

"The Inn. That's the operation center. Now what did you need to tell me?"

"About the man. The man with Aubrey."

He stopped and turned toward her and she almost bumped into him. "What man?" he demanded.

"There was a man with Aubrey tonight. I didn't have a chance to tell you. She called him her fiancé. Said they had a meeting with George. He waited for her by the door to the backroom, waiting, while Aubrey was insulting me. Then when Aubrey went over to him they got in an argument and he left. Sheil was watching them. I didn't see it."

"Hold on a minute. Let me get this right. This woman Aubrey, who is she?"

"She is the secretary in the restoration department at the museum. She does all the paperwork and scheduling for paintings and their transportation."

Nick understood, "So she knows where the paintings will be and when. She can tell the thief. I wonder if Marty looked at her when he checked backgrounds at the museum. Now tell me about the man."

"Aubrey said he was her fiancé and they had a Very Important Meeting with Mr. Dunning." May tried to imitate the self-satisfied tone. "The man was waiting for her by the door to the back room. Then Sheil came over to talk to me and gave me a running commentary on Aubrey as she went back to the door and her fiancé. They were arguing and then he left. Aubrey went in the back room alone. That was all before you got there. Before the auction. I'm sorry; I should have told you right away."

"It's OK. I didn't give you a chance to tell me anything." Nick called Ryan and told him about the man. And added that they would be there in two minutes.

They went to the house again and arrived just as Marty and the Sheriff drove up.

Nick looked at Ryan and said, "They don't know about the other guy do they?"

"Haven't had a chance to tell them. May, you tell them."

May wasn't sure she wanted to admit she had forgotten to notify them, but repeated what she had told Nick.

"Can you describe him for us May?" Marty asked.

"He is probably on the Cabinet's security video tape," she said.

Marty looked chagrinned, "Why didn't I think of that?"

Nick smiled and said, "Yup, that's my girl."

"We'll need a warrant. For that feed. Later," Marty said. "Now, here's the plan. Four of my Agents are parked in the alley blocking any escape. We just watch the video and wait for all the buyers to show up. They probably won't be using cash, but will make electronic transfers. We go in, with warrants to access their computers and to freeze any bank accounts immediately. We arrest them, and collect the paintings."

"They're still waiting for someone I think. Neal said one buyer was there and another buyer or seller was due," May repeated.

"But it looks like the sale will go ahead without him. They've been arguing about that."

Ryan interrupted then. "They have stopped arguing and are going ahead without the other guys."

"OK, we're out of here. We'll run the op from the alley." Marty and David left together.

May, Nick, and Ryan watched the feed. Everything would be recorded. May could feel the tension in the room. These two professionals were nervous? That surprised her.

"Why didn't you two go with Marty?"

Ryan responded, "I'm on a leave of absence and it's not my case. Nick here is still undercover and he is not a Federal Agent. Wouldn't do for him to be seen helping law enforcement. We're going to try to keep this arrest quiet for a few days, until Nick arrests his drug runners."

They watched as Dunning pulled out the four paintings and set them up. "Here they are, Russon. The three you ordered and this fourth is for another buyer. You could put in a bid for it though," he suggested hopefully.

"Nope. Won't fit in my collection. Not interested. Let's get on with this." He walked over and examined each painting in detail and said, "Pack them up for me to take back to the Inn. I've been here too long already." He sat down at his laptop and said, "Give me your account number and I'll wire the money."

"I get my share in cash first," Aubrey demanded. "I found Dunning and the guy to boost the paintings after you ordered them. I arranged everything. I knew how to steal the paintings and get them out of the museums. You pay me first."

"Your money is there in that briefcase. We didn't need to meet. We don't all have to be here. It's not smart." Russon put the briefcase on the table and opened it. "Count it."

Aubrey looked at the money greedily and touched it lovingly. "I trust you. Let me know when you want something else. But I think I will count it," Gloating, she began counting while Dunning read off his account numbers.

Ryan was grinning. "Thank you, Dunning. That was thoughtful. I'll freeze the accounts as soon as the transfer goes through."

"You going in Marty?" Ryan asked on his cell just as there was a knock on the back door and Marty walked into the backroom with his team.

"Everybody freeze. Right where you are and don't make a move. Federal Agents."

Aubrey grabbed the briefcase and kicked the agent closest to her as she turned to run out the door. David caught her and shoved her face first into a wall where he handcuffed her. Two other agents were cuffing Russon and Dunning while Marty read them all their rights.

The agents bundled the three crooks outside and into two vehicles to take them to the federal facility. Another agent collected the paintings, both the three crated, and the fourth still in the rack. Marty sat at Russon's laptop and read off Russon's account number for Ryan. He continued, "We'll take the laptops and art work to HQ. IT can work on the laptops, maybe they can find links to our thief or the other buyer and the guy who left earlier. We'll probably be at it most of the night." He looked around, "I don't believe it went just as we planned. Those guys were sitting ducks. We knocked and walked in the back door. George left it unlocked. Idiot. We didn't even have to draw a weapon. The only one who gave us any trouble was that woman. Ryan can you get warrants to search all three of their residences? And offices? We'll do a search of the whole Cabinet, maybe tomorrow."

"Ryan, we might want you to come down and help with the interrogation. That's your specialty. One of them might give us the thief for a lighter sentence. Probably have to wait till they talk to their attorneys. They don't like each other and I'm sure one of them will turn. I think the woman is going to be the weak link. Thinks she is brilliant and that these guys screwed up. Just the other way around. It was stupid to have this meet."

Marty looked at one of his agents and said, "I want you to stay here until I send a relief. I'll talk to Neal on the way out. No one comes back here. As soon as the festivities are over out there, lock up the whole building. Put up a sign 'Closed by the Fire Marshall'.

"For right now, Nick, no one knows anything happened. No one knows we made a bust here tonight. We should be able to keep it quiet for a few more days. Long enough for you to get that drug ring. I'll talk to Neal, tell him that Dunning was called away for a while and we have a man in the back room. No love lost between those two from what we can tell."

Nick spoke up, "Thanks. No telling what my drug gang would do if they heard the Feds made a bust here."

"OK, I see Neal now and I'm leaving the camera running. Talk to you tomorrow." With that statement he went out front to talk to Neal.

"That's it," said Ryan. "The Feds are out of your hair Nick."

"Me too," May piped up. "I am now officially relieving myself from any involvement with any law enforcement operation. In fact, I am starving. I think I'll go home and make a grilled cheese and do some more sewing."

"I'll go with you; you can make me a grilled cheese too," Nick said.

She just looked at him and shook her head. "No, you're not coming home with me."

"Hold it kids, stop fighting. Liz made pot-roast and salads for dinner. There's enough to feed us all." He had to smile at them. Nick must really have it bad. He was trying to be almost subtle. Not a normal behavior for Nick. Normally he came on strong with his women.

May, Nick, Ryan, Liz, Jesse, and one of Jesse's friends sat down for dinner. May shared her observations on the painting class and the auction. For a while they talked about the Jones boys and Amy. After dessert of chocolate pudding cake, May said it was time for her to go home and Nick insisted that he would walk her.

On the way back, they talked about 'The Event' until they reached May's stairs.

Then he had another thought. "That guy didn't see you tonight did he May?"

"Probably saw Aubrey talking to me. I saw him looking at us. But Aubrey thinks I'm just empty headed, arm candy. She wouldn't even mention me." A pause. "I'm sure. If she did it would be something derogatory and belittling."

"Good," Nick was holding her hand again. "Can I come up?" he asked.

"No, Nick," she said patiently.

He pulled her close and leaned down and kissed her slowly. Warmly. Just a lip kiss. A little touch of tongue on her lower lip as he broke off. He didn't want to end the kiss. It wasn't enough, but he either stopped now or…

He looked at her. She was a little flushed. Wanted to kiss her again but instead said goodnight and walked off, whistling. He could wait.

Week 5: Monday

She had fallen asleep in the rocker, pinning little animal shapes onto the quilt squares. She had gone to bed after 3 AM. Her clock said it was only just 8, now.

The sky was blue with puffy white clouds. People were walking around on the dock, sitting at tables, talking, drinking coffee, socializing. Life was going on down there. Everything was normal. Boats were streaming out of the marina. She noticed that Nick's boat was gone, so he must be on a charter. She could hear the seagulls.

After a simple breakfast, she took up the quilt. She had the zebra half sewn. She would finish that and start the elephant. Wanted a bunny too. It was going to be fun.

Later she opened the shop and looked around. Vintage had been busy Sunday. Well she knew it had been busy. She and Sheil had stopped in for a minute yesterday and stayed for almost an hour. Both of them had made sales in that time. Sheil had called Doris to come in and help, the shop was so busy.

May busied herself straightening clothes on hangers and hangers on racks. The green taffeta had sold and the blue gingham was also gone. Along with three other dresses. A banner day.

May had just finished one of the skirt racks and was starting on another when Doris breezed in, talking. "I brought Sunday's paper; it was too busy yesterday for me to read it."

"You sold so much, yesterday. What a great day. Though, I think I am going to miss that blue gingham. It was so perfect Vintage and yet so now."

"Yes, isn't it exciting? And I sold that same woman a skirt and top for her daughter. She also bought two scarves and two necklaces to match. We didn't have a purse to go with the gingham, but she bought that coco clutch to go with the skirt. I can't remember when we had a day so good. I'll get started straightening the jewelry." She went to the counter, talking all the way. Doris never stopped talking. It cheered May a little as she straightened one tops rack and moved to a second. Then she realized that Doris was talking to her. Not just talking.

"What? I was thinking. I didn't hear what you asked."

"How are you and Nick doing? You went out together last night. He is such a nice young man."

"Nick? Last night? What do you mean?" May was really baffled; she had lost her place in this conversation.

"When you went out to dinner together at Liz's. He behaved himself didn't he?"

"Went out to dinner together to Liz's?" Now she was sounding like a parrot.

"Yes dear, last night," Doris said this patiently, as if to a slow learner.

"What makes you think Nick and I went out to dinner? Or ate at Liz's?" she asked truly confused.

Doris laughed, "This is a small town remember. Everyone knows everything. There are no secrets."

Too right, it was a small town. Though May could think of one or two secrets no one knew yet. One had to do with art theft and the other, drugs runners. But May hadn't realized her personal secrets were part of the gossip. She needed to put a stop to that right away.

"Ryan invited me to dinner. Nick was also invited and he offered to walk me over and back. That's all there was to that. We did not go to dinner together as you implied. We were not together. We were just going to the same place." There. Did that even make any sense?

Doris smiled at her, nodding, "Yes, dear. And the kiss when he brought you home? That was just a thank you for walking you home?"

"Er, yes. That's all that was." Someone had seen that? People were talking about that? That was personal. "That was personal. And people are gossiping about it?"

"Of course, dear, but only in the nicest way. We all love to see you and Nick together. You're perfect for each other and we're hoping you two will realize it. We love both of you and want to see you happy. We're rooting for you."

May was flabbergasted. She opened her mouth to speak and nothing came out. She didn't know which part of that statement to address. The idea of people assuming that she and Nick would make a nice couple stunned her. She closed her mouth. And then fell back on her two sentence mantra.

"Nick is a 'for a while' kind of guy. He wants a girl for a little while. I am a 'forever' kind of girl. I want love and marriage, a little house with a picket fence. Two point five kids and a dog." Was that two sentences? Probably not, she needed only two for Nick. They had discussed it enough. "We are not going to get together."

"Beside I'm married, remember," she added.

Doris said, "I know dear."

"And soon I will be a single Mom. And no guy is going to buy into that. Especially a guy looking for a short term affair."

"Oh. If you say so. I guess you're not noticing the way he looks at you. Or the way you look at him dear."

May gave up. "Let's just not discuss it anymore. Nick was a perfect gentleman last night. As you must already know if someone was watching us and talking about it."

Doris changed the subject, "I just remembered. Come over here and see." She took May's hand and dragged her into the other room. "Look!"

"What? What am I looking at?" May asked as she looked for something new.

"The wall!"

"Yes, I see the wall." Baffled and then comprehending. "I see the wall! I can see the wall!" Yelling now. "The mauve ensemble. It's gone. Did you sell it? Oh, tell me you sold it. Don't tell me you just moved it." She was trying not to be excited. Trying not to jump up and down. She grabbed Doris' hands.

"Sold! Sold it. Last night! Sheil sold it!" reassuringly

"Oh, wow! How much did she have to discount it?" Afraid to hear the answer, ready to be disappointed. 50% off would be a reasonable price. But just the fact that it sold was exciting.

"She didn't."

"Didn't what?"

Didn't discount it. Sold it at full price. You just made yourself a week's pay or more."

"Really? Really? Someone bought it at that outrageous price?"

"That was not an outrageous price dear. Unless it was outrageously low. That woman, who bought it, didn't blink an eye. Thought she was getting herself a real bargain. She did too. Your next outfit should be priced even higher," Doris paused and then continued. "What an idiot of a first husband you had. He had you and never even recognized the treasure you are or the talent you have. Now go get yourself a cup of tea. Sit and read the paper. I'll finish with this rack and come and join you."

Doris joined her a few minutes later. "I put out the open sign, it's early, so we probably won't have customers. We can sit and read over tea together. Give me the society pages. I like to start with those. Have to keep up with the gossip you know," said it with a smirk.

"Just as long as the first customer in isn't that woman returning the mauve outfit," May joked still giddy.

"See, you can joke about it."

May was still a little in shock. Sold at the full price. It was unbelievable. It would add to her reserve for the baby. Her insurance at Vintage wouldn't kick in for three months and wouldn't cover her preexisting condition. So up through the birth would be out of pocket expenses for her. And that amount was a little higher than expected, so this was a really nice cushion. Gave her a little comfort. The baby, though, would go on her insurance immediately. Thank goodness for family plans. So finances were manageable. She used to be poor and knew how to budget and how to stretch a dollar. This sale would make that easier.

She thought of the cradle. She wanted the cradle, but knew it should wait just a little while longer.

Sheil walked in while they were having tea and handed May a check. "Per our contract. This is your percentage for the sale of your Designs by May. It also includes a commission for the Vintage accessories the customer bought to go with the outfit. Pour me a cup of tea too and we'll celebrate."

May jumped up and kissed Sheil. "I'm going to buy the cradle with the commission. I never thought about a commission. I am going to buy it today. Thank you. Thank you." She danced around and hugged Sheil again. And then hugged Doris.

"Get out of here. I didn't do anything but make some money off of you. We both are winners. In the right spot at the right time with the right talent and the ability to recognize the talent. And we're going to continue to be winners. There is another new shipment. You and Doris go through it and tag and log in the good items. May, you take anything that does not meet Vintage standards. And don't forget, you will be going with me to the Dock meeting tomorrow. About 11, coffee and donuts."

It was always an adventure to touch and feel the new items. Today they logged in everything as all the clothing was perfect. And Doris was disappointed. "You know, I always hope that the whole shipment will be perfect. And today all the clothing is ready to be put on the floor and I'm frustrated. I wanted you to have new material. I'm a bad person."

"We're not done yet, Doris. There's one more package behind you. You can still hope." May laughed at her as she got the last box which held linens. Faded and worn around the edges.

"Looks like you got your wish," May said, already planning. The fabric was a soft cotton percale. Wrinkle free. The print on one set was a happy blue rosebud with pale green leaves. The another set was a floral petunia in bold colors. There were extra matching sheets in solids of blue and green. A wealth of vintage material. She would be very busy designing and sewing.

"These are wonderful fabrics and prints. I can't wait to get started. This blue rosebud will make a great dress. It will hang soft and smooth.

And there is enough for matching a little jacket. I can almost see them. Maybe a Mom and daughter set." She looked at Doris and they both just laughed.

"Let's finish this and then I need to take a break, I need to make a purchase." She could buy the cradle. She could afford it now and the baby would need a cradle. She could hardly wait for her break. She caught herself humming as she worked. Of course they were busy so she didn't get her break until supper when she rushed over to The Cabinet.

Closed. They were closed 'Per Order of the Fire Marshall'. She had forgotten. It wasn't fair. And she was partly to blame. Well, she would just wait for them to reopen. It couldn't be too long. Maybe Ryan would know. No. The cradle wasn't important enough to call Ryan. Her shoulders slumped as she started back to Vintage and bumped into Nick coming out of Cougars Cove Photography. She didn't see his guilty look or notice him hide a receipt in his pocket.

He'd seen the picture through the window as he walked by. It stopped him up short. Mesmerized. It was a picture of him and May in front of The Cabinet. Must have been right after the auction. When he had whispered in her ear. She was looking up into his face. She was flushed and radiant. From adrenalin or his breath on her ear? Both probably. He went in and ordered an 8 x 10, matted and framed. Why? Where would he put it? He didn't know. But he snarled when the owner gave him a smirky, know it all, grin.

He caught May by the shoulders when she stumbled into him and said, "What's up? Where are you going?"

"Oh, I was just going to run into The Antique Cabinet to buy something. But they're closed."

"Marty's completing a thorough inventory. He shouldn't take too long. Needs to make sure there is no other contraband in there. They put up the sign to explain the locked door. What were you going to buy? I thought it was all junk."

She answered dejectedly, "The cradle." And then indignantly, "The cradle wasn't junk. Just looked like it." And then wishfully, "I want the cradle."

He had a twinge of guilt but he didn't tell her he had the cradle. In Hal's shop. Stripped already. The look on her face, longing, when she first saw it and touched it was more than he could resist. He had gone back and bought it that same day. He had another twinge of guilt. Because she looked sad and longing and he could fix that by telling her.

"They will be open again soon. Don't be so disappointed." And, he thought, I should have the cradle finished by that time. "Wasn't it pretty expensive? And it needed a lot of work didn't it?"

"Not that you really need to know, but I sold a dress." She'd almost said ensemble but figured he wouldn't understand. And she didn't feel like explaining. "So I have unexpected income. And I can use a little of it for that cradle. My baby has to have a cradle. And I can just see that one refinished, in a honey oak. With a pretty ice green liner and blanket. With my baby quilt. And my little girl laying in it smiling and drooling." Now she must be getting hormonal. She went on the defensive. She did need a cradle, why was she justifying herself to him? "I want it."

"Come on, I'll buy you supper and you can tell me all about this dress you sold. Why don't I know about it?"

"Because I didn't know myself until this afternoon." She flipped her hair, very short hair now, so that didn't work so well. "But I would expect the whole dock knows about it by now. So I guess you're just out of the loop." She turned to walk away, mad at herself. She didn't owe him any explanations.

"Let me buy you dinner and you can tell me about the dress. Please? I haven't eaten. And you need to eat. And I can tell you what Marty is doing. I'll get you a grilled cheese with tomato and ham? And fries???" He was begging now. Not sure why it was suddenly important for her to sit down and eat with him.

He looked so adorable that she relented. She had to eat and she could eat with him, but, "The dock folks will gossip. They'll see us eating together and it will fuel their belief that we are an item," she complained.

"OK with me."

"Of, course it's OK with you. I want coleslaw too. Baby needs veggies." A way to remind him that he wasn't dealing with a for a little while girl. And she had a lot of baggage. Good to remind herself too. A meal with Nick would be nice though. It was just a meal, not a date.

"Me too." He grabbed her hand and led her to what they both now considered their booth at The Fry Pan.

The waiter came over and said, "Two grilled cheese with tomato."

Nick took charge. Pushy? No just ordering dinner for a date. "Two grilled cheese with tomato and ham, two sides of sweet potato fries, and coleslaw. Iced tea?" he looked at her.

"No, make mine a lemonade," May said.

"Two lemonades then."

When the waiter left, May said, "What about Dunning and his buddies. How is that going?"

"Same as last night. They all lawyered up. But Aubrey is sending out feelers through her attorney, to Ryan. She liked him. Marty is doing that inventory and his IT guys are working on all the computers. They should find Dunning's contacts on his computer. It was password protected, but that didn't give IT much trouble. And his files are coded. It will take some time to work through them"

"Aubrey's laptop has everything on it. That woman apparently doesn't know about passwords. Has no idea that she should have been hiding her files. Marty has all her contacts and plans. She wrote them all down and save them." This with a shake of his head. "Hard to believe she was smart enough to pull these thefts off and dumb enough to leave her plans on her laptop."

"Except for the thief. He's not there. Aubrey never knew who he was. The guy that you saw her with? He's still a mystery. And facial recognition from the video doesn't help. No match so far. Marty wants that guy. He may be the other potential buyer, also. Marty is trying to find payments that link him to the stolen paintings."

The food arrived and they started to eat. May salted her fries. Nick used ketchup. Then she asked, "And you? What about your drug case? What about Bobby Frances and his soap?"

"David thought Bobby was going to meet his supplier and make a buy this morning. But it didn't pan out. I really want that source. We'll bust Bobby and his buddy and we want to do that inside Soaps. A bust inside will give us all the legal justification we need to search the shop.

And tie the buddy to the drugs. We have identified his buddy. He is high up in the organization. Has always kept a low profile though. He had a very long rap sheet, but no convictions before he turned 18. Since then, nothing. Kept himself clean by getting rid of anyone who could testify against him. Through intimidation, beatings, and murder. A very, very dangerous man. I doubt if Bobby really appreciates just how bad this guy is and I hope he doesn't find out the hard way. That's where we are now. Dead in the water again. A waiting game." But soon, soon Bobby had to buy more drugs. Nick was still betting on Wednesday because that was soap making night.

"Ryan is still running both operations. And that's it. Now tell me about your dress."

"Sheil hung my rose and mauve skirt and top on the wall and put a huge price tag on it. Added a Vintage blouse and purse to make a complete ensemble. And Sheil sold all of it last night." May's eyes were sparkling. "I can't believe anyone would spend that much money on used vintage fabric. On any dress. Of course they are actually paying for an original Design by May," she said tongue in cheek.

"Now you have lost me. Explain what you mean by your skirt and top."

"Sheil and I have an agreement. She was impressed with the yellow outfit I made for myself from a discarded Vintage dress. She gave me the Vintage discards I used to make outfits for the twins. Sheil and I have a contract that says that I can buy any damaged clothing from Sheil at her cost. The garments become mine to do with as I want. I take them apart and redesign the usable fabric into a current style. Sheil sells the item and takes a cut. I get the rest. Or I can sell them on my own and give her a cut, or I can give them away. I get to design and sew and sell my creations. And apparently, I'm going to make money while doing what I love. That's the way it works."

"So I wanted to buy that cradle with some of the money from last night's sale," she said wistfully. Then she brightened, "But I can wait. No one else will want that cradle. And I have plenty to keep me busy. I have damaged linens in Sheil's newest shipment and I can start designing."

"Wow, you make clothing from linens?"

She didn't hear him. She had an idea how she would make the Mom and kid outfit perfect. An easy way to resize them for the right buyer. Almost one size fits all. Just a little extra in the seam would work.

She suddenly snapped back to the present to see Nick watching her with an indulgent smile on his face. "Sorry, I just got lost in a design there."

He was shaking his head. "Yep, sure did. Do you need to write that down?"

"No, it was just basic stuff. But a really good start. The beginning is always the hardest part of any project."

Wasn't that the truth, he thought. She had looked so serious. Her eyes shining. Her face full of life. He wanted to kiss her again.

"Eat," he said and then watched her dive into her fries with enthusiasm. He ate also, always aware of her across the table. He was learning her moods.

She asked about charter fishing and he told her he would be happy when this particular job was over and he could get back to real police work. He'd had longer undercover jobs, more dangerous jobs. Nothing quite this boring. Part of the problem was that he couldn't take full day charters; he had to be around in case there was a development. The other part was that he really didn't like being a charter captain.

"Actually, I'm pretty happy to only be chartering half days." he said. "Seems like my customers are first timers who can't spell fish and need a lot of training. Or they are 'experienced fishermen' sure that everything I do and everyplace I take them is wrong. Haven't tossed anyone overboard yet but it's been a close thing. Three hours is just about my limit." He paused and added, "Fishing is fun, chartering is hard work and long days. With bad-tempered people."

"And I haven't been able to get even a nibble on any drug deals. Can't figure out why. No one of the criminal persuasion will talk to me."

"Why should they? You're a cop. How can you be undercover when everyone knows you? And knows you're a cop?"

"Well I'm supposed to be on paid leave while under investigation for pocketing contraband drugs and then selling what I didn't use myself."

"I haven't heard that. All anyone ever says is that you're from around here. Home town boy, come back home to settle down. A cop. Uncle to the twins. No one has ever said you might be under a cloud. Or into drugs." She looked at him and continued, "No one buys your cover story. They never even mention it. They all say you're retired from being a cop. Shame too, they say. So I guess they think you were a really good cop."

"I didn't know that. They're supposed to be saying I'm a crook."

"Nope. No one does. You sure wasted that cover story. Might be why you can't get any bad guys to sell you dope. Or try to buy it from you."

He thought about that and realized that everyone had acted happy to see him. No one had ever implied that they thought he might have done anything wrong. Humh.

"So where do you live? And I don't mean on the boat. Where will you move back to when you get Bobby and his partner?" She was curious. "What part of the state? Is it an apartment or house?" Why not Cougars Cove?

"I have a condo in Miami. Down town. Overlooking the ocean. Nice place. I work out of the Miami office. They gave me this assignment because I know the people. Thought that would give me a head start. But I guess we hadn't thought that one through. These people all think I am the good kid who came back, hunh?"

"Ya. Do you think you'd ever move back here? Everyone seems happy you are back." Maybe get married? Settle down? She didn't ask those questions.

"This visit has sure reminded me of what it's like to live in a small town. Everybody knows your business and has an opinion and feels it's their responsibility to share that opinion." He knew that he sounded disgusted, and that was because he was thinking of them all saying nice things about him instead of repeating his cover story.

"But it's actually kind of nice to know so many people care. I can see me moving back. I still have the family house. Hal takes care of it for me. Rents it. Banks all the income, taking out expenses. It's near his house. I could show you. You'd like it. Small pink house with a picket fence. Maybe you would want to go look at it with me sometime," he suggested. He wanted to know what she thought of his house. His house. He had only recently started to think of it that way. About the same time he had started thinking of May as his woman. His woman in his house.

What did that mean she wondered? Why would he ask her to look at his house? "Why?" she blurted out. And then immediately said, "I mean I could look at it with you. Someday maybe." Then she changed the subject. "You wouldn't find the town too boring for you now? After the excitement of the big city?"

"Miami is only about an hour away. Not a long way to drive to for a fun time." And he turned the question back to her. "You're from the big city too. And part of the social elite. You've been here about a month now, are you bored? Don't you want to go out dining and dancing? Do you miss all the functions? Do you hate being a shop girl?"

"Bored? Are you crazy? I've been too busy. I love the peace here. The quiet. The nosey people who care. I never really liked the big city and the noise. And I didn't really belong in that social group. I would rather be a shop girl as you call me. I want to be home where I can always find something to do. Read or sew." She thought about that a minute and noticed the almost sneer on his face. "Yah, I guess I do sound pretty boring don't I?" She laughed, "That's me, the shop girl, dull, boring May. And soon I will be dull, boring, Mommy May who would rather read a book by the fire then make conversation around a bar. And proud of it, too."

There didn't seem to be any more to say on that subject. They were two different people looking for different things. Sad, because she could really get to like him. Already really liked him. Liked kissing him. Especially liked him kissing her. She dragged her mind back before it got lost in that back room bed scene again. Barely. And saw him looking at her puzzled. She thought she might have turned a little pink.

"Where did you go, May?" he asked. "I don't think that was designing again. At least not dresses."

Now she was sure she was red so she just did the adult thing and ate more French fries and changed the subject. "I'll probably start sewing classes at Marge's soon."

"You're taking sewing lessons?"

"Not taking. Teaching. I am giving sewing lessons at the fabric store. Marge asked me. She's setting up the classes. I decide what to teach and how to teach it, at least for this first series of classes. This first series will be for beginners. Later lessons might build on that." She was pensive for a minute as she thought about that first lesson. She would have to check with Marge about the student levels. For beginners she should explain pins, needles, threads, fabrics, and patterns. Probably should do at least a review of how those all fit together.

They ate in a companionable silence. Nick insisted he was buying, she said she would do the tip. But he insisted on that too. She noted he paid in cash and left a nice tip. That made her feel good. Another mark in the plus column for Nick. He just got better and better.

He walked her back to Vintage. "I'll get back with you to go look at my house. It's empty right now and Hal says I need to make some decisions. Repairs and or upgrades. You can help me decide."

Another chaste kiss kept her awake.

Tuesday

May went with Sheil to the Dock meeting. Jeremy started, "The cost for advertising The Event was well below our normal budget for the start of the season, even with all the freebies we handed out. Visitor numbers were way up. Sales were remarkable. For all of us." The overall attitude was one of pleased satisfaction for The Event. Everyone had a profit from the weekend and for most, it was their best weekend ever.

"The tourists were happy. Almost every one of them left with something free and a sack full of purchases. That's a promising start for the season. Wayne says the website is getting hits and lots of orders for pictures and for enlargements. So the Polaroid idea worked well. Good advertising and public relations for all of us."

He looked at May and said, "You done good, girl. You done real good." They all clapped then, adding their own comments of 'right on, too right, more." She was moved.

Jeremy continued, "I know many of you plan on holding more mini events and we probably should have a calendar and a coordinator so you don't overlap. May should do that. Go to her if you want to have a mini event and she'll schedule it. Might even have two or three together. Let's start thinking about our Thanksgiving and Christmas programs."

"The donations for Amy. We have the Jones' contribution at the auction. We raised even more with the jars. I think folks were stuffing the ballot boxes. There were even a few hundred dollar bills," he said with amazement. "Amy will be coming home Friday. Right to the local airport, if anyone wants to go and greet her. She'll have day care and therapy for three weeks. We all did a good job on this. Feel free to take over food or offer time to visit or to give a break to her parents."

May decided that she would be there at the airport when Amy came home. She would start being a part of the community. Probably should find out where the airport was and where Amy lived. She would ask Sheil later. She made a mental note to put that on her Friday calendar.

That was it for the meeting. They ate and told stories about some crazy weekend exploits.

May wasn't sure about being in charge of the schedule, but Sheil just said, "Get out of here. Go to town and get a calendar and a pencil. Then just keep track. You'll know when you need to make an announcement or ask for advertising. Or, you can use the computer in the shop. Both maybe."

"OK. And I have some more ideas I'll jot down. How do I get to the airport to meet Amy? Or can I go to her house? Where is that? I want to be there to greet her."

"That's so sweet. You would need a car for the airport. You can ride with me." Sheil smiled to herself, she really liked May and was thrilled with her interest to become involved with the community.

Back at the shop there was a message for May to call Marge at the fabric store. When she hung up she looked at Sheil dazed.

"Well tell me. Tell me. What was that?" Sheil couldn't figure out what was happening.

"Marge has a sewing class lined up for me on Thursday morning. She said eight people have signed up. I can't believe it. This is all happening so quick."

"Get out of here. You're going to teach sewing at the shop?" She ran over and hugged her.

"I can't believe it," May said. "Marge asked me if I might be interested and I said yes. I didn't really expect anything would come of it. Or at least not this quickly. I'm stunned." She sat down. "I need to go in tomorrow so we can decide on a project. And money. She's going to pay me. More money for baby."

"Oh honey this is so wonderful. See, I told you. Can I go with you? I want to see what you're going to do."

May looked at her and took a breath, "Will you? That would be great. I'd appreciate it. And I need to get thread for the sheets. And I need to pay you for the sheets."

"No. I'll take the payment after you make your sales."

"OK. OK. I'm giddy. Let me straighten racks and get myself grounded. I am so lucky."

"Maybe lucky. But more like in the right place, at the right time, with the needed talent, making a good impression on the right people. You put yourself out there to help people and we noticed. And we might be taking a little advantage of a good thing. But everyone will come out a winner. Go to work and coast down."

That evening May laundered all the linens, she would mark off the bad portions the next day.

Wednesday

The meeting with Marge went well. They decided that for the first class the students would make a simple top. And part of the student's 'tuition' would cover the pattern, fabric, and thread.

May had made notes for a general step by step introduction to sewing in four one hour classes. "I'll start with how a pattern determines fabric, an explanation of fabrics, and how the fabric will determine the thread. How they are all connected. Then the students will pick out their fabric from a selection predetermined by us. They'll look at the patterns while I will explain how they work. The first day they will take the fabrics home to wash and iron. The second class, we'll place, pin, and cut. Third class will be pin the parts together, and sew them. Fourth class will be any adjustments, ironing, and hemming."

"I would expect each of the classes to run a little long. But that's OK with me," May finished. "Here's my written outline. Do you think that will work?"

Marge beamed, "Wonderful. I couldn't have done better myself. Here are three patterns we can use. I think maybe the students can decide which they want. Any of them would work well with this selection of fabrics over here." Marge led May and Sheil over to the stacks and touched the fabrics. A nice combination of colors and patterns. "Let's not start with stripes. Good idea to let them pick their own."

"Alright, let's talk money now. Do you want to be an employee or an independent contractor?" Marge asked.

May looked at Sheil who said, "She wants to be an independent contractor. She has her own design line which she is selling at Vintage as an independent contractor. In fact, that may be a good advertising plus for you for your sewing class."

She looked at May for confirmation.

"Yes, independent contractor will work better. I can pay my own social security and withholding taxes." At least she thought she could. Add accountant to her list of professionals to hire, lawyer, obstetrician, and accountant. Whew.

"I was hoping you would say that," Marge said, "I think four classes of one to one and a half hours for a total of $40.00 a person. Minimum of 5 students, maximum, we can decide. I have limited the first group to eight. The first ten dollars will cover fabric, pattern, and supplies, the rest is yours. You can decide if that works for you."

"And," Marge continued, "You get a 50% discount on anything you buy here."

"Get out of here," Sheil said.

May had hoped for half of the amount Marge was quoting her, she was thrilled. "After. After I have a successful group. You pay me after." When she got a nod from both Marge and Sheil, she said with a smile, "But I want my discount today. I have a list of things I need."

"My brother will draw up a contract and send it over," Sheil said to Marge while May picked out what she needed for her new 'sheet' designs. Then she and Sheil went to get Bryce and take him out to lunch. A business lunch. Bryce took notes and said he would send the contract to Marge and then bring it out to Vintage.

May and Sheil shopped a little and then bought a few groceries not available at the dock. Sheil dropped her off late in the afternoon.

As May put her groceries away, she looked at her life from Sheil's perspective. On the way home Sheil had said, "You know, your Derek is worse than a jerk. Look how you have thrived since you've been here. You have a great job, because you sold yourself. You have friends, because you are a friend. You live in a community which not only respects you, but considers you family. We all recognize your ability and your talents. You took the chance when presented with the opportunity, and now have begun two separate, independent, businesses. All in the space of, what, five weeks? He could have had an exciting successful wife. But he wanted a pretty wall hanging. You are so fortunate to be free of him. You go girl."

That evening she pressed the sheets removing the soiled and faded borders and cut the patterns from the linens to pin before the sewing class tomorrow. She was thinking, smiling to herself. Sheil was right, I am good; I'm not a boring person. A night off work and all she wanted to do was sew. She laughed at herself. She was happy. And she knew baby would be happy too. "Thank you Derek," she thought, "Thank you for setting me free."

Thursday

The sewing class went well. Actually it was a lot of fun. And she was surprised to see Marla and Carol there. They told her later that they wanted to learn to sew and could pay her for her knowledge. Also they wanted to keep their Sunday morning as a gossip session. That made May feel special.

She polled the other women to find their reasons for attending. Two women were Stay-at-Home Moms who wanted to sew clothing for their kids. Two were high school age girls who thought it would be interesting. They were curious. One of them wanted to make her own wedding gown. "Not that I have a boyfriend or even have a man in mind. But it has always been a dream of mine. I even have some sketches of what I want. But I have no idea where to start. I have never even sewn a stitch."

"Maybe you should start with a boyfriend," the girl with her drawled. They all laughed at that.

"Me too," May said. "I always thought I would make my own gown. But, my ex insisted on a name designer. Should have known right then that he wasn't my type. Maybe next time around."

The last two women worked with teen girls and wanted to add sewing to their list of activities and training. At the very least, they wanted to show the girls how to sew on a button, fix a hem. Chores that seemed to have become lost.

May told them that she would spend a little time on those during class.

She told them a little of her background, her education and training, the parts which qualified her to teach the class.

And then she explained what they would learn at each of the four sessions. Today you select one of these patterns, your fabric, and thread. The cost comes out of your tuition. The women had not realized that their materials were included and were thrilled to be getting the fabric and patterns free. It allowed May to begin the class on an even more positive note. Marge had made a very good decision there.

"Next week, after you take home your fabric and wash and iron it, we pin on the patterns and cut them out. Time permitting we will then pin the fabric pieces together. We'll finish the pinning the following week and sew the pieces together. The last week, we finish sewing; we iron again, and measure, and hem. You should be able to wear them home.

"Let's look at the pattern book, simply tab though for what you are making. Dress or slacks or top. The more expensive books generally have more intricate construction and detail. She showed them the pattern names and numbers they could choose from. "Write down the number and then go over to the appropriate drawer and find it in your size."

"You'll get to a point where you will just simply know the best fabric, but the pattern envelope will still be helpful in your decision making."

She then took them over to the fabrics and explained how different fabrics draped and fell. Showed how to test elasticity and stretching. She also demonstrated how to bunch up fabric and squeeze it in her fist. Letting it drop out so they could see the wrinkles and another piece so they could see it stayed wrinkle free. "How many of you like to iron?" she asked with a laugh. Most of the women shuddered.

One of the women said, "I love to iron."

"You don't," another woman said shocked.

"Oh, I do. I love to get into a bed with freshly laundered and pressed sheets. I feel so decadent. And when I am ironing, I have full control. I can think or sing. It's relaxing. It's time to myself. If I am feeling angry or frustrated, I can flatten those creases and wrinkles."

"Give me a good book," said one.

"A glass of wine will do me," said another.

"I might need to try that flattening part, especially in a dress shirt," said a third.

They all laughed again.

May continued, "You'll need to press out all your seems." She showed them how to drape the cloth over a shoulder to see how it would fall. Recommended they buy a half yard more of some prints so they could match up the designs.

After they made their selections she took them over to the large work table and had them open their patterns and find the pieces they would need for their tops. "You should have at least a front and back and facings for the neckline and arm, front and back. She explained that the facings were important for garment construction and a professional look. "Some of your patterns might have a seam down the front or back. That's OK. Sleeves are a little more difficult."

She explained how they would pin the patterns to the fabric and then cut them out and pin the fabric pieces together next week. "After you wash and iron the fabric during the week. This is one of those times you must iron or you will build mistakes into the garment."

She answered their questions and Marge came in to remind them of the time. The class had run about an hour and 15 minutes. Perfect. They spent another few minutes laughing and gossiping before everyone left. Marge handed May a check for the first session.

May pressed it to herself. "I feel like I should save it and frame it," she said.

"No. No, no, no. I'll make a copy and you can frame that. This you cash. Buy the baby something pretty."

Had May told Marge about the baby? She didn't think so. But pretty much the whole town knew her story by now.

May decided she deserved a grilled cheese and took her sketching to The Fry Pan. It should be quiet at this time of day and she would be able to linger over her meal and lemonade and she could people watch.

She had just been served when she looked up to see Bobby pulling out a chair.

"Hey, May. How lucky for me that you are sitting here all alone. And I'm alone too. Can I sit?" he asked as he sat.

Politeness saved her because she was tongue tied. She had been looking forward to a quiet afternoon sewing. Alone. And she didn't like him. And he was a crook. She really didn't want him to sit, but he was already sitting motioning to the waiter and asking, "What's good here?" looking at her grilled cheese and sweet potato fries and grimacing. "Anything healthy?"

She found her polite voice. "Um, I like everything I have tried. Try the lemonade."

He looked down his nose at the waiter. How did some people do that she wondered? He had to look up at the waiter but still managed to look down at him.

"Bring me a menu," he ordered. "And what type of water do you have?"

"Bottled water, sir," he holding out the menu to Bobby and winked at May.

She coughed. Holding in the laugh. Bobby was a pale imitation of Derek. An irritating imitation. Not as smooth. If he said he wanted 'Fine' or 'Bling' water May would choke.

"Let me see that," Bobby said grabbing the menu and turning to drinks. "Right, 'bottled water'. He looked at her and said, "Must be why you drink the lemonade." And then to the waiter instructed, "Bring me an iced tea. Unsweetened, I can do that myself. You do make that here?"

"Yes sir, sun tea," he said that proudly, after all it was one of their specialties. Along with the sweet potato fries.

"Do you have anything not fried?" Bobby asked closing the menu.

May wondered what part of 'Fry Pan' Bobby didn't get.

The waiter gave May an eye roll as he leaned over, opened the menu, and pointed, "The egg white omelet or the boiled shrimp salad in a vinegar, oil, and wine dressing."

"Bring me the salad. I suppose I can try that," dismissing the waiter.

He looked at her plate again, disapprovingly. She cringed. It put her on the defensive and she said feebly, "I only do this once a week." Wincing at her lie. "Eat here. They make it so good. And it is comfort food." She was blathering. Apologizing and explaining. She heard herself and stopped. This man was so like Derek it was spooky. Superior, and contemptuous, and critical. She was revolted by the person she had been when married to Derek. How could she have been so weak? She kicked herself. This jerk was not going to intimidate her.

She spooned over three or four fries and said sweetly, "Here, try." Though she was sure he wouldn't, and she wasn't disappointed. After all he hadn't even considered the lemonade. But she decided right then to be nice and see if she could learn anything that would help Nick. She remembered how frustrated he was in his surveillance. Maybe she could think of something to ask Bobby.

"Isn't Wanda with you?"

"Over at the shop. She had some kind of a meeting," he said dismissively. "I'm taking her to Miami for three days. I have a very important client there. Very important. We'll be staying at his villa. On the beach." Bragging. And then in disgust, "But, of course she had to have some meeting here first. As if her brother can't run that shop by himself. Any idiot can make the soap, but she has to be here. And now I have to wait for her to finish." This was Bobby whining. She should sympathize she supposed but before she had a chance he continued, "So I am eating while she talks with him and too bad she misses a meal."

That's Wanda's punishment May realized. Wanda had made a decision and had to be punished. Bobby was so like Derek. Anytime May had stood up for herself, she had been punished. May really had to speak with Wanda.

"I was supposed to meet him here tonight. But he had to leave town to set up transfers and pickups for us. He'll be back Sunday and we close the deal Monday evening. A lot of money to be made in that meeting, I want you to know. I am talking high six figures. Then I can really take Wanda off to celebrate. I'm thinking of chartering a boat. A charter and buy deal. Including crew. I have been looking at these yachts and have almost decided. It will be either the 60 footer or the 80 footer. After the deal Monday, I'm thinking the 80 foot Hatteras motor yacht. It will be perfect for me. Your boyfriend's dinky charter boat will look like a VW compared to it."

Why was he telling her all this? Bragging again. Idiot, she thought. And then, "Boyfriend? What boyfriend?"

"That guy you introduced me to in the shop. Isn't he your boyfriend?"

She managed a laugh, "No. I'm not seeing anyone. He's a relative of the shop's owner."

Bobby was eating his meal now acting as if it was barely palatable and immediately he looked interested. "Oh, well maybe next time I'm here, you can show me around? We can have dinner."

She was taken aback but agreed, "That might be fun. Will that be Monday?"

He looked at her confused for a moment and then said, "No, I won't be here Monday. Let me get back to you."

"Here comes Wanda," May said and he looked around for the waiter and asked for his check. Rather demanded it, complaining about the food. No surprise there May thought even though his plate was empty. A little off he said. Then he turned to Wanda and said, "I got hungry and had to eat without you because you had to work."

May watched as Wanda tried to hide her disappointment, and saw that it pleased Bobby to be able to rub it in. But Wanda looked at May and said, "I need to thank you."

"Why"

"Because of your idea for our lotions for the winners of the drawings. The hotel in town is ordering a supply of them as amenities for their guests. The small delicate jars are exactly the touch they want for their penthouse suites, and to sell in their gift shop. That will be a manageable number, barely, for us. If the lotions work out here in town then he'll put them in his other hotels. Big, big, step for us. Just this hotel in town means, borderline, we will have to hire another person. If he puts them in his chain, I can leave my job and be here full time. It's exciting."

May got up and gave her a hug, "I'm so happy for you. It's your soaps that got you his attention. It's your soaps that got you the deal.

I'm so excited for you. We'll need to celebrate when you get back." May turned to look at Bobby and surprised an angry frown on his face. "Isn't this great Bobby?"

"She shouldn't give up an important, prestigious, profession to become a shop girl. We have talked about this before Wanda, you know how I feel." He looked at her with that disapproving frown.

"Oh, honey, let's not fight. All that is far in the future," Wanda said, to mollify him.

May looked at them and said, "I need to go to the ladies room." And added to Wanda, "Come with me. You have a long drive and you can freshen up."

As soon as they shut the door behind themselves, May said, "That is a nasty mean thing he just did to you. Multiple nasty mean things. I can't keep my mouth shut and just watch. I have a husband just like that and I wish someone had told me I deserved better. So I'm telling you, no matter if I'm out of line. You deserve a man who wants to wait for you before he sits down to a meal. Not one who will eat without you and tell you it's your fault. You deserve a man who is happy with your successes, not one who puts you down when you succeed. Excuse me, but this guy is slime. You deserve better. I hope you didn't ruin his weekend by being a successful business woman."

May saw the damage her words had done. "I'm sorry, that was out of line. If you ever want to talk, you know where to find me." She changed the subject. "Think about how great your mini lotion series is. And how it's going to be even better when you add a mini soap series. Because I bet you have one planned? Right?"

Wanda looked at her surprised and nodded. "How did you know?"

"Because I recognize an up and coming business woman when I see one. The soap series is a logical next step. Come on, we better get back before he gets too angry."

When they got back to the table, Bobby was waiting impatiently. May supposed they had made him late. She turned to Wanda and hugged her and said, "You are a smart, talented woman."

Bobby didn't want to talk about Wanda's success and quickly dragged her off complaining that they were late.

May watched as they walked off together and then the waiter said, "Sure hope you are not trading Nick for that, uh, idiot."

"No, don't worry; I don't need to be around a self-important jerk. He sure is mean to Wanda. Sorry he was so ugly to you."

"You don't need to apologize for him. There is always one of them around to make sure someone like me knows my place. Your lunch is on me today."

Smiling, he turned and went over to another customer before she could respond. She decided she would accept lunch but leave him a large tip. She really did love the people here.

She would have to tell Nick what she found out. His boat was in, maybe she would walk over after she finished eating. But, just as she picked up her fork, her eyes wandered to the entrance. Marty? Looking like a business man in a hurry. Acting a little like Bobby, in fact. Looking at his cell in his hand. Shaking it. Raising it to his ear. Looking at it again. Looking around, his eyes pausing for a second on her, with a tilt of his head and a question in his eyes. Then back to his phone.

Curious. Oh. Her cell phone. He wanted her to look at her cell? She pulled it out and saw it was off. Saw Marty shake his head and walk outside with the phone to his ear.

She pushed the speed dial and when he answered said, "Ooops. Sorry."

"I tried to call, but you had your phone off," he chided. "I wanted to let you know that we're done here. When I couldn't reach you by phone, I decided to go by the shop and saw you over here. Was that Nick's guy you were eating with?"

"Yes. And he said some things Nick needs to hear."

"Like what?"

"He's going out of town now and won't be back until Sunday. He meets with an important client Monday evening to close a high six figure deal." She got it all out in one breath and was rewarded by a stunned silence from Marty.

"How in the world did you get him to tell you that? Wait. Tell me word for word what he said."

She repeated everything as near as she could remember and he said, "If this is what it sounds like, we do need to tell Nick. Are you done eating?"

"I am now." She grabbed a handful of fries as she waved for her check. Remembered to leave a big tip because the check was just for lemonade, the meal was gratis.

"Meet me at Ryan's," Marty said.

She found Ryan and Marty waiting for her. David was heading over. As was Nick, who had to secure his boat first. Ryan made tea and coffee.

When everyone was present, they made May tell her story three more times. When they started on a fourth time, she threw up her hands and said, "Look, that's it. I'm not repeating it again. Anyone of you can tell it as well as I can now."

Nick took her hand and when she looked at him he said, "I know it seems repetitive. It is. But it is also important. People remember new things when they repeat a story. See how you just remembered that part about them staying at a villa on the beach. That probably isn't important, but it could be. So bear with us and let's do it again. How about if this time, as you walk through it, we ask questions? OK?"

Marty said, "Let me start. Why was he even talking to you?"

"I don't know why he told me. He said he saw me sitting there. I think he was bragging. Trying to impress me with how rich and important he is. That's the feeling I got. And he was trying to punish Wanda for not doing what he wanted, and doing it immediately. So he gets to hurt her twice. First by sitting with another woman and second by eating without her. He was being spiteful. I recognize that type of meanness. I'm married to the same type of person and he would have done exactly the same thing." Did do it, she thought. More than once. And she had let him manipulate her.

They went through it two more times and then decided it was all they were going to get. They had a GPS finder on Bobby's car, so Nick called his people in Miami to follow him to the villa and find out where he went and who he was seeing. With an extra caution to keep an eye out and make sure that Bobby did stay in town for three days.

"We can't take a chance. It does sound like they will be at Soaps Monday night. But we still have to be prepared that they might be there sooner. Or later," he added as an afterthought. "There is no way we can check flight schedules to see if a man we don't know left the country and where he went. Or when he will be back. OK. That's all we can do tonight," Nick finished up. "And probably we don't need to worry until Monday night. But let's still keep an eye on the shop. I don't want us to get overconfident and screw up." He turned to May and said, "Come on May. I'll walk you home."

But Marty said, "Wait a few minutes. I need to talk to May. This Bobby stuff got in the way. You guys might as well hear this also. Everyone from the art theft arrest is out on bail. None of them have talked so far. And, this is the bad part; it won't be long before they have access to all our information. Florida is an open state and legally they have access to everything we have. Including that May contacted us. Her name will be out there. They will know that May is the one who called us in. There was no way for me to keep that out of the reports. So May, just keep an eye out. It shouldn't be a problem but I wanted to give you a heads up."

"Are you saying that they, or one of them, might be angry at me?" she asked confused.

"I don't really think so. They're all professionals and take an arrest in stride. All part of doing business. But I wanted you to know that they're free and might know that you were involved. So keep your wits about you if you see one of them and give Ryan or Nick a call. OK?"

"Sure." Did he really think that one of those crooks might come looking for her? It was too late now to go back and do anything different and she wouldn't anyhow. She would just be wary.

"Also, because of your expertise, I want you to go through a crate full of garments. Look like costumes, but I have no idea. None of our people can tell. There's some glass mixed up with the costumes also."

"OK. Let me know when."

"Whenever you get a chance, but the sooner the better."

And then she said, as they were all getting ready to leave, "I have a question about Bobby and maybe a statement also." When she saw she had their attention she asked, "Why do you believe Bobby when he says his partner left the country to close a deal? He has lied about everything else and exaggerated what he didn't lie about. Is it possible that the partner is in jail? Not out of the country. I mean he is a crook, isn't he? Doesn't it make more sense that he might have been arrested?"

Nick broke the stunned silence. "That's my girl," he said proudly. He looked at Ryan and suggested, "We should put her in charge of this investigation. She's the only one thinking."

Shaking his head, Ryan agreed. "Christ, how did we miss that? How is she always one step ahead of us? We can work with that. Checking arrests for the past week, even two weeks, is manageable. David and I will get on it. I knew you were a keeper the day you walked in my office and rescued me," he said to May.

She knew she was blushing. "Now I am going home. I had planned a nice boring evening home alone. Quiet time for me and baby and I'm going home and try to salvage a bit of that. Alone," she repeated as Nick got up.

"No. I am walking you home."

She didn't fight him. They were at her stairs when he took her hand and said, "I don't want you eating dinner with Bobby. You're my girl." He couldn't help himself, he was jealous.

She snatched her hand away from him. "What?" she said annoyed. "What do you mean your girl?"

"What I mean is I don't want Bobby to think he can move in on my girl. I don't want you eating with him. You're my girl," he said again.

He leaned over to kiss her, to prove it. A short, chaste kiss, like the last one. That left him wanting more so then he kissed her again. A long, slow kiss. He licked her lip. Then licked it again because it felt so good the first time and she opened for him with a little moan. Now he invaded her mouth for a long deep thrust. He pushed her against the wall. Gently. Moved from her mouth across her jaw. Kissed right at the joint. He had been watching that spot. Wanting to taste it all night. Her hips arched into him. That felt good. He kissed slowly down her neck. Went back to her mouth and almost got lost in there. But he was on a mission now. Again he kissed her jaw line, the corner of her jaw. And again she arched into him. Oh, that did feel right. That response. Good to know.

She didn't want it to stop. Not ever. Well, yes, he could stop when he got her upstairs in bed, naked. Naked? That word, that thought, broke the spell. He had his hands under her shirt, at her waist moving up to her breasts, when she murmured, "No." Her insides were mush. Her knees weak.

"Stop, please," she pleaded. She couldn't stop. He had to.

She was getting ready to do something stupid, like drag him upstairs, when he did stop. Rested his chin on her head. Her heart was pounding and she looked up into his face. She looked into that satisfied smile and her heart took a double beat. She almost felt like she was under a magical spell. How could he affect her so much with what started as a single, almost innocent, kiss? Well, it started innocent. Derek never had such an effect on her. Never kissed her with so much passion. Sex with Derek had been like eating leftover, burnt, green beans. Her body seemed to know that sex with Nick would be incredible. And her body wanted to find out. But her mind was still in charge. Almost. Sort of. She'd better get control of herself or she would end up one more of Nick's women. One of the many who spent the night on his boat. One night. That fear sobered her up.

"Wow," she whispered. Found her voice, "Wow." She reached up but didn't dare touch him. "Too bad. Too bad for me. But I am never going to be a for a little while girl," she murmured almost to herself. Took a deep breath and repeated the mantra in a normal voice, "I am never going to be a for a little while girl. You are never going to be a forever guy." Another breath, "Thank you for walking me home," she said unsteadily. And for stopping when I couldn't, she thought silently.

"Sure, but you're wrong. Thanks for your help tonight. See you tomorrow." And he walked away. Nonchalant. Or he would be once he got a really cold shower. But grinning to himself just the same. Doing a mental high five. His plan was working. He knew that if he had pushed, and he almost had, she would have caved. But that wasn't what he wanted any longer. He wanted more. Not the one night stand. He wanted forever with this woman. Him. Nick London. Wanted more from a woman then a one night stand. He walked back to his boat, whistling to himself. Yup, a cold shower.

May was too wound up to even think about sleeping, so she got out her quilt and worked on that. She was wrong he'd said. Wrong about what? Not the kiss certainly. That was heaven. And she could still feel the burning imprint of his hands on her. And since when was there a direct connection from her jaw to her sex? What happened there? She had never read or heard anything about a jaw joint disorder that connected to your groin. That had never happened with Derek. She would have been embarrassed about that but it was simply a reflex action, like a knee jerk. Sure, she was the jerk if she believed that. Knee jerk reaction to Nick's kisses? She was in trouble.

How did she feel about him? Was she falling in love with him? He didn't know. He couldn't know, could he? She was falling for him. Correction, she had fallen for him the first time they met. Even when he was ugly and mean, she had liked him. And that made her realize that he hadn't been ugly to her in a long time. What was that all about? What was she wrong about? Sleeping with him? Did he know that if he had pushed just a little, she would have invited him upstairs? The forever girl, hungry for a one time fling? Is that what he meant?

She wasn't quilting. She gave up and went for a long soak.

Friday

Half awake, May finally found the phone and answered it. Again, she had fallen asleep in the rocker. Sketching? No, thinking, worrying. About her reactions to Nick. The long soak in the tub hadn't helped. "Hello?"

"May? This is Bryce. You are now officially May Johnson. The decree is final. It was delivered this morning. Do you want to pick it up? Or I can bring it by this afternoon?"

"Yes, yes, I want to pick it up. I can come in now. Well, soon. Thank you." She hung up thinking. This was it. All her hopes. All her dreams. They were over. The idyllic marriage that turned into a prison sentence. Over. Get over yourself, she thought. It wasn't a prison sentence. Stop being melodramatic. It was just a marriage to a man who wanted a puppet, not a wife. A mannequin he could control. Not a woman with a mind of her own. She was lucky. She would have kept trying to make the marriage work, never understanding that Derek didn't want a wife. He wanted an object that he dressed and wound up to act as he instructed. She'd have disappeared if she had stayed married to him.

She laughed at herself. The forever girl. Forever was 10 months. She felt alone. Discarded. She was now that which she had often pitied. A single mother. Or she soon would be. She laughed at herself again. So her path to motherhood was different from most, the end result was the same. She would still be a woman raising her child by herself. Alone.

She put her hand on her stomach and rubbed. Thinking it's OK baby. I am free now. We can do this. We have already begun on our path. We are strong and resourceful and talented. She straightened her shoulders and went to get dressed.

She could do it. She knew she could. She had already started. Was already successful. She had come to the perfect place to raise her child. She had a job, a home, and friends here who would support her. She was not alone.

She wanted that decree. She would pick it up and then she would see if Ryan wanted to share a celebratory cup of tea.

Bryce was waiting for her. He still wished that she'd let him renegotiate the divorce. But she told him again that both she and the baby would live better lives without any influence from Derek. If she took money from him, he would be able to control how she lived. Where she lived. How she raised her child. Being poor and free was far, far better.

"Congratulate me," she said. "I have begun a new life with many opportunities and many new friends. This world, your world, is real. Derek's world is fake and empty. I was a little afraid that he might realize what he was throwing away and change his mind. And not sign the decree. Now I don't have to worry. I have what I want and he can never come after me or my baby. Thank you for helping."

Ryan wasn't at the Inn. The clerk on duty said Ryan had gone to town for the day. It was only then she remembered the meeting last night. Decided against The Coffee Spot. Didn't want to talk to anyone. Or see anyone. May decided that she really wanted to be alone. She went up to her apartment and sat on the couch and stared at the floor.

A long time later, she moved her head and noticed the window. I can't just sit here all day she thought, and got up and walked over to look out. Normal out there, nothing changed on the dock. Another bright pretty day. Suddenly she wanted to be a part of normal. Time to get on with her life. A life that was looking pretty good. She stood up tall and took a deep breath. With new enthusiasm, she changed and went downstairs to work early and found Doris was already there.

"You seem quiet, what's wrong? It's not like you to be somber," Doris said. "I don't like to see you sad."

"Oh, just got up on the wrong side of the bed, I guess," she said with a fake smile probably not fooling Doris. "No, that's not true. I'm now divorced. As of ten thirty this morning when Bryce gave me my divorce decree. I am now a single woman. A single, pregnant, woman. It's scary."

Doris said, "The divorce is final. That's why you are sad. How terrible."

May agreed. "Yes, it really hit me this morning. I'm alone. Discarded, worthless. A 10 month, short term affair. No picket fence around a white house, no dog, no two kids. Just me and my baby. And, yes, I'm feeling sorry for myself."

"Oh, child, you have that all bass-ackwards." She went over, took May's hand, and lifted her face. "I said it's terrible because that hateful man threw away the best thing that ever happened to him He was so lucky to have you. And he will regret doing this to you. But you are fortunate to be out of that marriage. You live in a great town. You have made a lot of wonderful friends here. Nosy, but wonderful. You have helped a lot of people in just the short amount of time that you have been here. You are now a favorite son. So to speak." She laughed. "Make that the favorite daughter. And you are not alone. You are so lucky; you have your whole life ahead of you. It's OK and expected for you to be a little disheartened. But don't belittle yourself while I am around. I won't have it. You hear?"

May tried to put on a brave smile. The words comforted her. "You are so sweet. You make me feel better already. I'm sorry for the pity party." May stood back and straightened her shoulders.

"Pity party? If you think that's a pity party child, you have never really been to one. I'll call you the next time someone has a real pity party. Lots of people divorce. Some remarry."

When Sheil walked in and Doris said, "She's sad because she is now divorced."

Sheil took a minute and said, "OK, we're closing the shop and going to The Coffee Spot to celebrate. And I want to know why you keep calling us nosey."

Janine sat down with them when they told her they were celebrating the divorce.

"Everything's on me. This is going to be a real party. Let me get a platter of hot muffins and scones. Hey, Jeremy," she hollered as he walked by, "come join our celebration."

So they explained to Jeremy. He took her hand and patted it. "I'll marry you," he said, "No, I can't. Forget I said that. Nick would kill me. After the way he kissed you last night. No, I didn't say that. Don't tell him I even suggested it."

"What? What? You saw that? You saw him kiss me?"

"Get out of here. What kiss? Tell me," Sheil demanded at the same time

"We saw Nick and May kissing last night," he said smugly.

"We? What do you mean, we? Was the whole dock out there spying on us?" May was outraged.

"Um, pretty much, all of us. Yes. If you want to kiss in private, you probably should do it indoors. There was a whole bunch of us sitting around having a quiet drink when you two came by. And we were not spying. You think we're not going to watch our two favorite people having fun together? And man, that looked like hot fun."

He let that settle in and then said, "You're turning red. Sunburn?" He gave a great belly laugh.

May only smiled and shook her head. "I thought we were alone. I'll have to remember that next time. What am I saying, there isn't going to be a next time."

"Ah, hon, you just keep telling yourself that." They all laughed at her.

Folks would wander over and sit with them. Drink a little coffee, eat a muffin. Pat her on the back and then go to work. The celebration lasted about an hour. There was enough of a crowd that they had to pull over another table to fit all of them. Everyone seemed to have seen the kiss last night too. Did they sell tickets she wondered? They were right; the kiss last night was hot. She felt her insides tremble each time someone mentioned it. And everyone did of course.

May felt both embarrassed and loved. These people, her new friends, had taken time out of their busy schedules to stop and first sympathize with her and then tease her and then celebrate with her. They cared. She hadn't had this with Derek. She hadn't been allowed friends. She had given up so much and not even noticed. Her new friends left money on the table for their food. No one expected Janine to pay for it all.

Nick got in from his half day charter and cleaned the fish, hosed down the boat, and went over to fuel her up. He would be happy when he was no longer a charter captain. Some of his customers were real idiots. Sometimes he thought he would just pull out his gun and make them walk the plank. He was laughing to himself over that thought when he saw Jeremy. Jeremy was shaking his head looking at him with a crafty, funny expression. Could Jeremy be laughing at the same image of a plank walking idiot? That was a stupid thought. And then Nick realized that he had been getting funny looks this morning too. What was that all about? Might as well find out he thought.

"Why are you looking at me that way?" he asked.

"Oh, just thinking of that kiss you laid on May last night."

"What kiss? What do you mean?"

"When you walked her home. That sizzled."

"She told you that?" Angry now. She was the one that didn't want any gossip. And she'd told Jeremy? And how many others? There were a lot of people looking at him slyly this morning. Now he was really angry.

"Never mind," he snarled at Jeremy and stalked off to confront May.

He stomped up the dock and into the shop scowling. May and Doris had been watching through the window. "Oh, oh," Doris said. "He looks mad." And then, "Hi, Nick, how are you today?" with a cheery smirk.

"You too?" he growled. "She told you too?"

"Ooops," Doris said and edged toward the back room, "I'll be out back if you need me." She didn't go very far into the back room though, stayed near the threshold. Didn't feel the least bit guilty about eavesdropping.

"What are you talking about Nick? And you better think for one minute before you say another word," May warned him in a dangerous voice.

Her tone held a warning that made him take a breath and look at her. Remembered her reaction to the kiss last night. Kicked his brain on. Then mentally he kicked himself too. Almost screwed this up, he thought. Hope it's only almost screwed up. He was on dangerous ground.

"I didn't say that. You didn't hear that. I'm leaving. Don't say a word. I was never here." He left. Went out the door. Took three deep breaths and came back in with a warm smile.

"Good morning May. Well good afternoon." He walked over to her, leaned in, and kissed her gently on the lips. Backed away before she could react. But her anger was gone and replaced with confusion. Good.

"You know. I think some of the dock folks, dock busybodies, might have been watching me kiss you last night. I don't think we are a secret anymore." He laughed. He had figured it out. He knew these people. And he knew May would never kiss and tell.

She smiled at him, "You think? The way I hear it, they were all out there having a nightcap when we put on a show for them. I'm a little surprised they didn't clap and cheer. And hold up numbers." She couldn't help the giggle.

"They probably thought they should be respectful of our privacy. But you're right; I think I did see some numbers this morning. Mostly 9.9s, and 10s." Now it was his turn to smile smugly.

He thought he could get away with it one more time. With a gleam in his eye, he leaned in and kissed the smile on her lips. And backed off quick. Before he forgot and got caught there again. Before she could react. There was a giggle from the back room.

For sure Doris was watching. But he knew she wouldn't gossip. And as if reading his mind, May said softly, "Doris won't talk, but there are at least five people looking in the window." And May giggled again. She was happy. He had come in angry to accuse her, had actually started to accuse her, but stopped when she asked him to think. Referring to her earlier request that the next time he got ready to accuse her of something, he should stop and think first. He had. She loved that, it was gratifying. His kisses today were sweet and full of promise.

"This town is full of the nosiest people I have ever met. They have no shame," she said with a note of pride in her voice. "They got all over me this morning for kissing you in a public place," she confessed. She glanced past his shoulder, "And there are three of them still looking in the window. This is not such a public place."

"They have been taunting me," he complained. Before he could say more, his phone buzzed. He looked at it and frowned. "Of course, now, they know something," he said to himself. "Hold that smile sweetheart. I'll be back to pick up where I left off. Duty calls." And then he kissed her nose and was out the door.

Sweetheart? He called her sweetheart. Made her feel warm all over. One word and she melted. Well, no. There were those simple sweet kisses. She really shouldn't let him. But it made her so happy just to be near him. And his kisses were heaven. She touched her lips. She could still feel his there.

"Sweetheart?" Doris said smugly bringing her out of her reverie. "He called you sweetheart. That's so, um, inconsiderate."

May laughed, as she was meant to.

Sheil picked her up at dinnertime to go visit with Amy. The twins were with her.

"I made a casserole. Let me go get it," May said. She had cooked it the night before, when she got tired of quilting.

"Is it healthy?" Melanie asked.

"Well, it does have nutritious vegetables, but it also has lots and lots of fat and flavor. And you can pick out chunks of fried potato and chicken. And leave the veggies behind. But I think you'll like the whole thing. Well, Amy will like it."

It turned out that Amy and the twins were best friends. That made the visit easier on May. As soon as they stepped in the door Melanie said, "May has got one of her scrumptious killer casseroles. All fat and calories. I can't wait to try it."

They visited together and then the women went to the kitchen for tea and coffee, leaving the girls to get caught up on gossip. May felt like she belonged.

Saturday

Saturday she started pinning the outfit. She wanted to give herself plenty of time for the layout. Make sure that each pattern piece fit on the fabric. She would cut the pieces after work. Again she laughed at herself. After work Saturday night and she would happily be cutting pattern pieces. Not nightclubbing or attending an important social event. She wanted to stretch like a lazy cat and just enjoy the peace and contentment. She hummed while she worked. A princess style dress with jacket for both Mom and daughter. She knew how to build room in the seams for alterations. She had enough fabric for a maternity top for herself. One she could wear after the baby too.

She liked this blue rosebud with the pale green leaves and it would match the green sheets. Maybe she should use it for the cradle. It would be better than the plain green she had imagined. She hoped she would have enough cloth. Was sure she would. The Cabinet would be opening soon, Marty had said a week, and she could get the cradle. She couldn't wait to finish pinning and actually be able to see all the pieces laid out.

The pink and blue bold floral petunia pattern would make a long fitted skirt and vest. The plain blue, a blouse that blended with the skirt. Maybe a granny bag to finish off the outfit.

She knew there would still be pieces left over. Hopefully enough to make tops or shorts for her Sunday gossip group friends.

Again she thought of her future. Things were working out. A good job. A nice apartment. Two added incomes from the remade vintage and the sewing classes. They were all jobs she could do while pregnant or after the baby came. She didn't want to count her chickens yet, but the future looked good for her and baby. It had all seemed so easy.

And then there was Nick. So short term. Not part of her future. But could she enjoy him just for now? Not to get involved with. She knew she wouldn't survive if she fell for him. Who was she kidding? She had fallen for him the moment she saw him. It would be a short affair. Maybe they could be friends for a little while longer? Friends? No, they weren't friends. She hoped she could be strong.

Thinking of Nick, she looked out the window. His boat was out, so he must have a charter. Idly wondered if it was a whole day? He had said he would get back to her. He left in such a hurry, she hadn't had time to tell him her divorce was final. Would it make a difference? If so, how? Would he ask for more? Or back off? And what would she do? She knew she didn't want him to back off, but it might be better. And why was she thinking about Nick again? Get a life girl. You have a life. Just pay attention to your sewing.

The next time she looked up it was time to go to work.

It was a good day with steady, friendly, customers all afternoon. Lookers and buyers. And then late in the evening, Wanda came in. She looked a little teary and asked May if they could talk.

"I just need someone, female to talk too. I think I want to break up with my boyfriend. And you said I could talk to you?" A hopeful question.

May looked at Sheil who told her to go ahead and take lunch.

They went to The Fry Pan and both got the shrimp. With fries, sweet potato fries, thank you very much. May started because she was pretty sure she knew what was wrong. Wanda had all May's symptoms. "This is probably my fault. I shouldn't have said anything about the way I feel. You probably spent the whole weekend looking at him through my eyes."

Wanda broke in before she could finish her apology, patting her hand. "You didn't say anything that Paul hadn't already said. I was so infatuated with Bobby. He is so handsome and suave, that I didn't notice the putdowns. But you're right. This weekend I did look at the way he treated me and I didn't like what I finally saw. How small and insignificant he made me feel. How much he detested the shop girl in me. He has wanted me to turn the shop over to my brother and work at moving up in the accounting firm. But I want to be in the shop. I want to make the lotions that I want to design soap formulas."

"We selected the Cove because it seemed to have the necessary tourist traffic and an extra-large storeroom area for supplies and cooking. Our initial costs for equipment were minimal. We found everything we needed on line including the ingredients and packaging. At the beginning the work is all labor, no automatic equipment. But our five year plan includes assembly line machines. And actually, it looks like we will reach that goal sooner with this hotel contract."

"I want to be a small business bookkeeper and tax advisor on the side. That's what I realized this weekend. Thanks to you. He wants me to be someone else and being her will not make me happy. Why didn't I see that before?"

"Because men like Bobby, find women like us. We are their specialty. They show us what we want to see, while changing and molding us to be their fantasy. It took me months to catch on with Derek. By the time he kicked me out though, I was chaffing under the constant control and belittling. I would have been gone pretty soon anyway, I hope. But let's not talk about me. I want you to be sure of what you are doing before you make a life changing decision."

"You know he told you he was my fiancé, but he has never asked me to marry him. Never even mentioned marriage. He just didn't like being called a boyfriend."

"He didn't ask you this weekend?"

"All I got this weekend was that I had to act like a proper lady. He even picked out my clothes."

"Sounds just like Derek. Bought my clothes and told me what to wear each day. Made my schedule and told me what to say. Told my hairdresser how to do my hair. All the while implying I just wasn't quite smart enough to make those decisions myself and was lucky to have him."

"Yes, that was Bobby this weekend. I wasn't obedient and that made him angry. I ruined his weekend. And he's going to have to work overtime to make up for the damage I did. He said we'd talk about my problems next weekend. So I'm supposed to think about my behavior and be ready to apologize. I am probably supposed to be scared he'll drop me. And I have a week to worry about it."

"I think the ruined weekend started when you made him eat alone. Because he couldn't wait for you. I don't think he even enjoyed the food. Too plebian I think. But, oh my gosh, this shrimp is sooo good." May laughed. "Poor, poor man."

"I know. This is especially good with the fries. Sweet potato fries was a good idea. But Bobby would be dismayed. He finds it hard to patronize a fast food restaurant like this."

"Yes, I was married to a man just like him. I got to tell you that you deserve someone a lot better."

"I'm just realizing that myself. But I think I'll wait for the weekend and find out my punishment before I break it off." And then changing the subject, "How about that handsome boat captain? Is he yours?"

May just knew she was blushing but owned up to where she was. "I'll be truthful. I like him a lot. A really, nice man. Kisses like a dream. I want him. But I will deny I ever said that. I have already messed up my life with the wrong man. I want a husband and a home, a family. I want forever, happily ever after. I know I won't get it, but that's what I want. Nick's a short term guy. Today, tomorrow is as far as he wants to plan with a woman. But, ohh, I really do like him. I wish I could do the one night stand thing. He makes me want to. But I'm afraid that it could get habit forming. A line of men in and out of my bedroom and how would that look to my daughter?"

"I was with you right up to daughter. A line of men is actually pretty expected in this day and age. But I don't see you doing that. And I don't understand the daughter part."

'You must be the only person in town who doesn't know I am pregnant."

Wanda raised an eyebrow, "So tell me."

"My control freak husband threw me out when I got pregnant, by him. Claims he is sterile. He's not, I am pregnant. And as of yesterday

I'm divorced. Don't look at me that way. Don't feel bad for me. I'm excited about my life here and my future and my baby. Because my future is here, in this great town, with these wonderful, caring people. I get to start over and I'm going to try not to mess up this time. Because I have found my home, so to speak, and my family.

"I guess, if you can do it under your circumstances, I can too. My situation is so much simpler. And I will give your captain a pass. I'm not really a one night stand girl either. But, I don't know. There aren't too many men like your boat captain. Might be worth it. Really, there have got to be some fine men out there looking for us."

"Too right. I know. I keep on thinking, just one night. It's not a big deal. And I'll have the memory. Enough of me. Are you going to be alright now?"

"Yes, talking with you has helped more than you can know. Thank you."

They talked some more finding many things in common. May mentioned that she would need an accountant for her side jobs. They agreed to get together one more time before the fateful talk that Bobby had scheduled.

Wanda went back to Soaps and May went back to Vintage where she knew that Sheil would make her tell all. She had gotten permission from Wanda to share. May knew too, that soon there would be subtle support for Wanda from her neighbors.

She wondered if this was information Nick or Ryan needed and then decided it wasn't. They would know that Bobby was back in town. The status of his love life wouldn't matter. But she would tell Nick the next time she saw him. Or maybe he should know now. No, this is just an excuse to call him, hear his voice. She was able to put it off, but she pulled out her phone during a lull at work and hit the speed dial. She almost hoped he didn't answer.

"Leave a message," her phone said in her ear. OK. She did, just as short. "Wanda came to see me. They're back. Umm, do you need to know that Wanda is probably breaking up with him? Bye." Love you, she said to herself. Love you? Where did that come from? She didn't say it out loud did she? She looked around. OK, it was just some remnants of her talk with Wanda. It didn't mean anything. Ohh, she was really in trouble.

She gave up, threw her hands in the air and went back to wait on a customer.

Sunday

The Sunday tutu sewing group discussed ironing. Marla and Carol told them about the sewing class. Then the topic moved to Amy. All of them had visited and were hopeful for her full recovery.

Carol wanted to know why May had lunch with a strange man. At first May was afraid she meant Marty and she didn't know how she would explain him. "Oh, you mean Bobby."

"If that's his name. Where was Nick?"

"I don't belong to Nick," she reminded them. And herself. "You know Wanda who owns Soaps? That was, is, unfortunately, her boyfriend."

"Unfortunately?"

"I don't really like him and I shouldn't speak badly about him, but he is really mean to her." She went on to explain, reminding them that this was just her point of view. Having recently been married to the same type of man she felt she might be an expert.

"What do you mean recently been married? Your divorce? It came through?" Carol demanded excitedly.

May nodded, a little unsure again of her emotions. "Friday. It's all over. I am a single lady again. Soon, a single Mom."

"How do you feel?" Marla asked.

"Relieved, most of all. A little sad that it didn't work out. Glad it is over."

Carol said, "OK girls we need to plan a party. Maybe a BBQ. To celebrate. I'll set it up and get back to you."

"Oh that will be fun," Marla agreed. They would plan a special split-up party.

Later, at work, May was looking through the newspaper for the Dock advertisement while Doris was, of course, talking about the gossip in the society pages.

"I don't know why you think you can't get involved with Nick. You're divorced now. It's OK."

Why did everyone want her to get involved with Nick? And Doris was the older more staid generation. Encouraging her to be promiscuous. May already couldn't stop thinking about Nick. He hadn't called back either. So either her message wasn't important or he didn't want to talk to her. Or both. Or neither. She was so confused.

Doris didn't notice that she wasn't listening. "And look at this article here. This big, rich, society guy is getting himself a new wife. Let me see, says here that his quickie divorce was just finalized and he already is announcing wedding plans in the newspaper. I'm sure you have heard of him. He's been in the news a lot lately. Derek Stratton and Corinne Smythe are going to tie the knot next month. A wedding announcement right after his divorce is final."

Doris looked up getting ready to finish that thought and saw a stunned May.

"Oh, my God. That's him? That's the creep? It is, isn't it?"

"Let me see that," May said grabbing the paper and reading.

The front door bell chimed and Sheil came in just as May was saying, "Corrine? Corrine Smythe? He's marrying her? Next month? He announces it now? How can he know already? Oh, that's what Aubrey was talking about. That's who he's been going out with. Just waiting for the divorce to be finalized to make his announcement. That... that... Did he have that planned when he kicked me out. Did he make up that sterile story to get me to leave? Was he planning this all along and I just fell into his trap? Quickie divorce, no alimony, no child support. Does he get off scot free?" She was rambling. Yelling. She heard herself. Saw Doris and Sheil, too, looking at her. She shut her mouth and took a breath. Than another.

Looked at them. Took another breath. She should be angry, should be spitting mad, stomping around the back room. Instead she felt, nothing? Relief?

Sheil looked at Doris for an explanation. Doris passed her the article. "May's ex. Looks like Derek dear got his divorce decree and made his little surprise announcement."

Sheil read the article as May sat bewildered. Sheil was dismayed. She looked at May and said, "You were actually married to this piece of worthless crap? Get out of here. He must really have got his hooks into you in a weak moment. You are so lucky to be out of his reach now. What scum."

May just looked at her. At both of them because they were both nodding their heads. "So he conned me into marrying him and then conned me into a no fault divorce?"

Sheil went to her and sat her down. "That's probably exactly what he did."

"And I'm carrying his child. And he kicked us both out. Because he said he couldn't have children. Accused me of cheating. Was he planning then to marry Corrine?" She sputtered.

"If you had known about this Corinne before you signed the paperwork, would you have contested the divorce, May? Think about it," Sheil said.

May tried to sit quietly and think. She was so, so… not angry. Not angry. Just disappointed. In Derek. If she had known that Derek was fooling around with Corrine, she might have killed him, but would she have dragged him through an ugly divorce? He didn't love her, never had. And she hadn't loved him. She knew that now. Because now she knew what love might feel like? She had been infatuated. She took a deep breath and looked at Sheil.

"Give me a minute here. He disowned his child, got rid of me with a no fault divorce. He is going to marry Corrine." She stopped and looked at Sheil and then Doris. "He wasn't fooling around with Corrine. He is a lot of things, but he wouldn't have done that. So Corinne is new."

A new thought hit her and she laughed. "Hah, he is going to marry Corrine", grinning, "The selfish social slut. I bet he regrets it even before they finish their vows. They are a perfect match. A marriage inspired by the devil and made in hell. OK. That's a fitting punishment for both of them." She took a breath. "That imagery helps. A marriage made in hell. The slut and the dictator. That is going to be so bad for both of them."

"I, on the other hand, am going to be a single Mom with a wonderful baby. I have a nice place to live in a wonderful town. I have lots of new friends, family, nosy but wonderful and caring. I'm happy. Have a good job, a terrific boss." She took another breath. "And I am a successful designer and seamstress who has just sold her first redesigned vintage ensemble at a huge profit." She stood and said a loud. "YES. Take that Derek, no good, scum of the earth. I have a new exciting life. Eat your heart out. I give you two weeks to realize your mistake and then just try a no-fault with Corrine."

"How's that for positive attitude? I wouldn't have contested the divorce. I wouldn't have fought him for money. I would have walked. Maybe I would have taken more time and more stuff. But I would have walked. And I didn't need more stuff for a new start. I would have walked and I probably wouldn't have ended up here. So I'm the lucky one. The lucky happy one," she finished up.

The transformation was amazing. From sad, to mad, to triumphant. She giggled.

"I'm OK now. You both can take a breath. Thank you Sheil for making me see that I am just where I want to be, with the people I want to be with and I don't really care what Derek does with his poor, pitiful self or who he does it with. Thank you."

"But you may have a moral dilemma. Should you warn them to use contraceptives?"

May opened her mouth to answer, but she didn't know the answer. "Um, they won't believe me. So no, I don't tell them."

"Forget about that idiot you left behind. Think about Nick."

"Sheil, no," she was aghast. "I will not think about Nick," she said in what she hoped was shocked outrage. But she was. Thinking about Nick. How sweet he was. She had to shut her mouth tight because she could feel the smile there. The smile she got whenever she thought about Nick. She was silly. And hopeless. Because there could never be anything for her with Nick. And she hadn't heard from him at all yesterday.

Sheil just laughed at her.

"Let's close the shop and just have lunch in the back room and gossip about everybody." So that's what they did. And later, Sheil wanted to see the sheets and May's plans for them.

"Oh wait until you see my sketches. You'll love them. And I already have the first ones cut out."

On her next break, May went over to Soaps. Paul was in the shop waiting on customers, so May decided to pick out some of the lotions for the tutu group.

The jars were delightful shapes and the colors of the fragrances, though the price was steep. She also picked up one for Sheil and a purple, lilac, one for Doris.

Finally, Paul was done and came over. "I don't know what you said to Wanda, but it sure was magic. She finally sees that jerk for what he is. A narcissistic, egotistical, conceited, overbearing jerk."

May laughed, "Aw, come on; tell me what you really think." Then she continued, "I just told her about my narcissistic, egotistical, conceited, overbearing jerk of an ex and let her draw her own conclusions. I couldn't just watch what Bobby was doing to her without saying anything."

"Well, thank you. She isn't going to make any hasty decisions, but at least now the blinders are off and she is aware of his shabby treatment. And you will be happy to hear that she called the jerk this morning and begged for forgiveness. He is making her wait until the weekend for the 'discussion'. Wanda actually got a kick out of his attitude. I think she's enjoying this part of it. She was actually smiling when she did it. Letting him dig his own grave."

"Good. Is she here? I wanted to check up on her."

"She'll be in tomorrow evening to start working on the lotions for the hotel. She's going to stay until she has them all done, she's anxious to have them finished and delivered. She can't wait to see how well they do. This is a major step for the business.

May laughed again and passed him the jars she wanted, "I need to buy these. I just love them and they will make great gifts for my friends. And I will be first before they get to be the fad of the glitterati."

"For you, half price. No arguments." He wrapped each one in sparkly tissue paper which matched the color of the jar. "These sparkles get all over everything. Your friends will chew you out for the mess. But each time they spot a sparkle on the floor they'll think of you and your lovely gift."

"Tell Wanda I'm next door, if she needs to talk. And thank you for the discount."

She couldn't wait and immediately gave Sheil and Doris their lotions and was rewarded with happy exclamations and hugs. They both sniffed and used their lotions right away and then shared. May pointed out the shiny sparkles on the floor and Sheil just laughed. "We'll leave them. The wonderful fragrances and the sparkles will send shoppers right over to Soaps. It will be good advertisement."

May had another discussion with herself and sent a text to Nick about Wanda working this evening. That way, he didn't have to answer a call or reply.

May was anxious to get back to her designs. So it looked like PB&J for supper and a bowl of chicken noodle soup to go with it. She thought she might have some leftover dessert. She was again laughing at herself, going home to sew like an old maid. PB&J and soup like a kid. But she was happy.

She wondered about Derek. Was he happy? Could he ever be happy? She had never seen him happy, now that she thought about it. Successful and powerful yes, but that didn't mean happy. He was always looking for the next power play. The next conquest. Never sat back and enjoyed what he had. Of course, that was why she was discarded. He was ready for a new conquest. Corinne? She felt sorry for him. And her.

She looked around her small apartment and thought, I'm happy. I'm successful. On my own for six weeks almost. It's time to stop looking back. She got out her sewing and smiled. Yes, I'm a success.

Week 6: Monday

The dresses were taking shape. She had both of them partially put together. She had worked late so she could go to bed knowing how the dresses would look. Better then she had imagined. She had not cut out the jackets or her top. But she was happy with the results so far and decided to take the morning off. Go to The Coffee Spot and have breakfast and watch the dock come to life. Maybe take her quilt, just in case she felt like working. And who was she kidding? She was hoping to see Nick. Hoping he would come sit with her. And smile that killer smile. And she was single now, maybe… She would bask in that smile, enjoy it. But she knew she wouldn't follow through.

She spoke with Janine about Amy. They both agreed that she looked good and it was great she was home. And then she settled in and, yes, worked on her quilt between bites of sticky bun. She was a little disappointed that there was no sign of Nick. His boat was in. And had been in yesterday afternoon too. Was he avoiding her? Had he gotten tired of the game he was playing with her? Wasn't it just Thursday that he had called her 'my girl'? Wasn't it just four nights ago, that he laid that kiss on her that she still felt all through her body? The kiss the whole town was talking about? Had he heard about her divorce? He had been called away before she had a chance to tell him. Had he decided that his game might be too dangerous now? She stopped herself. She wasn't going to get involved, so why did it matter? And it had only been two days since she had heard from him. She was acting like a schoolgirl.

And then, there he was. Pulling out a chair. "We have to talk."

She rushed in without thinking, "I'm divorced. It was official Friday. You rushed off before I could tell you."

His face went flat. Expressionless. That made her more nervous.

"I didn't want you to learn about it through the rumor grapevine." She was uneasy now. What did that expression mean?

"Say something…. Please," she begged.

He stayed silent.

"I really can't tell what you're thinking." She was beginning to be annoyed. And with that came strength. And a little bit of her old self. "I can feed you some words and you can just nod at the right ones. You don't have to speak. Let's try, Congratulations!" She said it with the proper excited tone. No response.

"Sorry, your marriage didn't work out," sympathetic now. She waited.

"You are better off without him," again she waited. Please let him just agree.

"Let's go to bed," she said half serious. She said that? Out loud? Had she actually said that out loud? She closed her mouth and covered it with her whole hand. Not letting anything else slip out. But it was too late, the damage was done. The words were out there. Her words. Her words which revealed her feelings.

And that sentence worked! Now she got a seductive smile. He was smiling that killer smile. It made her tingle. She felt warm all over. And she was lost. She was sure she was blushing. Yes, she was. She could tell because his smile changed and he raised an eyebrow at her with a question.

He stood up reaching for her hand, "Let's go."

She put her hands over her eyes. "No. No. I didn't say that. I didn't say that. It just slipped out."

He sat back down. "I didn't really think you would follow through, but I had to try. You know that's where we're going to end up. And I think you did mean that. It didn't just slip out, you were thinking it. The idea was there."

She still had her hands over her eyes. Wouldn't look at him. "I am not saying this, but, yes, I might have been thinking it." Now she looked at him through her fingers, with hunger, "Yes, I was thinking it. But I can't. I am not a one night stand." She had promised to always be honest with him.

"Sweetheart, it wouldn't be one night," he assured her. He was laughing because she was weakening. Falling for his plan. And she did look a little pitiful, hiding behind her hand, peaking through her fingers.

He had been speechless when she told him the divorce was two days ago. Angry. Two days. Two days lost. And she hadn't told him. But then he took a minute to remember her instructions to promise to take another look before condemning her. And he thought. So big deal. Two days was nothing. And he was the one who had left abruptly.

And when she said, let's go to bed, he had found his voice and grabbed her hand, not really expecting she would follow him.

Now he wondered out loud, "So I wonder how come none of the dock people raced over to tell me? That should have been great gossip."

"Good question. I don't know the answer. Maybe they thought you already knew. But you would think that they would be hassling you."

"What time do you work today?" he asked changing the subject. He had an idea.

"Today I go in at noon."

"I don't have a charter, thank god, and you said you would look at my house with me. We both have the time; we can do it now, after coffee and buns."

She looked at him a little wary, suspicious.

'No funny business. Well, no romancing. Not until you're ready," he promised. "I'll try to always warn you ahead, though sometimes I might get carried away. You do that to me. But you can always say stop and I will. Whatever we do will be up to you," he cautioned her.

That should have made her feel relieved, but she remembered how difficult it had been to say stop before, when he kissed her in front of the whole dock. She didn't know if she would be able to stop again if he kissed her. Smart thing would be to stop him before he kissed her. But then she wouldn't be kissed. Oh, poor her. She could remember that kiss with her whole being. Who was she fooling? If he wanted to kiss her, she was going to let him. She only hoped she wouldn't beg him to kiss her. If she was really smart, she would just say, thanks but no thanks and get up and walk away. Like that was going to happen. She had never played with fire before.

"OK."

He could almost read her thoughts as they moved across her face. That little bit of red, right before she said that very weak OK, gave him hope. He smiled. He was winning. And he hadn't even had to bribe her.

"Good. And I can fill you in on the status of the case."

"OK," she said again and they finished their coffee companionably.

He had her hand again. His fingers laced with hers. It felt so good as they walked together. He walked past Sheil's house and he stopped in front of the weathered pink house. An old Florida, cracker house, with a wraparound porch and a shiny silver tin roof.

"This is yours?" she said surprised. "I love it. But it should be blue. Oh, I'm sorry. That's just what I thought when I saw it before." She was rambling now because she was embarrassed. "When I went to the BBQ at Shiel's I saw this pink house with a picket fence, but I thought it should be blue. I don't know why I thought that. Pink is good."

He looked at her. Blue? His house was blue in his dream. A kind of peaceful blue. He wanted to grab her and kiss her. But, no, he had promised he wouldn't. But he wanted to.

"It's OK. That is why I brought you. To say what you think," he said, putting her at ease.

"It's almost an original cracker house." He looked to make sure she knew what he meant. One built by the first settlers. "My parents bought it new. Dade County pine frame will last forever. The roof is tin and was replaced two years ago. The wrap around porch goes all the way around. Let's go inside. Like I said, Hal's been taking care of it for me. Renting it out. He didn't want to make any improvements until I could decide what I wanted to do. I know what I want now."

He didn't say, I want you. In my house. In my blue house. Forever. It was too soon. She wouldn't believe it. So for now he led her through the house. Room by room. Inside the front door an open layout with the living room on the right, dining room on the left. Kitchen behind the dining room. Master bedroom with bath behind the living room.

An open hallway to the ell off the back which had a family room and two more bedrooms separated by another bath. A lot of windows, high ceilings, and fans in every room. It was larger than it looked from the outside. It was delightful.

He could tell she liked it. "Hal wants to update the kitchen and baths. You can help with that. I don't know much about that kind of stuff. And he wants to paint, says it is way past time. Inside and outside. I like the idea of blue on the outside. It sounds peaceful. Maybe you can help with the colors."

"Why doesn't Sheil help?"

"She'll help you. I asked her and she suggested you make the decisions. Because you are a designer, good with colors and dimensions. And I want you to help me."

"Oh. But you need someone who can get around town. Or online. I don't have a car or a computer."

"You can go with Sheil. You can use the computer at Vintage or come on my boat and use mine."

"I could use the one in the shop, as long as it is OK with Sheil. Not your boat. Not because I don't trust you," she said quickly. "I do. But the neighbors will talk."

"OK, any other problems? Will you do it?"

"OK. I still don't understand why you want me to do it." Emphasis on me. "I don't know anything about kitchen appliances or bathroom fixtures. But OK." She paused a moment and added, "I need a ballpark price that you want to spend. Do you want top of the line, or make do, or rejects from other projects?"

He breathed a sigh of relief. Hadn't realized he had been holding his breath. "Fix it the way you would if you were going to live here for the next 50 years. I have plenty of money."

"I would run everything by you first, before I ordered anything. To make sure we are both on the same track."

"Whatever makes you feel comfortable. The first thing you should do is pick out the blue paint." Would it be the same blue as his dream? "And the porch and trim will stay white?" he asked.

"That's the way I see it. Peaceful blue. It should have a touch of gray. And bright white porch and trim."

He took her to the swing on the front porch. "When I said we have to talk, I meant about the case."

She felt herself turning red again.

"But I'm happy to hear about your divorce because I don't sleep with married women. Now about the case." He went on before she could respond. "Thursday night both David and Ryan checked arrests in the south Florida area. We had the guy's picture from the Soaps video so it didn't take too long to find him. He was arrested in Ft. Lauderdale. Alberto Gonzalez. Got caught in a drug sting over there. The judge wouldn't set bail because they were selling drugs with minor children in the room. So Alberto is in jail."

"Meanwhile their last shipment seems to be lost in the mail. But it's paid for, and the buyers are calling and threatening all types of mayhem. Bobby keeps telling them to be patient and the packages will show up. But crooks are not known for patience. Bobby and Alberto need to get a replacement shipment out quick. They'll need to go to their source so they can make that shipment. We want that source."

"That's why Bobby went to the east coast this weekend. To get his partner out of jail. We got the judge to set bail and Bobby paid it, and Gonzalez gets out today."

"You would think they would have built a little play into their schedules for jail time. Anyhow, Ft. Lauderdale cops will follow Gonzalez back here and hook up with us and then, hopefully, we follow them to the source. They want to arrest them there not here, too many civilians here. And I want the source. But because sometimes things don't go according to plan. We need to ensure everyone stays safe. You are not going to like our plan."

"What is it?"

"We need to put a man in your apartment. Wait before you say anything. We can move you to the Inn."

"No."

"No, what?" he asked.

"No, I am not going to the Inn. You can put someone in my apartment with me. Who will it be? Do I know him? I could say my brother is visiting. Better make it a cousin, I don't have a brother."

He just looked at her.

"No, not you. You can't stay in my apartment overnight; the whole dock will be talking about us in the morning." And, besides, she didn't know if she could resist having him that close for that long.

"Let me finish telling you the plan. Then we'll discuss your objections. OK?"

She nodded. She didn't think there was any way he could convince her, she was safe listening.

"This is bureaucracy at its best," he said with a scowl. "We had to cut a deal to get Gonzalez out of jail. The Ft. Lauderdale cops get the take down at the drug factory. They will confiscate the factory. And they get the credit and publicity. David gets to seize Bobby's' condo and Gonzalez's home. He gets Gonzalez, because he's operating on David's turf and he also gets Bobby. Soaps is off the table. That was part of the deal. Wanda keeps Soaps. FDLE, that's me, just assists by watching Soaps and ensuring nothing goes wrong. And Ryan, as FBI, provides the overall command and backup. We all get some recognition when everyone is rounded up. So I didn't pick this job of watcher, I was assigned it."

"In a perfect sting, Gonzalez and Bobby will go to the factory together and it will all be over. Everyone is pretty sure that's the way it will go down. But we have to plan for Bobby maybe meeting Gonzalez here at Soaps. In that case, David and I will take them down. Outside. So, me, here, will be mostly sit and wait."

"When?"

"Tonight. I will come by at around eleven. No one should see me. I'll be careful. And if nothing happens, I'll sneak out by 3:30, and we repeat the whole thing Tuesday night. We're pretty sure it will happen by then." He waited for her to think.

"And you already promised me no funny business?" was what she asked though.

"No. All business. We can revisit our issues when those guys are all in jail." Sure he thought. He could do that. And then continued, "Your messages about Wanda and Bobby breaking up and Wanda working in the shop late were part of the reason for the compromise with Ft. Lauderdale. I can be close by to protect her, if I'm upstairs here. My boat is too far away."

"OK."

"That's it? OK? No more questions? Problems?"

"No. We can do that. Two nights. You can be discreet. Especially if it keeps Wanda and Soaps out of it. She hasn't done anything to be penalized."

"One more thing," he said and waited.

Now what? How could there be one more thing? "What?"

"The Cabinet. The FBI is going to confiscate everything. It's not going to reopen, at least not anytime soon. Here are the keys. Marty says you can look at those things in there for him, at your leisure. Says he already talked to you?"

"The cradle. I won't get the cradle." She felt a tear. That was so silly when there was so much going on; she was crying over a cradle.

"Don't cry," he pleaded. "Please don't cry."

"I know. It's silly. Give me a minute." She tried to collect herself.

"I have the cradle," he blurted out.

"What? What do you mean?"

"I bought it. That day you saw it and got all gooey eyed. I went back and bought it."

She stared at him in disbelief. And simply repeated what he had said. "You bought it?"

"It's in Hal's shed. I saw how much you wanted it. I was pretty sure the FBI would seize the Cabinet. They do that. Once the property was seized there was no way that cradle would be up for sale. I just bought it. For you. OK? And I sanded it," he added almost defensively. "You can tell me how you want it finished."

She was speechless. One word sentences sounded good.

"I need to think. I have to go to work." Well maybe not right now, but she got up and started off the porch.

He jumped up after her and grabbed her hand again. "I'll walk you back." He didn't know what to say, so he didn't say anything.

"Tonight," he reminded her when he dropped her off at Vintage then turned and walked away.

May worked with the twins. But her mind was a mess. Being near him always made it sluggish and slow. He wanted her to see his house. Thought she should select his colors. He bought her the baby cradle. Is this what a guy did for a one night stand? Was this the way they acted? Whatever was she going to do with him in her apartment all night? She was afraid. She knew what she wanted to do. That's why she was afraid. One night was all it could be. There was some safety in that thought. He'd be gone as soon as he got Bobby. She was afraid that she was going to do it. When he kissed her tonight, she wasn't going to stop him.

She could only hope that Bobby came to Soaps tonight and that Nick would be busy arresting him. Because otherwise, May was going to become a one night stand. What was the worst that could happen? Get pregnant?

Decision made. Maybe. She went back to work.

Wanda came in hoping for dinner together. She was all excited because she was making the lotions. She had two more batches to go and expected it would take her till the wee hours.

"I could help," May suggested.

"I wasn't really hinting for help. You don't have to do that."

"But if I do, you'll get done sooner won't you?" May really didn't want Wanda in Soaps if Bobby came by.

"Sure, with help I could have the lotions all made and leave them to cool."

"I'll come by after work and we'll knock them out. It will be fun." And Wanda would be out of the shop well before Bobby was due. They were firming up their plans back at Vintage when Sheil arrived.

"Get out of here. May you just go and help her now. You girls are not going to work all night over there. Do you hear me? You finish up by ten and go home. Both of you. Get going now. The twins can manage by themselves."

May gave her a kiss.

"What a great boss you have."

"Ya. Now let's get to work and be out of here by 9:30 or she'll be over here chewing us out and shooing us out."

Though May was anxious about Bobby, making the lotions was fun. And Wanda had lots of funny stories to keep her laughing. "How can so many funny things happen to accountants?" May asked. "I thought it was just boring numbers. You make numbers sound like fun."

"I really enjoy them and making them work. I also like to see my customers make money. I love to see my advice pay off. And I am really good at what I do. I want to work for myself and pick my customers. This shop will let me do that and also let me make soap which I love."

"I am doing what I love. Designing and sewing. Teaching sewing. It's fun. I didn't even need a college education to do what I am doing. Like you, I never thought of supporting myself by doing things I loved. Remember, I need a bookkeeper or accountant. I don't even know the difference. I need lots of tax advice for independent contractors or designers. I don't know if I should start my own business. And if I should, when should I do that. I am totally lost with all the rules and don't have a clue which way to turn. I was going to ask you if you can recommend someone to me."

"I can do it. I think your account would be a great way to start my business. Maybe I should pitch it toward business women. Smart business women, though. And I'll move upstairs. That's why we haven't rented that apartment. I want to live there. And if the hotel is happy with these lotions, I can get started."

They were just finishing up around 10 when Sheil knocked on the door. The twins were with her. They sat on the stools at the soap counter as Wanda passed out sodas. Sheil was enthusiastic when Wanda told her about her business plans and said, "My brother has been doing my bookkeeping and he hates it. He gave me final notice last week to get someone else. His legal business is taking up all his time. Do you think you could do my books?" she asked.

"Sure. I would love to. I am so happy I decided to work late here tonight. Two new clients. When should I start?"

"Bryce will turn over the books whenever you say the word."

"OK. Let's get together Wednesday. I still have a job in town and I better get going," Wanda said.

They split up heading home and May went up the stairs. A dark solid shape was up there waiting for her.

Nick. She had forgotten all about him. How could she have? Especially after her decision. She should have been worried and nervous all evening.

"What?" he said. "Did you forget I was coming over tonight?"

"Yes. I'm sorry. No, I didn't. Well, yes, I did, but only for the last couple of hours. I was busy."

"Yes, I saw, on the video. Don't get your panties in a twist. I didn't eavesdrop. Just checked in every few minutes to make sure you were OK."

"Well, come on in," she said as she unlocked and opened the door. She went around turning on lights and kicked off her shoes.

"Maybe you should close your curtains before anyone sees me up here," he suggested.

"OK." Though, if she was going to seduce him, the whole town would know about it anyhow. But closing the curtains was still a good idea for now.

He was setting food out on the counter. She had smelled Chinese and suddenly she was hungry. She hadn't eaten much at dinner, making her decision had made her stomach nervous. But with the decision made she was hungry. More ways than one.

"Smells good. I love Chinese. Want me to make tea?"

"No, I have that too."

She sat down with him. "What's the plan for tonight?"

"Keep the cell on. Keep the iPad on. Watch TV until something happens at Soaps. No funny business til then. We can listen in on the sting too when it goes down."

She cleaned up after they finished and he found a football game on TV. Both his cell and his iPad were out and on and kept half his attention.

"Boy, I am so excited to be able to watch football," she said sarcastically. "I just love it."

"Me too. We can watch together."

"First I want a shower. Then I will sit and pin and sew. If you will excuse me."

She stepped into the shower a little angry. He was acting as if she were just one of the guys. So much for her seduction plans. Probably just as well, she wasn't at all sure she knew how to go about a seduction. Beyond what she saw on TV.

The shower made her feel better and she put on her frog pajamas. Not the least bit sexy. Guaranteed to turn off any man.

She got her sewing and was getting ready to sit in the rocker when he patted the couch beside him. She looked at him doubtfully.

"No funny business," he said again. He hoped. It was going to be damn hard to keep his hands off her though. It killed him imagining her in the shower. Imagined joining her, taking her there. Yesterday, this had seemed like a good idea. Today though, he knew it had been ill advised. He hadn't thought about her taking a shower and he had to stop thinking about it now.

She put her sewing on the cushion between them and sat on the far side.

"Besides, I would never attack a woman in green frog pajamas," he joked. He couldn't wait to get them off her. Who'd have thought they would be a turn on?

"What?" she said groggily. Why did she feel like she was wrapped in a warm comforter? A lumpy comforter. She opened her eyes and was looking at Nick's chest. She raised her head and looked into his face. There was such need on his eyes she caught her breath.

"How did I get here?" She was in his lap, his strong arms wrapped around her.

"I pulled you over when you fell asleep. But there wasn't any funny business. I woke you because it's time for me to leave. Nothing is happening at Soaps tonight. And I was just waking you up with a kiss.

She had felt it. Even though she had been half asleep.

"Do it again. I slept through most of it."

"No. If I do it again, I won't stop. I won't go."

"I don't want you to. Go, I mean. I do want you to kiss me. I do want you to stay."

"You know how it will end, if I kiss you." He moved his hips to emphasize his condition. "You can feel how it will end."

She nodded. Started to hang her head to tell him to stay, but instead, looked him in the eye. "I want you to stay and make love to me."

"You sure?" His heart beat faster and he felt himself get harder.

"Take me to bed. Make love to me."

He picked her up and carried her to the bedroom. He set her on her feet and pulled the spread off the bed. Looked at her and leaned down and kissed her. A kiss that melted her inside.

When he broke it off, she whimpered, but he was pulling off the frog top. Stroking her, licking his lips. "God, you're beautiful." And then he was stripping her of the bottoms. "Beautiful. You are beautiful. I knew you would be. You had me hard all night imagining what was under that frog."

He pushed her back and down on the bed. Wanted to touch her all over. Reached out and smoothed his hand down her front, just lingering on her breast. "I knew. I knew you would be beautiful. Soft, smooth as silk." He brushed his hand across her breast again. He straightened and stripped off his clothes and knelt between her legs. Just looking at her. Then he leaned forward and went back to the kiss, laying on top of her he settled between her thighs. Stopped to nuzzle and lick across her jaw to hit the spot at the corner of her jaw and her hips arched right against his erection. "Oh, yeah, I like that spot," he breathed in her ear.

She was breathing heavy and only nodded, grasping his shoulders. Holding him close. She wanted him.

Then licked his way down to her breast. Licked and circling with his tongue, sucked it to an erect point. She moaned softly. Then he went back to her mouth Tasting her. She responded hungrily, as if she was afraid she wouldn't get another chance. His tongue moved in and out, demanding, as his stroked down her side. He broke off and repeated the whole tantalizing process on her other side. Licking her jaw line and when he kissed the joint there he was rewarded with similar reaction. The arch of her hips against his erection was almost unbearable. "Oh, sweetheart, I won't last long if we do that again," he told her.

Moved on to her other breast. Licked and then sucked as she bowed into him again with a small cry, her hands busy in his hair. Rubbing over his shoulders. Nails down his back.

He looked up into her face, her eyes were closed, and she was shaking her head back and forth. He reached down between their bodies and found her center and stroked her. She arched against him again, whimpering.

"You're ready and I can't wait. OK?"

She didn't have any breath left to speak with. She was breathing too hard, could only nod.

He entered her fast and hard and paused. "That feels so good. You're so tight." She was hot and stretched tightly around him. He could feel her pulse as he kissed her deeply. She crossed her legs around his waist, pulling him closer, deeper. "It feels so good," he breathed, could feel that he was losing control. Fighting his own reaction. He slid partway out and stopped. Back in again, slowly. Feeling the friction. The heat. Repeated the motions. His tongue mirroring the strokes. And then he did it faster. "I'm sorry, I can't wait." He pumped hard two times and felt her reaction, coming with a scream a fraction of a second before he exploded into her.

It felt so good, was over too quick. He collapsed on top of her, still inside of her.

When his breathing returned to normal, he rolled off her and lifted his head to touch her cheek. "You're crying. Did I hurt you?" Worried. He had been out of control.

"No, it was wonderful. I'm crying because it was so perfect." She pulled his head down and kissed him gently. "That was so good." She sighed. "I never did that before.'

He was puzzled for a minute. Then shocked as he realized. "You never came before?" still holding her.

"No. And, God, I feel so good now." She took a breath. "I need to rest. But, in a little while, can we do it again? For now I just want to lay here and enjoy. With you close to me."

"We'll do it again. Slower next time. I was a little out of control."

"Oh, man, if that was you out of control, you can stay that way. Anytime. It worked for me." And it had too. Her first orgasm she thought smugly.

He looked at her smiling. Moved over, kneeling between her thighs, pulled her hips up on his legs and blew softly on her, still swollen from their lovemaking. She almost screamed as her body shuddered and he held her down. "What are you doing? Don't"

He didn't answer, "Sh, sh, wait, feel." He spread her more, stroked her, and then leant over and licked her. She thought she would go crazy. Her whole body, still tingling from her first climax was building toward her second. It was unbelievable. "Don't." she whispered through clenched teeth.

His tongue was circling her clitoris and his hand was kneading her breast when she said don't

She got out another breath, "Stop."

His tongue was entering into her when she said stop. The words reached his brain as his tongue was mimicking what he had just done with another part of his body. "What?" He stopped.

She tried to breathe, got her breath, and forced the words out in a hurry. "Don't Stop. Don't Stop. Don't Stop." Over and over. He smiled and continued, licking her. Sucking her.

She couldn't catch her breath. She could feel it coming and then the waves of pleasure washed over her. "Oh my God, Oh my God." She screamed, spasming. He held her through the contractions. She was still quivering, trying to breathe. Crawled back up her body, kissing her all the way. A short stop to lick her nipple, and then to her mouth for a long kiss.

Finally, she could breathe. But she was boneless. He still held her close.

A short time later, when she could, she whispered, "Was that you in control? Because if it was, then I've changed my mind. I want you always in control. I've never done that before. Oh, my God."

"Never?" he asked with a smug, satisfied smile.

"Never. Not like that," she was still basking in the glow.

"Are you certain you're pregnant? How did you get that way?" he asked.

"Well, not that way for sure," she laughed. "I want to do it again. Once more. One more time before you go. Can we do it again?"

"Oh sweetheart we are going to do that all over again very soon. But slow and easy this time. And then we'll do it again. There is plenty of time. I am going to work you over good."

Tuesday

They didn't get much sleep before he had to leave.

"I'm going to stay right here," she said luxuriating in how her body felt. Well used, spent. "And just enjoy how I feel. I think I like being a one night stand. I could get used to this."

"You are not a one night stand, May," he said crossly. "You mean a lot to me. I don't just sleep with anybody. And you aren't sleeping with anyone but me." He was getting ready to say more when she put her hand on his lips.

"That's OK. I'm OK. I knew what I was doing. You don't owe me any explanations. Last night was wonderful." And she was surprised, she meant it. She wanted more, but she had known going in that he would be leaving and she had promised herself one night with him. Without guilt. Something to remember. "Go. Go to work."

"Don't forget I'll be back tonight."

"Oh good. Not a one night stand. I'll look forward to it. Maybe I'll buy a see through night gown," she said sleepily. Her body felt so good. And she allowed herself another smug self-satisfied feeling.

"You won't need it. Wear those frogs again. We have to work for a few hours before we can play and I can spend that time looking forward to taking them off you. And we need to talk." He bent over and kissed her hard, running his knuckles down her cheek. She looked so sated. She was already half asleep. He let himself out. He would tell her tonight, that he wasn't leaving.

She did finally get out of bed. But only because she had to. She felt marvelous. And beautiful And, she hated to admit it, but he made her feel this way. Not just physically. That was new for her. Sex with Derek had never been great. Never been so extraordinary. Derek treated sex like a required task that he performed perfunctorily. Nick had not only made love to her body, but to her mind. He had complimented her, appreciated all of her, enjoyed her. Made her feel like the most important person in the world.

It was a wonder that the twins hadn't seen more than two women on his boat. If he treated all his women the way he did her, there should be a line around the marina, waiting for their chance. She laughed at the picture. Man, she felt good. If she hadn't been in love with him before, she certainly was now. She was in deep, deep trouble.

She straightened the apartment. Laundered the sheets. She had left her sewing all over the couch. At half time, Nick had gone back for leftover take out and brought her some too. Then he had done all the cleanup. He had noticed that she didn't watch the game at all and found a chic flick. Brought the comforter and pulled her close when she said she was chilled. He brought her water when she said she was thirsty. That was probably all part of a practiced routine though. One he did to ensure he got laid. He didn't know he didn't need it.

He did let her go to the bathroom alone. Again she laughed. He had held her hand a long time when she stood. As if he was afraid she wouldn't come back. She had mocked him and he just grinned and finally let her go. Sweet.

She dawdled over her coffee and toast. In no hurry to do anything. But she did work on the quilt. Nice memories would be built into it with the elephant and giraffe and zebra. And she would tell baby about the wonderful man she knew for a little while.

It was a quiet Tuesday at work. A new shipment came in. That kept her busy. She was by herself today. Again something to be thankful for. She didn't think she would have been able to hide her good spirits from Doris or Sheil. All the clothing in the shipment was in perfect condition. Which was probably a good thing as she had plenty of fabric to keep her busy already. She labeled the garments and then ironed them. Printed out the data for Sheil. Took pictures and hung the items. These were really nice vintage fashions and should sell quickly. The shipment kept her busy most of the day. She had brought her lunch so she didn't even leave the shop. And she did make sales, some of the new stock.

She worried how Nick and Marty were doing and hoped that they could catch both Gonzalez and Bobby early. Then she would have a whole night with Nick. She slapped herself and thought you dirty, no good, stay-out, slut. Ya. With a satisfied smile. Like the cat who ate the canary. And that thought made her embarrassed.

She was planning on doing the look through of the Cabinet tomorrow for Marty. He only wanted her to check that crate. She knew that most of the stock was just junk, so it shouldn't take her very long.

Finally the day was over and she closed out and locked up and went up to her apartment. She hadn't heard anything from Nick all day, but he was waiting in the shadows by her door. He motioned her to stay quiet and slipped in behind her. She went over and closed all the curtains and then turned on the lights.

"What's happening?" she asked.

"Gonzalez led us to their supplier. FDLE let him leave with the product before they made the bust. There was a firefight and some of the crooks were injured. The cops are in the process of cleaning that mess up. Meanwhile the deputy trailing Gonzalez, lost him. David's waiting at Bobby's to see if he shows up there."

His cell buzzed. He looked at the text, sent back an acknowledgement, and said, "Bobby isn't at his apartment. David can't spare anyone yet, so it's you and me for a couple of hours. We stay here and watch and wait. If they show up, when they show up, we call and we wait until we get reinforcements. There's no hurry. They should be making soap for a couple of hours. Everything should work out fine," he said, as much to comfort himself as her.

He looked at her hungrily, but said, "No hank-panky. It's all work tonight. Sorry."

"Me too. Well, maybe after," she said hopefully.

He laughed at her. "After, I have to go downtown. Paperwork and interrogation."

One night stand, she said to herself. One night stand. But she'd already decided it would be enough. She didn't think forever would be enough. "No food tonight? I haven't eaten, how about a grilled cheese and soup? You can always depend on me for those," she said brightly as she walked into her kitchen. She wasn't going to show her disappointment.

"We need to talk about us," he started.

"No, you don't need to. I told you, I made my decision to sleep with you and I'm happy I did. Please don't tell me it was a mistake or that you're sorry. I don't think I could bear that."

"I wasn't going to. It has never been like that before for me. Probably because I have never been involved with the woman before. Last night was the best thing that has happened to me in a long time."

"You call a month a long time, hunh?"

"What do you mean?"

"The twins said you had a couple of different women over to your boat. Remember, they were bragging on you that day in the shop? I didn't mean to bring that up. What you did with me has nothing to do with anything else. I understand that."

He went over to her and turned her around. "Sweetheart. Look at me. I haven't had a woman in over a year. You are the first woman I have even looked at in that long."

"Really?" That pleased her, even if it might not be the truth.

"Now you're just looking for compliments. Yes. Really." He took a breath, "Those women that the twins saw were agents."

Now she looked puzzled. "So if you have sex with agents, it doesn't qualify as sex?"

"No, I didn't have sex with either of them," he said irritated. "Stop thinking like that. I don't lie either. They were part of my cover. To make it look like I had women coming for the night." He heard what he had just said and saw a smirk on her lips.

"And that is a gross play on words. Let me rephrase that. "The agents spent a couple of hours on the boat to make folks think I was a player. One read a book, the other spent the time texting her kids. I was working on a schematic the twins had given me for landscaping my house. Nothing happened between me and those women."

"I said you didn't need to explain. I really did mean that. But I'm glad you told me. Thank you."

"I'll open the soup," she said as she got out the bread and cheese?

His cell played the William Tell overture.

He looked at it and said, "Someone is going into Soaps. Can't tell who it is yet." He was all business. Pulled out the iPad and brought up the cameras. "Looks like Bobby's car. And here comes Gonzalez's van." He texted David Then he turned to another screen and they watched the two men enter the back door. Bobby was complaining, "I had other plans for tonight. We could have done this tomorrow."

"Tomorrow we could both be dead. That last shipment and is coming out of your share. Quit your whining and get started. This is the last time I'm doing this. What a mess. After tonight, I don't want to see soap ever again. I don't want to see you again. If I do, I'll kill you. Shut up and work."

Bobby was sweating. May thought it was good that he should feel threatened. He deserved it.

Nick and May watched quietly for a couple of hours as the two men worked through the steps until the molds were half-filled and cooling. And then Gonzalez said, "I'll get the stuff out of the van."

May was getting anxious. "How soon before David can get here? Looks like they're on the last step."

Nick sent a text to David and didn't appear happy about the results. "Be awhile yet," he said shortly.

Just then the door to the main shop opened and Wanda walked into the back room. "Bobby? Bobby what are you doing here?" she looked at her watch and said, "It's two in the morning?"

Bobby looked like he was ready to jump out of skin. Looking all around for a way out.

"Wanda, what are you doing here? You're supposed to be home."

"What do you mean; I'm supposed to be home? I came after work to set up a spreadsheet for the hotel lines. They wanted to add small soap designs to their order. I must have fallen asleep. And why am I explaining that to you? What are you doing in my shop?" she asked again.

"You need to leave Wanda."

"I, need to leave?" she asked confused. "You are a little confused. This is my shop." She was looking around. "Are you making soap? Well of course you're making soap. I can see that. I didn't even know you knew how to do that. Oh, that's right, you spent a lot of time with us when we were making the first batches, so of course you know how to do it. The question is why are you making soap? And why are you in my shop? How did you get in? Did I leave the door unlocked?"

"Look I am just making a batch of soap. For a friend. Leave now and I'll explain the whole thing tomorrow."

"Bobby, you really are confused. You are the one who should leave now and explain the whole thing tomorrow. I want you out of my shop now."

"But I'm not done," he whined.

"Get out or I'm calling security and they will arrest you for breaking and entering. I don't believe this." She was pulling out her cell.

"I'm begging you, be quiet and leave. Right now." He was looking anxiously toward the back door as he was shoving her through the inner door when Gonzalez came back in with his load and saw them. "What the shit? Who's that? And what's she doing here?"

Wanda stopped and looked at the two men. "Who are you?" she asked putting her arms across her chest. "Who is this man Bobby?"

Bobby walked toward Gonzalez placating. "This is my fiancé. She owns the place."

Gonzalez put down the package and pulled out his gun. "Well she picked the wrong time to be here."

"She won't talk. I can manage her," Booby promised Gonzalez.

Gonzalez looked at him considering, and then said to Wanda, "Get over in the corner there, sit down, and shut up." He waved the gun at her. She stumbled backward to the stool and sat. When she found her voice she said, "What is this Bobby? What's going on?"

"I said shut up," Gonzalez repeated.

"Please Wanda be quiet. Don't make him mad."

"I want you to leave, both of you. Now," she demanded as she stood up.

Gonzalez took a step toward her and threatened her with the gun. She cringed back.

"Shut up," he threatened. "Shut up or I will shut you up."

"Don't hurt her. She'll be quiet. Won't you Wanda?" Bobby begged her. "Please."

She nodded slowly, wide eyed.

"What are you going to do? You're not going to hurt her are you?" he asked Gonzalez.

Gonzalez looked at him and smiled. "Of course not. We just leave her tied up here. Let's finish. Forget her. Put the envelopes in the soap molds, load them in the van, and let's get out of here. Hurry."

Nick had jumped up when Gonzalez appeared to be going to hit Wanda, ready if things escalated. He couldn't get down there in time if Gonzalez decided to shoot her. Then he relaxed some as things calmed down and the two men went to work.

"He is going to shoot them, isn't he?" May said quietly.

Nick thought about lying, but it was pretty obvious that Gonzalez wasn't going to leave anyone behind to point a finger at him. "Ya. Probably. But we are not going to let him." He texted David again, "I need back up here. Now."

"Fifteen minutes. David can be here in fifteen minutes. That is not going to be soon enough. I'm going down. We need a distraction," he said looking around with no idea at all.

"I can do it, I can be the distraction."

He looked at her, "How? I sure hope you have an idea, because I don't"

"I can take down our sandwiches. Make believe that Wanda and I do that all the time."

Nick was shaking his head.

"I can channel Doris, you know I can channel Doris."

He was still shaking his head so she hurried to convince him. "I did it for you. Remember at lunch the other day." She had been joking about how Doris just talks and talks. And then she had done a three minute spiel on soaps and colors. She'd only stopped because they were both laughing too hard for her to continue. "That was all Soaps stuff I did, so I already know all the words. It can work. You know it can. I can distract Gonzalez long enough for you to get the drop on him."

He was still shaking his head. The idea of May walking in there by herself made his mind freeze. "I can't let you do that."

"You can't let him kill them either."

He looked back at the screens and saw that Bobby was taking the soap molds out to the van.

"Nick. Let me help. If I was an agent, you wouldn't hesitate."

"If you were an agent, you would have had training."

"Would that make a difference in this situation?" she was putting the sandwiches on plates, getting ready.

His eyes went from the screens to her and he knew that was the only choice, otherwise he would have to watch two people die. He knew that Gonzalez was going to shoot them. In the shop. He wasn't going to leave them there alive. He wasn't going to walk them out and take them for a ride either. If Nick tried to bust in there, Gonzalez would shoot them before Nick could take him down.

"OK. I don't like it, but OK. If you get hurt," he was shaking his head. "Don't get hurt," he ordered. He grabbed her and kissed her, "I love you," he said. "I love you. Don't get hurt."

She looked at him in shock and saw it in his eyes. "Me too," she said. "I love you too."

He pushed her away, "Go, I'm right behind you. Walk right in and to the counter, get his back to the door. I'll be right there. I won't let him hurt you."

She ran out and down the stairs and walked straight in the back door of Soaps. She started talking before she got to the door. "Wanda, I have our sandwiches. I hope you have sodas because I don't have any upstairs. I made grilled cheese and I have to go back for the soup. I only had the red clam chowder I know you don't like it too well. You don't have to eat it. And I put mayo on both the sandwiches. Truly decadent." She took a breath and without looking around went over to the counter near the stool and set down the plate.

"I'm so glad you stayed tonight, I was feeling a little lonesome, and needed some girl talk." Her mouth was dry but she kept up the chatter and acted like she had just noticed the soap. "I love the color of this soap. That's a new one isn't it? I don't think I ever saw the gold flakes before. You have to tell me how you do it." And she kept on blabbering as she went behind the counter beside Wanda. They would have a little protection by ducking down behind the counter she thought.

Where was Nick? He was supposed to be right behind her. She had to keep talking.

"I'll just put the sandwiches here. My, you really have been busy tonight. I can help you clean up. Or maybe we can make some more soaps. I would love to try out those flakes with the green lime bars. Did you ever notice that soaps and shampoos have the same names as beverages? And the same colors too? Cool Lime. Refreshing watermelon. Lemony yellow." God how much longer did she have to keep this up. Where was Nick. And what was Gonzalez doing, she was afraid to turn around and look. Surely he wasn't going to stay quiet over there too much longer. Granted she hadn't given anyone a chance to get a word in edgewise, but still.

She prattled on a little more and then said, "Did you say you have drinks? Maybe in the main store. Do you want to go get them? I can come help you." She said brightly, maybe they both could get out that way. Could it be that easy?

"Stop it. Shut up. Jesus lady will you be quiet."

She acted shocked and surprised as she spun around. "Oh. Wanda. You have a friend here. Oh, I'm so sorry; I didn't bring three sandwiches, but we can share. Or… Oh dear, I didn't mean to interrupt an assignation." Did anyone even say that word anymore? Where had she gotten that? Don't stop talking May keep on she encouraged herself.

"Though, if you're making soaps together, you probably aren't planning anything romantic." Keep going girl she told herself. "A new boyfriend, I'm so glad because I really didn't like that Bobby fellow. Can you introduce me?"

Nick was there. Thank goodness. She turned back to Wanda so Gonzalez wouldn't see her look of relief and to block his view of Wanda. Good thinking, Wanda's eyes were extra big watching at Nick. "You didn't tell me you were dating a new guy. This is really cool. That's one of the things I wanted to talk with you about." She grabbed Wanda and pulled them both down behind the counter.

And she heard Nick say, "Don't even breathe asshole. Don't even think it. That's a 45 in the back of your neck." Nick reached around and took Gonzalez's gun. "Put your hands on the counter and lean onto them. You know the position." He pulled his handcuffs out and reached around for one hand pulled it behind Gonzalez's back pushing his head on the counter and cuffed both hands together. "Now get down on the floor. Now asshole. On your stomach."

And it was all over. Where was Bobby and what took Nick so long? He was supposed to be right behind May. "I stopped to cuff Bobby. Handcuffed him and locked him in the van. Bobby was too scared to do anything. Even peed himself." Nick had been afraid the delay might make him too late.

But May had kept Gonzalez distracted and ducked at the right time. She had done really well here. Now she was comforting Wanda who was crying. "It's OK. Nick's a cop. He'll explain everything. Let's go upstairs to my place." She looked to Nick for confirmation and he nodded. She took Wanda by the hand and was walking her out past Nick when he caught her and held her close a minute. "Later," he promised. "We'll finish later."

May poured Wanda a brandy and then poured one for herself too. It was another ten minutes before she heard sirens. Finally.

Another half hour went by and a deputy knocked on the door. "Ma'am," he said. "Agent London wants you to know that he is going downtown and will be there the rest of the night. He said he will stop by when he gets free."

May sat with Wanda and told her what she knew and held her while she cried. Then May put her to bed and curled up on the couch to try to sleep and wait for Nick.

Wednesday

They were both up and showered when Nick texted that he would be a few more hours and it would be OK for Wanda to go to work, but Wanda wasn't to say anything about the arrests.

"I am so not going to talk about this," Wanda promised. "I am so glad I broke up with that creep. I guess I better see an attorney and find out if I'm going to be liable for anything, but I don't know who."

"Sheil's brother. I'll call him for you, as soon as Nick gives the OK," May said.

After Wanda left, May sagged back on the couch. It was the first time she could let herself think of what had happened. Everything was a blur, except for Nick declaring that he loved her. That made her feel warm all over. She didn't know what it meant in terms of the two of them though, so she wasn't going to allow herself to think it meant forever when it could just mean a little longer then a while. Or that he loved her at that one moment.

She was pacing around her apartment nervously, too anxious to sit and sew and remembered that she was going to look through that crate for Marty. She got a notebook and the keys and went over to the Cabinet.

When she walked in the back door, she waved to the camera and told it she was there to do a look over the crate. Just in case the camera was still running.

She looked at the frames, smiling as she thought of the ugly frame and all it accomplished. Then moved on to the crate. There was only the one crate, in the corner.

She got the top part way up. It was heavy so she slid it down the back. The garments were lying right on top. She caught her breath. These were not Halloween costumes. These were rare authentic ladies apparel. She was almost afraid to touch them and couldn't believe they were just piled in the crate. The delicate and fragile fabrics required special handling. The agents must have sifted through them not realizing their antiquity or value. She would need to be very careful handling them.

She laid them flat on the counter after she had wiped it down. The pieces were beautiful. Their value? Well she just couldn't estimate. They all looked pristine but they would have to be examined in a museum. Tens of thousands of dollars each probably. Marty wasn't going to be happy that these had been left behind. But then, clothing and fabrics were not his specialty and men often considered them worthless.

She began to take out the wrapped items that were in the bottom of the crate. Curious that junk should be so well wrapped and protected. When she got the first vase unwrapped she almost dropped it in shock. It couldn't be! It wasn't possible that this could be a porcelain vase from the Imperial Porcelain Factory! She held her breath as she walked back to the desk and put it down gently. She examined it closely and decided that it was indeed. Its value would be about a million dollars.

She went to pull out her phone and discovered she had left it behind. She held up the vase and told the camera its value. Then added that she would be unwrapping more treasures. She hoped someone was watching because she was too excited to stop and go get her phone. Wait, maybe the phone at the front counter worked. She ran to it, lifted it, and got a dial tone and stopped. She had been using the contact list in her cell and had no idea of phone numbers. Sheil. Vintage. She called Vintage because the number was the letters. Lucky for her Sheil answered. "Sheil, you have to reach Nick or Ryan. Tell them I'm in the Cabinet and I have found... Um. Tell them to call me here. On the landline, I don't have my cell. Don't tell anyone but Nick or Ryan, or maybe David. I found some stuff. They'll understand. Don't ask any questions, just do it please. I'll explain later. It's very important they call me." She hung up and went back to the crate.

The next item she unwrapped was a twin of the first. She put that on the desk also. Then a lovely piece of Chinese Meiyintang porcelain. Breathe, she told herself. She had forgotten to breathe. It was so beautiful. It also would be valued at over a million dollars. She looked back in the crate. At least another dozen items in there. The paintings they had recovered had nowhere near the value of these porcelains. The FBI had totally overlooked them. Now she was really anxious for Nick to call. She couldn't wait to unwrap the rest.

An hour later she had all the porcelains arranged on the desk. Fifteen pieces. Close to twenty million dollars total. They were breath taking examples and belonged in a museum for everyone to see. What were they doing here? Probably the same as the paintings. Waiting to be sold to the highest bidder. She wondered if Aubrey knew about them. Or George. She had the impression that Aubrey only knew about the paintings. She heard the back door rattle. Finally Nick was here. Thank goodness. She went to meet him and instead a stranger stepped in. She stopped short

"I'm sorry, we're not open."

"Who are you? No one is supposed to be here," the stranger demanded.

"I'm May. Who are you? Where did you get a key?"

"George gave it to me. So I can pick up my crate. Who unpacked the vases?" he screamed when he saw them on the desk. "What are they doing out." He turned on her angrily.

Now she was scared. She was here alone. She backed up. And, oh my god, she recognized him. He looked different, but he was the man who had been with Aubrey. And she was here alone with a thief and millions of dollars' worth of porcelain.

"Tell me," he screamed in her face.

She had to backtrack to remember what he had asked. "I… I did. My boyfriend, um, Neal, he asked me to come in and, uh, unpack and label things." She was making it up as she went along. If the man was friends with George and Aubrey, he wouldn't know Neal's girlfriend.

She hoped. And it would be normal for a girl to be nervous in the face of such fury.

"Put them back. Put them back now." The man was boiling with rage.

"I'm doing it. OK. Hold your horses. They're just pretty vases. I was going to use one for the fake flowers on the counter." Good, she was thinking again. She was pretty sure that channeling Doris wouldn't work with this man. But she knew very well how to do intimidated, wimpy, female. Derek had taught her. She cringed a little for effect.

"I didn't mean to do anything wrong." That was her, I am so sorry I made a mistake, little girl voice. It had always worked with Derek. "Neal called me last week to come in and today was the first time I could get here. He just said to get the delivery unpacked. I saved all the wrapping; I can put them all back the way they were." Yes, explain. Explain how you made the mistake and can fix it.

It seemed to calm the man down. Next step, change the subject. "Where is George? And Neal? Shouldn't they be here? The store says it is closed, but Neal never mentioned that."

"Just shut up and get those vases wrapped and packed. And be careful."

"I'm doing it. I'm doing it." She picked up the Chinese Pheasant vase and continued, "I just love this one. I was going to ask Neal if I could buy it. It would look great on my kitchen table. Do you want to sell it?" she asked seriously. Trying to distract him.

"Just wrap it and shut up lady."

"Geese, what a grouch," she said half to herself, but loud enough for him to hear and assure him she was just a stupid female. May wrapped just as slowly and carefully as she could. She was hoping for Nick to show up. Or Ryan. Anyone. She was hopeful the guy was just going to take his vases and leave. Without hurting her. But she knew that wasn't going to happen. He wasn't going to leave her alive. The only question was how he would dispose of her body.

"Hurry up," he ordered.

She was shaking a little as she wrapped the vases and it wasn't all faked. She acted as if she almost dropped the Chinese pheasant.

"Be careful," he screamed at her.

"I can't help it you're making me nervous, standing over me like that and yelling. Can't you just sit down and stop glowering?" she whimpered.

That worked. He wasn't happy, but he didn't want her to drop anything. Hopefully, he wouldn't try to rush her again.

Even so, too soon, everything was rewrapped and placed gently into the crate. And no one had come to her rescue. She would have to rescue herself.

"Can you help me with the cover? I can't lift it up?"

"You got it off. Get it back on."

"Well, ya, but all I had to do was slide it to the edge and let it drop. I didn't have to lift it." She pouted.

He walked over and she maneuvered so he was against the wall and then as they were lifting the top she shoved it into him knocking him into the wall and down. She ran for the door and was just pulling it open when he grabbed her. She kicked him and connected somewhere, she wasn't sure where. She knew she was fighting for her life. He wouldn't leave her alive now. She got the door open and started to run through when he knocked her down. He was on top of her and reaching for her throat. She was kicking and biting. She poked his eye and he screamed and let go. She rolled him off her and started to crawl away when he reached out one hand and grabbed her ankle. She twisted out of his grasp, got to her feet and started to run and ran into a hard body. She panicked and started to hit and pound.

Nick it was Nick. And there were men all around. Nick gathered her in and wrapped her up close to his body. Stroking her head, "It's OK," he whispered. "It's OK. I have you. You're safe. It's OK." Making soft sh sh sounds.

Because now she was crying. Trying to glue herself to him. Slowly, she calmed down. "I thought he was going to kill me. I was so scared. It wasn't like last night when I knew you were there. I was all alone. I was so scared I could barely think," she whispered softly.

He turned her face up. "Sweetheart, if this is how you act when you can barely think, I want you on my team all the time." He forced a smile, but he was still scared himself. Still shaking.

His cell had vibrated when she entered the Cabinet. The security alert for the Cabinet. He had smiled when she talked to the camera. That's my girl he thought. Then he had turned his phone off and gone into the interrogation room with Ryan and David. They had been in there two hours convincing Gonzalez that they would trade a death sentence for life without parole if he named names. When he was writing it all down, Nick took a break.

He turned on his cell and had 5 texts from Sheil. All the same. "Where are you? May needs you." His heart stopped. His body froze. He had trouble clicking the Cabinet security key and then time stopped. The room turned white. Even sound stopped.

His vision came back and he opened the door to the interrogation room, "We gotta go now," he said to David and Ryan still inside. They didn't question, just followed him out. He was playing the video as they ran for the car. David jumped in the driver's seat.

"Use the sirens. We need the sirens." He had to force himself to breath. To calm down. He wouldn't do her any good if he was shaking. There was time. He hoped there was time.

"How do you want to handle it when we get there?" Ryan asked him. That was good, he needed to think, and he needed to plan.

"Bust in. He hasn't drawn a gun. She's on the other side of the room. We get between them and take him down."

"Hurry, hurry. He has a weapon. She's making him help her with the top of the crate. Good girl."

They screeched to a halt and were jumping out of the car when May came through the door. Not too late. Not too late. The guy right on top of her. Watched her gouge him and break free. And run right into him.

Two more squad cars screamed into the alley.

Nick was still shaking. He patted her head one more time and pulled her even closer. Holding her tight. He could kill the guy for scaring her like that. Scaring him. "Your hands. You scraped your hands. Let me see."

He looked at her hands as Ryan slapped cuffs on the man. David read him his rights.

"You two OK?" Ryan asked?

"We will be. I'm taking her upstairs and I'll get her cleaned up." He started to lead her away. Holding her tight. Ryan and David got the guy into the squad car. Not gently.

Nick looked up and found a crowd had gathered around. Sheil was there. He owed them all some explanation. "May just took down an art thief. She's fine. Just shaken up. And we are going up to her apartment now and discuss our future together. We don't want to be disturbed." Otherwise they would all be following and trying to help, offering food. And he needed time alone with her.

He doctored her hands and then wiped her face and sat down and pulled her into his lap.

She whispered to him, "I'm sorry I'm being so wussy. But I was so scared. I'll be better in a minute. I promise. Thanks for cleaning my hands. I hadn't even noticed. I guess I fell on them when he jumped on me."

"I could kill him for that. But he's going to jail for a very, very long time. Now give me a kiss."

She smiled weakly and did. And then looked up at him and kissed him again. He made her feel safe and oh, it felt so good. So right.

"Hold me. Love me," she whispered.

Later, when they were both showered and dressed, he told her, "We need to talk. We haven't had a chance since the other night. I love you," he told her.

"I know," she said, "I love you too. And I will be with you as long as you want. I'll take what I can get, for as long as you want me around. For as long as you're in town."

He reached out turned her head to look him in the eye. "Look at me," he told her. "I'm not leaving Cougars Cove. I'm staying. David is hiring me, his vacant detective position. I have given my notice to FDLE. I start with David as soon as I get off vacation. I'm staying here. I'm moving back home."

"So when you get tired of me, when I get fat and awkward, I'll see you around all the time with the flavor of the day," she said it sadly. "I can do it."

"Either I am not saying this right or you are not listening, lady. You are mine. I am staying because of you. I want you. I want us together. I want that little blue house with the picket fence. My house. I want you in it with my 2.5 kids and a dog."

"And the baby I'm carrying?"

"I want the baby. I don't care who is the baby's father," he told her.

She wasn't sure what he meant by that. "Are you saying you don't care if my ex-husband is my child's father or some other man?"

"No. Don't put words in my mouth. And don't try to misunderstand. I meant that I don't care that your husband is the sperm donor. The baby is mine. I'm the father. I will be the father." He continued, "I fell in love with you the first time I saw you. In that moment I knew that it was you and it was forever. I tried to fight it. Lord knows I tried to fight you. But then I realized that my future is a life with you. I want to be your husband. I want to be the father of your baby girl. I want us to live in my house and have more children. A boy next time. Can you do that, sweetheart? I have vacation time coming. We can make it a honeymoon. Will you marry me?"

"Oh, yes, Oh, yes. I will."

Two weeks later

"So when's the wedding?" Liz asked a few days later. They were all gathered together at the Inn so Ryan could update them on the cases.

Nick shook his head, disgusted. May grabbed his hand and said, "Three weeks. Nick wanted to go to Vegas. I said no. There are too many people who live here who want to see us married. And I want to make my own bridal gown. I've always wanted to make my own gown and I'm going to do it. Marge has already ordered the fabric, an almond satin. But we have to do it before I show. My dream gown isn't a maternity dress." She laughed. "And Nick agreed he could wait. That gives him time to remodel the house and paint it blue."

"The dock committee is arranging the wedding. It's so sweet. We don't have to do anything but show up."

She looked at Ryan and said, "Hal is best man, will you walk me down the aisle?"

"I'd be honored," he stammered.

Nick changed the subject, holding her tight. "Status on the cases?"

"First the drugs. It worked pretty much the way we guessed. Bobby came with Wanda and her brother when they made their first batch of soap. He had been completely bored whenever she spoke of her plans to open the shop. Half listened when they set up their business plan and determined rental costs. Anyhow, when he saw the baubles, for want of a better word, he immediately thought of the problems he was having with distribution and runners. If he could get a package that would fit the mold, he could distribute his product in the soap through the mail. He made a wrong assumption: that the soap fragrance would confuse the dogs. But otherwise this was a pretty smart operation.

He copied Soaps' business plan, setting up his company "Idyllic Mood Soaps". Ordered soap supplies from the same supplier. Idyllic is even registered as a real company and pays taxes. Has a bank account for the online sales and purchases. His advertisements say he includes gold flecks in his soap, using his secret recipe. He buys the gold online. So his income and expenses are transparent and not way out of line. He doesn't even pay much in taxes.

He met his customers at various bars and hotels in town with a small sample product. All buying and selling is done on the website which requires a password. The buyer would go to the website. The home page is simple, extolls the virtues of the gold flecked, bauble soaps. Idyllic Mood soaps secret recipe would make you feel happy and pampered. The page reminds the buyer that he had attended the meeting, tested the product, and signed up for a password. The instructions tell him to click 'Order". That brings up a page to enter the password. And that connects to the order page that lets the buyer order soap containing ten ounces of gold flakes or drugs. Pay online. Of course include the name and address for shipping. Email to notify when the shipment was sent. Idyllic Mood would pick up the postage and decide on the fragrance."

"Time out for a little business math. Figure gold is going for about $1,800 an ounce and coke for about $2,800. So he marks up the gold to the equivalent of coke and charges $2,800 for a bar of soap containing an ounce of gold. And the coke is marked up also. Of course, the gold purchases and sales are a method of money laundering. That's a nice profit for Bobby, and he keeps the gold and trades it on the web for coins.

Bobby and his buddy would sneak into the shop in the middle of the night and make enough soap bars to fill the order. Put them into a mold to dry. Then they would take them back to his apartment where they boxed and labeled them. Got a few hours' sleep and took the packages to the post office.

The post mistress was very curious. You noticed that she seems to be a gossip. And she loved the fragrances. Each time he made a shipment, he brought her samples."

"Now for the art thefts. With the capture of Carson, that's the guy you got May, we cleared a number of international burglaries. You were right about that Nick. This guy is wanted all over Europe. And not as a gentleman thief. He could be hired to steal, or to steal and dispose of the owners. He was not above rape either, once he was in a home." Ryan looked at May. "You were fighting for your life there girl. And you did a good job."

"We have found a number of locations where he hid his own pieces. Not hidden too well, all we needed to do was track his cell phone. Guess he figured he would never be caught so he never bothered with any encryption or hidden files. Each location was listed, including the Cabinet. And we found a master inventory.

"The insurance companies are still tallying the other items we found. As you might imagine, the value of those recovered objects will go into the tens of millions. There are rewards for the recovery of most of the objects."

"We also found some items that were not even listed as stolen. Generally those were from collections where the owners were murdered. Ugly business. Apparently he turned over the items he was hired to steal but kept a few select treasures for himself. Those will take longer to catalog."

"It's so sad. That people can be so greedy," May said.

Ryan nodded and continued, "Since May was instrumental in the capture of the thief and the recovery of the pieces, those rewards will go to her. For the items in the Cabinet, that will be over a million dollars. She will get a smaller percentage of the other recoveries, but it will still be a pretty nice number."

May gasped and Nick reached out for her hand. "I'm marrying a millionaire?"

May looked at Nick, "I want to be a designer and a seamstress. I want to sell vintage clothing. I want to continue to do what I'm doing. You want to be a cop. It will be hard for us to do those things if we have a lot of money. Would you feel comfortable if we put it in trust for the children?"

"It's your money sweetheart. It's what you want to do."

"No. It's our money. You have a say. Please."

"Trust for the kids, works for me. Maybe share a little with someone needy. Like Amy."

"Oh, that's why I love you." She kissed him. This is what she wanted. She wanted to live in this town. With this man. In the blue house with the picket fence and three kids and a dog. This was perfect."

www.ingramcontent.com/pod-product-compliance
Lightning Source LLC
Chambersburg PA
CBHW061923130726
47909CB00012B/520